About the Author

Claire Leggett has loved dragons, magic and everything fantastical since she read The Enchanted Wood by Enid Blyton. As a child she used to sneak to the bottom of the garden in the hope of finding fairies. Alas she never found any, so she brought them alive in her own imagination. Her stories are full of magic, adventure and escape.

When Claire's not writing she can be found creating her own handmade journals, swinging on a sidecar, or in the garden attempting to grow something other than weeds.

Claire lives in Western Australia with her husband, who loves even her most annoying quirks, and is currently learning how to crochet.

You can connect with Claire by joining her reader group. http://www.claireleggett.com/reader-group/.

Also by Claire Leggett

Fantasy

The Emperor's Conspiracy
The Daughter's Duty
The Assassin's Gift
The Healer's Curse
The Servant's Grace

Claire also writes contemporary romance and romantic suspense under the pen name Claire Boston.
www.claireboston.com

The Servant's Grace

The Emperor's Conspiracy

Claire Leggett

First published by Bantilly Publishing in 2021

The Servant's Grace: The Emperor's Conspiracy 3
EPUB format: 978-1-925696-63-9
Mobi format: 978-1-925696-64-6
Print: 978-1-925696-70-7
Large Print: 978-1-925696-71-7
Hard Cover: 978-1-925696-72-1
Cover design by Lana Pecherczyk
Edited by Ann Harth
Proofread by Teena Raffa-Mulligan
Map by Shona Husk

Good leaders must first become good servants.

Robert K Greenleaf

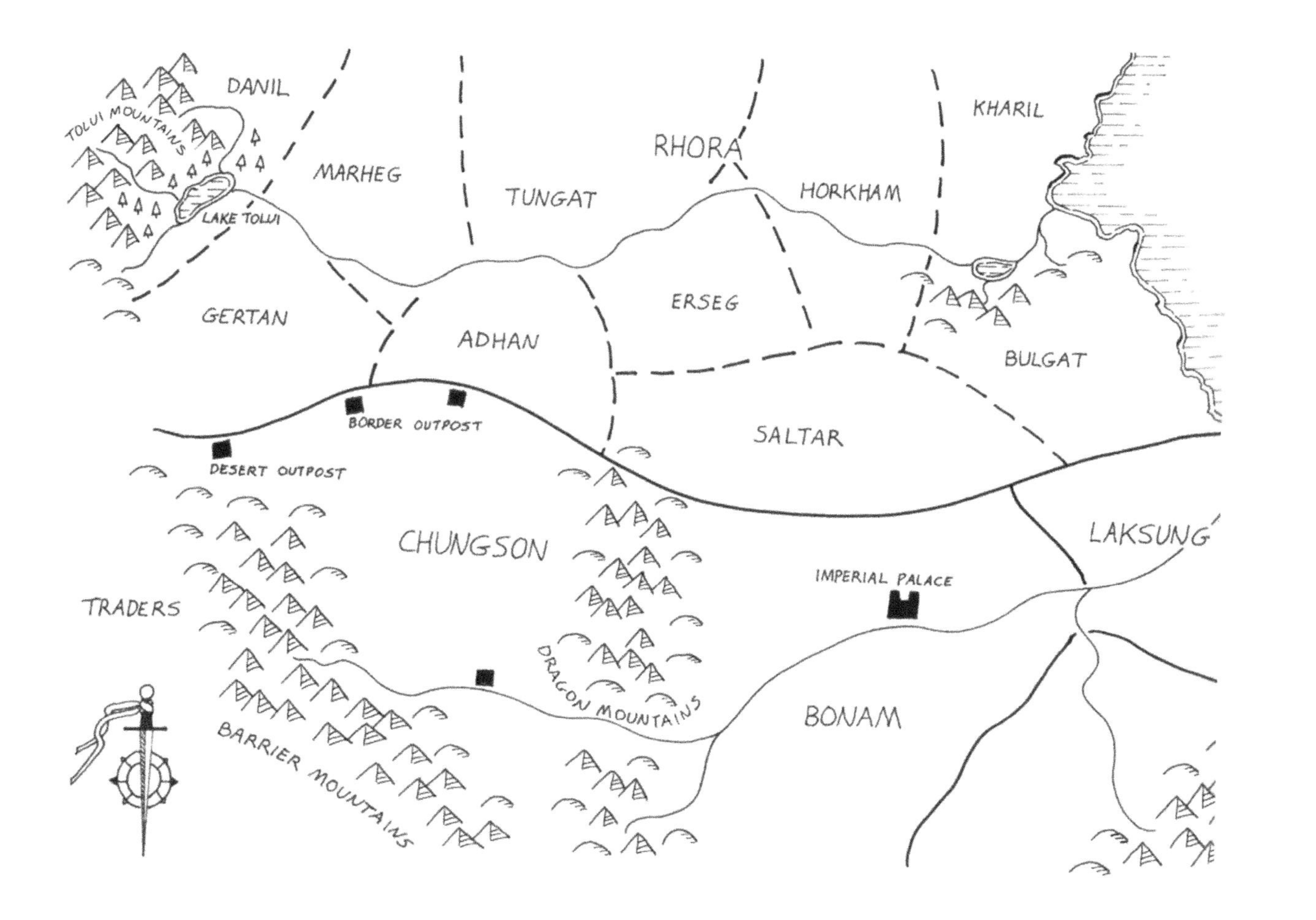
DANIL
TOLUI MOUNTAINS
LAKE TOLUI
MARHEG
TUNGAT
RHORA
HORKHAM
KHARIL
GERTAN
ADHAN
ERSEG
BULGAT
BORDER OUTPOST
DESERT OUTPOST
SALTAR
CHUNGSON
LAKSUNG
IMPERIAL PALACE
TRADERS
DRAGON MOUNTAINS
BONAM
BARRIER MOUNTAINS

Chapter 1

"You will be my bridal companion."

Lady Daiyu's words jolted Shan from her contemplation as she brushed her mistress's hair. "Me?" The uncertainty of where she would work when Daiyu moved to Bonam had plagued her in the days since it had been announced that Daiyu would marry Prince Kun, the heir to the Bonamese throne. "But my lady, I thought you weren't allowed to take a maid with you."

"I am not, but I would be lost without you." She smiled. "However if you come as my bridal companion, the emperor can't refuse. It is one of Chungson's most important wedding traditions." A lovely tradition which enabled a new bride to take a friend with her when she moved into the new household, but the companion only stayed a year. "I can't bear the thought of training another maid."

Yet Daiyu had given no thought to how difficult it might be for Shan to move. The imperial palace was in a whole other country, far from the lord's residence and Shan's family's village. What would happen to her after the year? Would she be left to fend for herself in Bonam? Would she ever see her family again? Even as her thoughts whirled, Shan inclined her head. "As you wish." No other response was acceptable. As the lady's maid of the sister of the ruling lord of Chungson, dissension could lead to death. "When do we leave?"

Daiyu's shrug was delicate. "When my brother tells us. There are still many things to organise before the wedding, but I hear the emperor would like to meet me beforehand. I believe he wants to ensure I am a suitable bride for his son, and to be the future empress."

That was something Shan hadn't considered. When her mistress married Prince Kun, she would be in a position of power. Perhaps she would be able to whisper in the heir's ear, change things for Shan's family and other poor people like them.

"You will make a fine empress," Shan said. "All who look upon you will fall in love and praise your beauty." She was truly pleased Daiyu had been given such a good marriage and prayed the prince was kind.

Daiyu's laugh tinkled like a bell. "You are sweet, Shan. What would I do without you?"

Shan placed the hairbrush on the dresser and fetched Daiyu's nightgown, the pink silk soft to her touch. Daiyu lifted her arms and Shan slid the outfit over Daiyu's head.

Someone knocked on the door.

Daiyu frowned. "It is late for a visit." She waved at Shan to answer it. Few people visited Daiyu's bedchamber, and even fewer at this time of night. It had to be Lord Anming.

Sure enough, when Shan opened the door, the lord stood before her, his posture erect, the crisp line of his vest meeting the well-pressed crease of his pants. She bowed. "My lord."

"Leave us." He walked past her and greeted his sister. "I have had word from Bonam."

Shan hesitated. This sounded important, and it related to her future. She checked no one was looking at her and focused her gift inward, visualising its golden glow and embracing the tingle on her skin as she willed herself invisible, and then closed the door. It was a gift she'd discovered while training. Servants, even ladies' maids, were meant to be invisible—on hand to see to every whim, but unnoticeable at all other times. One day, when Bingwen, the man she'd been sold to, had furiously berated her for a minor mishap, she'd simply disappeared.

She shifted towards the bed. Her gift had landed her one of the most prestigious serving positions in all of Chungson, so that Bingwen could monitor the ruling family.

Daiyu's attention was on her brother. "And?"

"The emperor wants you at the palace within a half moon," Anming said.

"That's hardly enough time to have all my wedding outfits sewn," Daiyu complained.

"You can have them made there," Anming replied. "We must leave tomorrow." He scanned the room, his gaze passing over Shan. "Do you remember the secret code we created as children?"

Daiyu laughed. "Of course. I haven't thought of it in years."

"Good. You must not tell a soul what I am about to tell you."

Shan froze. She should leave. What she didn't know, she couldn't report back to Bingwen. But it could be equally dangerous if Anming noticed the door open.

Daiyu frowned and then immediately smoothed her expression to one of serenity. "It shall be our secret."

Anming paced the room, restless like a tiger. "I put my life in your hands when I tell you this," he said. "To inform another will mean my death."

Nausea welled in Shan's stomach.

Daiyu placed a hand on her brother's arm to stop him moving. "You're scaring me, brother. I swear whatever it is, I will tell no one."

Anming ran a hand through his hair. "Prince Kun is

unlikely to ever be emperor."

"Why not?"

"There are rumours that Kun's cousin, Prince Bao is still alive."

"Bao? But he died over eighteen years ago with his parents."

Anming shook his head. "He didn't. The rumours are true. Bao plans to oust Emperor Xue and retake the throne Xue stole from him."

Shan's mouth dropped open, her heart pounding. Such talk was treason.

Daiyu's hand shook as she clutched the front of her gown. "How can that be? Brother, what you say could get you killed."

Anming nodded. "It is the truth. Bao's parents were murdered and he only just escaped with his life. Emperor Xue was behind the attack, which is why Bao couldn't reveal himself. Bao hopes his uncle will relinquish the throne, but we do not believe it likely. I need you to be my eyes and ears at the palace. You must send me word of any rumours, any information the emperor might have."

Shan pressed her lips together to stop from speaking out. The lord was asking his sister to do the impossible. Daiyu was far too sweet for such a task. She was a musician, a dancer, a patron of the arts. If she ever needed to scold a servant, she sent Shan to do it for her. If she ever fibbed, she blushed a deep red.

"Use our code and write to me every moon," he continued. "I must know what is happening inside the palace."

Daiyu shook her head. "I cannot. It will get us both killed."

"You must. My life is in your hands."

What a horrible thing for the lord to ask of his sister. If the emperor thought Daiyu was a spy, she and all of her servants would be killed.

Unease skittered along Shan's skin. This would not end well for any of them.

"I dare not tell you anymore. The less you know, the better. Simply report any rumours of a revolt, any mention of Bao, or if the emperor appears to be preparing for battle."

"I imagine I will be in the women's quarters or the guest quarters," Daiyu said. "I doubt I will hear anything."

"You will spend time with Prince Kun," Anming said. "You may hear things through him. Become his confidante. It makes perfect sense as you will be his wife." He strode to the door. "I have much to prepare for your departure. We will talk again before you leave."

Shan waited until the door closed behind him before she exhaled.

Daiyu wandered to the window and peered out at the darkness beyond. Shan waited a few moments and then reappeared and walked to the bed to adjust the thick layers of quilts.

Daiyu gasped and whirled around. "Shan, you scared me. I didn't hear you return."

Shan smiled at her. "That is how it is meant to be. Would you like me to light a fragrance for you, my lady?"

"Please. Something soothing. I've had some distressing news."

Shan went to the wooden cupboard by the dresser and removed an oil burner and some oils. She combined a mixture of fragrances and lit a small candle under the bowl. When she finished, Daiyu was already in bed.

"What may I do to help?" Shan asked.

"Nothing. My brother tells me we must leave for Bonam tomorrow."

"Shall I pack your things?" Shan suggested. "In the morning you can see that I have what you need."

Daiyu sighed. "Yes, please. I don't know what I would do

without you, Shan."

Shan turned the lamp on the dresser down low. "Then sleep well, my lady. I will take care of everything." Was there any way she could protect her mistress from the task the lord had asked her to do?

She left the room and went next door to Daiyu's music room and library, putting what she had heard firmly in the back of her mind. She had a job to do and it was none of her business what the ruling class was planning. Except she was supposed to report rumours like these to Bingwen. Would moving to Bonam mean she was finally free of the hold her former master had over her? She prayed it would be so and then studied the room.

She needed perhaps a dozen chests for packing.

She moved through the servants' passages to the storeroom. The old storeman was snoring, slumped over the table. She smiled and rapped on the wooden top to wake him.

He snorted and sat up, almost losing his balance and falling off the chair. He blinked a couple of times. "What can I do for you, Miss Shan?"

"I need a dozen chests delivered to my lady's music room immediately," she said. "We are leaving for Bonam sooner than expected."

The man got to his feet. "You're going with her?"

She nodded, her chest tightening. Away from her whole family and into the home of the man who had taken away their freedom.

"I'll deliver a trunk to your room as well," he said.

"Thank you." She would only need one for her possessions.

"Who else is going with you?"

"No one."

The storeman frowned but didn't comment. "Is there anything else you need?"

The desk contained blank parchment and some ink. "May I have a few pieces of parchment? I won't have the chance to say goodbye to my family, so I'd like to send them a letter."

"Of course." He pushed the items towards her. "If you write it now, I'll make sure it gets sent with the morning mail." He shuffled off to fulfil her order.

Shan sat at his desk. What could she say to her family? They relied on her income and the last she'd heard, they were frantic because the rice harvest had been infected by weevils. They would have little money for close to a year, and her wages would take far longer to travel from Bonam—if they made it past the robbers on the main highways.

She would speak with Daiyu in the morning. Perhaps she could arrange an early payment to tide them over.

Quickly she dashed out a letter to her family, pretending she was enthusiastic about the move. It wouldn't do to worry them. Then she wrote a shorter letter to her little sister, Zan who was twelve. Her heart squeezed. Zan's birth had been a pivotal day for Shan. She'd been thrilled to finally have a sister after having five brothers, but her father had been disappointed to be stuck with another girl. It was then Shan had vowed to do everything she could to support her sister.

Two years later Shan had been sold to Bingwen. Though she only had the chance to return home once a season, and only for a day, she adored the time she spent with Zan. She was such a lively spirit who loved to learn. Shan always slipped her an extra coin, took her books—books she'd saved up to buy or others that Daiyu no longer wanted.

How was she going to support Zan from Bonam?

My dearest Zan,

Though I am travelling far from you, you will always be close in my heart. I will write when I can. Study hard, take care of yourself and let me know if you need any help.

Your sister, Shan

Finally she scribbled a note to Bingwen, informing him of

her travels, hoping it was the last time she would ever have to write to him.

She sealed the letters and addressed them, leaving them on the storeman's desk as he returned.

"The chests are on their way," he said.

"Thank you." She pushed the letters to him. "Could you see these go with the first mail?"

"Certainly."

Shan returned to the music room as servants carried in the trunks. After they left, Shan surveyed the room and sighed. This would take all night.

~*~

The sun blushed below the horizon as Shan wrapped the last lute and placed it gently in the final chest. The room was finished. She hadn't packed everything, leaving the guzheng which was too large to pack and the things Daiyu had never shown an interest in.

She completed the inventory and left it on the table for Daiyu to examine. If Shan was fast, she had time to pack her own things and have something to eat before she would be required to wake Daiyu.

She passed several other servants in the halls and nodded greetings. Some of the higher ranked maids ignored those under them, treating them with as much disdain as their masters treated them. But not her. She could have easily been one of them. If Bingwen hadn't seen her turn invisible, she would have been trained as a scullery maid, or a courtesan. She rubbed her arms, remembering the calculation in Bingwen's eyes.

She entered her room. The benefit of being a lady's maid was having her own space. It was small in comparison to Daiyu's chamber, but bigger than the one her sister shared with their brothers at home. The chest the storeman had delivered was in the centre of the floor. She worked quickly, folding her clothing and placing it at the bottom to pad the trunk. Her collection of hair pins was next. As was habit, she depressed a small button on the side of the long chopstick-like needles and a thin blade rasped out. She checked its sharpness and then clicked it back into place, removing a lone strand of her long, dark hair from around the pin. She'd never used them, but Bingwen had insisted she learn how to fight. It was her duty to protect her employer at all costs. Shan practised weekly to make sure she could extract the pins from her hair quickly. She'd perfected clipping back her hair with smaller pins and clips so the daggers were decorative only.

Next was the chest of drawing supplies Bingwen had given her. If others saw it, she could say it enabled her to practise her art, but in reality Bingwen wanted her to send him reports about the lord and his family. He held her family's livelihood in his hands, and she daren't disobey him. Inside the box was the precious drawing she had done of the village and the weeping willow by the pond. Sorrow crept over her. She shouldn't think of it as home. It was almost two decades since she'd lived there, and yet the picture gave her peace. She examined the other drawing, that of her mother and Zan, so lifelike it was as if they stared back at her. It was all she had to remember them.

Finally, she lifted a loose floorboard under her bed. The papers in there were dangerous, the headlines enough to have her lashed. Ban Indentured Servitude! Equal rights for all! Stop child slavery! She should have never held on to them, but if she was caught disposing of them, she would be in just as much trouble. They were pamphlets peasants had handed her when she'd been in the town. Shan agreed with much written in them and had managed to source the writings of several scholars who spoke of change.

The lure of a society where parents didn't have to sell their children into servitude just to survive was strong. There had to be a better way.

Carefully she folded the sheets as small as possible and placed them in the drawing chest. She would find some way to dispose of them on her journey. Perhaps she could leave them in an inn or bury them in the forest.

Shan scanned the room. All her possessions were contained in a single box. She was lucky to have that much.

She splashed water on her face, hoping to wash away the fatigue hovering over her, and changed into a fresh outfit. Already the birds were singing their greetings to the day. Daiyu would sleep until later if her brother let her, but Shan had to be ready for anything.

She hurried into the kitchen and greeted the old cook with a deferential bow. "Good morning."

"Miss Shan, you are up early today," he said.

She smiled. "I have not been to bed. I had to pack my lady's things."

"I heard you were leaving soon." He gestured to the pot he was stirring. "Rice porridge?"

"Yes, please." She sat at the long wooden table where the servants were permitted to take their meals, sighing as the load left her feet. She helped herself to the tea nearby.

Perfect.

The cook placed a bowl in front of her. "Enjoy."

"Thank you." She ate slowly, savouring the food. It was a privilege to be served, to eat food she didn't have to cook herself. Her mother had taught her never to lose sight of that.

She closed her eyes as the painful memory struck her. Her parents too poor to keep her, needing the income her sale would provide in order to survive. Her mother's tearful goodbye and her father's stoic disinterest. Girls were never worth much.

But she'd proved him wrong. The money she sent home regularly had helped them greatly, had brought in almost as much as a good harvest.

"You can't do that!" The screech shocked Shan's eyes open.

Two grey-clad servant girls ran into the kitchen, Mei resolutely ignoring Chen who clutched at her sleeves.

"Please don't tell. They'll throw me out." Chen seemed to realise where they were and wailed.

"Shut up," Mei snapped. "You are not worthy of working here."

Shan sent a prayer to her ancestors for strength. She had heard similar arguments too many times over the past sixteen years. "Girls." She barely raised her voice, but the girls whirled around to face her.

"She ruined the dowager's dress!" Mei yelled.

"It was an accident. The berry slipped from my hand."

"You shouldn't have been eating while you worked."

"It was my breakfast."

Shan held up a hand. The cook snorted and turned back to his pot, muttering something about useless little girls. His comment stung. Why were females always considered useless? "If I understand correctly, Chen spilt berry juice on the dowager's dress and Mei is going to report her?"

Both nodded.

She sighed. "You should be ashamed of yourselves." As the girls' mouths dropped open, she continued. "First of all, some vinegar on the stain will remove it within an hour. As a washing maid, you should know that." Chen's eyes widened. "Secondly it does not speak well to your character that you would be so quick to turn your fellow worker in." She raised an eyebrow at Mei. "We are all fortunate to be working in the lord's residence and mistakes are occasionally made." Mei opened her mouth to protest, and Shan cut her off. "I understand your fear of the dowager's unhappiness,"—it was legendary—"but put yourself in Chen's position. How would you feel if you're the one who makes the next mistake, and you are thrown out on the street without a reference?"

Mei's face fell.

She wanted to say they were the many compared to only a few, but that kind of talk would get her arrested. "Now return to the garment and treat the stain with vinegar. Work together to clean it and let there be no more telling tales about mistakes."

The girls bowed. "Yes, ma'am." They hurried away.

"Do you think they'll remember the next time?" the cook asked.

"I hope so." A servant's life was tenuous, relying on the whims of their owners or masters. It was hard to think about more than the immediate future, because at any moment your circumstances could change.

Like her move to Bonam.

She finished her porridge and cleaned her bowl. "Thank you." Now to find the lord's manservant and ask if he knew when they were leaving. She hardened her heart. Still, so many years after his rejection, it was difficult to face Lin.

He was the only one who made her stomach swirl and wish she could remain invisible, the only servant whom she saw almost daily and each day it hurt as much as the day before, even as she tried to convince herself he was a horrible person. But he was charming to everyone, including herself when they were with others and his charm tied her in knots.

The way it had when they'd been younger and she'd been in love with him. Had been certain he felt the same way about her.

And when the breakup had come, she'd been so unprepared, so shocked, she'd said nothing. Over the years she'd replayed the moment over and over again in her head and each time she'd reacted better, had been cold and biting, or aloof and uncaring, or yelled at him and called him an unfeeling pig. The fantasy made her smile and eased some of the pain.

"Why are you so happy this morning?"

Lin's voice shocked her out of her daydream, and she gasped. He stood in the dim light of an intersecting corridor, just outside the lord's personal chambers. Even in shadow he cut an impressive figure, tall and lean, standing with the poise and confidence of a lord, his dark eyes always seeing into her soul.

She would never show him how much pain he still caused her. She embraced all the sweetness she could muster and inclined her head. "I was merely thinking of my tasks for the day."

"You need to pack. The emperor has ordered Lady Daiyu to be at the palace by the end of the moon."

"I packed my things after my lady's music room. When my lady wakes, I will add her clothes and we will be ready to leave." His eyebrows shot up, and satisfaction swept through her. "Do we leave today or tomorrow?"

"Tomorrow. The contingent of soldiers to accompany us are late. Anming says they should be here by evening."

It irritated her that he used the lord's name rather than his title. He had no right. Then his words sank in. "Us?"

A smile slipped over his face. "Anming and I are to accompany you."

It was hard enough to avoid him in the residence when the lord and his sister often ate together. On a trip across the country, it would be nearly impossible. "Is that necessary?"

"Anming wants to ensure his sister arrives safely."

She couldn't argue against that. "Of course. Shall I send my lady's trunks to the storeroom for loading?"

"Please do."

She bowed only low enough that it couldn't be considered disrespectful and hurried away. She felt his gaze on her all the way down the hall.

Chapter 2

Later that day, Shan returned to Daiyu's rooms after running an errand to discover the lord and Lin there.

Daiyu whirled around to her, distress covering her face. "Shan, perhaps you can reason with my brother."

Uncertainty and discomfit crawled onto her shoulders, but she said, "Of course, my lady. What are we discussing?"

"He tells me I may only have nine trunks on my journey."

Shan's mind whirled. She'd already packed a dozen and hadn't begun on Daiyu's clothes. But she weighed her words carefully. To upset either sibling could cost her her position. "It does seem a low number," she said. "I am sure he has a reason."

The lord nodded. "We must travel lightly in order to arrive at the palace in time. You will have the funds to purchase additional things in the imperial city."

"But I have too many favourite things. How will I ever choose?" Daiyu clenched and unclenched her hands.

Daiyu's anxiety would build if Shan didn't diffuse it. "Might I suggest we pack what you will need on arrival, and perhaps your brother will be kind enough to send the rest of your things at a later stage."

"But that will take too long!"

This wasn't good. Every now and then Daiyu became

fixated on an idea and clung to it no matter how ridiculous it was. Shan couldn't afford this to be one of those times.

"I'll be expected to look my absolute best," she said. "They will watch my every move, judge my every outfit and I can't possibly be seen in the same outfit twice."

She had a valid point. Daiyu was marrying the heir apparent.

"I need my musical instruments to show how accomplished I am and my choice of books will prove my intelligence."

Shan moved to her side. "My lady, we can come up with a solution. Perhaps some of your things can go in my trunk."

Lin cleared his throat. "The nine trunks include your things."

Her displeasure at his comment must have shown on her face because his eyes widened, but he said no more.

Shan calculated how long it would take to procure more dresses and items after they arrived in Bonam. The cost made her heart stutter. "Perhaps if we knew what funds you will have, we can better decide what to leave behind." It wasn't a question she could directly ask her lord.

"But I don't know how much things cost."

"I can help you," Shan said.

"Oh." Daiyu turned to Anming. "Brother? How much will I have?"

Anming named an amount which had Shan stifling a gasp. It would feed her entire village for five years. "The capital has everything you could want. The seamstresses will be dying to supply the new princess."

He was right.

Daiyu glanced at Shan to confirm it would be enough. Shan nodded.

"Fine. Nine trunks it is. Shan and I will repack." She waved her hand to dismiss her brother, and both men left the room.

"My lady, shall I cancel your tea with Lady Zi?"

Daiyu sighed. "No. I am far too upset to deal with this mess. I trust you to pack while I'm gone."

When the door shut behind Daiyu, Shan let out a deep breath, fatigue already circling her. It was going to be a long day.

~*~

It was late by the time Shan had reasoned, cajoled and manipulated Daiyu into agreeing to the final contents of the nine trunks. She arranged for them to be taken to the storeroom and went to find her own things.

When she arrived at the storeroom, Lin was inside. She turned to go, not wanting to deal with him, but the storeman saw her and called out, "Miss Shan, you have two letters."

Her heart jumped and she hurried in, nodding a greeting at Lin. "Thank you." The writing on the first envelope was her sister's.

"Courier said that one was urgent, said he was made to wait while they wrote it."

Unease curled around her stomach like smoke. She slipped the letter out and read.

She swayed as her head went light. No. They couldn't do that.

Firm hands gripped her arms. "Dire news?"

It took her a moment to register what Lin was asking, to realise he was holding her, his hands steady. She longed to step forward into his arms and seek comfort like she had when they were younger, but instead she nodded and stepped out of his grasp.

The money she'd sent wasn't enough to pay her family's debts. Her sister was about to be sold to Bingwen as Shan had been all those years ago.

She wouldn't let it happen. Then she spotted the second letter—from Bingwen.

Nerves crashed with fear as she slid her finger under the flap. She braced herself as she read. He wasn't happy about her leaving, though he was looking forward to receiving Shan's sister. He had a man who needed a concubine. But he also had a place for a scullery maid if Shan was willing to send him information from the imperial palace.

The chains tightened around her neck. She would never be free. But she wouldn't let her sister suffer the same fate as her. There had to be a way to pay the debt.

"My trunk." She faced the storeman. "Where is my trunk?"

"It's with the rest of the things going to Bonam." He pointed to the room next door.

Quickly, she located it. She had little of actual value except her clothing, and she could persuade Daiyu to buy her a couple of outfits when they arrived in Bonam. She separated her possessions into piles; clothes to sell, items she had to take with her. When she finished, her treasured box of drawing equipment was all that remained. Her heart ached. It would get some coin, maybe enough to tip the balance of fate. She moved it into the sell pile.

"What are you doing?"

She whirled around. How long had Lin been watching her?

She hesitated. She'd once confided her secrets to him and though she hated to make herself vulnerable again, she needed to sell the things quickly, and he had contacts she didn't. "There is only enough room for me to take these items." She gestured to the pile to her right. Where were Daiyu's trunks? She spotted the one she wanted and quickly added her clothes and hair pins to it. She faced Lin. "I would like to sell the rest. Do you know of anyone who would buy them?"

Lin moved closer, examined the items. "You do not need to sell them. There will be room in a later wagon."

She swallowed hard. "My family needs the money now."

"Your things won't fetch much. How much do they need?"

Far too much. She hesitated, not wanting him to know how bad it was. But what did it matter? She told him.

He shook his head. "You'll be lucky to get half that with these."

Shan gritted her teeth. "It is all I have."

His eyebrows raised. "Where are the rest of your clothes? You understand your move to Bonam is for a year?"

"I am no imbecile." She glared at him. "You have seen everything I own." She gestured to the chest. "Every extra coin I earn goes to my parents." She'd confided that to him back when they still shared such things.

"Was the drawing chest a gift?"

She closed her eyes, praying for patience, drawing on her training, her grace. Bingwen would be appalled at the way she let Lin rile her. He'd taught her better than this. She folded her hands in the proper submissive position and acknowledged his truth. "You are right. My fealty to my parents isn't absolute. I indulged, keeping a copper or two each pay to save for the equipment." Lin couldn't know the truth. To have two masters was forbidden. Better he think her less pious than to realise Bingwen had given her the chest and still controlled her.

Shan turned to the storeman. "Do you know of anyone who would purchase these things?"

He shook his head. "They are far too fine for my pocket, though my wife would love one of your gowns." He hesitated and then said, "Perhaps I can ask around, see if anyone can help."

There wasn't enough time, and she knew how little the other servants earned. She was rich in comparison. What other options did she have? "What time do we leave in the morning?" she asked Lin.

"At first light."

She might make it home and back in time, but what was the point? She didn't have the money to stop her father selling her sister into a life of servitude.

Shan blinked rapidly to stop the tears, the ache in her chest pulsing throughout her body.

"Here." Lin held out a hand and she automatically reached for it. He dropped a handful of coins into her palm.

Far more than she needed. Her mouth dropped open. How did he have so much? "I can't accept this." She thrust it back at him.

He stepped back, his expression fierce. "You can. Consider it a loan if you must."

Unease stirred. "With what payment terms?"

"Two coppers a moon."

It was incredibly generous, but that meant he wanted something else from her. She'd heard too many stories of the extra payments a girl could make to lessen her debt. Though Lin had made it clear he wasn't interested in her in that way, there may be others he would offer her to. She closed her eyes. They would be things her younger sister would be forced to do. There was no choice. Her fingers closed around the coins. "Thank you. Let me write a contract."

"There's no need," Lin said.

"Yes, there is. Please take the things I left out as a partial payment."

He shook his head. "You will need them in the palace. They wear many outfits a day and it wouldn't be appropriate if you wore the same things."

She almost asked how he knew and then remembered he had visited Bonam with Lord Anming on occasion.

Instead, she pulled a chair alongside the table and opened her chest.

Someone called for the storeman and he left.

Shan searched for a fresh sheet of paper and uncapped her

bottle of ink. She dipped her quill in as Lin came to stand behind her.

"Do you understand what to write?"

She nodded. Her training had been extensive, ready for any position Bingwen might need her to serve in and not much was needed aside from the details of the loan and the repayment schedule. Lin stood behind her for a moment, checking her words, and then shifted to admire the drawing box. It was a beautiful piece of bamboo wood with copper inlays. She wrote the final terms on the bottom and placed her quill in the jar. "It's ready to be signed." She glanced at Lin, saw he had a very familiar pamphlet in his hands and was reading it with a deep furrow on his brow.

Her heart lurched and she leapt to her feet, lunging for the paper. "That's private."

He held it out of her reach. "It's addressed to all who are unhappy with the regime."

Icy fear slid down her back. "It is something I was handed on the street and I thought it wise not to let it disseminate further."

"Why not destroy it then? Or show it to your Lord?"

Your Lord, as if Anming wasn't his lord too. "I forgot about it."

"I don't believe you." Lin crossed the room and shut the door, closing them in together. At his dark expression, Shan backed up until she bumped into the table. What would he do to her?

He nudged her aside and signed the contract she had written. Then he pulled the other pamphlets from the chest and read them.

Shan wanted to be sick. This was it. At best she would be lashed and banished, at worst she would die. Neither would help her younger sister. Both would bring additional shame to her family. There was only one thing to do. Pray Lin had a heart, that the moments they'd shared years ago still meant something to him.

"Please, you don't understand."

"No? It appears you are unhappy with the emperor. You do not agree with the social structure of the land, you chafe against its restrictions. Is that correct?" His tone was unreadable, and his eyes revealed nothing.

"My twelve-year-old sister is about to be sold into a brothel because my father's harvest failed. She is less valuable than a son and not as useful as his oxen. Do you think it fair?"

He said nothing.

"My family starves yet our lord and lady can afford to buy new outfits worth five years of food, because our emperor has decided we must arrive at the palace at a certain time. That money could pay my father's debt and the debts of hundreds of the poor, but they are invisible to the rich. Is that right? Is that just?"

A bang from outside the door made her jump. Lin folded the pamphlets he held and tucked them inside his tunic. "I'll keep hold of these for you. I suggest you get rid of any others you have."

He walked out of the room.

Shan collapsed into the chair, her heart racing. What would he do now?

She spotted the signed contract on the table. Would he have signed it if he was going to turn her in? He'd never get his money back. She carefully folded it and packed it in her chest. Her muscles tight, skin tingling, she added the box and the rest of her clothing to Daiyu's trunk and tucked the money Lin had given her into a pouch. She would deliver the money to her family.

Then she would worry about Lin.

Chapter 3

A knock on her bedroom door woke Shan before sunrise. She yawned, fatigue sitting heavily over her as she called out, "Just a moment."

"Time to rise," Lin said.

She tensed. He hadn't said anything to the lord about the pamphlets he'd found—at least not that she knew. Maybe this was it. Maybe he was planning to ambush her while she was sleepy and unprepared, but at least she'd sent the money to her family. "I'll be right there."

She lit a lamp and washed quickly before dressing and placing her hair in the simplest design with her hair pins. She wrapped her ribbon garrotte around her wrist and took a final look around her room to make sure she had left nothing behind. It was empty aside from the bowl of water on the table. One of the other servants could deal with it.

She opened the door to find Lin waiting for her. Would he say anything about yesterday? She inclined her head. "Good morning. Is our Lord ready?"

"Yes."

Curse it. That meant they would all be waiting for her and Daiyu. Not the impression she wanted to give them. "My apologies. I will see to Lady Daiyu now."

"There is time for that. Anming wishes to see you."

Her footsteps faltered. "Now?"

Lin nodded.

Nausea rose in her. What had Lin told him? She swallowed. "Where is he?"

"Follow me."

They moved through the hallways of the manor house, passing only a few servants who were preparing for the day. Shan's steps slowed and she glanced at the man she had once loved. Would Lin really betray her after all they had been through together? It could be his way of getting her out of his life for good.

Lin knocked on a door and entered without waiting for a response. Anming turned from the window. "Thank you for coming, Shan."

Shan bowed low, clenching her teeth.

"I have something to ask of you and it is imperative you tell the truth."

"Of course, my lord."

"Did Bingwen teach you the art of defence?"

She blinked. This wasn't what she had expected. "Yes, my lord." She'd thought that had been one of her selling points. A maid who could protect her lady was most sought after.

"Do you still practise your skills?"

"Yes, my lord."

"Show me your weapons."

She glanced at Lin who stood next to her watching with as much interest as Anming. Slowly she slid the hair pin knives from her hair and presented them to him. Would he use them to kill her?

"Is this all?"

She unwound the ribbon bracelet around her wrist and showed him the thin piece of wire embedded in it, making the perfect garrotte.

He took the ribbon from her. "Good." He placed the weapons on the table. "Tell me, when did Bingwen ask you to spy for him?"

Shan held herself rigid, not daring to show her surprise, though her body went cold. Her mind whirled but she could see few options. "Just before I came here to work." Heat rose in her cheeks. "My lord, please. I never wanted to spy for him. He threatened my sister, said he would buy her and sell her into the worst brothel in the imperial city if I didn't do as he asked. I never wanted to betray Lady Daiyu or yourself."

His gaze was hard. "What information have you passed to him?"

Would he kill her family as well as her? She braced herself. "I told him only things I thought were general knowledge; if we were going to the summer residence, or when a dignitary was in town. I mentioned the occasional argument you had with your father, but simply that you were upset with each other, and not the cause of the dispute. I made it seem as if Daiyu was never informed of matters of the state." She hesitated. Would it be worse or better if he knew she'd heard him tell Daiyu about the emperor?

"Your sister means so much to you that you would betray your ruler?" Lin asked.

How dare he question her? He knew what their lives were like. She bit her tongue. The punishment for what she'd already told them was death. But perhaps she could save her family. And if they were all going to die, at least she would have a chance to have her say.

"I told him as little as I could," she said. "I did what I could to protect my little sister who has no control over her life, no freedom to follow her dreams. It is not her fault she was born to a poor family. No one should have their lives dictated because others have more wealth than they do. And the rich are so blind they don't even see her except for how she can be used."

Lin and Anming frowned.

"If Daiyu was in a similar situation, wouldn't you do everything you could to save her?"

"She is in a similar situation," Anming growled.

"You think becoming empress is as bad as being sold into a brothel?" Shan couldn't keep the incredulity out of her voice.

"None of us has any power while the emperor is in charge."

Surprise made her pause. That was incredibly dangerous talk. "Will the new emperor be any better?"

Anming's mouth dropped open. "What are you talking about?"

"The prince who survived, the one you told Daiyu about. You asked her to spy for you." She clenched her hands, waiting for him to order her death.

Only a twitch of Anming's eye showed his surprise. "You were in the room last night. You were invisible."

She gasped. "What do you know of that?"

"Last night Lin told me what you can do."

Hurt speared her. After a decade of keeping her secret, why would he betray her now? Lin focused on the wall across from him.

"Show me."

Her heart raced. This was it. She would not survive the day. But she would not be ashamed of what she had done. She visualised herself disappearing, drawing the golden ball around her, and her skin tingled.

Anming's gasp told her he couldn't see her. He stepped closer, hands out and touched her shoulder. "I can feel you."

She dropped the illusion and stepped away from him. "Yes. I can still be heard and felt, just not seen. A servant's duty is to be as unobtrusive as possible."

Anming glanced at Lin. "Do you really trust her?"

Why was Anming asking Lin's opinion?

"Yes."

She gaped at him, unable to believe his words. "You hate me after..." She wasn't going to mention their past in front of her lord.

Regret fluttered across his face but he said nothing.

"Then we should tell her?" Anming asked.

The lord was being deferential to Lin; it made no sense. It was as if Lin was in charge here. Suddenly everything fell into place. She whirled to him. "You're the prince everyone thought was dead?"

Lin's gaze didn't leave her. He nodded once.

Her mouth dropped open and her head spun. She stumbled to the divan and Lin—no, his real name was Bao—grabbed her arm to hold her steady. He smiled. "I never thought I'd see you rattled."

Shan couldn't speak. She'd lived side by side with this man for the past sixteen years, had at one time shared with him all of her hopes and dreams, and he never said a word. He'd let her talk of a future together knowing full well they would never have one. Had it all been a game to him?

The betrayal cut her deeply. He knew the life her family was forced to live and he had the power to fix it.

And he had done nothing.

"Why have you been hiding here for so long?" she demanded. "Why haven't you taken your rightful place and changed things?"

Anming responded. "It is not that simple," he said. "Until recently, the emperor had some powerful people at his command. They would have slaughtered any who rebelled against them."

Surely it couldn't take eighteen years for Bao to retake his throne. A prince wouldn't like being forced to do menial tasks the same as her. But he had worked by her side.

Hope blossomed. Would he change things? Could life improve if he were emperor? She remembered the days when they'd been friends and he'd been kind; his raucous laugh when something amused him always cheered her. She stood. "Let me go to Bonam with my lady. I can gather the information you want without Lady Daiyu being involved. I will have access to the servants and the ladies in the palace and with my gift, no one will see me."

Bao waited for Anming's response.

Determination filled her. This was her chance to improve society. "We all know my lady is too sweet for such a task. She would be caught for sure."

"You're right," Anming said. "Daiyu will be a hopeless spy."

"How do we get the information out?" Bao asked.

"You could teach me the code," Shan said. "Or I could tell Daiyu what I have learnt and she can write the letters."

"Best if she write the letters," Anming said. "There is no reason for you to write home regularly."

She stilled her expression, biting back her retort. She was poor so therefore she couldn't possibly want to communicate with her family. He really didn't understand.

"We'll do both," Bao said. "I'll teach Shan the code in case she can't speak with Daiyu freely and we can bring her sister to the manor, give her a position here, so that Shan can write to her."

Shan's heart expanded, warmth filling her, and she swallowed the lump in her throat. "You would do that for me?" Bingwen couldn't touch her sister here.

Anming nodded in agreement. "That way if you betray us, your sister will be punished."

The warmth fled. Of course. It wasn't something done out of the goodness of their hearts, it was a means of control. She inclined her head, her posture stiff. "I understand. May I go?"

"There's one more thing," Bao said. "Prince Kun may be an ally. He knows I am alive and has promised to help me reclaim the throne, but we are not certain whether he can be trusted. He does not know that you and Daiyu are aware of what is happening. Maybe you can confirm whose side he is on."

"I will do my best." She was going into a dragon's lair, where the only person she could trust was herself. Nerves and hope clashed in her stomach. Times were changing and maybe, just maybe they would be for the better.

"You may go," Bao said. "We leave in an hour."

She bowed to Anming. "We will be ready."

~*~

Shan had little time to think about Anming's orders as she hurried to help Lady Daiyu prepare for the journey. Daiyu was unhappy about being woken early and grumbled the whole time Shan did her hair. But it wasn't long before Shan sat next to her in the carriage which would take them to Bonam and the imperial palace. A contingent of soldiers surrounded them and Anming and Bao rode alongside. She was pleased they weren't starting the journey with Bao in the carriage, the close confines would have been too much. She hadn't completely adjusted to the news he was a prince, no, the rightful emperor. She shook her head.

Crowds lined the streets out of town, cheering and waving their lady goodbye. Daiyu waved out the window, smiling, ever so gracious, without a hint she was tired. It was an honour to Chungson that their lady had been chosen to marry Prince Kun, though Shan imagined neither Daiyu nor Kun had had any say in the matter. This was a political alliance between the emperor and Lord Anming.

Her lord was sacrificing his sister to put Bao back on the throne. Why did the men of Bonam and Chungson not value their women? When had women become such second-class citizens? She'd heard stories from her grandmother, whispered at night away from male ears, of a time when women were protected and valued as mothers and partners.

A time prior to the current emperor. Would Bao bring back those times, or was it too late? Were the men happy with the situation, and not willing to give up the power they held?

She would do all she could to convince Bao to make changes. He said he trusted her—though not enough to tell her the truth about his birth. Now she knew, she understood why he had rejected her—an emperor couldn't marry a servant.

They travelled all day, stopping only for a midday meal. The road grew bumpier the further they got from the city. She was relieved when they finally arrived at the inn where they would stay the night. Shan helped Daiyu out of the carriage and she winced at the stiffness in her joints. When the door closed behind them in Daiyu's bedroom, Daiyu groaned and stretched. "I feel as if my joints have been stuck into place. I never realised sitting in a carriage all day could be so exhausting."

Shan smiled and rubbed Daiyu's back. "It's the sitting still," she said. "Perhaps tomorrow we can ride for a short while."

Daiyu shook her head. "I cannot. Now that I am betrothed to Prince Kun, it would not be appropriate for me to be seen on a horse." She sighed. "I envy my brother his freedom."

Shan glanced at her. "You surprise me, my lady. You always seem perfectly happy with your life." Her life would be further restricted as wife to the heir.

"I am happy, but that doesn't mean I don't recognise that my brother and my servants have more freedom than I have."

Annoyance welled in her. "I would respectfully disagree."

Daiyu raised her eyebrows. "Why is that?"

"Your servants have little freedom, my lady."

"In their free time they may do whatever they like, whereas I am constantly watched and my actions are judged.

I must always be the perfect lady. Only when I am alone with you or my brother may I be myself."

Daiyu had little concept of a servant's life. "My lady, your servants have no money to do what they like; they also have very little free time. They must watch their actions just as keenly as you, in case someone from a higher class takes offence and they lose their position. Like you, they are only truly themselves when they are with people they trust."

"Is that so? I never realised."

Shan hesitated. "It seems as if people in all classes are unhappy, but only the emperor or empress can change things."

Daiyu gasped. "Do you think I could improve things when I am empress?"

Shan nodded. "The ladies and consorts follow the empress's lead." She gestured for Daiyu to sit and began to undo her hair from its elaborate style.

"I will not be empress for a long while," Daiyu said. "I do not believe the emperor will like such talk, and I do not know what Prince Kun is like at all."

"He sent you a letter, did he not?"

Daiyu smiled and relaxed as Shan brushed her hair. "He did and his words were sweet, but how do I know he wrote it himself? He may have asked a court poet to write it."

"We will find out what he is like soon enough."

There was a knock on the door and Shan answered it to find Bao outside. "We have arranged dinner in the dining room. Anming would like to speak with you both."

Shan inclined her head. "We shall be there shortly." She shut the door.

Daiyu sighed. "I should have known he would want to eat with us. You'd better tie back my hair again."

Shan did as asked, sweeping Daiyu's dark hair into a simple bun and threading a ribbon through it. Before they left the room, Daiyu touched Shan's hand. "What you said about servants earlier… are you truly yourself around me?"

Shan jolted. What could she say? The concern in Daiyu's eyes was sweet, but would telling the truth hurt her?

Daiyu stepped back, dismay crossing her face. "You aren't, are you?"

"No, my lady. I was taught it was disrespectful to be overly familiar with my mistress."

"That's silly. I thought we were friends."

Shan swallowed hard. Daiyu wanted honesty. "My lady, you still have the power to send me away if I do something which displeases you. I daren't ever do anything you don't approve of. I need this job too much. My whole family depends on my income."

Daiyu placed a hand over her mouth. "I never realised. What do your family do?"

It was the first time she had ever asked about Shan's family. "They are rice farmers, my lady, at the mercy of the weather each year. This year their whole harvest was infected."

"We must tell my brother. He can send them some money."

"And what of the other farmers in similar circumstances? My family is not alone in being uncertain where their next meal or coin will come from."

Daiyu's hand shook, showing her distress. Shan feared she had said too much. Her lady was far too gentle a soul to be burdened by such things. "It is the way of the lower classes," she said. "We should go. Your brother will be waiting for us."

Daiyu nodded and led her silently from the room.

The private dining room was guarded by Captain Wei, one of Lord Anming's men. He opened the door when they arrived. "The lord is waiting for you."

"Thank you." Shan followed Daiyu into the well-lit dining room with a large round table in the centre. Anming and Bao stood with cups in their hands and turned when Daiyu entered.

"Sister, how are you after the long journey?" Anming asked.

"I am tired." She took the cup Bao had poured for her and sat.

"I shall see that dinner is brought quickly." Bao left the room.

Shan stood behind Daiyu's seat waiting for instruction.

"We need to discuss what I told you about the emperor before we left." Anming sat in the chair nearest his sister.

Daiyu gasped. "We should not discuss such things here. Someone might overhear."

"Lin will see to it that no one can."

Shan glanced at the window which looked out onto the road. One of their own guards walked by. They must be people Anming trusted.

"I have spoken to Shan and she has agreed to gather the information we need," Anming said. "She will tell you what to write to me."

Daiyu glanced up, her eyes wide. "You would do that for me?"

Shan inclined her head and smiled. "Of course, my lady."

"Thank you." Daiyu reached out and clasped her hand. "Please, you should sit."

"Yes, my lady." Shan went to sit and Daiyu cried, "No. Don't sit because I asked you to, sit if you want to." She glanced at her brother. "How is it you are close to Lin? You two are more like brothers than master and servant. Shan has just confessed that she is not her true self when she is with me."

Anming raised his eyebrows at Shan. "Shan's upbringing was different from Lin's."

"What should it matter? They are both servants."

Shan continued standing, not willing to sit until after

dinner had been served. Daiyu mustn't know Bao's true heritage. A wise decision given Daiyu's inability to lie without giving herself away.

"Have you ever asked Shan about her background, about her family?"

Daiyu hesitated. "She told me just now that her family are farmers."

"And she has been your maid for sixteen years," Anming pointed out. "Perhaps you haven't been a friend to her."

Shan stayed silent. All this talk of being equals and yet they were talking about her as if she weren't in the room.

"What do you know about Lin's family?" Daiyu asked.

"That is not for me to tell," Anming said. "Now remember, make sure Shan is with you when you write to me. She will pass any important information to you."

"What if the emperor catches us? I don't want Shan to be arrested."

"Then you must be very careful. Tell no one what you are doing. No one."

Daiyu nodded. "I won't."

Bao returned accompanied by serving girls carrying plates of food. The rich spicy steam from the fish smelled divine. After Bao had dismissed the girls, he sat next to Anming and at Daiyu's prompting, Shan sat as well.

"We made good time today," Anming said. "If we can continue at this pace, we should be at the imperial palace within the half moon."

"How long will you stay, brother?" Daiyu asked.

Anming and Bao exchanged a glance. "Not long, but I will return for your wedding."

If Bao was the true emperor, would people in the palace recognise him? Was it wise for him to be with them? And what was their plan to overthrow the emperor? Would war be involved? Would anyone even be safe in the imperial palace? She had too many questions without answers.

"Who else will be at the palace? Have you met any of the ladies there?" Daiyu asked.

"When I was there, the empress resided in the summer palace and I do not know when she will return," Anming said. "Prince Kun's sister died recently, but I believe a number of the emperor's consorts will be in residence."

"What about State Princess Lien?"

"She was married to the Rhoran Khan a few moons ago," Bao told her, a hint of a smile on his face.

Shan reviewed her history. The state princess was the niece of the emperor, which made her Bao's sister. But the Rhoran were barbarians. Why would he seem pleased his sister was married to one of them?

"The poor girl," Daiyu said. "It must be horrid living on the steppes with those nomads."

"The Rhoran are not as barbaric as we were led to believe," Anming said. "There is no need to fear them."

"I think I should die of fright if I ever saw one," Daiyu declared.

Shan watched the men carefully. There was more to this. They must have interacted with the Rhoran or the state princess at some stage. There wasn't any other explanation for their attitude when for years the Rhoran had been used by parents to scare their children into behaving. Even her mother had told her if she didn't behave, the Rhoran would come for her. She'd been terrified.

Though she longed to, it was not her place to ask questions.

But if Lien was Bao's sister, and she was married to the khan, did that mean the Rhoran supported Bao's claim to the throne?

Dread swirled in her stomach. This was far bigger than she'd realised. She and Daiyu would be trapped in the imperial palace, at the emperor's mercy. If any hint of Anming's involvement came to light, they would be arrested and killed.

Shan would keep them both safe. From here on, she would practise daily with her knives, and never be without her ribbon. It would be up to her to protect Daiyu.

What kind of tiger's den was Anming sending them into?

Chapter 4

The next few days were long and uneventful, except for when Anming and Bao joined them in the carriage to teach Shan how to write the code. The key to indicating her letter was encoded was starting with the phrase, 'I have such wonderful news to tell you.' What followed was a little confusing, and focusing on the writing while the carriage jolted over the rough ground made her queasy, but at least it distracted her from Bao's presence.

When she wasn't learning, Shan did her best to entertain Daiyu by singing, or telling her stories. The bumpy road had made writing poetry difficult, so instead Shan drew from the vast well of tales she'd learnt while training with Bingwen. Some were perhaps a little too risqué for her lady, but she'd told them anyway and Daiyu had been delightfully shocked.

She was telling one such story about a sprite and a human when Daiyu stopped her and pointed. "There's a river up ahead. Maybe we can stop for a rest." She waved to her brother who rode outside and called, "May we stop at the river?"

"No!" Bao barked, his expression fierce and Daiyu shrank back into the carriage, her face a little pale. "Did you hear the way he spoke to me?"

Shan nodded, stroking Daiyu's arm but watching Bao. His

posture was stiff and she'd never seen him so alert, his gaze scanning the surrounding countryside. But when he looked back at the carriage, grief clouded his eyes. Her heart clenched. Why was he upset?

Suddenly shouts of alarm came from outside the carriage. Horses whinnied and men yelled.

"What's going on?" Daiyu shifted to look out the window and Shan pulled her back as an arrow flew through and thunked on the opposite side of the carriage.

Daiyu shrieked.

"Quiet." Shan placed her hand over Daiyu's mouth, her pulse pounding in her head as riders dressed in brown peasant clothing rode out of the surrounding forest. "Slide to the floor and stay still."

Daiyu's eyes were wide as she obeyed without question. Shan drew the curtain across the window and peered out the corner. Men fought, steel clashing as swords struck each other and arrows thunking as they hit the carriage. Chaos.

Though their attackers wore farmers' clothing, their skill spoke of military training. They weren't ordinary highway robbers, or simple farmers hoping for some easy money.

The carriage lurched and their driver fell from his seat with a scream. The reins cracked and the horses lunged forward, galloping through the fighters. As they rushed through the mayhem, Bao and Anming fought for their lives. Shan's throat closed and she prayed for their safety.

"Get up." She helped Daiyu back to her seat.

"What's going on? Are we safe?"

"I don't know." They had cleared the fighting, but who was driving the horses? She pulled the curtains further back. No soldiers accompanied the carriage. She shifted and stuck her head out the window, trying to get a glimpse of the driver. All she could see was the brown of his clothing.

Not one of their guards. Shan frantically tried to remember the things Bingwen had taught her about being kidnapped.

She retreated inside. "One of our attackers is driving the carriage."

Daiyu paled and swayed. Shan shook her. "Don't faint. We will get out of this. Do exactly as I say." She kept her tone calm and authoritative, even though she trembled inside. Daiyu couldn't know how scared she was.

"What do we do?"

The carriage was moving too fast for them to jump from it without getting injured. She could wait until they stopped and turn invisible, but she'd never tried to make someone else invisible and their kidnappers would touch them the moment they climbed into the carriage. It was possible she could attack the driver when they stopped, but he might take them to a camp full of people and she couldn't fight them all.

She swallowed and breathed deeply to contain her panic. Could she climb out the window and overpower the driver? He wouldn't be expecting a woman to defend herself. She examined the carriage, figured out her path to him as it rattled and bumped over the road. It wouldn't be easy, but it was their best option. "Stay here." She withdrew one of her hair pins and extended the blade. "Take this."

Daiyu's hand shook as she took the knife. "Why do you have this?"

"To protect you."

"Then why give it to me?"

"In case something happens to me." Shan glanced out the window. Bamboo forest lined the road and there was no sign of their guards or attackers chasing them. They were alone with only the driver to contend with.

Daiyu grabbed her arm. "What are you doing?"

"Taking back control of our carriage." She squeezed Daiyu's hand. "Trust me. If someone comes in the door, aim for their eyes and neck." She demonstrated.

Her lady gaped at her.

Shan couldn't waste time here. The further they got away from their guards, the more in danger they were. Who knew where they were being taken?

Her heart raced. The driver sat closer to her side of the carriage. He might not see her in his peripheral vision.

Shan pulled herself out of the window, sitting on its edge and reaching for the railing which ran along the roof. She ignored Daiyu's squawk of surprise, too desperate to hold on as the carriage jolted over a large rut. She gritted her teeth. What was she doing? She'd never attacked anyone and certainly not while on a galloping carriage.

Still no sign of pursuit.

Her feet tangled in her dress and she used one hand to pull it over her knees and then hauled herself up so her feet rested on the window ledge. Their trunks were tied to the roof, but there was a slight gap between them and the rail. She climbed, gripping the rope tying the trunks to the roof and balancing on the small space as the carriage bumped across the ground. The driver hadn't noticed, his gaze on the bend in the road ahead. He was taller than her, stockier as well, and gripped the reins as he whipped the horses faster. She wouldn't be able to knock him off the seat. She would have to kill him.

Her stomach clenched as she withdrew her other hair pin. Across the neck was the fastest, simplest way.

Just like killing a pig.

She crawled closer and a jolt made her sprawl forward, almost dropping the knife. The driver whirled around with a shout.

Curse it.

He reached for his sword and she lunged, thrusting her knife at his face. It pierced his eye and he screamed in pain, dropping the reins and lashing out, punching her. She fell onto the seat next to him and grabbed the side to stop herself from falling. His fists flailed and hit her, but there was little strength behind them. He seemed to have forgotten about his sword. She stabbed him again, aiming for his throat, but another jolt skewed her aim and her knife pierced his chest instead. Pain and fury mixed on his face.

Another bump threw her across the seat away from him and she steadied herself before bringing her legs to her chest. Using all of her force, she kicked him square in the side and he lurched over the carriage edge, desperately reaching for something to hold on to. She sliced at his hands and pushed him away. He grabbed her.

No! His weight was too much, pulling her towards him. Shan flailed and dropped her knife as she clutched the railing around the carriage roof. But she was too late. The driver's weight pulled her down and her fingers slipped from the bar.

She fell.

Daiyu screamed.

Shan hit the ground hard, the air leaving her body and pain sweeping through her. She groaned, wanting a moment to recover. Where was the driver? She rolled along the dirt road, reaching for her garrotte. Gasping for air, she got to her knees. The driver lay where he fell, unmoving.

She took a second, pushing past the pain radiating from the myriad gravel scratches on her body, and brushed her stinging palms against her dusty top. The carriage disappeared around the bend. Daiyu! She prayed to the ancestors for the horses to stop with no one whipping them.

Every movement was torture as she climbed to her feet and stumbled to the man. His neck was twisted at an unnatural angle and his eye was a bloody mess.

Dead.

She'd killed the man. She vomited, retching until nothing was left in her stomach. Taking a clean corner of the bottom of her dress, she wiped her eyes and mouth. The road was empty, the surroundings silent except for the chirp of insects. She was alone, in the middle of nowhere. Daiyu was vulnerable. The sun reflected off the driver's sword and she undid his sword belt and tied it around her own waist, the weight heavy.

Should she drag the body into the forest?

Yes. Better no one find him. She hauled on his arms and dragged him a few yards into the trees. Now to find Daiyu.

Determined, she jogged down the road after her lady, ignoring the pain as she stepped on rocks her thin slippers couldn't protect her against. Around the bend showed an empty road. Her spirits sank. How long would the horses run? She continued forward and at the next bend she spotted the carriage in the middle of the road, the door open. Relief filled her and Shan ran. "Lady Daiyu!"

Daiyu stumbled out of the forest, tears flowing down her face, the knife still clutched in her hand. "I thought you were dead!"

"I am unharmed."

Daiyu froze, horror on her face and Shan looked down at herself. Smears of blood covered most of her clothing. "It is not mine."

Fear crossed Daiyu's face, but Shan ignored it. "My lady, you need to get back into the carriage. We cannot stay here."

"Where do we go? Is my brother still alive?"

Fear for Bao gripped Shan, clutching her in its claws, but she didn't let it show. "I'm sure he is, my lady." She took her lady's arm and led her back to the carriage where the horses waited, panting. "We will go forward to the next village and wait for him there."

"Shouldn't we go back for him?"

Shan shook her head and helped her up the step. "No, he will follow us as soon as he's dealt with the attackers. He knows which way we've gone. We will be safer waiting in the village, especially if the attackers are fleeing towards us."

"But who will drive the carriage?"

"I will." She closed the carriage door.

Daiyu stuck her head out of the window. "Have you ever driven a carriage before?"

Shan smiled, putting on her most serene front. "No, my lady, but I have driven oxen and it can't be too different." She climbed into the driver's seat, flinching at the blood on it. Her knife was wedged in the crack between the seat and the carriage so she extracted it, cleaned it on the bottom of her skirt and replaced it in her hair, refusing to dwell on where it had been. Then she gathered the reins and set them on their way.

~*~

It took another hour to reach civilisation, a travellers' inn on the side of the road. The crooked window shutters and layer of grime on the two-storey building suggested it had seen better days, and there were low weeds all around the building. Did anyone even live there anymore? Shan pulled the horses over for a closer look and a stable boy ran out. He halted when he caught sight of the blood covering her clothes and gaped at her.

"Fetch the innkeeper," Shan ordered. "We were attacked by highwaymen and my lady needs a room and protection."

The boy ran inside the inn.

"Are we stopping here?" Daiyu asked, appearing at the window.

"Maybe." She wanted to assess the innkeeper first. If the highwaymen were from around here, he may be more inclined to turn Shan and her lady over than protect them. He obviously didn't have the money to keep his inn in good repair.

A tall thin man strode out, a frown on his face. "Who demands to see me?" He swore at her appearance and then he turned his attention to the carriage. He straightened, recognising the crest on the door. He bowed to Daiyu, who still stared out the window. "My lady. Welcome to my humble inn."

Shan spoke. "Lady Daiyu needs a room to rest. We were attacked on the road by the bridge and are waiting for our guards to reach us."

The innkeeper paled. "That's an unlucky spot. It's where Emperor Huang died, you know."

Bao's father. She gasped. No wonder Bao hadn't wanted them to stop. "I didn't know. Do you have a room for us?"

"I shall have my wife prepare one immediately. Come into the dining room and rest." He seemed genuinely concerned.

She debated whether to ask him if there was any law enforcement in the area, but the skill of their attackers made her hold her tongue. They would recover here, wait overnight if need be for Lord Anming and Bao to catch up with them. If they hadn't arrived by morning, they must be dead. She prayed they arrived soon. "Thank you."

The innkeeper helped Daiyu out of the carriage and Shan turned to the stable boy. "Keep them harnessed but brush them for me," she said. "If you see any soldiers ride by wearing a grey uniform, stop them and tell them Lady Daiyu is inside. I will see you get a coin when they arrive."

The boy nodded and took the reins.

Shan entered the inn behind the innkeeper and paused at the door to allow her eyes to adjust to the dim light. Two travellers were inside the tavern section, eating a meal. They looked up, but weren't overly interested.

"This way, please." The innkeeper led them down a corridor to a separate dining room. The window faced the road. Perfect.

"Thank you, sir," Shan said as Daiyu sank into a chair. "Please bring us some tea."

"Certainly." After he left, she checked the door. It couldn't be latched from this side, but she could block it with a chair. She strode to the window and pushed it open, straining to hear any riders approaching. Bao had already survived one attack at the river. Would he survive another? She prayed again for his safety.

She turned to find Daiyu staring at her as if she was a stranger. "What is wrong, my lady?"

"How can you be so calm?" Tears poured down her face. "We were attacked, you killed that man and my brother may lay dead on the side of the road." Her voice rose.

"My lady, I was trained to protect you, taught to focus only on keeping you safe." She longed to sink into a chair as well, but her job wasn't finished. "Until you are back with your guard, I must consider any risk to you."

"I'm not in danger here. No one would be foolish enough to harm me."

Shan raised her eyebrows. "Someone was foolish enough to attack a full contingent of soldiers guarding you. You don't have that here."

Daiyu's gaze darted to the door as someone knocked.

It was probably their tea, but Shan pulled Daiyu to her feet. "Wait by the window. If I am attacked, climb through it and find somewhere to hide."

Daiyu sobbed as she moved.

Shan opened the door to find the innkeeper holding a tray of tea. She gestured him in and then checked the corridor. It was clear.

"Can I get anything else for you?" he asked.

"Not at the moment," she said. "When our guards arrive, please show them in."

He nodded and left. Shan dragged a chair to the door, blocking it.

"My lady, sit down. I'll pour you a drink." Her hands shook as she set the cup on the table. They were safe for now.

"Are you all right?" Daiyu asked.

Shan nodded. She couldn't be overwhelmed. Not until Bao and Anming arrived.

A thunder of hooves reached her ears. She and Daiyu raced to the window. A group of grey-clad soldiers galloped down the road, with Lord Anming and Bao in the midst of them.

"There they are!" Daiyu cried.

Relief filled Shan and she pushed the window wider as the stable boy ran out to wave down the riders. "Over here."

The soldier in front shouted and the group stopped outside the inn. Bao spotted her and relief filled his expression. Her heart thumped. They were safe.

As the men strode inside, Shan ran to remove the chair from the doorway. She pulled the door open as Lord Anming strode in and Daiyu threw herself into her brother's arms, sobbing. Shan stood back, her heart clenching as brother and sister clung to each other. Bao moved straight to her, pulling her into his arms and hugging her. "Are you all right?"

Shocked, she nodded, a lump forming in her throat as she hugged him back. It had been years since she'd been in his arms and it still felt as safe as it had then. "Are you?" She lowered her voice. "The innkeeper said the river was where your parents died."

He pushed her away, his expression closed. He nodded once. "You're covered in blood."

"It's not mine." She touched his arm. "The attack must have brought back terrible memories."

He stiffened and pulled away, glancing at Daiyu. "Whose blood is it?"

He didn't want to talk about his parents' murder. The rejection stung. "The man who stole the carriage."

Bao closed the door and then led Shan to the table. "Sit. Tell us what happened."

Anming helped Daiyu into a chair and then looked at Shan.

She swallowed. Would they be horrified? Would they

arrest her for murder? She clasped her hands together and told them what she had done.

"You killed him?" Anming asked.

She nodded. "I had hoped to simply knock him from the carriage, but I failed."

Neither man said anything.

"I wasn't sure where he was taking us, didn't want any harm to come to my lady. He was committing a crime." Would she be killed for her actions?

"I am impressed," Anming said. "Thank you for protecting my sister."

She bowed. "It is an honour, my lord."

"What happened to the men who attacked us?" Daiyu asked. "Who were they?"

"I am uncertain," Anming said. "They were all killed."

"Despite their clothing, they weren't farmers," Shan said. "Please don't punish the nearby villagers."

"What makes you think that?" Bao asked.

"They were far too skilled," she said. "And their weapons were of high quality." She showed him the sword she'd taken from the carriage driver. There was a symbol on the hilt she didn't recognise, but Anming swore.

"Bonamese."

Bao nodded.

Shan frowned. That made little sense. Why would they attack the Chungson delegation, and inside their own borders?

"Why?" Anming asked her question.

"Perhaps he knows," Bao answered. "Or maybe it was arranged by someone not wanting Daiyu to marry Kun."

Who were they talking about? "You think they targeted us?" she asked. "But that is foolish. We had soldiers protecting us."

"There are many families who would like their daughters to marry the heir of Bonam," Anming said. "This is why I wanted to travel fast and with a large guard."

Daiyu's hand shook. "They wanted to kill me?"

Anming nodded.

"Will I be safe in the palace?" she asked. "We must tell the emperor what happened."

"We will," Anming assured her. "I am certain you will be safe after we arrive." He stood. "We should keep moving. The further we get from where we were attacked, the safer we will be."

Bao turned to her. "I'll find you a change of clothes before we leave."

Surprised, she nodded to him. "Thank you."

Shortly afterwards, they were back on the road. Bao had found her a simple dress to wear, and she'd washed herself and made sure the stable boy received his coin. In the carriage Daiyu was silent, staring out the window.

"How are you, my lady?" Shan asked.

She didn't answer.

Shan closed her eyes. Would Daiyu send her away when they arrived at the palace? Shan wouldn't blame her. What she had done was against the law, against God. She had taken another's life.

Shan's chest squeezed as the image of the man's eye bursting came to her. She stroked her stomach to soothe it. She couldn't be sick, not here. When she was alone, then she would have time to remember what she had done, time to grieve for her crime.

The man's yell echoed in her head. She placed her hands over her ears, but it was no use. Images flashed behind her closed eyes as if she was replaying the entire event. Tears battered her eyelids and she refused to open them, refused to let the emotion win. She had done what was required to protect her mistress. That was her job, her mission, her purpose in life.

Her body shook with the effort to keep herself together.

"Are you all right?" Daiyu touched her arm.

Shan swallowed hard. She nodded, opening her eyes, and tears leaked out. Quickly she brushed them away. "I—" the words stuck in her throat. She cleared it and tried again. "I didn't… mean to… kill him." The tears formed faster than she could blink them away.

Daiyu stared at her for a moment, her concern and uncertainty clear.

Shan hiccoughed and pressed her lips together to hold everything inside.

Daiyu slid her arm around Shan's waist. "Of course you didn't. You were very brave. You saved my life. Thank you."

Her soft words and the comfort of her touch were too much. The dam broke and Shan wept.

Chapter 5

After the attack, Anming decided they would ride through the night, stopping only for a couple of hours' rest and to change the horses. He and Bao rode in the carriage with them to ensure everyone's safety. Daiyu's emotions were all over the place, with her snapping and crying at the smallest grievance, and Shan was exhausted trying to keep her happy.

She had little chance to speak to Bao, and none in private. She wanted to ask him about the attack, make sure he wasn't too distraught, but she couldn't raise it with Daiyu present.

Bao had spent the first day staring out the window, his bow within easy reach, not looking at any of them. Anming hadn't made an effort to involve him in the conversation though his concerned glances were enough to tell Shan he was worried about his friend.

She wanted to place her hand on Bao's knee to comfort him, but she daren't. The second day when Daiyu was fretting about the confines of the carriage, Bao turned to her. "My lady, permit me to take you far away from this carriage." Though his smile was full of mischief as he launched into a tale involving dragons and conspiracies, his eyes didn't sparkle the way they normally did when he was happy.

As they approached the imperial city, Shan insisted on Daiyu's behalf that they stay for a full day in a safe inn so they could all rest. It wouldn't be appropriate for them to arrive in their exhausted state. Daiyu's first impression on the emperor, Prince Kun and the whole palace had to be positive. Luckily Bao had sided with her.

Shan helped Daiyu to bathe and then they'd spent most of the first day sleeping. When they awoke, Shan tidied Daiyu's nails, pampered her with a face mask and then arranged a massage. When Shan was satisfied Daiyu had recovered enough to continue, she told Anming, and he sent word ahead to the palace of their imminent arrival.

As they reached the imperial city, Shan lowered the curtains on the carriage. She desperately wanted to take in the city that would be her new home but it wasn't appropriate for Daiyu to be seen.

The sounds of the city reached them. Vendors calling their wares, bells ringing and children playing. The smells followed; dumplings and flowers with the occasional unpleasant scent as well. Heat swirled around the carriage, increasing the temperature inside. This was the home of the emperor. She'd heard Lord Anming tell Daiyu stories of it. Huge red walls surrounded the city, with paved streets and buildings everywhere. The palace itself was protected by a wide moat and more walls, though apparently there were a few small gardens inside the courtyard for contemplation.

The carriage stopped and voices raised in discussion, but not loud enough for Shan to hear what they said. A few minutes later, Bao came to the carriage door. "My lady, Prince Kun has sent his personal guard to escort you to the palace."

Behind him was a soldier dressed in red.

Daiyu inclined her head. "I am honoured."

Bao closed the door and Daiyu smiled. "That is a good sign," she said. "It bodes well that the prince is thoughtful enough to send his personal guard to accompany me through the city."

"He must be looking forward to meeting you." Shan wouldn't tell Daiyu it was more likely one of his advisors had recommended it. "How are you feeling, my lady?"

"Nervous." Daiyu rubbed her stomach. "This will be my home. I hope Prince Kun is kind."

So did Shan. Being in the emperor's court would give them even less freedom than they'd had in Chungson. How many women would be jealous of Daiyu?

The carriage rattled across a bridge and soon after someone called a halt. Daiyu fussed with her hair. "Do I look all right?"

"You look beautiful," Shan assured her.

Shan had spent several hours that morning making sure Daiyu's hair was designed in an intricate woven knot. The pale pink silk gown she wore gave a slight blush to her skin, highlighting her delicate femininity. The carriage door opened, and Captain Wei announced, "My lady, Daiyu of Chungson."

Shan waited on her seat as Daiyu stepped out of the carriage. Where was Bao? He should have been the one to announce Daiyu. As Daiyu moved forward, Shan followed her. The guards formed a passage and at the end stood Lord Anming with another man about his age. He was dressed in the finest deep amber silk, and behind him stood a red guard of soldiers. He must be Prince Kun. He stood tall, his eyes focused on Daiyu as if a little surprised. At least one of Daiyu's concerns could be forgotten. He was a fine-looking man.

Daiyu bowed and Shan bowed a little lower.

"Lady Daiyu, permit me to introduce your betrothed, First Prince Kun of the Bonamese," Anming said.

"It is an honour to meet you, my lady." Prince Kun stepped forward and offered her his hand.

She took it. "The honour is mine, Your Highness."

He frowned when he noticed Shan. "Who is this? I

thought the emperor permitted no servants."

Daiyu inclined her head. "Shan is my bridal companion. It is a Chungson wedding tradition."

Kun frowned. "I shall inform the emperor."

"If required, Shan can return home with us, though we hope the emperor will allow us this one tradition," Anming said.

Kun nodded. "Very well. Permit me to show you the imperial palace."

"Thank you, Your Highness," Daiyu replied.

Shan dropped behind her mistress and Lord Anming and took in her surroundings. The area was bigger than any courtyard she'd ever seen; it seemed more like a city block. A wide stream meandered through the area with only three bridges allowing people to cross it. In the centre stood a large building which the prince identified as the Hall of Clarity, and little pavilions were set up around the only patches of garden in the otherwise bricked area. There was little shade and the heat reflected off the pavement in an unpleasant haze.

They crossed the stream and moved past the Hall of Clarity to one of the pavilions. "Rest here in the shade, my lady," the prince said to Daiyu before gesturing to the buildings around them.

"This is where government business is carried out. The Office of Internal Scrutiny deals with upholding the law, the Office of Ministers is where the emperor's advisors work, and the building over there is the scholars' library."

In front of them was a huge wall and guards monitored the courtyard from above. A servant came out of the small door to the side of a huge set of gates.

"Those are the Gates of Heavenly Virtue," Kun said. "Beyond that are the emperor's private quarters. You will have a palace inside until we are married."

Daiyu nodded. "And then where will we live?"

He smiled and it softened his features. “I have a palace inside the quarters as well. All the imperial family does. No one outside the family is allowed inside without our permission.” He glanced at Anming and lowered his voice. “I’m afraid your brother may not enter. My father has banned any outsiders from entering the private quarters. You may have heard the rumours my cousin, Bao is alive. We do not believe it true, but it is obvious someone has their eye on the throne.” He turned to Anming. “I’m sure you understand.”

Anming nodded. “The emperor is wise to be careful.”

Shan caught the long, loaded look Kun gave Anming.

“One of my men will show you to your quarters, Lord Anming. I will show my betrothed to hers and then we shall gather at the Hall of Clarity for dinner with the emperor.”

Shan’s muscles tightened. Dinner with the emperor already? She had expected it would be several days before that occurred, days where they could learn the proper protocols for meeting the most powerful man in the world. She followed Prince Kun and Daiyu through the Gates of Heavenly Virtue and into the private quarters. It was far quieter in here. Any servants stopped what they were doing and kowtowed as the prince walked past. How bothersome. How would they ever get anything done if they had to keep stopping when the imperial family walked by?

There were several small palaces on either side of the road. “The Lotus Palace was where my cousin, Princess Lien used to reside, and is now occupied by the Third Consort. Next to that is the Second Consort’s palace.” As Kun told Daiyu who lived inside, Shan made a mental note. Most were the concubines of the emperor. Kun stopped outside a building where a number of servants lined up. They fell to their knees in kowtow. “This is the Jasmine Palace.” Sadness crossed his face. “It was my sister’s before she died.”

“I am terribly sorry for your loss,” Daiyu said. “May the

ancestors greet her warmly and protect her."

He nodded and ordered the servants to stand. "These will be your servants," he said. "You only need to ask for whatever you require."

"Thank you, Your Highness."

Kun smiled at her. "I will leave you to rest and acquaint yourself with your quarters. Someone will bring your luggage and then I will fetch you in time for dinner."

Daiyu inclined her head and watched him leave.

"Shall we go inside, my lady?" Shan suggested. The longer they stayed out here, the more likely they would run into one of the concubines who would want to talk, and Daiyu needed to rest.

"Of course."

One of the servants, an adolescent boy, hurried to open the door for them.

Inside it was blessedly cooler. The main room had a table for entertaining, as well as a place for a variety of instruments including a guzheng, which was surrounded by chairs so visitors could sit and chat or listen to the music. To the left was the bedchamber, the bed low to the ground and surrounded by curtains for privacy.

"Please, introduce yourselves," Daiyu said to the servants who had followed them in.

A woman, perhaps in her thirties, stepped forward. "My name is Zhi," she said. "I am to be your lady's maid."

Daiyu glanced at her and then Shan. "Shan has been my lady's maid for many years, and I could not leave her behind. I am sure I can use you for something else."

Shan winced internally. She was supposed to be Daiyu's bridal companion. She would have to remind Daiyu when they were alone.

Zhi's smile was forced. "As you wish. This is Ting," she indicated the young girl with a round face and wide eyes, "and Yun." The girl with a tiny mole above her eye bowed.

"Hai is your eunuch." She gestured to the boy who had opened the door.

"It is lovely to meet you all," Daiyu said. "I thank you for your service. Could someone fetch me some tea? It has been a long journey."

Ting bowed and scurried away.

"If it pleases you, my lady," Zhi continued, "ring this bell and we will come to you. We are only a room away. Perhaps I can show Shan to the servants' room."

"That would be lovely." Daiyu sat at the table and sighed. "The rest of you may go."

Shan followed Zhi through a sliding door concealed behind a pillar. It led out to a corridor with several doors. Zhi's body was tense as she spoke. "The far door is the servants' entrance," she said. "At the other end is the storeroom and utility room, and here is our bedroom." She pushed open the middle door. A small sitting area had a room leading off either side. One room contained four beds, and the other a single bed. The room with the single bed had personal effects already inside. Should Shan claim the room as was her right as Daiyu's companion? Privacy would be welcomed but she didn't want to make an enemy on her first day.

Shan smiled. "It is lovely. Did you all serve First Princess Fen?"

"No," Zhi said. "The emperor ordered all of the princess's servants killed for failing to protect her."

Shan stiffened. "What happened?"

"She was killed by highway robbers on her way to the summer palace."

How horrific. Only a cruel man would blame a servant for being unable to save the princess.

"We were handpicked by the empress to be the lady's maids," Zhi continued.

"I am sure Lady Daiyu will be honoured to hear that. Is

the empress back from the summer palace?"

Zhi nodded.

Ting passed the open doorway carrying a tray of tea.

"I must go and serve my lady. Excuse me." Shan returned to Daiyu's quarters where Ting was setting up the tea. Someone knocked on the door and Shan opened it to find porters with their trunks. "Please come in and put them in the bed chamber." She directed them as Ting poured the tea. Her first task would be to unpack.

"Shan, would you like some tea?" Daiyu called.

"No, thank you, my lady. I will see to your things first. We will need to find a suitable outfit for you to wear to dinner tonight." The perfect ensemble was in trunk five which currently stood behind all the others. She sighed and got to work.

~*~

It took Shan all afternoon to unpack Daiyu's things. She was thankful for the help of Ting and Yun who steamed out the wrinkles in several of Daiyu's outfits so Shan could continue unpacking. Hai was useful as well to move the trunks and take the empty ones to the storeroom.

Zhi spent the afternoon talking with Daiyu, telling her about palace life. Shan listened so she could learn as much as possible. Finally all that was left were Shan's things. "Hai, could you take this trunk to my room?"

He carried the trunk away. She could let him decide where she was going to sleep. She went into the main room. "My lady, we should start preparing you for your dinner with the emperor and the prince."

Daiyu nodded. "Ting, could you arrange me a bath?"

"Yes, my lady." Ting hurried away.

"What will you be wearing, my lady?" Zhi asked.

Daiyu turned to Shan in question.

"I thought your pale blue gown would be perfect," Shan

replied and indicated where it hung in the bedroom.

"Oh, my lady, the emperor dislikes anything that's blue," Zhi said, her eyes wide in worry. "Perhaps you have another outfit."

The other outfits which had been steamed were beautiful, but more for day wear than for an audience with the most powerful man in the world. "We will need to steam another one," Shan said. "Perhaps you could help us choose." Zhi knew far more about palace life than either of them.

Daiyu nodded her approval and Zhi joined Shan in the bed chamber. She went through the wardrobe and frowned. "Is this all she has?"

"Yes. Lord Anming restricted her to only a few trunks. We plan to purchase more now that we've arrived."

Zhi tutted. "Men don't understand these things. If our lady is invited to visit the other women in the palace, she will need a different outfit for each visit. She could go through her whole wardrobe in a week."

Shan closed her eyes. She'd be spending all her time helping Daiyu dress at this rate. "Perhaps tomorrow we can visit a seamstress."

Zhi shook her head. "No. It wouldn't be proper for the heir's betrothed to go into the city. The seamstress will come to her. I will arrange it."

"Thank you."

Finally Zhi pulled out a pretty mint green outfit. "This will do. Yun, see this is steamed immediately," she called.

Yun ran to obey. Meanwhile Daiyu's bath had arrived and she was washing herself.

"Show me the jewellery our lady has," Zhi ordered.

Shan clenched her teeth. Following Daiyu's orders was one thing, but this woman was her equal. It wouldn't hurt her to be polite. She brought out the box full of jewellery and hair ornaments.

Zhi grimaced at the selection. "I will arrange for a jeweller to visit tomorrow as well." She glanced at Shan. "These pieces may have been suitable in Chungson but in Bonam we expect a higher standard."

Any one of the pieces would have fed Shan's family for a year. They were gorgeous designs in gold, silver and bronze. "I'm sure Lady Daiyu will be pleased to have something new."

She went to wash Daiyu's back and it wasn't long before Daiyu sat in her gown ready for her hair to be done. "How would you like it?" Shan asked.

Daiyu glanced at Zhi. "What is the latest fashion at the palace?"

"I can show you if you like."

"Please."

Zhi smiled with satisfaction as she nudged Shan out of the way and took the long comb from her. "Excuse me."

Shan smiled in return though Zhi's behaviour rankled. She would need to speak with Daiyu and clarify her role before Zhi got too upset. Zhi worked quickly, but Shan watched in order to replicate the style if required.

It was another hour before Daiyu was ready. She sat on the edge of her seat, posture straight, not a hair out of place and looked every bit the royal princess. "You look beautiful, my lady," Shan told her.

"Thank you." She clasped her hands, the only sign she was nervous.

"Which one of us would you like to accompany you tonight?" Zhi asked.

Daiyu frowned. "What do you mean?"

"A lady's maid always attends the banquets. She is able to tell the servers what the lady wants so she is not disturbed unnecessarily."

Daiyu hesitated.

"My lady, why don't you take Zhi? She will be able to advise you about the correct protocols and I can finish arranging and tuning your instruments."

"All right."

Zhi bowed. "With your permission, my lady, I shall freshen up."

"Of course." After Zhi had left, Daiyu turned to Shan. "I feel my days will be more monitored than they were in Chungson. There is so much I need to learn about the palace."

Shan smiled at her. "Don't fret. I am here for you, and Zhi will be a helpful ally."

"What do I do about her?" Daiyu asked. "I don't need two maids."

"I am supposed to be your bridal companion," Shan reminded her. "We still don't know whether the emperor will allow me to stay. But if he does, do not fear about offending me. I will do whatever you require of me."

"Thank you."

There was a knock on the door and Daiyu inhaled sharply.

"You will be full of grace tonight, my lady. Prince Kun appears to be quite taken with you already."

She blushed. "He was very kind, wasn't he?" She gestured for Shan to open the door. A black-clad servant stood there. "Prince Kun advises it is time for Lady Daiyu to attend the dinner. He has sent her a sedan chair."

Behind the man was a cream silk sedan chair and four bearers. "She will be out momentarily," Shan said.

Zhi had returned and helped Daiyu to her feet.

"Have a lovely time." Shan waited until Daiyu was seated in the chair and they moved down the paved road back towards the main palace before she closed the door.

Alone, at last.

She sighed and returned to her own room. Hai had left her trunk in the room with four beds. Ting and Yun jumped to their feet as she walked in.

"Is everything all right?" Shan asked.

They nodded.

"Then why are you standing?"

"We must stand when a superior enters the room," Ting said.

Shan waved them to sit. "Don't be silly. I am not your superior. We are all servants of Lady Daiyu."

Yun's eyes widened. "I thought you were Daiyu's friend, her bridal companion."

Of course. "She is also my mistress, and in that regard, I am her servant."

"You are far more important than us, at least that's what Zhi says."

Tread carefully. "Zhi may require you to stand when she enters, but I do not. Heavens, you'd be up and down all night."

Ting smiled. "Is there anything we can do to help?"

"The rest of Daiyu's clothes need steaming," Shan said. "My lady was limited in what she could bring with her, so Zhi is arranging a seamstress to visit tomorrow, but we must be ready for any number of invitations."

"The palace has a whole department for clothing the women's quarter," Ting said. "Many seamstresses would be pleased to clothe our lady."

Good. It was one less thing to worry about. "If you could show me to the steam rooms, I can help you with our lady's things and then do my own."

Yun shook her head. "It is not appropriate, Shan. You can't do the things we do."

"Why not?"

"It is not part of your role."

She had to remember she was Daiyu's companion. "I'm sure I can help."

Yun shook her head. "In the palace each person has defined roles. Zhi's is to attend to our lady when she is visiting or when she is in her palace. We run all the errands, clean her clothes, prepare her bath, clean the room, and Hai is available for any heavy work."

"Surely it won't matter if I help you," Shan said.

"It will. The other ladies will shun you. They will tell the empress about your inappropriate behaviour and then she might shun Daiyu."

What kind of world had she moved to? "Am I allowed to do my own clothes?"

"It is best if you leave it to us," Ting said.

Shan stifled a sigh and went to her trunk. "Could you please steam one of my outfits so I have something to wear tomorrow, and then do the rest of our lady's outfits?"

"Of course." The girls bowed and hurried away, calling to Hai to help them carry everything.

Shan sat on her bed. The sooner she understood the protocols the better. Could she trust Zhi to teach her? Yun and Ting could help, but they wouldn't know everything involved in being a lady's companion. The last thing Shan wanted was to embarrass Daiyu or do something which would make her an outcast.

Though she was hungry, she couldn't eat yet. She didn't know where to go for a meal or where Ting and Yun had gone to ask them. In the meantime she would tune Daiyu's instruments and prepare her bed for when she returned.

She crossed the hallway into the main room. A thump in Daiyu's bedchamber made her frown. Daiyu couldn't be back already. Perhaps it was the others getting Daiyu's clothes. She crept towards the doorway and peered inside. A strange man wearing black servant clothing was inside, going through Daiyu's drawers. Shan's heart raced. Who was he? What was he looking for? She debated turning invisible and watching him for longer, but he might find whatever it was he'd come for.

"Can I help you?"

The man yelped and spun towards her. "Who are you?"

His voice was low, raspy as if he had spent his day yelling.

"That was going to be my next question," Shan said. "I am Lady Daiyu's bridal companion."

"She wasn't supposed to bring anyone with her."

Her skin went cold. "That is beside the point," she said. "Now, who are you and why are you going through my lady's things?" She didn't know whether there was anyone nearby who would hear her call for help. If she made a fuss and he had a legitimate reason for being here, she would hurt Daiyu's standing.

"There wasn't supposed to be anyone here." His square jaw jutted out.

So he had no right to be here. She touched her wrist ribbon and glanced towards the doors but no one was outside. "Yet, here I am. I suggest you answer my question before I call a guard."

"There are no guards. He made sure of it." The man stepped closer to her.

Who had? Shan's skin crawled. "What do you want?" The man was taller than her and though his outfit was loose, she could tell he was muscled underneath it. Her ribbon garrotte would be of no use and she didn't want to kill the man, just get answers from him. A bronze statue stood on the table a few feet away. "Why are you here?"

"It is none of your business." The man's gaze flicked to the doorway behind her and she moved away from it, further into the bedchamber, glancing to make sure no one else was there.

The man lunged towards her, a knife glistening in his hand. She leapt backwards, missing his strike and lost her footing on the loose carpet. She flailed, blocking his next attack and regained her balance. Heart racing, she backed away towards the table, dodging his next stabs, but the knife caught her sleeve and ripped it. Desperate now, she grabbed the bronze statue and swung it at him, hitting his hand.

The man swore as the knife flew out of his grasp. Could she reach it before he did?

She swung the heavy statue at him again and he leapt back. Shan lunged for the knife on the ground, her fingers closing around the hilt, and spun around.

He was gone.

She crept forward, eyes searching for movement but then a door slammed. Not letting down her guard, she entered the main room and scanned it. It appeared empty, but she checked behind couches and curtains until she was certain the man had gone.

Letting out a breath, she lowered the knife.

What should she do now? Would anyone believe her if she reported it? She examined the blade. Nothing unique about it. Its wooden handle was similar to a knife seen in a kitchen.

Shan hurried across to her sleeping quarters, but the other servants hadn't returned. She didn't want to cause a fuss, draw too much attention in case it wasn't appropriate. She'd have to wait until someone came back to discover the proper protocol.

Her hand trembled and she sank onto her bed, her heart racing. She'd almost been killed, again—almost been forced to kill, again.

She blew out a shuddery breath. As soon as she'd discovered Bao's secret, she'd known life at the palace would be dangerous, but she hadn't anticipated the attacks would happen immediately.

She closed her eyes, exhausted.

Perhaps if she drew the man's face while it was fresh in her mind. That way she'd have something to show people when she reported the break in.

The thought of having something to do calmed her. She fetched items from her drawing chest, lit a lantern and sat at the table to record his portrait.

Chapter 6

It took Shan an hour to finish the drawing, making sure the squareness of his jaw and his narrow, nervous eyes were correct. She packed away her things and returned to Daiyu's rooms, laying the drawing on the table. The drawers were still open, and things had been thrown to the floor. She shook her head and tidied, her nerves fragile, constantly checking the doorway in case someone came in. She should have done this first, before she'd drawn the portrait. Her priorities were skewed.

When the room was put to rights, she prepared Daiyu's bed. Ting and Yun returned with Daiyu's clothes and Shan leapt away from the door as they walked through. She placed a hand to her heart as they stared at her. "Sorry. You startled me."

Yun frowned as she hung the clothes in the wardrobe. "Who did you think it would be?"

Shan didn't respond, but her stomach rumbled. "Ting, could you show me where the kitchens are before you retire? I haven't eaten since this morning."

"Of course." She bowed. "I hope you've been added to the list."

"What do you mean?"

"As Daiyu's companion you come under a different

bureau than Yun and I and therefore get different food rations."

Shouldn't they all get the same? As they walked through the main room, Shan collected the drawing from the table.

"Who's that?" Ting asked.

She hesitated. "I'm not sure. Do you recognise him?"

Ting frowned. "No. Did you draw that?"

"Yes."

"Where did you see him?"

"He was just someone walking past." She wouldn't say anything until she'd had a chance to speak with Daiyu. She wasn't certain who to trust.

A rustle and the clink of metal outside the front door had her spinning around. It sounded like Daiyu was back. She tucked the paper into her top and hurried to open the door. Daiyu stood on the front step with Prince Kun, an appropriate distance between them. Shan bowed low, averting her eyes.

"Thank you for accompanying me back to my palace," Daiyu said.

"It is my honour," Kun replied. "I hope you enjoyed dinner tonight."

"It was lovely. Though I shall be sorry to see my brother leave tomorrow, I feel truly blessed to be living here with such lovely people."

Relief filled Shan and she smiled, pleased Daiyu had enjoyed herself. It boded well for her future.

"Sleep well, Lady Daiyu." Prince Kun took his leave and Daiyu swept into the room, sighing in pleasure. After Zhi entered, Shan closed the door behind them. Daiyu sat on her divan and clutched her hands together, a huge smile on her face.

"Did you enjoy your dinner, my lady?" Shan asked.

"It was wonderful," she replied. "The people were lovely, the food was amazing and Prince Kun…" She blushed.

"He was extremely attentive all night," Zhi said.

"I am pleased. May I help you get ready for bed, my lady?"

"I couldn't possibly sleep yet," she said. "My heart is too full. Tomorrow the empress has invited me to tea." She sat straighter, her happiness gone. "What if I do something wrong? What if she doesn't like me and calls off the betrothal?"

"I can teach you the etiquette in the morning, my lady," Zhi said. "You needn't fear. The empress will love you."

Shan nodded. "All your clothes have been steamed and pressed." Her stomach rumbled again and she flushed.

"Have you eaten?" Daiyu asked.

"Not yet, my lady. I will find some food when you are in bed."

"Nonsense. Zhi can help me. Why haven't you eaten?"

"I wanted to ensure everything here was perfect," she said.

"Have Ting show you the way to the kitchen," Zhi said.

Shan glanced at Daiyu for permission.

"Yes, go. I will see you in the morning."

The paper pressed against her breast reminding her she hadn't told Daiyu about the intruder. But she didn't want to disturb her happiness. She'd talk to Hai about a guard for the front and rear doors of the palace when she returned.

She found Ting and Yun in their bedroom getting ready for bed. "Could you tell me where the kitchens are?"

Ting glanced at her pyjamas and winced. "Sorry, I forgot."

"I can follow directions," Shan told her.

"Thank you." Ting smiled. "Turn right out of the servants' exit and follow the road until the end. Turn right again and you'll reach the kitchens."

"Thank you."

"Remember to stop and kowtow if you see any of the concubines or imperial family," Yun added.

Shan nodded. At this time of night there should be few people out, unless they were returning from the banquet. She exited the building and took a moment to breathe the warm night air. It was far warmer here than in Chungson, possibly because the brick soaked up the heat during the day. A few lanterns flickered on the walls, lighting her way and making shadows dance. Her muscles tensed and bumps rose to her skin.

Where had the intruder gone? How safe was she out here? When she returned, she'd tell Ting and Yun about the man, ask them for advice. Although she hated to upset Daiyu, Daiyu's safety was paramount.

At the end of the road she turned right. More palace entrances lined the road and though lanterns lit their doors, no one was around. At the far end was a building where lights glowed in the windows and people moved back and forth. The kitchen.

She was almost there when she heard footsteps ahead of her. Fear made her press against the wall and turn invisible. She moved to the junction and peered around the corner. A servant spoke with a man who wore a navy-blue official's uniform, the cut of the fabric revealing he was a man of importance. She stayed where she was, unwilling to call attention to herself.

"You said no one would be there!" the servant rasped.

Shan's heart pounded as she recognised the voice of the man who had attacked her.

The official shushed him and lowered his voice so Shan couldn't hear his answer.

Her soft-soled slippers made no noise on the pavement as she kept to the shadows and crept towards them.

"She came to Bonam with Lady Daiyu," the servant said.

The official made an annoyed sound. "Daiyu was told she couldn't bring any servants. The emperor commanded it."

"Well she did. The maid saw my face."

"You should have killed her."

"I thought her body might cause too many questions."

"And you breaking in won't cause an uproar? I'm surprised guards haven't been called already." The official looked around as if expecting men to run around the corner. The lamp illuminated his face, and Shan memorised his narrow eyes, thin pointed nose and the shape of his long moustache.

"What do you want me to do now?"

"Leave. Go as far from here as you can."

"But what will I do for work?"

"You should have thought about that before you allowed yourself to be seen," the official said. "I can't be associated with you now."

The servant grabbed him. "I did what you ordered me to do. You have to give me something. A recommendation at least."

The official shook him off. "No. Go now. If you're caught, you'll be hung for being in the women's quarters."

"You lied to me," the servant yelled. "You said the emperor would reward me for my work and now you're banishing me?"

"Quiet," the official hissed. "The emperor only rewards people who succeed."

Shan's mouth dropped open. The emperor had ordered Daiyu's room to be searched? What did that mean for Daiyu?

The servant growled and lunged forward, snatching something from the official's belt. It took Shan a second to make out the glint of the blade and she was too late to stop him as he stabbed the official in the stomach. Shan gasped.

The servant looked in her direction, eyes wide and then the official groaned. "Help! Someone help me."

The servant stabbed him again as the door to the kitchen opened. He frantically looked for escape and then turned and ran. The woman who came out of the kitchen screamed and half a dozen more people ran out. They hesitated on the verandah as if too scared to come closer. Though the official had ordered Daiyu's room to be searched, Shan couldn't let him die. He might be able to give her more answers. She dropped her illusion and ran to him, falling to her knees, and placing her hand over his wounds. A couple of eunuchs ran towards her. "You, get a physician," she ordered the first one. To the next man, she said, "Call the guards." She glanced at the people still gathered around the kitchen. "Someone find me bandages or cloth," she called. One of the women ducked back into the kitchen.

The official's warm blood ran down her fingers and he gasped, his eyes wide and full of pain.

The woman ran over with dish towels. They would do. Shan folded them and then pressed them hard against the wounds. The official groaned. "I'm sorry," she said. "I have to stop the bleeding."

Footsteps pounded on the pavement and two guards ran up. "What's going on?"

The woman backed away and looked at Shan to answer. "He was stabbed in the stomach by a man wearing black servant's clothing," Shan said. "The man ran down there." She nodded in the direction.

"That's Prime Minister Cong," one of the guards said, horror on his face.

"We've sent for a physician," Shan said. "If either of you know what to do, I'd appreciate your help, otherwise you should go after the man so he doesn't escape."

"The gates are shut. There's nowhere he can go," the guard said, but he left to raise the alarm.

How hard would he be to find amongst the hundreds, if not thousands of servants working at the palace?

Another man ran up carrying a large leather bag. He knelt next to Shan and asked the guards, "What happened?" He shoved Shan aside so he could look at the wound.

Shan knelt back, annoyance running over her. "He was stabbed twice in the stomach. The blade was about four inches long."

The physician glanced at her. "You saw it happen?"

Ancestors, she shouldn't have said anything. Caught now, she nodded. "I walked around the corner as it happened," she said. "I couldn't stop it."

"What did the man look like?" the taller guard asked.

"I could draw a picture of him," Shan said. "Would that help?"

Prime Minister Cong groaned.

"I need to get him inside," the physician said. The two eunuchs hurried to help him, and Shan moved out of the way, her hands still covered in blood. Her stomach clenched and she breathed to control the nausea. A scullery maid stood to the side, her eyes wide in shock.

"Excuse me, could you show me where I can wash?" Shan asked, desperate to wipe the blood onto her gown but she couldn't afford to ruin another outfit.

The girl blinked and then gasped as she saw Shan's hands. "This way."

The taller guard grabbed her arm. "Where are you going?"

"If it pleases you," Shan said. "I will wash my hands so I can draw the picture for you. Do you have some paper and charcoal I could use?"

The guard stared at her a moment and then said to the maid, "Show her where she can wash and then take her to the Office of Internal Scrutiny." To Shan he said, "What is your name?"

"Shan. I am the bridal companion of Lady Daiyu of Chungson."

He nodded and waved them away.

Shan followed the maid into the kitchen and the maid poured her a bowl of water. The scent of food turned Shan's stomach. She wouldn't be eating tonight. Not after this.

"Thank you." As Shan washed her hands, she asked, "What is your name?"

"An."

"I appreciate your help."

An stared at her. "I don't know how you're so calm."

Sadly she was getting used to the violence, though her hands shook as she dried them. "My Lady's carriage was attacked on the way here," she said. "That was far more terrifying than this."

Why was the Prime Minister spying on Daiyu? Had the emperor really ordered it?

She placed the towel on the table. "Could you show me the way to the Office now?"

"Of course. Do you need to send word to your lady?"

"No. She told me to retire after I had eaten. She will be going to bed herself shortly."

When they exited the kitchen, a group of guards was gathered outside. The tall guard motioned to her. "That's her. She saw it all."

The man he spoke to turned and Shan dropped to her knees, kowtowing, her heart racing. They'd called Prince Kun. Zhi had mentioned servants were expected to kowtow for any of the imperial family and with her role not yet defined, she didn't dare simply bow.

"Rise," Kun said. He frowned. "Who are you?"

"Your Highness, I am Lady Daiyu's bridal companion," she said, not surprised he didn't remember her.

"You saw the attack?"

"Yes, Your Highness."

"Come with me." He strode away.

Her nerves jumped and clamoured as Shan followed him through the streets until they reached a large, ornate palace. The guard on the door opened it and then bowed low as Prince Kun swept inside. Shan hesitated before following him. The receiving room was double the size of Daiyu's with an intricate parquetry floor. A glossy black table stood in the centre of the room and Prince Kun sat. A servant ran to pour him some tea.

"Fetch me paper and writing tools," Kun said.

Shan stood a yard from the table, her hands behind her back, waiting for his instruction.

"Tell me exactly what happened."

Should she admit to hearing some of the conversation? If the emperor really was behind the trespass, it could be very dangerous. It would reflect badly on his honour and she would be punished for lying even if it was the truth. She skipped to the part where Cong had been stabbed and told him what she had done afterwards.

"That was quick thinking," Kun said.

"Thank you, Your Highness."

"Lord Anming tells me you saved Lady Daiyu when she was attacked."

Shan jolted then nodded. "I protected my lady as best as I could."

"The emperor didn't want Daiyu to bring anyone with her. Why did you come?"

Her skin pimpled. "I am her bridal companion, Your Highness."

"Will you leave with Lord Anming?"

"I will do what I am ordered to do, Your Highness."

He pursed your lips. "Stay. I will have a word to the emperor. You have proven yourself useful, and Daiyu will be happier with someone she knows."

She bowed. "Thank you, Your Highness."

"You believe you can draw the man you saw?" Kun asked.

The paper already under her top burned. "Yes, Your Highness. I have been told my drawings are quite life-like."

The servant returned with paper and charcoal.

"Then sit." He pushed the items towards her. "Show me what you can do."

Shan's hand trembled as she picked up the charcoal stick. Was the prince as cruel as his father? No, he seemed to care about Daiyu's happiness. She swallowed and allowed herself to calm. She'd drawn the man once, she could do it again.

When she was finished, she pushed the paper across to the prince who had watched her work. "This is him, Your Highness."

"Your drawing is indeed fine," Kun said. "If the ladies discover your talent, they will want you to draw their portraits and those of their children and pets as well."

She inclined her head. "I will do whatever is asked of me."

"Then I ask you do not make it common knowledge that you draw so well."

What a strange request. "Of course, Your Highness."

He studied her. "Where does your loyalty lay?"

Surprise stole her voice. What did he mean? She swallowed. "To the emperor, of course, Your Highness."

"And after him?"

Was she supposed to mention the entire imperial family individually? "To the imperial family and then to my lady, Daiyu."

"And if I told you your loyalty should be to Daiyu first?"

He was testing her, but why? "I would do whatever you bid me."

He was silent a long moment. "Then these are my orders. You are to tell no one of them, is that clear?"

Her heart thumped. "Yes, Your Highness."

"Your priority is keeping Lady Daiyu safe. If anyone gives you orders to the contrary, you are to tell me immediately, is that clear?"

"Yes, Your Highness." He must know something was wrong. She hesitated. "Your Highness, how will I contact you?"

"No one will question you sending a message to me. You can say it comes from Lady Daiyu."

She nodded, her stomach a swirling mass of nerves. Not even a day in the imperial palace and she was already involved in intrigue.

Prince Kun picked up her sketch. "I will take this to the guards. You may return to your room."

She stood and bowed low. "Thank you, Your Highness."

She wished she had never come to Bonam at all.

Chapter 7

The next morning dawned clear and bright, a welcome contrast from the darkness the night before. With Daiyu still sleeping, Shan asked Zhi to teach her what was expected of a lady's maid.

Zhi frowned. "Lord Anming told the emperor you were Daiyu's bridal companion. Are you not leaving with him today?"

"No. Prince Kun confirmed I was to stay last night."

"When?" Zhi demanded.

Shan hesitated. Word would spread quickly about the stabbing. "There was an incident last night." She told Zhi what had happened. "His Highness asked me to stay."

"The emperor ordered Daiyu to come alone."

How was Zhi aware of what the emperor wanted? "Prince Kun said he would speak with the emperor." She bowed her head. "I will do whatever is asked of me."

"Lady Daiyu cannot have two lady's maids. She is not yet of the correct status for such things."

"Then we can continue to call me Daiyu's bridal companion," Shan said.

Zhi splayed her fingers over her chest. "But that would mean the prince could choose you as his concubine."

What? Shan's chest tightened and discomfit filled her. "In

Chungson, a bridal companion helps the bride with wedding preparations and to settle into her new home."

"Here it means more like a sister bride, a first option for the prince's consort."

She couldn't bear that. She shook her head. "Then we will choose a different title."

"You do not wish to be the prince's consort?" Zhi was horrified.

"In Chungson it is not common for a man to take concubines and consorts." Shan chose her words carefully. "I would be honoured if the prince wanted me, but I would not want to upset Lady Daiyu."

"Strange how little Bonam customs are followed in its vassal states."

Shan ignored Zhi's judgement. She was pleased Chungson had managed to hold on to some of its customs in the nearly twenty years since Bonam had invaded and taken over its rule.

The bell from Daiyu's room rang. Zhi rushed to answer it and Shan followed more slowly. Until Daiyu told her differently, she would continue to act as her maid. While Zhi helped Daiyu dress, Shan arranged for Ting to get her breakfast.

"My brother is leaving this morning," Daiyu said as she swept into the receiving room. "I must say goodbye before he goes."

"My lady, you will need your betrothed's permission to leave the inner palace," Zhi said.

"Why?"

"Ladies in the women's quarters are not permitted to leave without the emperor's consent, or in your case, Prince Kun's. Their honour and virtue must be guarded at all times."

"How tiresome," Daiyu said. "Fetch me some paper so I can write to the prince."

Shan retrieved it. "Would you like me to deliver it for

you?"

"You do not know the way."

Shan bowed. "I do, my lady. I was there last night." She explained what had happened.

Daiyu covered her mouth with her hand. "How awful. Do we know if the Prime Minister is all right?"

"No, my lady. I shall ask the prince when I see him."

Daiyu folded the note and placed her seal on it. "Hurry. I am not sure what time Anming is departing."

"Yes, my lady." Shan left the palace and retraced her steps from the night before. The paths didn't seem as narrow now, and the shadows were a friendly reprieve from the sun. When she reached the prince's palace, she rang the bell and waited, head bowed. A manservant answered the door.

"I have a message for the prince from Lady Daiyu."

The man took it. "I shall see that he gets it."

Shan stopped him from closing the door. "If it pleases you, the message is urgent. If Prince Kun is here, I will wait for an answer."

The manservant scowled at her. "Wait one moment." He closed the door.

She clasped her hands in front of her while she waited. Inside voices murmured and behind her servants strode along the paths going about their morning duties. There was no bird song, or wind blowing through the trees. Little natural noise at all.

The sun heated her back as she waited, but she didn't shift into the shade. And still she waited.

Just as she was debating whether she should ring the bell again, the door swung open and Prince Kun stood there, his rich mahogany two-piece suit unwrinkled and perfect. Shan kowtowed.

"Please stand. I will send word to Lord Anming. Tell Lady Daiyu I will be there within the hour to accompany her to the Hall of Clarity."

Shan bowed. "Thank you, Your Highness." She hesitated. No, it wasn't appropriate for her to ask how the Prime Minister was, or if they'd found his attacker. She would leave that for Daiyu. When Kun gave her leave, she bowed again and returned to the Jasmine Palace.

"Prince Kun will accompany you to visit your brother," she told Daiyu. "He will be here within the hour."

Zhi gasped. "That is not enough time to get her ready!"

"I am sure we will manage together," Shan said. "If you are happy for me to choose her gown and jewellery, you can start on her hair."

"Show me what you want her to wear," Zhi said as if Daiyu wasn't in the room with them.

"My lady, I thought the purple gown would be nice."

Daiyu nodded. "Please. And the silver earrings."

Shan fetched the outfit, which Zhi approved, and helped Daiyu dress. While Zhi did her hair, Shan returned to her room for the letter she'd written Anming last night. It included the image of the man who had broken into Daiyu's palace. He might be able to find out more about the incident. She tucked it into the small bag she carried.

When she returned, there was a knock on the door. Zhi gasped. "That can't be the prince. Daiyu is not ready." Yun and Ting held sections of Daiyu's hair while Zhi arranged it in an elaborate twist.

"I shall answer it." Shan opened the door to find Prince Kun waiting. She bowed low. "Your Highness, Lady Daiyu will be a few more minutes. Might I offer you some refreshments?"

Prince Kun frowned. "No."

Shan hesitated. Daiyu needed more time. "If I may ask, Your Highness, how is Prime Minister Cong?"

He focused on her. "He is recovering. The doctor said he was lucky to have arrived when he did." The prince inclined his head. "Thank you for your quick thinking. I will make sure the emperor knows what you did to help."

"Thank you, Your Highness. It pleases me to know he survived." She paused. "Was the man who attacked him found?"

"Not yet." Kun's words were sharp.

"Then I pray to the ancestors that he is found soon." Behind her silk rustled and she turned as Daiyu glided to the door. She bowed to the prince. "My apologies for keeping you waiting, Your Highness."

"It is an honour to wait for a beauty such as yourself."

Daiyu blushed and together they walked down the steps to the waiting sedan chair. Shan and Zhi followed, walking next to the couple as they were carried through the Gates of Heavenly Virtue and into the main palace courtyard. They stopped outside the Hall of Clarity and Prince Kun helped Lady Daiyu from the platform. "Your brother waits inside."

Shan followed. Would she have the opportunity to give the lord her letter? She hadn't seen Bao since they'd arrived at the palace, but Anming would have another manservant.

They entered a small receiving room with a delicate parquetry floor. Lord Anming waited inside with Captain Wei. Bao was nowhere to be seen. She ignored the stab of disappointment. Both men turned as they entered and Lady Daiyu greeted her brother before they all sat around a small table. Zhi poured tea while another servant served the food. Shan made her way across to where Captain Wei stood against the wall.

He nodded. "Shan."

She slipped the envelope from her bag. "Please give this to our Lord."

He took it and crossed his arms behind his back, hiding the envelope. "I will. Trouble already?"

How much did Wei know about her mission here? Perhaps he was aware, but she couldn't risk it. "The letter explains everything." She glanced at the table and jolted as she met Prince Kun's eyes. Keeping her expression calm, she bowed to him. Had he seen her give Wei the envelope? Would he be suspicious about what it contained?

"Tell Mother I am well and happy here," Daiyu said. She smiled at the prince. "While she is honoured you chose me, she was sad about me moving so far away."

"She will see you at the wedding."

"Indeed," Anming said. "It will be a day for much celebration."

They spoke about the wedding for a little longer until Lord Anming stood. "We must go if we're to travel any leagues today. Take care of yourself, sister." He hugged her and glanced at Shan. She inclined her head. She would watch over Daiyu, would have done so without the order from her lord and the prince.

"Safe travels, brother." Only a slight quiver in her voice showed Daiyu was upset. They all walked out of the receiving room into the courtyard.

Anming bowed to the prince and his sister and strode across the courtyard with Captain Wei to where his retinue waited.

Shan and Daiyu were on their own.

~*~

When Prince Kun returned them to the Jasmine Palace, Lady Daiyu hurried inside and sat at the table, tears brimming in her eyes. She sniffed, dabbing at them to hide her reaction. Zhi tutted. "My lady, there is no reason to be sad. You should be honoured to be here in the centre of the universe, at the imperial palace, seat of his Heavenly Majesty."

"I am," Daiyu said. "But I will miss my brother."

"We all miss our family, but there is little we can do about it," Zhi said, her shoulders stiff. "We must do as His Majesty wills." There was an undertone of displeasure which belied Zhi's pious words.

"What time are you due to visit the empress, my lady?" Shan asked.

Daiyu gasped. "I'd forgotten about it." She glanced at the clock on the wall. "Mid-afternoon."

"We have time to prepare," Shan said. "Were you able to procure the palace seamstress for today?" she asked Zhi.

Zhi nodded. "I can send for her now if my lady wishes."

They both looked to Daiyu. She sniffed. "Please do. It will be good to be distracted, and I must have enough clothes. I would hate to bring dishonour to Prince Kun."

"He seems lovely, my lady," Shan said as Zhi ordered Yun to fetch the seamstress.

Daiyu beamed. "He is far nicer than I ever expected," she said. "I thought he might be old or so very serious, but he knows much about music and poetry. We spoke at length last night."

"I am sure he will enjoy hearing you play the guzheng, my lady," Shan said. What would happen to the betrothal when the true heir reclaimed his throne? Would Lord Anming still permit Daiyu and Kun to marry? He would still be a prince and a worthy match for Daiyu. But perhaps she would marry Bao instead.

Shan's stomach clenched, a foolish reaction. He had never been an option for her. Servants were rarely permitted to marry. She sent for tea and then the seamstress arrived with a bevy of eunuchs carrying bolts of silk in myriad colours. She moved out of the way, keeping her back to the wall as Zhi and the seamstress took control, helping Daiyu choose colours and styles for her new outfits.

She made note of who was there and memorised what the seamstress said were the latest styles, taking the opportunity to study the designs Daiyu was shown.

In between the measuring and discussions, Shan ordered Daiyu something to eat. It wouldn't do for her to turn up at the empress's palace faint from lack of food, or with her stomach grumbling. Daiyu nodded her thanks and picked at the food as she was wrapped in different colours of silk.

Finally, a messenger arrived with a note from the empress. They were to have tea in the garden. Daiyu dismissed the seamstress who promised to have the first outfit ready for fitting by the next day and as quickly as they had arrived, they were gone in a bustle of colours.

Shan told the messenger, "Lady Daiyu will be there shortly." She closed the door and Daiyu slumped over the table. "I'm exhausted. What should I wear? What do I say?" She turned to Zhi. "You haven't told me how I am supposed to respond to the empress."

Shan fetched Daiyu a fresh outfit as Zhi calmed her. "My lady, be respectful at all times. You may respond to the empress's questions, but do not ask your own unless you are enquiring about her health. She will want to know all about the lady who is going to marry her son, so mention your accomplishments, but do not brag."

"You will be wonderful, my lady." Shan held up the mauve dress for Daiyu's approval and her lady nodded. "Your mother has trained you for this. You know what is expected of you."

Daiyu sighed and smiled. "You are right. No one can be as exacting as my mother."

They helped her dress and then followed the messenger through the maze of streets and over a lovely ornate bridge into the emperor's garden. A large maidenhair tree stood at the entrance, and Shan stroked her hand along its bark. It reminded her of home.

"This is lovely," Daiyu said. "Am I permitted to come here whenever I like?"

Zhi hesitated. "The gardens are for the imperial family," she said. "You will be part of the family soon, but we will have to ask Prince Kun if you can come here before you are married."

Shan would ensure Daiyu asked him. It was quiet and peaceful amongst the lush bushes and Daiyu loved nature.

They wove slowly through the paths, past an empty pavilion and a beautiful herb garden, until they arrived at another pavilion by a small pond. The empress was already there waiting, stroking a black and white cat on her lap. Daiyu tensed as Zhi made the formal introductions and then they all kowtowed in front of her.

"Stand. Take a seat, Lady Daiyu. I am eager to speak with you. My son monopolised your time last night and now it is my turn."

Daiyu slipped into the seat across from the empress, and Shan and Zhi stood outside the pavilion with the other maids. Shan scanned the surroundings. The pond was still, reflecting the branches of the trees above it and a couple of birds flew in and out of the small flowering shrubs bordering it. On the other side of the pavilion, jasmine entwined up the posts, filling the air with its sweet scent.

The empress's maids were impeccably dressed, and their attention didn't waver from the empress, waiting for any command.

"Tell me, Lady Daiyu, what instruments do you play?" the empress asked.

"I play the lute and the erhu, Your Majesty," she said. "Though my favourite instrument is the guzheng."

"Why is that?"

"I enjoy its crisp sound. It soothes my soul."

"How poetic. Are you an accomplished artist?"

Daiyu flushed. "I must admit though I try my best, I am not as good as my companion, Shan." Daiyu gestured to her and Shan inclined her head at the compliment, pressing her lips together. She hadn't thought to ask Daiyu to keep her talent a secret. Would Prince Kun be angry?

"Is that so? You would allow your companion to be better at something than you?" The censure was clear.

"I truly believe Shan's talent is a gift from God. There would be few who capture the spirit of a scene like she does."

The empress looked at Shan, and Shan lowered her eyes. "Then I must see this talent. Come forward."

Shan's heart beat rapidly. She was honoured Daiyu thought highly of her artistry, but now was not the time to brag about it, especially not to the empress. She moved into the pavilion, her gaze still on the ground as the empress ordered one of her servants to fetch drawing utensils. She bowed low.

"Where did you learn to draw?" the empress asked.

"My master before Daiyu insisted I learn. He was very exact in his requirements."

"Do you draw landscapes or people?"

"Both, Your Majesty."

"Then I would like you to draw myself and Lady Daiyu here. We should have something to commemorate our first tea together." Her smile was a little bitter. "The current and future empresses of Bonam, should the usurper not have his way."

Her skin pimpled but Shan didn't dare comment on the usurper or show any knowledge of such things. "Yes, Your Majesty."

The servant arrived with a drawing board, paper and charcoal and with the empress's permission, Shan sat on the edge of the pavilion to draw the scene.

"Have you heard the rumours, Lady Daiyu?" the empress asked.

Shan concentrated on her drawing, her pulse racing. It was meant to be treason to even mention the idea of another emperor, but perhaps the same laws didn't apply to the empress. She held her breath waiting for Daiyu's response.

"No, Your Majesty, I have not."

"Perhaps such rumours haven't reached the stately homes

in Chungson yet. It is said the rumours started in the countryside there." Her tone was hard.

"Then I'm sure my brother will see they are stopped," Daiyu said.

"Don't you want to know what the rumours are?"

"If it pleases you to tell me, Your Majesty."

The empress sipped her tea and studied Daiyu. Shan didn't dare capture on paper the calculation in her eyes. "The rumour is that Prince Bao, son of my brother-in-law, Emperor Huang, survived the Rhoran attack and is ready to reclaim his throne."

Daiyu gasped, her cheeks growing red. "But why would he wait so long to come forward?"

"Precisely," the empress said. "It is lies spread by peasants. Tales they spin to pretend their lives could be better than they are, as if they aren't perfectly adequate under our Heavenly Majesty."

Shan pressed a little hard on the drawing and took a moment to breathe and release the tension in her shoulders. The empress knew nothing of the conditions in the country, or about how those who were poor struggled to live.

"Our Heavenly Majesty is indeed magnificent," Daiyu said.

"And yet you disobeyed him," the empress said.

Shan kept her eyes on the paper in front of her, her teeth clenched.

"What do you mean, Your Majesty?" Daiyu asked.

"You brought your lady's maid with you."

"Oh. It was not my intention to disobey the emperor," she said. "Shan was to help me on the journey and be my bridal companion. It is a tradition in Chungson."

"Why is she still here?"

Shan glanced up to draw the next section, her face expressionless.

"Prince Kun suggested she stay." Daiyu smiled. "He was

worried I would miss home and wanted a little something to help me settle in. He is exceedingly kind."

The empress's smile was pinched. "He is."

Why were they all intent on keeping Daiyu isolated and alone? Was Kun aware of the plan and trying to thwart it?

"Many ladies were surprised and disappointed when the emperor announced your betrothal," the empress said.

"It is an honour I am not worthy of," Daiyu said.

"You do not think you are a good match for my son?"

Daiyu's eyes widened. "It is not that. I am not certain any woman could ever be good enough for the prince, but I respect the emperor's faith in me and I will strive every day to be the best wife I can be."

Shan smiled. Daiyu had anticipated the empress's next comment—suggesting the emperor had got the match wrong—and neatly prevented her from asking it.

"My son is very worthy. He is an excellent scholar and poet, as well as a brilliant soldier." The empress sipped her tea. "I am sure he will write a poem for you before the wedding if he deems you worthy."

"I shall pray that he does."

Shan continued her drawing as the empress so politely grilled Daiyu about her upbringing, skills and thoughts on the world. Shan was proud of how well Daiyu deflected the implied criticism and responded with dignity and grace. Years of dealing with her mother's criticisms and exacting standards had been good for Daiyu.

"Has your servant not finished our drawing yet?" The empress glared at Shan.

Shan waited for Daiyu to ask her directly before she responded. "I need only a few minutes more."

The empress stood and Daiyu and Shan were forced to stand as well. Shan balanced the tablet she leaned upon against one arm as she drew, not daring to stop. She kept her gaze lowered to the paper as the empress said her goodbyes to Daiyu.

As Shan added the final strokes of the drawing, the empress approached her. She bowed low.

"Show me what you have done."

Shan held the drawing out with both hands and kept her head lowered.

The slight intake of breath from the empress was satisfying. A moment's pause. "I will take this. Do you paint as well?"

"Yes, Your Majesty."

"Then you will paint Prince Kun's portrait for me," she said. "I will send for you."

"Yes, Your Majesty." Her heart raced. She had not as much practice with paints, not having access to the water colours most often used. She would have to ask Daiyu to buy her some.

The empress left the pavilion with her maids and when she was gone, Daiyu let out a breath. "I think that went well."

Zhi nodded. "She is pleased with you, I can tell." She glanced at Shan. "It is a great honour to be asked to paint the prince's portrait."

Shan inclined her head. "It is. My lady, may I buy some paints so I can practise before the empress has need of me?"

"Of course. We must source them immediately."

They strolled through the garden and back to the Jasmine Palace. The temperature rose as soon as they left the shady confines of the garden and Shan wished she had something to drink. When they returned to the palace, Daiyu announced her desire to play the guzheng. She waved her hand at Zhi and Shan. "Zhi, please show Shan around the inner palace and teach her what she needs to know about palace life. If I need you, I will send Ting or Yun to fetch you."

"Yes, my lady." Shan and Zhi bowed and left her to play.

They entered their room and Zhi scowled. "The empress

doesn't like you."

Dread filled Shan. "How can you tell?"

"She asked you to paint the prince's portrait. The last three artists who she asked have all been banished because of the poor job they did. I would be very careful if I were you."

Shan had no words. "And what of our lady? Will she be punished if the empress is unhappy?"

Zhi nodded. "The master is always disciplined along with the servant. We must make sure Lady Daiyu is with you when you paint the prince. That way they can spend time getting to know each other. If the prince is fond of our lady, he can intercede and ensure she is not punished."

"I will suggest it to Lady Daiyu." And send word to the prince. If he truly wanted to protect Daiyu as he implied, he would be happy to spend time with her. "Thank you for your warning." Perhaps she had misread Zhi's animosity, or more likely, Zhi was concerned about the safety of her own job.

Shan sighed. As long as Daiyu stayed safe, Zhi's intentions didn't matter.

Chapter 8

Shan accompanied Zhi from the palace. "What protocol do I need to know?" The faster she learnt about all the ways she could make a mistake at the palace, the less likely she would be to cause Daiyu shame or dishonour.

"The servants in the inner palace are divided into four groups," Zhi said. "Eunuchs like Hai are the only men allowed in the inner palace with the exception of the emperor, Prince Kun and the Prime Minister."

"There are no entertainers?"

"Sometimes, but the emperor prefers female entertainers," Zhi answered. "If there is a male, the emperor generally sees him in the outer palace, at the Hall of Clarity. After the eunuchs are the wet nurses and tutors for the emperor's children."

Shan frowned. "I thought the emperor only had two children."

Zhi laughed. "Of course not. He has two children from the empress, Prince Kun and Princess Fen, who died tragically a few moons ago. His other children are from his concubines and range in age from babies to adolescents. They are mostly princesses but his favourite concubine has just had a son." She lowered her voice and stepped closer to Shan. "There is talk his new son might replace Prince Kun as heir."

Where would that leave Daiyu?

"The third group are the female entertainers and ladies' maids like us. The entertainers might be dancers, singers, musicians or artists. Their role is to entertain the emperor, empress and concubines. They may be called at any time of the day or night."

That was similar to the manor house in Chungson. Her sister, Zan might be learning the correct etiquette there right now.

"Finally there are the scullery maids, gardeners and cooks. Ting and Yun fall into this category. Each group is greeted according to their standing. The group lower than us should bow to us and we should bow to everyone else."

"Where do the eunuchs rank?" Shan asked.

"They are male, so they are the highest." Zhi gestured for Shan to follow her down a corridor.

"And what of the concubines and princesses?" Shan asked. "Do we greet them equally?"

"Oh, heavens no!" Zhi exclaimed. "There are degrees to each concubine depending on whether she is in or out of favour with the emperor."

"How will I know?"

"I will teach you, but in the meantime, if you see anyone of rank, turn your back and kowtow as they walk past, and pray they don't speak to you."

"And if I get it wrong?"

"Depends on who you insult. You might be lucky enough to get away with twenty lashings, but if you offend the First Consort or the empress, you may be banished or hanged."

Killed for an unintentional slight. This was what life was like for those who were unlucky enough to be born of the wrong class. Was it any wonder there were rumblings in the countryside? The rumour of a new emperor, one who might be better than the current one, would be incredibly enticing.

Shan followed Zhi along the road she'd travelled the night before.

"There are corridors for the fourth rung servants." Zhi pointed them out. "We can use them if we choose and sometimes I will if I do not wish to run into one of the concubines. Most of the time we will be with Lady Daiyu and therefore I will show you the main thoroughfares first."

The tour took in the Hall of Ancestors, several pavilions of contemplation and past the emperor's own private quarters. High on top of the outer walls, guards stood on walkways monitoring the inner palace. Would anyone be mad enough to try and sneak in?

Shan frowned. The inner palace was far bigger than she expected, much larger than the Chungson manor grounds where she had lived with Daiyu. Perhaps it was no surprise the Prime Minister's attacker hadn't been found yet. He could be hiding in any one of the numerous buildings, though she doubted anyone would dare shelter him.

She should have spoken to Hai, asked him to guard Daiyu while they were away from the palace. "Even though Hai is younger, does he have superiority over us?" she asked Zhi.

"Theoretically yes," Zhi said, "but he doesn't realise." Her smile was sly. "He is still in the eager-to-please stage of youth, and I aim to keep him that way for as long as possible. Plus, I believe he has a crush on me."

Which meant he would do whatever Zhi asked of him.

"You found the kitchens last night, didn't you?" Zhi asked.

"Yes, but I am not sure what my quota is."

"Lady Daiyu sets how much food and drink we may have," Zhi said. "The others are fed according to the masters of the eunuchs and scullery maids. We may have three meals a day and we can order Ting or Yun to fetch it for us or go to the kitchen ourselves."

It didn't sit comfortably with Shan to send others to do

something she could do herself.

Zhi gasped and her hand shot out to stop Shan. "It's the emperor!" She spun around, facing the wall and kowtowed. Shan followed her lead, holding her breath as the procession rounded the corner just next to them. The bricks were hot, burning Shan's palms and her knees through her dress. She gritted her teeth and lifted her hands so they hovered just above the ground as the sedan chair the emperor was on stopped just behind them.

"I want Cong moved to the physician's hall," a deep male voice bellowed. "He should not be recovering in the inner palace. It is not appropriate."

"I will see he is moved at once, Heavenly Majesty," another man said and footsteps hurried away.

"You, where's my parasol?" the emperor demanded. "It is far too hot to be exposed to the sun."

And yet he didn't notice or care that they were kneeling on the sun-baked bricks with their skin exposed. Was he being intentionally cruel or was he simply clueless? From what she'd heard about him, it could be either. Shan didn't dare shift position to allay the pain of the hot bricks. To bring the emperor's attention to her could be just as painful. Instead she counted slowly in her head, meditating as Bingwen had taught her, taking her mind to a different place, out of her body, away from the pain. She could endure anything, *had* endured far worse pain in her training.

Next to her Zhi whimpered.

Shan wished she could comfort the woman, encourage her to hold on, but it wasn't possible. They weren't allowed to move.

Silence filled the space behind them, but still the emperor did not continue on his way. Was he watching them, waiting for another whimper so he could punish them, or was his attention elsewhere, on something Shan could not see?

After Shan had counted to one thousand, the emperor

finally gave the order to move. She waited until Zhi sat before getting to her feet. Zhi's forehead was red and her hands blistered.

"Let's get you some ointment for your hands," Shan said. "Which way to the physician's hall?"

Zhi shook her head. "We are not allowed there. It is in the outer palace and for the imperial family and officials only. We must go to the wet nurse bureau."

Ridiculous. "Which way?"

Zhi gestured and limped forward. "Why are your hands not burnt?"

"I lifted them from the ground," Shan said. "My knees are sore though."

Zhi gasped. "That was dangerous. You must always connect to the earth when the emperor is around."

"Were my burning knees not enough?"

"No! Your hands and forehead should have touched as well. You are lucky he did not notice."

"I shall keep it in mind next time I see him," Shan said. She prayed to the ancestors it wouldn't be for a long time.

They made it to the wet nurse building without running into any more of the imperial family. Shan followed Zhi inside and stayed behind her as Zhi explained what she needed.

The wet nurse sniffed. "You want us to waste our precious burn cream on you because your skin is not tough enough to handle the sun?"

Shan bit her tongue.

"If it pleases you," Zhi said. "It was in respect for the emperor."

"You are blaming the emperor for your injuries? I should tell the empress of this."

"No! That is not what I meant," Zhi said. "I apologise. Of course I am fine." She spun around and left.

Shan eyed the wet nurse and followed Zhi out. "Is there

anywhere else we can go?"

"No."

"Then perhaps I can ask Lady Daiyu if we can purchase some items when we send for my paints," Shan said.

"Why would she do that? No one would refuse her request for medication."

"Our lady is kind," Shan said. "She will not like to see you suffer. Let's return to the palace and we can at least bathe our wounds in cool water."

Daiyu was still playing the guzheng, the music beautifully haunting, when they arrived back. They went into their rooms and Ting fetched some water from the barrel in the storeroom. Shan made a cool compress and laid it across Zhi's forehead while Zhi placed her hands in the bucket. "Stay there," Shan said. "I'll talk to our lady."

She slipped into the receiving room. Sitting across from Daiyu in rapt attention was Prince Kun. Shan jolted and kowtowed, staying where she was until Daiyu finished the song and Prince Kun said, "Stand."

"My apologies for interrupting," Shan said. "I did not realise you had a guest, my lady."

"Is there something wrong?"

Shan glanced at the prince. "Zhi has injured her hands," she said. "I wanted to ask permission to buy a few treatments in addition to the paints when you send someone into the city."

"There is no need," Kun said. "She can get treated at the wet nurse building."

She would make enemies amongst the wet nurses if she told Kun the truth and that could be bad for Lady Daiyu. But Zhi needed something for her blisters. "Your Highness, I must confess I am used to having access to a few things so that I can treat minor ailments without having to bother those who have more important things to attend to. It will also mean I can better attend to my lady should she have a minor injury."

The prince studied her, perhaps seeing through her words.

"I would hate to be a bother," Lady Daiyu said. "Maybe it would be wise to buy a few items."

"If it pleases you, my lady. I could go now."

"It is getting late," the prince said. "It would be dark before you got back and it is not wise to go into the city after dark." He gestured for his manservant who stood in the corner to come forward. "What do you need tonight?"

"Some ointment for burns and blisters."

"Go fetch the ointment for me."

The man hurried away and Shan bowed low. "Thank you, Your Highness."

"You can go into the city tomorrow morning," he said. "I will send one of my men with you to ensure you are safe." He glanced at Daiyu. "Did you want to go into the city, my lady?"

"It is not necessary if it is not safe."

"I can keep you safe. I can send a dozen of my personal guards with you."

So very kind of him.

Daiyu hesitated. "I would like to see more of my new home."

He smiled. "Then you shall. I will send my men to you mid-morning. I'm afraid I will be busy, but I shall ensure they take you to Jung Li's for dumplings. It was my sister's favourite place to go." Sadness crossed his face.

Daiyu touched his hand. "May she dance in the ancestors' hall."

He nodded. "Aside from treatments, what else did you need?" he asked Shan.

"Paints, Your Highness. Your mother has requested I paint your portrait, but I didn't bring any equipment with me."

"Did she?" He scowled. "I shall schedule time for it.

Perhaps Lady Daiyu would be kind enough to sit with me when you do, so I may have some pleasant conversation."

"I would be honoured." Daiyu smiled.

Good. She wouldn't have to worry about Daiyu's safety while she was painting. Shan stepped back, removing herself from the conversation, but not the room. With Kun's manservant away, it wouldn't be proper to leave the two of them alone.

At Kun's request, Daiyu played another song and Shan poured Kun a drink. She stayed out of the way until his manservant returned with the ointment.

"Thank you," Shan said as she took it from him. Along with the ointment, he handed her a note. "From the prince," he murmured.

She resisted glancing at Kun and tucked the paper into a pocket before excusing herself and returning to the servant quarters where Zhi still lay on her bed, her hands in the water. "I have something which should help," Shan said. "The prince was visiting our lady and he sent for it."

"Bless the ancestors," Zhi sighed.

Shan patted Zhi's hands dry and applied the ointment to her hands and forehead. "The prince has approved a trip into the city tomorrow morning so I may buy paint and some basic treatments. Our lady is coming with me and Kun is sending his personal guard with us."

Zhi sat. "I should go too."

"Perhaps you should use the time to rest and heal."

Zhi studied her and then glanced at her hands. Finally, she sighed. "Thank you. I will."

"Can I get some dinner for you?"

"Please."

Daiyu would soon want her meal as well, but it depended on when Prince Kun left. Was it improper to suggest the prince ate with her? Probably.

The bell rang and Ting ran to see what Daiyu wanted.

Shan followed more slowly, hovering in the doorway. The prince had left and Daiyu was ordering her dinner and a bath. As Ting left, Shan entered. "Can I get anything else for you, my lady?"

Daiyu clasped her hands. "I never imagined the prince would be so attentive," she sighed. "I could barely remember how to play with him so close to me."

Shan smiled. "He seems very kind."

"He is. I cannot wait to go into the city in the morning." She frowned. "Why do you need treatments? Is asking for help improper here?"

"We went to the wet nurse building and were denied," Shan told her. "I thought it best to stock our own supplies."

"Good idea. What happened to Zhi? Should I go see her?"

Better not to mention the emperor. "She's resting, my lady. I will fetch her dinner shortly."

"And what happened?"

Sometimes Daiyu's kindness could be a curse. "She burnt her skin on the pavement while she kowtowed."

"Who would have made her kowtow for so long?"

Shan said nothing and Daiyu's eyes widened. "Oh. You were not injured?"

"No, my lady."

Yun arrived with the first of many buckets of warm water for Daiyu's bath. "Help me take down my hair, and then see to Zhi," Daiyu said. "I will enjoy a soak in the bath."

"Yes, my lady."

A few minutes later, Shan hurried towards the kitchen. Kun's note rustled in her pocket but she didn't dare read it in the open. She ducked along one of the servant corridors Zhi had showed her earlier. No one was around. She opened the letter.

Come to me after Lady Daiyu has gone to bed.

She stiffened. There was only one reason a man called a

woman into his chambers alone at night.

What was she going to do?

Chapter 9

The Jasmine Palace was quiet and dark. Daiyu had gone to sleep, Zhi had retired to her own room to recover and Shan stared at the ceiling as the other servants slept in their beds next to her. She couldn't ignore an imperial order. To do so was death. Had the prince decided to take her as his concubine? She squeezed her eyes closed, trying to control the nausea swirling in her stomach. It didn't matter what she wanted. She had to go.

Quietly she dressed in the outfit she'd left out for the next day. No one stirred. She sneaked out of the palace and paused, scanning her surroundings. The lanterns flickered along the road and in the distance, she heard the murmur of voices, but aside from that it was still. The prince's note was in her pocket should she be stopped and questioned on her way.

Keeping as much to the shadows as she could, she strode through the servant corridors, pausing at every corner to check if anyone was there before continuing. Occasionally she checked behind, but she wasn't being followed. At the prince's palace she hesitated. Two red-uniformed guards stood outside the main entrance and two guarded the servants' entrance.

She would have to declare herself.

Swallowing hard, she moved away from the building and the guards' attention immediately fell on her. She went to the servants' entrance and bowed to the two guards. "Prince Kun asked to see me," she said. "I am Lady Daiyu's bridal companion."

"This way," one guard said and took her down the alleyway to the servants' entrance. Once inside the palace, he patted her down, checking for any weapons, his hands lingering over her breasts. She didn't react. He paid no attention to the ribbon she wore around her wrist, or the hair pins which held her hair in place. Should she tell the prince his men underestimated her? No, best she keep some secrets to herself.

The manservant who had been with Kun earlier that day came down the hallway. "Follow me."

Even the servants' passageways were beautiful with polished floors and bright lighting. The manservant knocked on a door and at the prince's call he showed her in. "Miss Shan is here to see you, Your Highness."

A single lantern stood on the table, but otherwise the room was dark. Thick curtains covered the windows ensuring complete privacy and the prince was dressed in a simple silk dressing gown. Her stomach clenched. It was not clothing suitable for her visit.

"Leave us," Prince Kun said.

"Yes, Your Highness." The manservant bowed and left the room, leaving Shan alone with Kun. He beckoned her closer, his eyes not leaving hers.

Nerves skittered across her skin. Was he really going to do this? How would Daiyu react? Men were notoriously weak when it came to resisting their desires. She stepped closer until she was two yards away.

"Closer."

Her pulse raced. She didn't want to do this. It wasn't appropriate, she wasn't attracted to him, she didn't want to upset Daiyu, and yet she obeyed the command, moving until she was only inches from where he sat. She kept her expression impassive.

Kun stood, brushing against her body, crowding her, but she didn't step back. His hands swept over her lower back and his head bent to her ear. "I apologise," he whispered. "This subterfuge is necessary."

She stiffened as he kissed her neck. What was he talking about?

"Daiyu was kind to bring a bridal companion," he said in a louder voice. "Kind to think of my pleasure."

She stared at him.

"You do know in Bonam, a bridal companion becomes a concubine of the husband?" he asked.

She fought back a cringe. "Of course, Your Highness."

"Call me Kun. I want my name on your lips."

Shan swallowed. "Yes, Kun."

He took her hand, led her through the receiving room to his bed chamber. When her steps slowed, he tugged her forward. "No need to be shy. You are as much mine as Daiyu is."

She had her knives, but they would do her no good. If she injured the prince, she and Daiyu would die. At the edge of his bed, he said, "Lay down. I will undress you."

Limbs shaking, she did as he asked. Heavy drapes surrounded three sides of the bed and as he followed her onto the mattress, he pulled across the final curtain. Darkness surrounded them with only the faint glow of the lantern outside giving any light to see.

Kun pulled her up and murmured, "The guards must believe you are here for my pleasure. They will not question your arrival or departure at odd hours this way." He knelt beside her, his voice still low. "Why did you not tell me about the man who broke into Daiyu's palace?"

She was here to answer questions? Relief made her dizzy,

but it was quickly followed by concern. How did he know about the intruder? Had Lord Anming told him?

"I expect an answer." His lips were close to her ear. He must be concerned about others listening.

She swallowed. "Prime Minister Cong said the emperor had ordered it, so I assumed you knew."

"When did he say this?" he growled.

Curse it. Maybe he didn't know. She swallowed. "Before the servant stabbed him."

"So you heard more than you told me?"

Every molecule in her screamed danger. What could she possibly say that wouldn't get her killed? "Yes, Your Highness. I was concerned the emperor was spying on Lady Daiyu when we had only just arrived, and I didn't know who to trust. Then when you told me my priority was Daiyu's safety, I decided I was right to stay silent."

"Tell me everything you heard."

She did as he asked, keeping her voice low. When she was finished, he asked, "Is there anything else which concerns you?"

Shan hesitated.

"Tell me."

"I was told the empress has been less than impressed with the last three people who painted your portrait."

"This is true. I will deal with Mother and ensure you and Daiyu are safe."

Relief filled her. "Thank you, Your Highness." His concern for his betrothed was admirable, but was there more to it? Had Anming asked him to keep Daiyu safe? No, he couldn't have. To imply Daiyu was not safe in the imperial palace would have been dangerous, particularly to the heir to the throne. But someone must have told him about the intruder.

"Does Daiyu know what you have been asked to do?"

"I have told no one what you ordered me."

"And what about the thing Anming told you to do?"

She was glad the dark hid her surprise. "He asked me to do nothing." She prayed the Gods forgave her for her lie. Every muscle was ready for flight, though she had nowhere to run. She couldn't abandon Daiyu.

Kun was silent. "You are to come to me every night at this time. Make yourself pretty so my guards suspect nothing. I want a daily report from you."

"Yes, Your Highness."

"Call me Kun when we are alone." He reached for her hair and removed one of her hair pins. "We need to make you look more dishevelled."

"No!" She grabbed his hand, pointing the end of the pin away from them not a moment too soon. The blade shot out and clicked into place. She froze.

Kun shook her hand off and examined the blade, holding it above his head so it caught more light from the lantern outside.

Shan's heart pounded and she held her breath.

"Ingenious. Are they both like this?"

Perhaps he would be more lenient towards her if he knew they'd been used for Daiyu's benefit. "Yes. They enable me to protect my lady. I used them against the man who kidnapped her on our journey here."

"How do you retract them?"

She showed him.

"Does Daiyu have them too?"

"No. She is not trained in how to use them."

"Perhaps you should teach her." He shook his head. "No, there is nowhere safe from spying eyes." He handed the hair pin back to her and she undid her hair, messing it up. When she'd been training, she'd seen consorts who had been bedded coming out of the magistrate's house. They always looked flushed and inevitably some part of their clothing was out of place. She pinched her cheeks.

"How long should I stay here?" Her cheeks heated as he chuckled.

"A few more minutes lest my manhood be questioned." He sounded amused. "Why are you loyal to Daiyu?" Kun asked.

The answer most servants would give is because she was her mistress, but that wasn't all it was. "She is kind," Shan said. "She understands mistakes can be made and she doesn't punish unnecessarily. Though she is unaware of much that happens outside her world, she is gracious and sweet to those in her world." And she'd stopped Shan from being fired when she'd made her biggest mistake.

"And you are aware of what happens?"

She hesitated. "I was born on a small farm outside our city. My family still works it and struggles when crops are bad."

"I would like to speak to you more on the subject, but it is time for you to return." He undid the belt on his dressing gown and slipped it from his shoulders. His whole torso was chiselled muscle. "Remember," he murmured, "I just pleasured you. You feel giddy and happy."

She smiled, unable to stop herself. "You were wonderful."

He flung back the curtains and a guard stepped into the doorway, glancing at them and then away. Shan pulled her dress tight and retied the belt. Brushing her hair from her face, she stood, smiling demurely at Kun. As she stepped away from the bed, he grabbed her hand and pulled her back, kissing her on the lips. It was like being kissed by her brother, but she endured it. "May I use your brush?"

"Of course, my dear." He retied his dressing gown and strode to the dresser to fetch it for her.

She adjusted her ties and redid her hair, placing the hair pins back into it. Every time she looked at Kun in the mirror she blushed. If there were people watching them, or listening to them, they would think she was no longer a virgin.

Would word get back to Daiyu? Should she say something in case it did, tell Daiyu the truth?

After she'd made herself presentable, she turned to Kun.

"You may leave," he said. "Return tomorrow at the same time. Do not tell your lady." He dipped his head to kiss her neck and whispered, "Tell her the truth."

"Yes, Kun," Shan said. "I am honoured you would choose me." She exited the palace via the servants' entrance and ignored the guards who were there. They didn't say anything, but she could feel their gaze on her as she walked away.

Every day she would have to keep up the pretence, report to Kun, send letters to Anming and keep Daiyu safe. The responsibility crashed around her. She had more masters here than she had in Chungson. Could she now cross Bingwen off the list of men who controlled her, or had Anming forgotten to send for her sister? It hardly mattered, she was helpless to do anything but obey all those who held her life in their hands. Would anything change if the emperor was replaced?

Or was she just a pawn in their games?

~*~

Shan woke early and checked on Zhi. The woman was still sleeping, but her blisters looked far less red today. Next she sent Yun to get Daiyu's breakfast and went to wake her lady. Kun's men would be there in a little over an hour to take them shopping in the city.

She pulled the bed curtains away from Daiyu's bed. Her mistress slept soundly, a smile on her face, no worries in the world.

How nice it would be to rest easily. Shan hadn't fallen asleep until the early hours of the morning, her mind too full contemplating what to do about all the orders she'd been given. At least she was fortunate that Anming and Kun both wanted Daiyu to be kept safe. That was something Shan agreed with.

"My lady, it is time for you to wake." Shan tied back the curtains.

Daiyu shifted and muttered.

"Kun's men will be here soon to take us into the city," she said.

Daiyu opened her eyes and smiled. "Is it morning already? I was having the loveliest dream."

"What was it about, my lady?" Shan fetched Daiyu's dressing gown and held it out for her.

She blushed as Shan did up her gown. "About the prince and our wedding." She walked into the receiving room as Yun returned with Daiyu's breakfast. Ting entered behind her and went to make the bed.

As Daiyu sat, Shan poured her some tea and Yun served the noodle soup.

"How is Zhi?" Daiyu asked.

"I left her sleeping," Shan said. "Her burns are much better today, but I thought it wise if she stays behind this morning and rests."

Daiyu nodded. "Good idea."

While Daiyu ate, Shan retrieved a couple of dresses from Daiyu's wardrobe. "What would you like to wear today, my lady?" As she turned to show Daiyu the options, Yun straightened from where she had been whispering in Daiyu's ear. Daiyu frowned.

"What did you do last night, Shan?"

Shan pasted a smile on her face. The rumours must have already reached the kitchens. "Nothing of any importance. Which dress do you prefer?"

"The blue."

Shan replaced the other one.

"I hear you came in late last night," Daiyu continued.

Yun avoided her gaze as she took the dress from Shan.

"I did, my lady." She walked into the receiving room. This

was not a discussion they could have in front of the other servants and if Kun would only speak to her on his bed, did that mean there were others similarly watching Daiyu?

"Where were you?"

"The story is not interesting, and I do not wish to bore you."

Daiyu's eyes glistened with unshed tears, but they were also set in determination. "Please. There is nothing else to entertain me while I eat."

Shan swallowed. "Perhaps I can tell you the story on our way into the city." A knock on the door interrupted Daiyu's response. Shan hurried to answer and found the First Consort's maid on the doorstep.

"An invitation for Lady Daiyu," the woman said.

"Thank you." She closed the door and took the invitation to Daiyu.

"She wishes to take tea with me this morning," Daiyu said. "Shall I tell her I have other plans?"

"I do not believe it wise to upset her," Shan said. And rejecting the offer in favour of going into the city would be seen as a slight.

"Shan is right," Zhi said, entering the room. She bowed. "My apologies for sleeping late, my lady."

"We thought it best to let you heal," Daiyu said. "Show me your hands."

Zhi held out her reddened hands. "I am capable of serving you, my lady."

Another knock on the door and when Shan answered it, she found the empress's maid at the door alongside the other maid who was awaiting a reply. "The empress wishes you to begin Prince Kun's portrait this afternoon," the maid said. "She will send for you mid-afternoon." The maid left, not waiting for a reply.

Not that there was any Shan could give aside from 'of course'.

"Who was that?" Daiyu asked.

Shan told her.

"Then you must get the paints you need this morning." She glanced at Zhi. "Zhi can accompany me to the First Consort's palace and you can go into the city. Take the money you need from the purse Anming left me."

Shan didn't want to leave Daiyu unprotected while she was in the city. "I could send someone with my list," she said. "Then Zhi can rest further and I can go with you."

"Nonsense. I am fine." Zhi's tone was hard.

Shan sighed.

"If Zhi feels able, then she can serve me. You know others will never get exactly what you need, and we can't afford to upset the empress."

Shan bowed low. "Yes, my lady." She would make it clear to Kun's guards that Daiyu was staying behind. Perhaps Kun had told them something similar about keeping an eye on Daiyu.

She and Zhi helped Daiyu prepare for her tea with the First Consort and then Shan brought the purse to Daiyu so she could retrieve the coins. "Would you like me to buy you anything while I'm in the city?"

"Perhaps if you see something I would like."

"Of course, my lady."

Kun's guards arrived as Daiyu was preparing to leave. Daiyu stepped up to the man in front. "There's been a change of plans. I am going to tea with the First Consort. Shan will go into the city without me."

"Yes, my lady." He ordered two men to go with Daiyu and dismissed the palanquin bearers and the other guards.

Daiyu stiffened. "Is no one going with my bridal companion?"

"I will, my lady," the officer in charge said. "She will be safe with me."

"Thank you." Daiyu walked down the steps and towards

the consort's palace with Zhi by her side.

Shan prayed Daiyu would be safe while she was away. She would have to be as fast as possible. She turned to the guard. "Which way?"

He gestured. "I am told you want to buy paints and treatments?"

"That's right." They walked side-by-side through the inner palace and the Gates of Heavenly Virtue. The day was warm and already the pavement radiated heat. She wished she could carry a parasol.

They left via the western gate, crossing the wooden drawbridge which spanned the wide moat surrounding the palace. The sights and smells of the city hit her as soon as she crossed into its streets. Vendors called their wares, people crowded the streets and dogs roamed as if they owned the place. "Stay close to me," the guard said.

The shops closest to the imperial palace contained high-priced items: beautiful fans, instruments, dresses and jewellery all of the highest quality. Shan paid attention to everything, including where they were going. It wouldn't do to be lost in the city. With all that was happening, she might need a quick exit for her and Daiyu. "How large is the city?" she asked the guard.

He glanced at her but didn't answer.

Had he been ordered not to answer her questions, or was he merely rude?

It was of no matter. The road they were on stretched in a straight line, towards the outer wall. Each street they passed was similarly straight, as if the whole city was a grid. They moved into a middle-class area. Here were shops for the artists, entertainers and successful shopkeepers. She spotted an art supply shop and stopped, reviewing the wares in the windows. She needed a full palette of colours, so she was prepared no matter what colour the prince wore. The shop had a beautiful set, in a bamboo box with a set of paintbrushes of multiple sizes.

"What are you doing?" the guard demanded.

"Shopping." She smiled at him, staying polite. "These paints look to be of a high quality."

He grunted when she entered the small shop. The shopkeeper bowed to her. "Mistress, how may I help you today?"

"I would like a paint set."

Her guard scanned the shop and then exited, standing by the entrance. At least she didn't have to worry about him breathing down her neck.

"Of course. What will you be painting?"

"Who," she corrected. "First Prince Kun."

The man gaped at her for a second before recovering. "Then you will need our highest quality paints," he said, walking to the back of the shop. He retrieved a set from under the counter and opened the marble inlay lid. As Shan examined the set, he fetched a set of brushes from the back room. "These are the best we have."

The brush hair was fine and perfect for what she needed. "How much?"

He named the price. "Mistress if you would be so kind as to tell others where you bought it, I could give you a discount." He handed her a card.

Daiyu had given her plenty of money and it wouldn't do to skimp on her materials, though the price was enough to make her heart race and for guilt to squeeze her chest. If only she could give that amount to her family, they wouldn't have to worry about their failed harvest. It would buy them food and clothing for a whole year. Zan could even afford a few books of her own. "I shall be sure to tell all who ask me."

They finalised the sale and the man wrapped the package carefully. A young boy entered the shop and Shan smiled at him.

"What are you doing in here?" the shopkeeper asked.

"My master asked me to buy some paper," the boy said, handing the shopkeeper a list.

"Let me finish with this lady first." The shopkeeper turned to get a woven bag for the paint set and the boy thrust a piece of paper into Shan's hand, his eyes wide.

She opened her mouth to ask what it was and he shook his head, placed a finger over his lips.

Her skin prickled, but she smiled as the shopkeeper turned back and handed her the bag. "Thank you."

While the shopkeeper served the boy, Shan paused at one of the shelves as if something on it had caught her eye. She unfolded the note. At first it made no sense, and then she recognised the code Bao had taught her.

Go to the Sun and Moon herbalist shop.

Her heart pounded. Could she trust it was from Anming? And if it was, what was he still doing in Bonam?

She went outside to where the guard waited. "The shopkeeper recommended the herbalist at the Sun and Moon," she said. "Do you know where it is?"

"It'll be this way." He gestured away from the palace.

Shan took her time as they walked, making note of the shops they passed, sometimes stopping to see if she could spot anyone following her. No one in the crowd was familiar to her.

Finally they reached a section of the city where herbalist shops lined the streets. Spicy scents filled the air and dried animal parts filled jars in shop windows. Shan scanned the names on the stores until she spotted the Sun and Moon. Her grip tightened on the bag she carried as her guard entered the shop ahead of her. The space was cool and only one other patron was inside, an older woman who was buying a packet of dried mushrooms. There was limited space between the shelves which filled the shop, barely wide enough for her to fit with her paint set. "It might be best if you wait outside again," she said to the guard. "Could I ask you to hold my bag?"

He scowled but reached for it and the bell over the door rang as he left with the older woman following him.

"What can I do for you?" The grey-haired shopkeeper bowed respectfully. His clothing was neat and the quality of cotton was of the highest grade.

"I'm looking for a few treatments." She handed him the list she'd written the night before.

"Wonderful. It will take me a few minutes to prepare them all. Can I offer you some tea while you wait?" He gestured through a door to the back of his shop. In the room was a table and chairs.

Her guard faced the street, alert for any danger outside.

She would deal with any danger inside. She inclined her head. "Yes, please."

She followed him through the door, her gift at the ready for any attack. Shelves full of concoctions lined the walls and aside from the table and two chairs, the space was empty.

"Let me heat the water." The shopkeeper left through another door which faced the back of the shop.

Shan didn't sit. She monitored both doors, ready to flee or yell for help at the slightest sign of trouble. The door the shopkeeper had gone through opened, and the shopkeeper entered with a tall, lean man.

Relief and surprise flooded her.

The shopkeeper carried a teapot. "Please take a seat." He sat the teapot on the table and then went back into his shop to prepare her order. Shan inclined her head at the man whose dark eyes seared her soul as he stood a few feet from the table, out of view of the door into the shop. What name should she use? His real name might be too dangerous. "Lin."

He smiled. "Shan. I hope you weren't too concerned."

Not too concerned… he had some nerve, though her relief outweighed her fear at the subterfuge. She smiled back at him. "What are you doing here? Aren't you supposed to be with our lord?"

"No," he said. "He left some people in the city in case Daiyu needed help." He glanced towards the door. "We don't have much time. How are things?"

"You mean aside from the intruder, the attack on the Prime Minister and the empress trying to trap Daiyu in a lie?" she said sweetly.

"What intruder?" Bao demanded.

"I sent Anming a message about him. Didn't he tell you?"

Bao frowned and shook his head.

"The day we arrived, when Daiyu went to dinner with the emperor, I caught a man in her room going through her things."

"What did he want?"

"I don't know. I scared him off." Should she tell him about Prince Kun's orders? She would be disobeying an imperial command.

"Where is Daiyu at the moment?"

"Having tea with the First Consort," Shan said. "Prince Kun's guards are with her."

He raised his eyebrows. "Does the prince not believe she is safe?"

"The prince does not confide his feelings to me."

He stared at her. "But you have spoken to him?"

She nodded. "He has been attentive to Daiyu and when I witnessed the Prime Minister being stabbed, he asked me to draw the attacker."

"Is that the only interaction you've had with the prince?"

She blocked the night before from her thoughts. "I will be with him this afternoon when I paint his portrait as the empress has requested."

"Will you be alone with the prince?"

"The prince has asked Daiyu to keep him company."

"Good. They seem to like each other." Bao smiled.

It was nice that he cared. "I believe so. He does not want any harm to come to Daiyu either."

"How do you know this?"

Shan hesitated. "He sent his guard with her."

"Is he fond of you too?" Bao studied her.

"I wouldn't know."

"No? You didn't speak to him when you went to his palace last night?"

How in heaven's name did he know about that? Deliberately she sipped her tea, not letting any emotion show on her face, but she couldn't stop the flush of her cheeks. "What we spoke about doesn't concern you."

"Everything that happens in the palace concerns me." His imperious tone smothered her embarrassment.

She narrowed her eyes. "Then you should know the palace is full of intrigue," she snarled. "Daiyu must measure every word she speaks, even the degree of her bow. There is judgement everywhere. The servants fear everyone's displeasure and there is competition to curry favour." Her heart raced with her indignation. "Just yesterday Zhi and I were required to kowtow on the hot pavement for the emperor for so long that Zhi has bad blisters on her hands. And then the wet nurse bureau rejected our request for ointments to soothe the injury." She took a breath. "While the palace looks beautiful, underneath it is as filthy as a pig pen."

"The servants are unhappy?"

She hesitated. Why had he focused on that? "No one dares say as much. To do so would be too dangerous."

"Perhaps you can talk to them, find out how they feel about the rumours of a new emperor."

She stared at him, the fear and anxiety of the past few days clashing together, creating a potent mix of outrage. "You are determined to get me killed, aren't you? You don't really care about my lady or me, you only care about that throne." She stood, her heart racing. "If anyone hears me asking such things, I'll be dead." She'd had a glimmer of hope when she'd discovered who he was, that maybe he'd truly cared for her, but this proved he thought her a tool to be used.

She didn't give him the opportunity to respond. She returned to the main shop, knowing he couldn't follow her. The shopkeeper showed no reaction, simply handed over her packages and told her the price. As she paid him, she thought she heard Bao say, "I care too much."

She paused before putting the change in her purse. What did he mean by that?

Chapter 10

It was midday when Shan returned to the Jasmine Palace and Daiyu was already inside eating her meal.

"How was tea?" Shan asked as she unpacked the treatments and arranged them in a drawer in Daiyu's cabinet. When Daiyu didn't respond, Shan turned. Zhi glared at her with intense dislike, but it was the devastated distress on Daiyu's face which made her gut clench. "Is something wrong, my lady?"

"Where did you go last night?"

Her spirits fell. She'd forgotten Daiyu had asked about that earlier. If Bao had known, then the whole inner palace was probably talking about the prince's new consort and they wouldn't have been kind to Daiyu. "May I speak with you privately, my lady?"

"You may answer my question."

Shan had never heard Daiyu so cold. Though they had known each other for years, Daiyu had believed the rumours. "First Prince Kun asked to see me."

"Why?" Daiyu's voice broke.

"He had some questions about you."

Daiyu frowned. "What did he want to know?"

Shan was aware Zhi was hanging on to every word. "My lady I am happy to tell you everything. Shall we go for a walk and get some fresh air?" Would Daiyu's anguish make her forget Anming's instructions?

"Our lady needs to rest, as I'm sure you do if you are to paint the prince this afternoon," Zhi said.

Curse it. "Will you be joining me when I paint, my lady? The prince said he would love you to keep him company."

Tears filled her eyes. "I couldn't possibly, not now that I know…"

Frustration simmered. Shan couldn't tell Daiyu the truth in front of Zhi and whoever else might be listening. The code. "I have such wonderful news to tell you."

Daiyu blinked and frowned. Shan waited for her to catch on and then stifled a groan as Daiyu gasped and glanced at Zhi. No, Daiyu would never make a spy. "Then perhaps we should go for a walk," Daiyu said. "Zhi, put some more ointment on your palms and rest a while. I will deal with Shan." Her tone hardened a little and Zhi smiled.

"Yes, my lady."

Shan fetched a parasol for Daiyu, and they stepped out of the palace. One of Kun's guards fell in behind them and Daiyu waved him back. They walked side-by-side and Daiyu said, "Explain yourself."

Shan flinched at the imperial tone. This was why she couldn't be herself around Daiyu. She kept her voice low. "My lady, the prince asked me to his palace and requested I pretend to be his consort."

Daiyu winced.

"But it was a pretence only, my lady. He asked me to tell you the truth so you would not be upset, but I couldn't tell you this morning with the others there. No one else is to know."

A frown marred Daiyu's forehead as she tilted her head to look at Shan. "Then what did the prince want?"

She told Daiyu about the intruder, the attack on the Prime Minister and what she'd overheard, and then about what

Kun wanted of her. "He wants me to report to him nightly, which is why I am to pretend to be his consort. No one will question my visits." She turned to Daiyu. "Truly, my lady, the prince only has your safety on his mind."

"Oh, but it is horrifying. Couldn't he come up with a different reason for you to be there? You'll be painting him this afternoon."

"We may not be alone," Shan said.

"All of the consorts were laughing at me," Daiyu said. "The First Consort was positively gleeful when she told me the gossip. Told me not to worry, it was good the heir had healthy appetites. And then she made it a point of enquiring whether people in Chungson take concubines, when she already knew full well they don't."

"My lady, you cannot take it to heart. Every word, every comment will be a test to see how you react. You must not show your true feelings otherwise they will use it to their advantage. You are surrounded by people who want to use you to better themselves. Be very careful."

Tears glistened in Daiyu's eyes. "This is a horrible place. I wish I had never come."

Shan didn't dare mention her meeting with Bao or remind Daiyu of her brother's plans. It would only upset her more. "Take heart, my lady. I am certain the prince genuinely cares for you."

Daiyu sniffed. "I hope so."

"Come now. Let's return to the palace and out of this heat. You can rest until it is time to visit your prince."

Daiyu touched her arm. "I am sorry for doubting you."

Shan smiled. "It is understandable. But please remember, everything I do is for you. If I ask to speak with you privately it is because there are things the others cannot hear."

"I shall ensure you have time alone with me every day."

"Thank you, my lady."

It would help, but there was little Shan could do about the

consorts' attempts to undermine Daiyu.

Daiyu was right. This was a horrible place.

~*~

The empress insisted Prince Kun be painted in the Hall of Clarity, in one of the imperial chairs. Shan gathered her things, and with Hai carrying her easel, she followed Lady Daiyu and Prince Kun's palanquin into the outer palace. Her nerves hummed as they passed multiple ladies on their journey, all of whom bowed to the prince and then glared at Daiyu after they had passed by.

She was surprised not one of them had decided to take Daiyu under her wing and show her around, try to win her favour. Perhaps they'd been warned not to. The empress hadn't seemed pleased by the match and she wasn't someone to upset.

They eventually arrived outside a receiving room off the main hall. Men guarded the door but stepped aside to allow Kun to enter. Shan's muscles tightened as she walked in. The empress sat on one of the divans, surrounded by her maids. Several guards lined the walls and Kun's men joined them.

"Your Majesty." Kun bowed to his mother as did Daiyu. Shan got to her knees to kowtow, waiting for permission to stand. The parquetry floor was hard and polished to perfection.

"You are late," the empress said, displeasure in her tone.

"My apologies. Had I known you would be here, I would have arrived on time," Kun said. "I asked Lady Daiyu to keep me company."

"Well she is no longer required if I am here."

Shan closed her eyes, her forehead pressing on the cold floor. That would leave Daiyu alone.

"Have you heard Daiyu play the guzheng?" Kun gestured towards the instrument in the corner of the room.

"No, I have not."

"Then please allow her to entertain us. She plays beautifully."

"Very well."

People moved around Shan, but she didn't rise until Kun said, "Stand, Miss Shan and set up your things."

The prince still spoke to his mother who would be behind Shan if she set up the easel in the most convenient spot. But the only time it was permitted to turn her back to the imperial family was when they were walking in the palace grounds.

The guzheng and other musical instruments were opposite the empress and Lady Daiyu sat there.

"What is taking so long?" the empress demanded. The question wasn't directed at Shan so she was not permitted to answer it.

The rules of etiquette could get a servant in as much trouble by following them as by not following them.

"Miss Shan?" Kun asked.

She bowed. "Your Highness, the best place to station the easel is directly in front of your chair," she said. "But I fear it means I will have my back to the empress."

"Can you sit further away?"

"I will not get as much detail further away."

Kun glanced at his mother. "Would you like detail in my portrait, Your Majesty?"

Her eyes were hard. "Get your guards to move the chair."

Kun gave the instructions, and Shan directed Hai to set up her easel where she would be facing all those in the room. She gestured for the guards to bring the imperial chair further forward. The chair required four guards to carry it. "Thank you."

While she prepared, Kun and his mother spoke. Daiyu sat quietly in front of the guzheng, her hands folded in her lap. It would be a boring few hours for her if the empress took all of Kun's time.

The prince glanced at her and seeing her waiting, he sat in the chair. "Do you have a preference for how I sit, Your Majesty?"

"Sit straight, like the emperor you will be."

It was a stiff pose and the warmth Shan had seen in him disappeared; he was replaced with a dispassionate, emotionless man.

"Perfect," the empress said.

Shan kept her mouth closed and focused on the drawing. This would have to be the best work she had ever done. Anything less than perfect could affect Daiyu's standing and harm them both.

"Lady Daiyu, I would be honoured if you could play some music to help pass the time," Prince Kun said.

"Of course, Your Highness. Do you have any requests?"

"Play whatever is your favourite."

Daiyu began a soft, traditional tune and the notes sang in haunting melody. The tune gripped Shan's heart, twisting it. This was the song that had played at an event she had attended at the manor house in Chungson, the first time Bao had secretly asked her to dance, in the days when they'd still been close.

He had held her in his arms and she had allowed her imagination to get the better of her, had pretended one day they would be allowed to dance together without needing to hide, had fantasised Daiyu and Anming would see their love and let them marry.

Foolish dreams.

She shook the melancholy away. She had no time for memories now. This prince had to have her full attention.

Not the prince who had broken her heart.

~*~

It was almost dinner when the empress announced she had had enough for the day. Shan exhaled quietly, relieved for the break. The painting required intricate layering and her hand was stiff from the unfamiliar motions. When the empress approached, Shan bowed and backed away from the easel so the empress could see what she had done.

Silence.

Shan's heart raced. The prince came closer but the empress waved him away. "You may look when it is finished. Return at the same time tomorrow."

"My apologies, Mother. I have business to attend to all day tomorrow."

"Then the following day." The empress left the room with her maids and guards.

Shan sighed and began to clean her brushes. Daiyu stopped playing and flexed her fingers. The prince noticed and walked to her. "I hope you have not played too long and hurt yourself."

Daiyu bowed. "It is an honour to play for the empress."

The prince lowered his voice, but he was still close enough for Shan to hear. "Yes, but Mother can be rather exacting at times."

She smiled. It was sweet how attentive Kun was to Daiyu.

She finished packing as Kun and Daiyu approached.

"Now Mother is gone, I can look."

He and Daiyu examined the painting. "It is wonderful, Shan," Daiyu said.

Kun nodded. "Your work is excellent."

"Thank you, Your Highness. Is there somewhere safe I might leave it to dry?" Carrying it all the way back to the inner palace seemed like a waste of time.

He gestured to his guard. "Put this in one of the storage rooms."

The guard lifted the canvas easily and strode away.

"Let me accompany you back," Kun said.

Daiyu and Kun were carried back to the inner palace and after bidding Kun farewell, Daiyu sank onto her divan with a groan and rubbed her fingers. “I never expected the empress to make me play the whole time.”

Zhi brought in a bowl of warm water and Shan retrieved the calming ointment from the items she’d bought that morning. “She will be impressed by your stamina,” Shan said.

“I hope so. I will win her approval somehow.”

Shan and Zhi arranged Daiyu’s bath and dinner and it was some time later before Shan was able to rest. She returned to her bedroom and sank onto her bed with a sigh.

Ting smiled. “Tired?”

Shan nodded. “It is quite nerve-wracking to paint the prince and have the empress watching. I hope she is happy with the final result.”

“You should be worried. The empress is not kind to those who disappoint her.”

“Is there anyone at the palace who is kind to those who serve them?” She bit her tongue. She must be more tired than she thought to say such things.

Ting’s eyes widened and she glanced around. “The prince is said to be kind.” She lowered her voice further and came to stand close to Shan. “Unlike his sister who was unpredictable.”

Shan longed to ask for more details, but she didn’t dare. “How long have you worked here?”

“Two years. I was chosen by the local magistrate in Laksung to come to the palace.”

“That’s a long way from home. How long are you here?”

“A minimum of five years,” Ting said. “Though some of the other maids have been here far longer. If the bureaus are pleased with my work, they may want me to stay.” Her eyes held despair.

“It is a long time to be away from your family.”

She nodded. “I miss them terribly. My little sister cried so when I left.”

The sharp pang in Shan’s chest was painful. Where was

her sister, Zan now? Had she been taken to the manor house as promised? She should have asked Bao when she'd seen him. "I understand. I was fortunate my family lived not too far from the Chungson manor and I could visit each season, but now I don't know when I'll see them next."

"We must do our duty as the emperor requires." The words were said with no ounce of piety.

"It is our privilege." Yun entered the room and Ting stiffened.

"Of course," Ting said quickly.

Interesting. Shan stood. "I must get some dinner. Would either of you like something to eat?"

"A pork bun would be lovely," Ting said.

Yun scowled. "We are fed plenty by the bureau. I do not need anything else."

Ting looked at the floor.

"We all have days when we are a little hungrier than usual. I feel as if I could eat a whole ox." Shan chuckled and Ting smiled but Yun's expression stayed unimpressed. No matter. "I will be back shortly."

As she walked through the inner palace, Bao's words came back to her. It wasn't safe to ask how happy the servants were, but perhaps she could listen to conversations without anyone knowing. The kitchen was a good place to start. As she neared the building, darkness surrounded her. She crossed to the window and there were only two maids inside cleaning. There was little conversation.

Shan entered and smiled at the girls inside. "May I find myself some food?"

The elder nodded. "Leftovers are by the fire."

Shan helped herself to the food, putting a pork bun on a plate for Ting, and then sat at the table to eat while they cleaned around her. When she was finished, she cleaned her dishes. As she moved towards the door, the younger maid was staring at her. "Is something wrong?"

"Why did you clean your plate?"

"I didn't want to cause more work for you."

She smiled. "Thank you."

The older maid scowled. "Don't thank her. If one of the masters sees, they might think everyone can clean up after themselves and then we will be left without a job."

"I am certain there will always be work for you at the palace," Shan said and left before she could be embroiled in an argument. She returned to the Jasmine Palace and gave Ting the pork bun. Then she freshened ready for her visit to Kun.

"Where are you going?" Zhi demanded.

"Prince Kun asked to see me."

Zhi's mouth dropped open. "Again?"

"Yes." She walked out of the room, unwilling to further explain herself. Zhi knew there was nothing she could do about a direct order from the prince. She hurried through the grounds. As she neared the prince's palace she heard soft sobbing. Shan paused and on a whim turned down a servants' corridor towards the sound. She found a young boy, no more than eight or nine years old, huddled in a ball, crying.

"What's wrong?" She knelt next to him and he gasped and sprang back.

He wiped his tears. "Nothing." He clambered to his feet.

"Perhaps I can help if you tell me."

He hiccoughed. "I'm hungry."

Shan frowned. "Did you not get dinner?"

"My master said I didn't work hard enough today to deserve it."

How could anyone starve a young child? She couldn't send him to the kitchen for her, because she'd just eaten. "If he refuses you breakfast, come to the servants' entrance of the Jasmine Palace in the morning and ask for Shan. I'll see you get some food."

He sniffed. "Thank you."

She smiled. "I'm sorry I can't help you tonight." She said goodbye and once again entered the prince's palace through the servants' entrance. As with the night before, Kun wore a dressing gown and sat at the table waiting for her. "You took your time tonight."

She bowed. "My apologies."

"In my bed now, before I change my mind." The terse tone had her tensing. Was this part of his subterfuge?

She hurried into his bedchamber and climbed onto his bed. The curtains had barely closed behind the prince, shrouding them in darkness, when he growled, "Tell me about your meeting with Bao."

Chapter 11

The air left Shan's lungs. How could Kun possibly know? How on earth was she meant to respond? Bao had said Kun might be an ally, but if he'd wanted Kun to know about their meeting, surely he would have given her a message for him.

She shifted away from him, kneeling back on her heels. "I am not certain what you mean, Your Highness."

"I know my cousin met with you at the Sun and Moon this morning. What did he want?"

"Your cousin?" Playing dumb was the only way to get out of this.

"Prince Bao, son of Emperor Huang, the rightful heir to Bonam."

She shook her head. "I met with Lord Anming's manservant," she said. "Not a prince. I was surprised he was still in the city, but he asked me about Lady Daiyu."

Kun smiled. "Lord Anming's manservant?"

Curse it. Hadn't he known who Bao had pretended to be?

He studied her. "What exactly did he ask?"

"Whether anyone else had been spying on her."

"How did he know someone had been spying?"

Her pulse raced. "I told my lord, so I assume he told his manservant."

"And how did you answer his question?"

"I told him I hadn't seen anyone else."

"Did he ask anything of you?"

She closed her eyes, frustration and anger swirling in her. No matter what she did, she risked her life each time she spoke to Bao and Kun. "You both seem to know exactly what the other is doing. Perhaps you should ask him directly."

Kun sat back as if she'd hit him with her fists. "He knows what I do?"

She pressed her lips together. She'd said too much.

"Tell me," the prince demanded.

She'd had enough of this game. "Your Highness, perhaps you don't understand the precarious position you put me in, perhaps you don't care, for I am after all only a servant. By spying on the man you tell me is the true heir, I risk death should he come to power and discover my betrayal, and yet how can I not spy for you, because to refuse an imperial order means death to me anyway. Tell me, in my position, what would you do?" A lump formed in her throat.

He was silent for a long moment. "I would do what I thought was right."

Would he? Would he spare her life after all she had said? Her question came out as a whisper. "And how would you know which is the lesser of the two evils? I know what life is like under the emperor, but how do I know if life under Bao would be any better?"

"Could it be much worse?"

The quiet question stalled her fears. She stared at the prince, wishing the light was better so she could read his expression. The silence stretched. She wasn't only risking her own life, but that of Daiyu's as well. Though what she had already said was enough to get herself killed. "Not by much."

"What makes his rule so awful for you?"

She shifted, kneeling into a more defensible position.

Maybe he would listen, maybe she could make him see. Should Bao fail to defeat the emperor, Kun was next in line. He could change things. She kept her voice to no more than a murmur. "People have little say over their lives," she said. "Many of the servants at the palace had no choice to come here and they miss their family. I passed a boy in the passageways who was crying because he was starving. His master had decided he didn't deserve to be fed today. My own family is so poor they sold me and are about to sell my sister so they can make ends meet." Next time she saw Bao she would ask him where her sister was. She took a breath. "Servants can be killed for the misdeeds of their masters, there is no choice, no freedom, and fear haunts their every step. It is no way to live."

Someone behind the curtain cleared their throat and Shan froze, terror ripping through her. Had they heard her words?

"Your Highness, the Heavenly Majesty is here to see you."

All the breath left Shan's body. She was dead. A whimper escaped before she could stop it.

"Send your concubine on her way," a man said. "I must speak with you."

Kun reacted first. "Hair," he murmured, tugging at her clothes so they didn't sit perfectly. "I'll be right there, Heavenly Majesty. Please have a seat in my parlour and I'll send for tea." Kun shook her and she snapped out of it. She could turn invisible if necessary. She'd have to run straight to Daiyu and flee with her, because otherwise Daiyu would be punished too.

Heart pounding, she adjusted her hair and clothes and then Kun swept the curtain aside. Through the doorway, the emperor sat at the table and waited. No guards were in Kun's bedchamber.

She followed Kun out of the room, keeping her head lowered.

"Stop." The imperial command made her stomach

convulse. "Who is this?"

Shan fell to the ground in a kowtow, not daring to move.

"She is Lady Daiyu's bridal companion, Heavenly Majesty," Kun replied. "My new consort."

"Stand."

She got to her feet, keeping her eyes lowered.

"She is beautiful," the emperor said, the approval in his voice making her skin crawl. "I didn't think the Chungson considered their bridal companions consorts."

"They are under Bonam rule," Kun said.

"True. But perhaps you should respect your betrothed's feelings," the emperor said. "She might not like you taking a consort, and I could do with a new woman."

Horror filled Shan. Oh, ancestors, no. The idea of having to sleep with the emperor, the man who cared not for the misery of his people, made Shan want to vomit. She would run away before she gave her body to him.

"You always say a woman must learn her place, must do whatever her husband bids of her. Daiyu's feelings are of no concern of mine. She must get used to the way things are here in Bonam."

Kun's uncaring, matter-of-fact tone was unlike the man she'd seen up until now, but she daren't look at him to discern if this was his true nature.

"You are right," the emperor said. "In future I expect you to get my permission. Had I seen her first, she would be mine. Go now, before I change my mind."

Shan bowed low and hurried from the room. Kun's manservant accompanied her out of the palace and she trotted down the road, her pulse racing, wanting as much distance from the palace as she could. She stopped in a space the light didn't reach and breathed slowly to control her heart rate and adjust her clothing and hair.

Why wouldn't the emperor simply order Kun to go to him? She frowned. Perhaps he'd been on his way back from one of his concubine's palaces. The reason didn't matter, but the information they discussed could be important to Bao and to Daiyu's safety.

It was her best chance to discover whether Kun really was to be trusted.

She scanned the darkness. No one was around. Keeping her steps light, she returned the way she came. When she reached the palace, she focused and faded away, drawing her power to her. Four guards stood at the servants' entrance, two of the emperor's and two of Kun's men. None of them spoke.

She slipped past and waited across the corridor from the entrance. How could she get inside without them noticing? The door opened and the manservant ushered a servant out. He held the door open as he called to the guards, "Let no one else through."

Shan ran on her toes through the door, brushing against the manservant as she entered the hallway. He gasped and murmured, "Ancestors protect me."

He thought her a spirit.

The manservant went into the room across from the prince's receiving room. If the layout of this palace was similar to Daiyu's that would be his room. He had probably been told to leave. Left alone in the hallway, she exhaled and crept closer to the door. It was slightly ajar and the emperor's voice carried.

"The rumours of Bao's resurrection are getting stronger in the country. My men tell me they've heard them in all the vassal states."

"I told you he means to retake the throne," Kun said. "For some reason he believes you had something to do with his parents' death." His tone was cold, uncaring, not at all like the warmth he'd had with Daiyu and herself.

"Shut up. Don't speak as if you believe he is who he says he is. Prince Bao died with his parents."

"Yes, Heavenly Majesty."

"I've recalled troops from the border," the emperor said. "We need them in the imperial city. The usurper will attack when he is strong enough. We need to ensure the people see our strength, make sure they fear me more than they support him."

"Would a more benevolent approach be better?" Kun asked.

"No. The people must know what will happen to them if they support the usurper. I've arranged for a demonstration in the courtyard soon."

"What demonstration?"

"I will have the guards round up people spreading lies about the usurper and behead them."

Shan wanted to be sick. The emperor had to be stopped.

"Have you extracted any information from Daiyu?" the emperor asked.

What? She peered through the gap in the door. Kun shook his head. "I haven't had much chance to speak to her alone. Mother was there while my portrait was being painted."

"I'll see you aren't disturbed next time. We need to know if Anming is behind all of this. You need to gain her trust, seduce her if you must."

Kun chuckled. "What do you think I'm doing with her companion? I had her willing to tell me everything when you arrived tonight."

"Ah. I didn't realise. Are you sure you don't want me to take over? I can promise her more than she could ever dream of and she is very beautiful."

"Better if I can work the two women off each other," Kun said. "Jealousy can be a wonderful tool. She was about to tell me about rumours she'd heard when she was in the city today."

"What rumours?"

"Something about the usurper. As I said, I didn't quite get it out of her."

"Send for her when I go. I want to know everything." The emperor stood.

"Yes, Heavenly Majesty."

Shan's mind raced and she eased back from the door. The emperor suspected Anming which was incredibly dangerous not only for Lady Daiyu and herself, but for the whole of Chungson. And she'd let slip that Bao was Anming's manservant.

But Kun hadn't mentioned it to his father. He'd made it sound like he was seducing her and he wasn't, not in the way he said. But he was listening to her concerns, was suggesting he supported her views and that was another type of seduction. Fool.

She reached for the door handle and saw her hand. Curse it. In her concern, she'd lost control of her illusion. She pulled the tingly coat back around herself, shaking a little at the effort. Normally she didn't hold it for so long. Quickly she slipped past the guards and when she was out of eyesight, she let the illusion fall. Time to get back to the palace. And figure out how not to tell Kun anything, while still telling him something.

She would not fall for his seduction.

~*~

When Shan arrived at the Jasmine Palace, she found all the lanterns lit and Ting and Yun hurrying down the corridor. Alarmed, Shan asked, "What is wrong?"

"Thank goodness you're back," Ting said. "Lady Daiyu is ill. We've sent for a physician but no one has come."

Shan raced into Daiyu's bedchamber. Zhi sat with her, a bowl held on her lap as Daiyu vomited into it. Her skin was pale and damp with sweat. "How long as she been like this?"

"An hour."

Shan went to the drawer with treatments. "Has she had anything to eat?"

"Not since dinner."

Perhaps something she'd eaten hadn't agreed with her. "What did she have?"

"Dumpling soup."

"Get me some boiling water." Ginger tea would soothe her stomach.

Hai entered the room looking a little bleary-eyed. "There's a messenger from Prince Kun."

Damn. She'd forgotten about him. "What does he say?"

"You are to return to Prince Kun's palace."

Daiyu's illness was the perfect excuse to refuse. "Tell him I will come as soon as a physician arrives for Daiyu."

Hai gaped at her. "You can't refuse the prince."

"He will understand." She hoped.

Ting brought in a teapot full of water and Shan added the ginger and peppermint to it. "Who prepared Daiyu's soup?"

"Yun fetched it from the kitchen."

"In the morning I want you to find out whether anyone else was ill."

"Yes, Shan," Ting said.

Shan carried the teapot and a cup into the bedchamber. Zhi was rubbing Daiyu's back and murmuring to her. "My lady, how are you feeling?"

"Awful." Daiyu groaned.

"In a minute you can have some tea." Shan glanced at Zhi. "When was the physician sent for?"

"At least half an hour ago."

Plenty of time for him to get here if he wasn't busy with someone else. But if the illness was caused by the soup, he could be busy with more important ladies. "I am sure he will arrive soon." Kun would arrange it when he heard Daiyu was sick.

Sure enough, as Shan poured the tea there was a knock on

the main door. Yun hurried in, her eyes wide. "The prince is here and he has the physician with him."

Daiyu groaned. "Don't let the prince see me like this."

Shan handed the tea to her. "I will speak with him."

She placed the pot on the table and went to the main door. "Your Highness, it is kind of you to come." She bowed.

"I heard Lady Daiyu was ill, so I brought my private physician."

"She is honoured." Shan directed the doctor to the bedchamber, but stopped the prince. "My lady would prefer you don't see her when she isn't looking her best."

Kun frowned. "What is wrong with her?"

"I suspect something she ate for dinner didn't agree with her, but the doctor will be able to tell us for sure. She has been vomiting for the past hour and is perspiring and pale."

He paced the entrance. "I do not like this."

"Illness happens to us all, Your Highness," Shan said. "If you would like, I can send word with what the doctor says."

He shook his head. "I'll wait."

"Then let me offer you tea." She gestured to the table and made sure the door between the receiving room and the bedchamber was closed while the doctor examined Daiyu.

"Thank you." He sat and she expected him to ask her more about Bao. Ting and Yun were inside the bedchamber and Hai had disappeared, probably going back to bed.

She poured the tea and stood next to the table while he drank.

He stared at the bedchamber door and when it finally opened, he stood. "How is she?"

The physician frowned. "She's stopped vomiting. I've told her to sleep and hopefully she'll feel better in the morning."

"You'll return in the morning to check her." It wasn't a request.

"Of course, Your Highness. I am sure she will be much

improved."

Shan accompanied the men to the door. "I will send word of how she is to you in the morning," she promised.

"Thank you."

She closed the door and exhaled. He'd disobeyed his father's orders to find out more information. Was it because he had forgotten in his concern about Daiyu, or did he not trust the Jasmine Palace was a safe place for such discussions?

Either way, she would have to invent a story for the next time she saw him.

In the morning Shan let Daiyu sleep. She left Zhi at the palace in case Daiyu woke and then headed for the kitchens with Ting to discover if anyone else had been ill. The kitchens were bustling as they prepared breakfast for each of the palaces. Ting joined the line of servants waiting. She spoke to the girl in front of her. "Did your lady have the dumpling soup last night?" she asked. "My lady was terribly sick after."

The girl shook her head. "My lady enjoyed the soup immensely."

Ting questioned the other maids around her but none reported any illness. Maybe it wasn't the soup. Lady Daiyu had eaten a couple of treats while with the empress, but there was no news of the empress being unwell and someone would have mentioned it if that had been the case. Besides, Kun had also eaten the sweets.

At Shan's turn in the kitchen, she retrieved food for not just herself but for Zhi and the others as well. One of the scullery maids said, "That's a lot of food for one."

"It is, but not too much for five." She heard murmurs of surprise as she left with Ting.

"They'll be talking about you for a week," Ting said.

"Why?"

"A lady's maid does not serve other servants. It is beneath her position."

"May she serve her new friends?" Shan asked.

Ting beamed at her. "They would not believe such things could happen."

Even amongst the lower class the divisions were clear. It made no sense. The happier people were, the harder they worked and the more loyal they were.

On the way back to the palace she spotted the young boy she'd seen last night. She stopped. "Did you get any food this morning?"

He shook his head.

She handed him one of the buns. "Here you go. Don't forget, if you need more, come to the Jasmine Palace."

"Thank you." He stuffed the bun in his mouth and hurried away.

"Why did you do that?" Ting asked.

"I saw him last night, crying because his master hadn't fed him. He doesn't deserve to starve."

"You are very kind," Ting said. "Not many in your position would notice, let alone care."

Hopefully one day that would change.

When they returned to the palace, she gave the food to Ting, Yun and Hai and she and Zhi went to check on Daiyu. Her sleeping gown was drenched in sweat, her skin clammy and her hair stuck to her face. She tossed and turned.

"She's no better today," Zhi said.

"No. Let's wake her and have her drink more tea. The physician should be back soon. I'll send a message to the prince and let him know she hasn't improved."

"You're getting quite comfortable with the prince," Zhi commented.

Shan said nothing. Instead, she prepared the tea and fetched a fresh bowl of water while Zhi woke Daiyu. When she returned, Daiyu sat in bed but her eyes were unfocused.

Zhi's concern was clear. Shan handed her the bowl of water and cloth. "Cool her skin. I'll send for the doctor."

She wrote a note to Kun telling him Daiyu hadn't improved and gave it to Hai. "Take this straight to the prince and then fetch a physician."

The boy nodded and ran off.

"Is there anything we can do to help?" Ting asked.

"She will need clean sheets and fresh water," Shan said. "Make sure there is always cold and hot water available."

Ting nodded.

When Shan entered the bedchamber, Daiyu had a little more colour in her cheeks. Zhi had washed her and tied her hair back neatly. Shan poured some tea and helped Daiyu sip it. "How are you feeling, my lady?"

"My stomach hurts," she said. "I ache all over."

"I've sent for the doctor. He might be able to give you something else that will help."

The doctor was surprisingly quick to return. "Prince Kun sends his regrets that he cannot come in person. He has other commitments today."

Daiyu smiled at him. "If you see him, please thank him for his kindness."

After the doctor examined her, he prescribed rest and plenty of fluids. As Shan walked him out, she asked, "What is wrong with her?"

He sniffed. "It's a minor fever. She will be fine in a day or two." He left before she could ask anything further.

Of course he wasn't going to pay too much attention to a woman's ailment.

Zhi helped Daiyu change into a dry nightgown, and Ting and Yun changed the sheets. When they were done, Shan dismissed them. "You can have the day to yourselves." There was no point in everyone hanging around the palace. Daiyu wasn't going to need much and if she did, Shan could send for them.

"Thank you, Shan," Ting said.

"If you see Hai, tell him it includes him."

Yun bowed and they left.

Daiyu was back in bed when Shan returned. "I'm going to rest a little longer."

"Sweet dreams, my lady. May you feel better when you waken."

Daiyu's breath deepened into sleep almost as soon as she closed her eyes.

Shan prayed to her ancestors for Daiyu's speedy recovery.

Chapter 12

Daiyu slept most of the day and Zhi and Shan took turns watching her. A couple of invitations arrived for her to have tea with various concubines but Zhi politely declined them and said they would arrange a time when Daiyu was well.

Yun arrived back with a bowl of clear broth. "I thought our Lady would appreciate something plain for dinner."

"Thank you," Shan said taking the tray. "I'll see if she will drink some of it."

Zhi was shutting the windows in the bedchamber. They'd alternatively opened and shut them all day as Daiyu had shivered and sweated.

"Why don't you take a break?" Shan suggested. "Go and have dinner and I'll feed Daiyu. Then we can swap."

Zhi brushed a hand over her forehead. "All right. Let me help her to sit first."

Over the day Daiyu had become weaker not stronger. Together they woke Daiyu and made her sit, piling pillows behind her for support. Rather than balance the soup tray on Daiyu's lap, Shan held the bowl and spoon fed her.

"I feel so useless," Daiyu murmured.

"You will get stronger. Don't fret. You have nothing to do but heal."

"I am supposed to be with the prince when you paint him

tomorrow."

"I am sure it will be cancelled when the empress discovers you are unwell." She would speak to Kun about it tonight. She didn't want to leave Daiyu for any length of time. She'd been debating sending word to Anming or Bao all day but had decided not to worry them. Daiyu was rarely ill and would probably wake feeling fine tomorrow.

Daiyu managed to eat about half of the soup and then went to sleep again. When Zhi returned, Shan stretched. It was too early to see Kun but she wanted some fresh air and something to eat.

"The others are back," Zhi said. "They offered to help should we need it."

Daiyu was on her third nightgown. "I'll ask them to wash Daiyu's clothes. She ate about half of the soup and I'll return the bowl when I get dinner."

Zhi smiled. "Go now. The kitchens weren't too busy when I left."

Shan had a word to Ting and then exited the palace, taking a deep breath of the warm air. The palace had been stuffy. She needed some exercise, so she strode in the opposite direction to the kitchen.

Many servants were out, carrying trays of food and running messages back and forth between the buildings. She smiled at those who hurried past and they stared at her as if she was strange before dropping their gaze to the ground.

No matter.

She reached the stream which divided the emperor's garden from the rest of the inner palace. How she would love to wander under the shady trees and inhale the sweet scent of the flowers growing there. But without Daiyu, she wasn't permitted in the garden. She followed the stream and came across the washing area. She hadn't been here before but she was glad she knew where it was. Two girls sat close together just beyond the laundry hut vigorously washing undergarments and whispering. She was about to continue when she caught the words, "Prince Bao is alive."

She eased closer, checking for watching eyes before she turned invisible.

"How do you know it's true?" the girl with a long braid whispered.

"Cixi told me. He's taking back his throne."

"What will that mean for us?" the girl asked. "Won't he kill all the servants in the palace and replace us with his own?"

"No. I've heard the prince wants to keep everyone. If we rise up and support him, he will reward us. We can choose to stay at the palace, or we can finally go home to our families."

"I don't believe it. The emperor says things he doesn't mean all the time. Why would Prince Bao be any different?"

"I tell you, it's true! Cixi said the Rhoran are amassing on the border as well. She says the prince's sister, Princess Lien is now the khan's wife and they will fight for the prince."

The girl with the braid shuddered. "They're barbarians. If the prince lets them into Bonam, he'll never get rid of them."

"No, they don't want Bonam, they want to be left in peace but the emperor keeps attacking them. We must be ready. When he comes we must fight for the true prince."

Shan was captivated by the conversation and almost missed the footsteps coming closer. She spun around and kicked a stone near her foot. The girls looked right through her and then another two washer girls rounded the hut and Shan ducked out of the way.

"Shush now," the older girl cautioned.

Shan waited a little longer to see if the subject was raised with the other girls, but it wasn't. Her mind whirling, she moved back around the hut out of sight and dropped her illusion.

The rumours were inside the palace. For the servants to discuss it so openly must mean they were unhappy with the emperor's rule. But it was clear there were two factions and no one knew who to trust.

The talk of fighting was also alarming. If Daiyu was in the inner palace when the fighting started, it could be incredibly dangerous, particularly when it became clear Anming was on Bao's side. Why had Bao not mentioned any plan to get Daiyu out?

Or were they collateral damage? And where did Kun stand in all of this?

She strode down the servant corridors and every time she turned a corner she interrupted people speaking in hushed tones. Once or twice she thought she heard Bao's name. Was she being paranoid, seeing intrigue everywhere she went? A man caught her eye, and there was something familiar about him. She slowed, watching him as he whispered something to the person he was with and turned.

Captain Wei.

What was Lord Anming's captain doing in the inner palace? Any males were eunuchs and she was fairly certain he wasn't. Before she could approach him, someone bumped into her and when she turned back, Wei was gone.

Her skin prickled. Wei's presence confirmed something more was going on. The tension amongst the servants was palpable. She couldn't rely on Kun or Bao to rescue them, couldn't trust them to remember Daiyu. She fetched a couple of steamed buns from the kitchen and strolled around the perimeter of the inner palace. She should have done this when they first arrived. High above the walls were walkways from where the guards monitored the grounds. On every corner was a watchtower and though there were a couple of doors in the thick walls, she was fairly certain they didn't lead to the outside. The only exits were the Gates of Heavenly Virtue and the small door next to it for the servants to travel between the areas.

If a revolt occurred, the gates would be locked.

She frowned. Maybe they wouldn't. It would depend on how many servants rose up to fight. There were thousands of servants and officials inside the inner and outer palace. Nowhere would be safe.

And if Anming surrounded them, the emperor couldn't escape.

Shan examined the walls. Far too high for anyone to scale and the archers would shoot anyone who tried. Besides, a large moat ran around the outside of the palace and Shan couldn't swim. She wasn't certain Daiyu could either.

The only safe option would be barricading Daiyu inside the Jasmine Palace. They could potentially hold off any attack until help arrived. But whose side would Daiyu's other servants choose?

Her muscles were tight as she made her way back. She prayed to her ancestors that the attack wouldn't come while Daiyu was ill and she prayed Daiyu would wake in the morning feeling well.

Did Kun know what was going on? Could he read the mood around the palace, or did he not pay enough attention to the servants?

She studied the Jasmine Palace. The servants' entrance came off a narrow path only wide enough for one person. If they could barricade the door, it would be difficult to knock down because there wasn't enough room to swing a battering ram.

The servant bedrooms had no windows, so no entrance or exit points there. Shan handed Ting and Hai the extra buns she'd collected for them. Yun wasn't there. The receiving room and the bedchamber would be the hardest to defend. Large glass windows let in huge amounts of light and would be easy to smash. Several people could breach the palace at the same time. The two divans could be pushed against the windows, which would hamper but not halt rioters, and the table could be used to reinforce the doors.

"Shan?" Zhi called.

Shan blinked and entered the bedchamber. Daiyu still slept. "How is she?"

"She hasn't woken since you left. Is everything all right?"

How could she phrase this so it wouldn't get anyone into trouble? It might not just be Zhi listening. She frowned and scanned the walls. If Prince Kun was worried about eavesdroppers in his palace, it must mean people could listen in here as well—but where? She would have to examine the walls to see if there were any hidey-holes, or perhaps there was space in the roof.

That could be a space for them to hide.

"What's wrong with you? You're staring around the room as if you haven't been here before."

Shan refocused on Zhi and cleared her throat. "I'm feeling off."

"Do you think you've caught what our lady has?"

"No, it's more of a feeling that something is about to happen. I can't explain it, but it's making me nervous." She rubbed her arms. "I got the same feeling before I was told I was going to serve Lady Daiyu." Far better to let Zhi think she had a premonition than to mention everything she'd heard.

Zhi nodded. "I noticed some of the servants looked more nervous than usual. Perhaps something is in the air. Is it a full moon?"

She shook her head. "Will you be all right with our lady for a little longer? I am meant to see the prince."

Zhi grimaced. "Yes."

Shan left the palace. Quite a lot of servants were still out which was unusual. She smiled at all she passed but no one made eye contact. When she arrived at the prince's palace there was only a single guard on each of the doors.

That wasn't right.

She walked to the servants' entrance and smiled at the

guard. He was not one of the guards she'd seen on her previous two visits. "I am here to see Prince Kun."

He stared at her. "The prince is not in at the moment."

Nerves began to swarm in her stomach. "Should I wait for him?"

"His Highness has gone away for a few days. I'm not at liberty to say when he'll return."

Shan frowned. Kun had sent no note to Daiyu and Shan was supposed to paint him tomorrow. "Thank you." She inclined her head and walked away. Perhaps the emperor had ordered him to leave, but the timing was too convenient. Something was definitely going on.

And Kun had left Daiyu to fend for herself. Some prince he was.

It was up to Shan to protect her. Her first task on returning to the palace was to examine the exterior for potential hiding places. Were the walls hollow to allow someone to spy on the palace occupants? She paced the distance while pretending to examine the flowers in the small garden beds outside. There was no obvious sign of an entry point aside from the servants' entrance and the main entrance. Letting her gaze rise, she checked the eaves. The darkness made it difficult to see clearly so she would take another look in the morning. Once inside, she paced the interior distance which was almost the same as the exterior. No hidden walls. She found the servants' quarters empty. Strange. Ting, Yun and Hai were normally asleep by now. Quickly she examined the walls for any hidden areas and then went across to Zhi's room to check.

Nothing.

She slipped into Daiyu's room. The heat from the day still lingered, making it uncomfortable. She strode across to open a window when she heard raised voices coming from Daiyu's bedchamber. Shan's muscles tensed and she faded so no one would see her approach. Treading lightly she went to the entrance.

"The empress insists Lady Daiyu drink this," Yun said. "It will make her feel better."

Shan frowned. Why did the empress care all of a sudden?

Ting frowned. "It smells horrid. How will that do anything except make her vomit?"

Hai was on Daiyu's bed, holding her upright, but Daiyu was as limp as a rag doll.

Zhi stood by the dresser, watching. She should be making the decision about what to give Daiyu, not distancing herself.

Shan brushed a hand over her hair, touching the smooth cool length of her hair pins and waited.

Zhi strode over. "If the empress ordered it, we cannot refuse."

Ting bit her lip and then burst out, "But the empress does not care for our lady."

Yun hissed and turned to her. "How dare you say that? It's treason."

"It's true!" Ting hesitated. "Have you not heard the rumours which have been whispered around the inner palace?"

"I pay no attention to rumours," Yun said.

"Perhaps you should." Ting turned to Hai. "You've heard them… about the true heir coming to reclaim his throne. Some think Lord Anming is behind the plot, which means Lady Daiyu may also be involved."

Shan's stomach curdled. Ting shouldn't be speaking so openly. Things must be at a tipping point.

"The empress wouldn't support Daiyu marrying her son if that was the case," Ting continued.

"Do you believe the rumours?" Zhi asked, her tone calm.

"I don't know what to believe," Ting said.

"I do," Yun said. "The nasty rumours are meant to upset the emperor and empress. Anyone who spreads such things should be arrested and beheaded." She glared at Ting who stepped back, her hand going to her throat.

"All the eunuchs are talking about it," Hai said. "Most of them believe it to be true, even if they don't support the true heir. They are preparing to fight for the emperor."

"We will all fight for the emperor," Yun said.

Zhi said nothing.

Daiyu coughed and shivered, her eyes fluttering open briefly.

"We must give her the soup," Yun declared.

Time to show herself. Shan eased out of the room and dropped her illusion before walking in. "How is Daiyu?"

All of them jumped and spun to face her.

"You're back earlier than I expected," Zhi said.

Shan smiled. "The prince wasn't available." She moved to Daiyu's bed and took her hand. "How are you, my lady?"

Daiyu didn't respond, just stared blankly at her before closing her eyes.

"We must give her this soup before she goes back to sleep." Yun tried to push Shan out of the way.

"I can feed her." She reached for the bowl and Yun jerked it away.

"I will."

"Don't be silly," Shan said. "It is late and you need sleep. I will see to it that my lady eats." She gripped the bowl and had a slight tug of war with Yun, soup slopping over the side before Yun let go. Shan sniffed at it. Ting was right, there was something off about the dish. "What is it?"

"Something the empress ordered," Yun said. "I believe the physician made it."

"Then I am certain it will be good for our Lady. Why don't you all go to bed? It's late and I fear we will all be needed to watch over Daiyu in the next few days if the soup does not help." She placed the bowl on a nearby side table and stared at Ting and Yun until they bowed and walked out. Zhi crossed over. "I can help."

Shan placed a hand on her arm and smiled at her. "You have done enough already. We will need to support each other while Daiyu is ill. Rest while you can. You have been with our lady for many hours now and I can have my turn."

"Hai can help you," Zhi said finally and left.

Which just left the eunuch who still held Daiyu upright.

The soup had stopped steaming, and a pot plant in the corner could be used to get rid of it. Shan wet a cloth and wiped Daiyu's sweaty brow.

Daiyu's eyes opened. "Shan?" she whispered.

"How are you feeling?"

"Weak. Ill."

"Are you hungry?"

"No."

Hai spoke. "The empress sent you soup to make you feel better."

"How kind. I will drink it in a moment."

Shan squeezed her hand and shook her head. "Perhaps you will feel better if you pass water."

Daiyu's cheeks flushed as did Hai's.

"Hai fetch the screen and the bowl," Shan said. "I can hold our lady." She slid her arm around Daiyu's back. While Hai fetched the privacy screen, Shan whispered, "Do not drink the soup." Perhaps Yun had added something to the dumpling soup to make Daiyu ill in the first place.

Shan directed Hai to set up the screen in front of the bed with enough room for the bowl. "I will see to our lady. You can wait in the receiving room."

He glanced at the bowl of soup before nodding. When he was gone, she adjusted the screen so it also blocked his view of the side table with the soup on it and she fetched a pitcher of water. "Let me help you up." She lowered her voice. "Do you need to pass water?"

Daiyu shook her head.

"Then stay there while I deal with the soup." She poured

the water into the bowl. When enough time had passed, she called Hai back in. She folded the privacy screen. "Please empty the bowl while I feed our Lady."

Hai glanced at the soup bowl and then nodded.

She waited until she heard the door close behind him and then poured the soup into the pot plant leaving just enough to make it look as if Daiyu had eaten some and returned to her lady's bedside.

When Hai returned she placed the spoon into the bowl. "You've done well to eat that much, my lady. You should rest now." She helped Daiyu lay down and fanned her. "Thank you, Hai. Can you take the bowl back to the kitchen and then get some rest? There's no point both of us watching our lady sleep. I will fetch one of you when I need a break."

Hai scowled but did as she asked.

Shan waited until Daiyu's breathing became regular and then stood. Yun and Hai were loyal to the empress, that much was clear. She couldn't count on their help should anything happen. Ting might help her, but Zhi was unknown and therefore couldn't be trusted.

She searched the bedchamber for nooks or crannies where they could hide. Again her gaze lifted to the ceiling. The roof outside was pitched, leaving a gap in the space above. Daiyu moaned. But even if there was, Daiyu was in no state to climb and she wouldn't be able to lift Daiyu in there by herself.

Shan retrieved one of Daiyu's bags and went through her lady's things, adding money, a change of clothes and sturdy shoes. She still had a water flask they'd used on the journey she could fill with fresh water. The next time she went to the kitchen she would request dried biscuits for Daiyu. They would last for several days. Now where could she hide the bag? Anyone seeing it would realise it was for travel and would question why it was needed.

As Daiyu continued to sleep, Shan went into the utility room and filled the pitcher and flask with fresh water. Her gaze caught on the roof. The square panels were made of bamboo. If anyone was up there, they would be located above the receiving room or the bedchamber.

She doused the lantern and waited a moment for her eyes to adjust to the dark. Then she climbed onto the water barrel and pressed the bamboo panel up.

The space was dark, but as she scanned it, nothing moved, and she could make out no figures.

Quickly she returned to Daiyu's bedchamber and stood on the table. Again she checked to make sure she hadn't missed anyone and when she was satisfied, she stowed the bag in the ceiling, counting the number of panels to the wall.

That just left the problem of Daiyu. She wasn't well enough to run away, and while Shan could possibly carry her, it wouldn't be far or fast.

If she was holding Daiyu, would she be able to make them both invisible? She'd never tried to extend her gift to another person. Placing a hand on Daiyu's arm, Shan concentrated, using her gift to fade, then she pushed it towards Daiyu. It stretched out, sliding over her almost like a tunic, and Shan panted as she tried to cover Daiyu's whole body. Her hand trembled at the effort, but eventually Daiyu's arm and then her torso disappeared. She gritted her teeth as finally Daiyu's whole body vanished from view. The strain was too much. She gasped for breath, letting go of her gift and they reappeared.

It wouldn't work, not for any length of time. Even if she managed to hide Daiyu, people would hear her panting and they couldn't stay still. But perhaps all that was required was practice.

She poured a glass of water and sipped.

Daiyu's life might depend on Shan's ability to shield her.

She wouldn't let her down.

Chapter 13

The rumble of an opening door woke Shan. She blinked to clear the haze from her eyes. Why was she lying on the floor? She sat, wincing at the aches in her muscles. Daylight shone around the edges of the drawn curtains in Daiyu's bed chamber. She must have fallen asleep some time during the night. The last thing she remembered was struggling to stay upright as she fought her exhaustion. She'd covered Daiyu in a blanket of invisibility over and over. Each time she'd been able to hold it longer than the last. Her head spun as she stood and checked Daiyu.

"How is she?" Zhi asked walking into the room and opening the curtains.

"Her colour is better," Shan said. "She's not sweating as much."

"The empress's soup must have worked then."

Shan nodded.

"Why didn't you wake me to take my turn?" Zhi asked.

"I was not tired." She smiled at Zhi. "And to be truthful, I don't think I would have slept in my worry for Daiyu."

Daiyu stirred and Shan fetched her a glass of water as she opened her eyes.

"How are you, my lady?" Zhi asked.

"Thirsty."

Shan helped her to sit and then held the cup to her lips. "Are you hungry?"

"A little."

Shan rang the bell. When Ting arrived, Shan said, "Fetch our lady some broth and dried biscuits."

Ting hurried to obey and Shan added restorative herbs to a pot for tea.

"Should we ask the empress for more of her soup?" Zhi asked.

"I don't believe it's necessary," Shan said. "Daiyu said it tasted ghastly and it seems to have already done its job."

"I would like a bath," Daiyu said. "Not too hot or too cold. I feel sticky and achy."

"I'll arrange it, my lady." Zhi left the room.

Shan placed a hand on Daiyu's forehead. It was much cooler than it had been. "You are looking better."

"Yesterday is a bit of a blur," Daiyu said. "But I feel there is something important I should remember."

"My lady, I fear you might have been poisoned," Shan murmured. "Do not drink or eat anything which comes from Yun or the empress."

Daiyu gasped. "Why would they hurt me?"

"The politics of the palace are not to be understood." She checked Zhi hadn't returned and a movement in the corner caught her eye. The pot plant she'd poured the soup into the night before was shrivelled and a leaf dropped off the main stem. Her heart lurched. "My lady, I poured the empress's soup into that pot last night."

Daiyu gasped. "The plant was healthy yesterday."

It was time to leave the palace. "The servants spread rumours about the true heir to the throne and I worry unrest will erupt soon. I have prepared a bag should we need to flee, but I have not had a chance to send word to your brother."

Daiyu frowned. "Surely we'll be safe here."

"No, my lady. I do not know who to trust."

"But Prince Kun will protect us."

"Prince Kun has left the palace, and I'm not certain when he will return." She gripped Daiyu's hand. "I only trust you, and you should only trust me. Your other servants are loyal to the emperor."

"As are we," Daiyu reminded her.

"Of course, but your brother asked me to keep you safe, and to do that I must ask that you trust only me."

Fear crossed Daiyu's face and she nodded. "All right."

Zhi returned with the bath, and Hai carried buckets of water to fill it. Ting arrived with the broth and biscuits and Shan tasted the broth before she fed it to Daiyu.

"You had many invitations yesterday," Zhi told Daiyu as she helped her undress. "Would you like me to respond to them today?"

Daiyu shook her head. "I still feel a little queasy."

"Another day's rest and I'm sure you will be fine," Shan told her, pleased she would be staying in the palace for another day.

"Shan, why don't you get your breakfast and I will stay with our lady while she bathes?" Zhi asked. To Daiyu she said, "She was up all night and I'm sure she needs food and rest."

Shan shook her head but Daiyu didn't notice. "Yes, go and eat Shan."

She couldn't ignore a direct command. Had Daiyu not understood what Shan had told her about the danger? "Of course, my lady. Thank you. I will not be long."

Hai and Yun were nowhere to be found which gave Shan some comfort.

The roads were busy with servants fetching breakfast for their masters. Shan weaved through those who had stopped to chat and arrived at the kitchen where a line snaked out the door. This would take some time.

As Shan neared the front of the line, Yun came out of the kitchen carrying a tray with soup which looked suspiciously like the soup the empress had sent the night before.

"Yun," Shan called.

Yun spotted her and ducked her head as if she was going to ignore Shan completely.

"Yun, come here please." With the tight etiquette of the palace, Yun couldn't ignore a direct summons from a servant who ranked higher than her, particularly not in front of all these witnesses.

"Yes, Shan?" Yun bowed, holding the tray carefully.

"I hope you're not taking that soup to Lady Daiyu."

"It's from the—"

"It doesn't matter who it's from." If the spectators heard it was from the empress, Shan couldn't refuse. "Lady Daiyu has already eaten and is bathing. Any more food will go cold and go to waste." She smiled. "Unless you would like to eat it. I'm sure our lady wouldn't mind."

Yun paled. "No, I couldn't. It's not right."

"All right. Then perhaps you can find someone else who wants it, but you mustn't take it to our lady. She will feel terrible about the waste and we don't need her feeling worse than she already does."

"Yes, Shan." Yun's posture was stiff as she walked away.

Shan reached the front of the line and requested more dried biscuits and steamed buns. The more food she could store the better. She trotted back to the palace and was quiet as she stepped inside. The hallway was empty and she entered Daiyu's receiving room to find Hai and Yun speaking in hushed tones, the bowl of soup on the table. They sprang apart and bowed to her.

"Is everything all right?" she asked.

"Yes, Shan," Hai said. "I was telling Yun that our lady is still bathing."

"Lovely. Why don't you eat while she's busy? You could

share the soup."

"Thank you, Shan," Hai said as Yun took a step back.

"You're welcome." As she crossed to the bedchamber there was a crash behind her and Yun gasped. "I'm sorry. I'm so clumsy."

The bowl had smashed on the floor and soup spread over the ground. Shan wasn't surprised. "Clean it and then fetch your breakfast." She continued into Daiyu's room.

The day passed quietly. Daiyu rested in bed and Zhi and Shan took turns playing music or reading to her. Shan carefully monitored what Daiyu ate and made certain no one went close to the water pitcher. At midday Daiyu exclaimed, "Oh, you are supposed to paint Prince Kun's portrait this afternoon."

"The prince has gone away on business," Shan reminded her.

"You must confirm. It would be awful not to turn up." Daiyu turned to Zhi. "Should we send a note to the prince, or the empress?"

"To the empress, my lady. Say you are a little unwell and won't be able to attend, but ask her if she would like Shan to continue the portrait."

"Is it wise to bother the empress with such things?" Shan asked. "Perhaps if I confirm the prince is away, that would be sufficient."

"It is the correct order of importance," Zhi said. "I can take the note for you."

Shan fetched the writing table and implements, and Zhi left not long after with the letter.

"What is wrong?" Daiyu asked.

"I do not want to leave you alone."

Her mistress sighed. "Are you not perhaps being paranoid? The others have been lovely all day."

"The pot plant is dead," Shan said. "That's telling

enough."

"Perhaps it was the heat of the soup that killed it."

Shan didn't comment. With Zhi gone, she had time to add the dry biscuits to the travel bag. She checked the receiving room to ensure no one was there and then retrieved the bag from the roof space and added the biscuits.

"What are you doing?" Daiyu asked.

"Collecting a few things in case we must run," Shan said. "There is enough space in the roof for us to hide should we need to."

Daiyu stared at her. "Did my brother know you're not a normal lady's maid when he bought you?"

"Yes, my lady. I was taught how to protect my mistress and that is what I will do." She slipped the panel back in place and climbed off the table just before Zhi entered the room.

"What did the empress say?"

"I was not able to see her, but I left the note with her maid," Zhi said. "I am sure she will send word if Shan's services are needed."

"Thank you." Daiyu yawned. "I'm going to rest now. I'm still exhausted."

"Of course." Shan helped her to lie down and then tucked her in. "We will be in the next room if you need anything."

Zhi and Shan left her to sleep. Zhi lowered her voice. "You are right. Something strange is going on."

Shan's heart skipped a beat. "What do you mean?"

"There are hundreds of servants throughout the inner palace. I've only seen the streets this busy when a celebration is planned and there's nothing happening until next month."

At least she wasn't the only one who had noticed. "What do you think it could be?"

Zhi crossed her arms and rubbed them as if she was cold. "Ting spoke of rebellion last night, and since then all I see are people whispering together or exchanging glances. I am worried she may be right."

Shan chose her words carefully. "If it came to that, do you think Lady Daiyu would be in danger?"

"I believe we all would. I once witnessed a riot and people went crazy. I saw friends attacking friends in the frenzy and afterwards they despaired over what they had done."

"Is there any way we can protect our lady?"

"She cannot leave the inner palace without permission," Zhi said. "If Prince Kun was here she could request a trip into the city, but I do not think the empress will grant such a thing."

It was unlikely. "Then we shall have to pray to the ancestors it does not come to a riot."

Zhi stared at her. "Shouldn't we plan something? Isn't it up to us to protect our lady?"

"What would you suggest if we can't leave the palace?" Shan couldn't trust Zhi with her escape plan.

"Could we ask Prince Kun's guards to protect us?"

"He should have taken his guards with him." But he hadn't. Not all of them. The guards on his palace were wearing the red uniform which denoted Kun's guard. So either he hadn't taken his full protection—which was strange if he was leaving the palace—or the guards on his palace weren't his. But why dress them as if they were… unless Kun hadn't really left. The muscles in her shoulders tightened. Where was the prince? "Should we tell the empress what we suspect?"

Zhi shook her head. "If we're wrong, we'll be punished for lying and Daiyu might be disciplined as well."

"Then we must wait and see. Make sure the others lock the palace when they come in and leave."

Zhi clasped her hands, uncertainty crossing her face. "I don't know if we can trust them."

What had changed to make Zhi confide in her? "Why not?"

"Just a feeling." Zhi sighed. "I hate this. I hate not knowing who to trust, having to watch my every word, of being trapped here when all I want is to be home with my family."

Something was off. Zhi was being far too forthcoming. "I miss my family as well." She smiled. "But we will do as the emperor and empress bid us."

Shouts outside caught their attention and they hurried to the window. Guards strode down the road dragging servants with them. The men and women were crying out their innocence. Shan froze. "That's Ting. What's going on?"

Yun burst into the room, her eyes wide. "The guards are rounding up everyone who has spoken about the rumours of… what Ting mentioned yesterday. They're going to be beheaded."

Nausea rose in Shan's stomach. "Ting was in the group."

Yun nodded. "I told the guards she was spreading rumours."

Shan clenched her hands to stop herself from slapping the young girl. "How many have they arrested?"

"At least a hundred. They're taking them to the main courtyard in the outer palace. They will show everyone what happens to people who betray the emperor."

The emperor's demonstration. She'd forgotten about it.

For a moment she considered running after the group, pulling Ting away and hiding her. Then Daiyu moaned in her sleep. She was Shan's priority. "I will pray Ting learns better in the afterlife." Her heart broke. Ting shouldn't have been so trusting.

Horror played across Zhi's face. "Ting hadn't chosen a side. She was merely informing us of the rumours."

Yun glared at her. "There is no choice. If she didn't immediately stand for the emperor, then she is against him. You didn't say anything at the time."

"Of course I support the emperor," Zhi said.

Yun turned her glare on Shan.

"I will always support the true emperor," Shan said.

Yun gaped at her. "You support the rumours?"

Interesting. Shan shook her head. "I said I support the true emperor. Your question suggests you believe the rumours are true and Emperor Xue is not the true emperor." She stared at the girl. "Should I call the guards to take you to the courtyard?"

"No! No, that's not what I meant. You confused me, I thought you meant the true heir which is what they've been calling the usurper."

"Funny how words can be misconstrued. You reported Ting for far less than what you just said."

Yun paled and she stepped back. "No. She didn't support the emperor immediately."

"And you implied our current emperor isn't the true emperor." She turned to Zhi. "Do you think we should call the guards?" Though it was one way of getting Yun out of the Jasmine Palace, Shan didn't want her to die. She was a victim of the society she was forced to live in.

"It is difficult to say," Zhi said. "If we are lenient, Yun may interpret that as us not supporting the emperor and report us."

"That would get us all killed, because we would tell the guards her words as well." She glanced at Yun. "I don't think Yun is quite that foolish."

Yun shook her head. "No. I wouldn't. It was a slip of the tongue. I'm so very sorry. It's not what I meant."

"Perhaps we should simply confine her to the palace for the meantime," Zhi said. "That way she would avoid any temptation."

Slightly concerned about Zhi's motives, Shan nodded. "Good idea." She grasped Yun's arm. "You can stay in your bedroom until this all blows over."

"But I did nothing wrong."

"Neither did Ting and she's dying because of it." Shan dragged her into the servants' bedroom. She scanned the room to make sure there was nothing Yun could use to escape and grabbed a spare set of clothes and her drawing chest. "You can wait here until Lady Daiyu wakes and she decides what should be done with you."

Shan closed the door and Zhi placed a cross bar over it to lock it in place. The fact the palace had a way of locking servants in their room was extremely telling.

"What do we do when Hai returns?" Zhi asked.

"Where is he?"

"I do not know."

"I shall ask the guard to bring him to Daiyu when he arrives." How much could she trust Zhi? There was little choice. They were the only ones able to protect Daiyu. She turned to her. "I am worried. The beheadings will either frighten everyone enough to stop any talk of revolt, or they will spark it."

"I agree."

"Then we need to be prepared. We should fetch non-perishable food and ensure the water barrel is full. Hopefully if we lock ourselves in the palace, people will leave us alone."

"Or they'll burn it to the ground."

Zhi must have seen some awful things. "That might be the case. Let's work on hiding first, and then we'll plan how to escape if we need to."

"I'll get the food," Zhi said.

"I'll check the water." She wasn't leaving Daiyu alone, but she might be able to send one of the guards for it. She didn't trust Hai not to contaminate it after she'd seen him speaking with Yun earlier. She entered the storeroom. The barrel was about three-quarters full. With potentially five people drinking from it, it would last a quarter moon if they rationed it. But with Daiyu still recovering, she needed to keep her fluids up.

She strode to the servants' entrance as Hai walked in. "Where have you been?"

The guilt on his face made her tense. "Nowhere."

"Clearly that's not true."

"I wanted to see what was happening to the people who were arrested."

"And what is happening?"

"They were taken through the gate into the outer palace and I couldn't follow," he said. "There are rumours the emperor is opening the gates to show the city people what happens to those who plot against him."

He would be foolish to do that. It would allow Bao and Anming to get men inside. "What do you think will happen after the servants are killed?"

"Everyone will stop spreading lies," he said.

Perhaps he was right, but he was naive not to expect the alternative. What was she going to do with him? "Could you fetch another barrel of water?" She could leave that barrel in the room with Yun and Hai. Then if he had contaminated it, it wouldn't be her problem.

"I thought it was almost full." Hai moved to pass her and she blocked him.

"Lady Daiyu has drunk a lot to keep hydrated. Go fetch it now."

"Yes, Shan." He bowed and left the room.

Shan went back into the main palace and checked Daiyu was still sleeping. Then she added her clothes to the bag in the roof.

The streets were empty. When Shan opened the main door, the guards at the entrance didn't turn. The stillness and silence were eerie. Was now the time to flee? But where could they go? The gates were guarded and those into the inner palace were probably shut. Even with her ability to be invisible they couldn't escape that way. Maybe the emperor's garden would be a good place to hide. The maidenhair tree had thick branches, but it wasn't ideal for a long time.

Footsteps echoed off the walls and she faded pulling the main door closed.

Two guards stopped in front of the palace. "The emperor wants us to confirm Lady Daiyu is still inside."

One of Daiyu's guards nodded. "She's been ill for several days."

"Good." The guard looked at the palace, his eyes going right through Shan and then continued on, turning the corner and heading towards the emperor's garden.

Shan eased back into the palace. Daiyu would definitely be the next person they came for. Perhaps the only reason they hadn't was because she'd been sick—or they thought the poison would deal with her.

Something banged in the palace behind her and Shan dropped her illusion. In the servants' hallway Hai was struggling with the new water barrel. Shan opened the door to their rooms. "Put it in here."

He frowned. "Why?"

"Because I said so." He shouldn't be questioning her.

With a scowl, he carried the barrel in. Yun pounded on the door. "Run, Hai. Get the empress."

Hai spun to face Shan and she withdrew her hair pin dagger, pointing it at him. "You're not going anywhere. You and Yun are staying here."

He shifted to the side and crouched.

"If you attack me, you will die." Her heart pounded. The time for subterfuge and guessing were gone.

Hai hesitated.

"You have two choices," Shan told him. "Either enter the room with Yun or die here now."

"I could yell for the guards."

She nodded. "And you'd be dead before you finished taking a breath." She kept her gaze steady.

His eyes darted to something behind her and before Shan

could turn, pain blossomed in her head and everything went black.

Chapter 14

Darkness surrounded Shan and her head thumped. She clenched her teeth to stop from groaning and blinked to clear her vision. It stayed dark, but as her eyes adapted to the lack of light she recognised the shapes in the room. She was in her bedroom, alone.

She sat, feeling the lump on the back of her head and dizziness swept over her. She clutched the mattress as nausea rose in her stomach.

Breathe.

Deep breaths calmed the nausea and some of the pain.

Someone had hit her from behind. They must have carried her in here and freed Yun. Which meant Daiyu was alone with them.

Shan stood and stumbled to the door, leaning against it while the room spun. She huffed. No time for weakness, her lady was in danger. When she pushed the door carefully to ensure it didn't make too much noise, it didn't budge. They would have barricaded her in here.

No windows, a barricaded door, wooden floors…her gaze drifted upwards. A panelled ceiling. She smiled, glad Yun hadn't thought of it.

Climbing onto the bed, she wasn't quite tall enough to reach the panels. Curse it. What else could she stand on? She reached for her hair pins to check whether the panels were loose, but they were gone. She swore. At least they hadn't taken her ribbon.

The water barrel Hai had brought in was by the door. Perfect. She was tempted to drink some water but she didn't trust it. Instead she climbed on to the barrel, careful to keep her weight on the edges of the lid.

Voices outside made her pause.

"We need to fetch the guards," Yun said. "The empress will want to question her."

"We don't need the guards. If we take her ourselves, we'll be rewarded," Hai replied.

Should she wait until they opened the door and then fade? No, the room wasn't that big and she might bump into one of them. Besides, with her thumping head she might not be able to channel her gift. Her energy was better spent helping Daiyu.

She pressed the panel up and to the side. It was a little lighter in the roof with daylight shining through the eaves.

A gong echoed in her head, making her ears ring and her head ache. Gritting her teeth, she braced herself on the sides of the panel and lifted herself into the dusty cavity. Then she lowered the panel back into position. The roof space was empty aside from the bag she'd stored there above Daiyu's room.

Would they hear her crawling above them?

She had no choice.

Below her Hai said, "I'm going in." A thunk as the brace was removed from the door and then a gasp. "She's gone!"

"She can't be. Check under the bed."

"She's not here," Hai said.

Yun swore. "We've got to get Zhi."

Shan scowled. Zhi was in on it. Perhaps she'd been the one to hit Shan from behind.

As their footsteps faded, she crawled across the roof,

pausing when she estimated she'd reached the space above Daiyu's bedchamber. She lay on her stomach and lifted a panel. Daiyu sat in bed and Hai and Yun were speaking in low tones to Zhi. The soup bowl on the table next to Daiyu's bed caught Shan's attention. Zhi had brought in more of the empress's soup. There was no question now. Shan would have to rescue Daiyu on her own. She unwound the ribbon around her wrist.

Timing was everything. She couldn't take all three of them. Not without the guards being alerted.

"Find her," Zhi growled and Hai and Yun ran from the room.

"Is something wrong?" Daiyu asked.

"No, my lady. Now, you should eat this soup the empress sent for you." Zhi picked up the bowl and walked closer, turning her back to Shan.

"I'd really prefer some biscuits," Daiyu said.

Good. She had listened to what Shan had told her. Shan lowered the panel and crawled closer. She stopped next to the bag she'd packed and lifted the panel. Zhi was below her, sitting on the bed, holding a spoon out to Daiyu. "My lady, it really is better if you eat."

Shan took a breath. She had nothing heavy enough to hit Zhi with and any scuffle would alert the guards. She would have to kill Zhi. It took some effort to fade, but when she had, she checked no one else was in the room and then lightly lowered herself from the ceiling. She slipped her ribbon over Zhi's head and pulled it tight, cutting off her airway. Zhi struggled and Shan let go of her illusion. Daiyu yelped, slapping her hand over her mouth to muffle the sound. Shan held on, keeping her body close to Zhi's to prevent her from attacking. "My lady, get up," she said. "Stand on the table and get the bag from the ceiling."

"You're killing her!"

"She was trying to kill you with the soup." Zhi stopped

moving and Shan held a minute longer to make sure she wasn't pretending. Daiyu hadn't moved. "My lady, we must leave. The whole palace is about to erupt in violence." Her head swam with fuzziness. Escape. She climbed onto the table and retrieved the bag, digging through it for a simple outfit Daiyu could wear. "Put this on." When Daiyu didn't take it, Shan thrust it at her and shook her arms. "I must get you to safety. They've already beheaded Ting for treason."

Daiyu gasped.

"Yun turned her in. They locked me in the servants' quarters and were talking about turning me over to the empress." She threw the bag over her shoulder.

Finally Daiyu moved, stripping off her sleepwear. She shook as she stepped into the dress. Shan pushed Zhi's body under the bed, ignoring the horror that wanted to rise up and take control. It had to be done. She moved to the window and peered out. The sun was sinking, meaning it would soon be dark, but they couldn't wait until then. Only guards strode the roads outside, alert and armed.

In the receiving room, a door opened and Shan ran back to Daiyu who had dressed. "Down," she whispered, pulling Daiyu behind the bed. She moved in front of her, shielding her with her body. If she faded too soon, she might be too tired to keep the illusion in place.

Hai ran in and he gaped. "They're gone! Yun, they're both gone."

Yun entered and Shan murmured to Daiyu, "I need you to keep completely still. I'm going to make us invisible."

"How?"

"I'll explain later." She held Daiyu's hand and faded, pushing the illusion out, and over Daiyu.

"Where are they?" Yun demanded and strode to the bed, throwing back the covers. "Check the cupboards."

Hai hurried to obey as Yun checked under the bed. She shrieked. "Zhi is under there."

Shan wasn't certain she could keep the illusion in place while they moved but she had no choice. As the servants bent under the bed to retrieve Zhi's body, Shan murmured, "Stand."

Should she knock out Hai and Yun or would it be better to slip out without them noticing? They didn't seem to want to bring Daiyu's absence to the guards' attention. Probably scared of being held accountable and punished.

"She's dead," Hai said as he dragged Zhi's body out. Tears glistened in his eyes.

Yun was pale. "They'll blame us for this, for letting Daiyu get away."

"We must be honest to the empress. She will believe us."

"You're such an idiot. The emperor didn't hesitate to imprison Prince Kun for treason. The empress will punish us for our failure. It doesn't matter that Shan is some kind of assassin with her hairpin blades, we will be at fault."

Kun was a prisoner. That explained why his guard was outside the palace still. Were they guarding the prince under house arrest?

"We can't lie to the empress," Hai insisted.

"Then you will die. We need to get out of here."

Shan smiled. It was nice Yun was getting a taste of what she'd put Ting through.

"I won't let you go." Hai grabbed Yun and they fought.

Shan tugged Daiyu's hand and they circled around the fighting pair towards the door, moving as fast as she dared, though the servants were too busy fighting to notice. They got through the door into the receiving room as Hai yelled, "Help! Guards, help!"

Shan pushed Daiyu against the wall and stepped in front of her again. Her hands shook with the effort of holding the illusion as the guards burst in through the front door and raced into the bedchamber. Though the front door was now clear, someone would see them if they went out that way.

She couldn't hold the illusion for that long. Instead she tugged Daiyu to the back of the palace. As she passed the table, her hair pins glinted at her. She swept them up and then peered into the hallway before pulling Daiyu inside and dropping the illusion. "We'll go out the back."

It was darker now and the lanterns in the hallway hadn't been lit. Shan tucked the pins into her hair.

"Then where will we go?" Daiyu whispered.

Bells clanged outside and voices raised in shouts. What now? Shan managed to replace the illusion before the guards on the servants' entrance rushed past. One man bumped her arm but he didn't seem to notice. "The palace is under attack," one guard called. "We must get Lady Daiyu to the empress."

As soon as they'd entered the main room, Shan ran, pulling Daiyu with her.

Outside was chaos. People ran through the streets, fear on their faces. They could get lost in the crowd. She kept Daiyu's hand firmly in hers. "We'll go to the emperor's garden," she told Daiyu. "There must be somewhere we can hide."

Daiyu's hand trembled in hers and sweat beaded her face.

"Are you all right, my lady?"

She shook her head. "Zhi gave me some tea. I didn't think not to drink it."

Curse it. "Just keep walking for me. Breathe slowly." She slid her arm around Daiyu's waist and Daiyu leaned on her. They rounded a corner, and at the clang of metal Shan pulled Daiyu to the side. Ahead servants fought with hoes and sticks against fully armed guards. She spotted the laundry maid who had whispered to her friend about Bao using a washer board to block the blade of a sword, her eyes wide with fear. Next to her a eunuch stabbed the guard with a staff, but it barely budged him. Shan swallowed. They would be slaughtered, but there was little she could do.

Kun wouldn't be coming to help them.

With the fighting blocking the whole street, it was too dangerous to go that way to the garden. "This way."

Daiyu stumbled and fell against Shan. Her eyes fluttered closed. "Stay with me." Shan's head pounded as she shook her and half dragged her along the road. Guards stood outside the palaces, ready to take on any who would dare attack, but she didn't dare ask for shelter without knowing who she could trust.

Down the next street lay bodies of servants groaning or dead. Shan scooped up the hat of one and placed it on Daiyu's head. It would hide her identity and the fact she was ill.

They were about halfway there.

"You there, what are you doing?" The guard stepped out from a building, his hand on his pommel.

"Returning to our dormitory," Shan said. "What's going on?"

"The palace is under attack."

She gasped. "Is the emperor safe?"

The man nodded. "He left for the summer palace this morning."

"Praise the ancestors," Shan said.

"You'd better get inside while you can."

"Thank you." She pulled a weakening Daiyu with her and hurried past the guard. Did Anming and Bao know the emperor wasn't in residence?

She half carried Daiyu through the streets, stopping often to avoid the fighting, sometimes having to fade them so they weren't seen. Her breath came in gasps as she finally spotted the bridge into the emperor's garden. Almost there.

Daiyu groaned and crumpled to the ground. Shan crouched beside her. "My lady." She shook her. "Not far now. We just have to get across the bridge and then we'll be safe."

Daiyu's eyelids fluttered, but she didn't speak.

Someone nearby screamed in pain and the clang of swords was far too loud. "Hold on to me, Daiyu." She slid one hand under Daiyu's knees and one around her back and lifted. She grunted with the effort as Daiyu clung limply to her neck.

She could do this. It wasn't far. Moving as fast as she could, she carried Daiyu across the open pavement, towards the bridge. Her eyes scanned the darkening garden but she couldn't see movement. The slope of the bridge seemed steeper than it had when they'd crossed it only a few days ago and she panted as she went down the other side.

Get as far away from the buildings as possible.

Hopefully others wouldn't enter the garden, too afraid of breaking the rules.

Moving off the main path into a copse of trees, she paused to get her breath back. "My lady?" She jiggled Daiyu.

Nothing.

Fear filled her. What had Zhi given to Daiyu? Would it wear off or was it stronger this time, designed to kill fast not slowly? The noises of battle were still too close. Shan continued through the garden carrying Daiyu, focusing on the next step and then the next, as her arms screamed at her to put Daiyu down. If she could find a sheltered spot, she could leave Daiyu, then search for a safer location more quickly.

She stumbled into the rock garden, where large quartz rocks jutted from the ground. Two rested against each other forming a sort of cave. It would have to do. She lay Daiyu gently on the ground under the rocks and checked her pulse. Fast, much too fast and her hair stuck to her forehead with sweat. Shan shook her and Daiyu's eyes opened. "Stay here, my lady. I'm going to get help."

Daiyu's eyes closed. No telling if she actually heard or understood, but there wasn't anything Shan could do about it.

The sun had disappeared below the horizon and only the last remaining rays shone above. Night was their friend. She took stock, running through her memory of the garden. The empress's herb garden. There might be something there she could use to break Daiyu's fever, something which might counteract the poison. But which way was it?

She would be systematic about it. Search the garden in lines until she found it, starting with the section furthest from the buildings. Less chance of running into anyone else fleeing the attack.

She strode through the fading light until she reached wall. No guards were on top, they were possibly too busy at the guard towers or fighting below. She jogged along it, keeping to the canopy under the trees. Then she heard voices.

Her heart leapt and she ducked behind a tree.

"Do you think it's the usurper attacking?"

"Who else? The servants know better than to revolt."

They were the same voices she'd heard before asking about Daiyu. She pulled her illusion around her, panting at the effort and peered out from behind the tree. The two men headed back towards the bridge.

What were they doing in the emperor's garden? Could there be somewhere she could hide Daiyu?

She waited a moment more until she was sure the guards had gone and stepped away from the tree, scanning her surroundings. A door in the wall. It was underneath a large tree and if she hadn't been looking for it, she might have missed it in the darkness. Her skin prickled. How many guards would be inside? Perhaps she could fade as she opened the door and take stock. She retrieved her hair pins and crept closer. No voices from the other side of the door, but it could be too thick to hear them.

Taking a moment to slow her breathing, she pulled the illusion to her, finding it more difficult this time. She opened the door a crack and peered inside. Two guards, one sitting at the table with his back to her and the other by the shelf with drinks. She slipped in and closed the door behind her. Bracing herself, she clenched her teeth and then sneaked up on the man at the table and slit his throat with her dagger, instantly silencing him. Her stomach convulsed as warm blood ran down her hands. The man by the shelving turned and yelled, dropping his glass as he reached for his sword. There was only one other door in the room and the guard strode towards it.

Shan shook with the effort to hold her illusion. Any sound would cause the guard to swing his sword, and if she was too close, he would hit her. What else could she use? A bow and quiver full of arrows leaned against the wall in the corner. It had been years since she'd used one, but it was her best chance. She crept to it and lifted the bow, notching the arrow as the guard came back into the room. She aimed and let the arrow fly. It hit his shoulder and he yelled, dropping his sword. She ran towards him as he reached for his weapon. Her illusion had gone. She swung her blades across his neck and then leapt back, out of his reach as the sword came up and then fell harmlessly away as the life left the guard's eyes. Guilt and nausea rose as she fought not to let it take control.

She panted, her eyes not leaving the man in case he wasn't quite dead. He didn't move. She grabbed his feet and dragged him out of the doorway. The next room was small and the torture devices that hung on the walls chilled her. A prison. Was Kun here, was he in any state to be rescued?

Keys hung on a hook next to the door.

She didn't have the energy to fade this time so she would have to move quickly. Fatigue made it difficult to lift her arm to take the keys and it took her a couple of tries to get the key into the lock.

She paused before turning it. What if it wasn't Kun but some violent prisoners? They could kill her and then Daiyu would die as well. She cleared her throat and called, "Is anyone inside?"

No answer. Was the door too thick? She knocked hard, wincing as the sound reverberated through the room. "Can you hear me?"

"Who's there?" A male voice which sounded like Kun.

"Shan. Who are you?" She held her breath.

"It's Kun. Let me out."

She twisted the key and the lock clicked open. Pushing open the door she found Kun inside, sitting on the straw-covered ground, dressed in his palace finery which was now ripped and dirty. He hauled himself to his feet, stumbling towards the door. In the better light she saw the bruises on his face.

"How did you find me? What's happening? Where's Daiyu?"

"This way." She led him into the main room and pressed him into a chair before pouring him a drink from the jug on the table. Kun gaped at the dead guards. "I'm sorry. I had to kill them."

She refused to look at them as she handed him a dried biscuit from her bag. "The palace is rioting," she said. "The emperor was going to hang over a hundred people for spreading rumours about the true heir and the servants revolted." If Kun went into the grounds dressed as he was, he would be a target. Bracing herself, she studied the guards. The one she'd killed first was about Kun's size. She pulled off his clothes. "I heard you'd been imprisoned and found this room while looking for the empress's herb garden. Daiyu has been poisoned. I've left her somewhere safe, but if we don't find a cure soon, she may die."

He stared at her as if in a daze. She hoped the beating hadn't damaged his brain. She handed Kun the pants. "Put these on, Your Highness. You can't go out there looking like a prince." Though would dressing as a guard make him any safer? He would at least blend better.

He scowled at her but took the pants and began to change.

Shan struggled to take the tunic off the guard. "I need you to tell me where to get a cure for Daiyu's poison."

"What poison is it?"

"I don't know. I believe the empress gave it to Zhi and Yun."

"My mother tried to kill Daiyu? But Daiyu is innocent in all this." His lips firmed and he bent to help her with the tunic. "We must save her."

Shan sipped some water while he dressed, some of the tension leaving her.

Kun grabbed the sword belt and sword from the guard and then looked around, spotting the bow and quiver of arrows in the corner. He swung them onto his back. "Let's go."

Outside it was fully dark, but the scent of smoke hung in the air. In the distance, a glow appeared. "They've set the palace alight," Shan said. "Where's the herb garden?"

"Close to the empress's palace."

They should get Daiyu before they went. "This way."

It was impossible to go too fast through the garden, though her eyes adjusted to the darkness quickly. Kun followed close behind and her shoulder blades itched. She prayed he could be trusted.

She stopped, a little uncertain of how far they'd come.

"What's wrong?" Kun whispered.

"Which way is the rock garden?" She thought they would have reached it by now.

"Through here." Kun took the lead, turning right and a short distance later they arrived. Shan hurried to the spot she had left Daiyu and pulled her out. She was shivering, her skin icy cold, but wet with sweat. "Daiyu, wake for me." She cradled her mistress and wiped the sweat from her brow.

Kun swore. "Who knows what Mother gave her. Let me

see if I can get help." He was silent, eyes closed, face a picture of concentration.

Shan frowned. "What are you doing?"

He didn't open his eyes. "Calling for Kew. She might be in the palace somewhere."

His answer made no sense to her. How could he communicate with anyone silently? "Is Kew a healer?"

"A dragon." He opened his eyes and grinned. "She's on her way."

Chapter 15

Shan tensed. She'd heard stories of dragons attacking men who went hunting in the mountains but had never heard of someone being able to talk to them. Daiyu moaned and Shan stroked her arms. "It's all right, my lady. Kun and I are here. We'll make you better."

A swooshing sound made her look up as a shadow dropped from the sky above, wings spread, and came to a slightly rough halt on the ground next to them.

Kun laughed. "You can fly now."

Yes. The tone of the voice in Shan's head held joy. *What is wrong with her?*

Shan stared as the dragon walked closer. Kew was larger than the biggest palace dog, but not quite the size of a tiger. Her hands tightened around Daiyu as if she could protect her from this beast. But was she a beast if she could communicate mentally?

I will not hurt her. Anming is a friend of mine.

The voice in her head was strange, light and adolescent, but if this creature could help Daiyu… "She's been poisoned, but I don't know what with."

Let me touch her. Kew pressed her nose and her paw to Daiyu's skin and was silent. *I am not familiar with it. Let me ask Geriel.*

"Is she here?" Kun asked.

Kew nodded.

Geriel? How did Kun know a dragon who knew Anming? Whose side was he on? Could the dragon be trusted or was she lying too? Shan sighed, reining in her questions. None of it really mattered if Daiyu couldn't be healed.

Geriel can help but we need to get Daiyu to her.

"Where is she?" Kun asked.

Near the Hall of Clarity.

Which meant moving the whole way through the inner palace, while avoiding the fighting. Would they be too late?

Kun lifted Daiyu from Shan's lap. "Take my sword. You'll have to protect us."

A surge of shock went through her. He trusted her to defend them. Quickly she retrieved the sword from his belt. It was far heavier than she was used to, but her hair pin daggers were no use against a sword. She swung it to get used to the feel and followed Kew and Kun through the garden.

I will help you avoid the fighting as much as I can.

They passed fearful servants running into the garden, but no one stopped or attacked them. They were trying to save themselves. Crossing the bridge brought the whole scene into stark focus. A couple of the palaces burned, and eunuchs had formed a line to the stream to pass buckets of water in an attempt to put out the flames. If they failed, the whole inner palace might burn. Shan hoped no one was trapped inside.

Stop.

She almost crashed into Kun at the sudden command. A group of guards ran past the intersection just ahead. "Will any of the guards protect you?" she murmured.

"I don't know how many know about the emperor arresting me."

"The men at your palace told me you'd gone away and

weren't sure when you'd be back."

He grunted and they kept moving, stopping only when Kew gave the order. They reached the Gates of Heavenly Virtue which were closed and heavily guarded.

This way. Kew headed towards the servants' gate further away. It was guarded as well, but as they drew closer Shan realised the guards weren't imperial guards, but heavily armed servants. She gasped. "Captain Wei."

He nodded to her. "Shan. Prince Kun. Kew. This way." He opened the door and ushered them into the guard room. Other men from the journey to Bonam were also inside. They cleared the way and opened the door on the far side.

The fighting was much worse in the outer palace. Big groups of men fought; officials, guards, eunuchs and soldiers, some with swords and arrows, others with sticks and knives. Across the way, the pavilion where Daiyu had rested in the shade was burning. A scream of pain made Shan jolt as nearby a black-clothed servant stumbled back as a soldier yanked his sword from the man's stomach. Blood spurted into the air and she flinched, nausea burning in her. Surely this wasn't the way to start a new rule—with so much bloodshed of your own people.

As they exited, several guards from the guard room flanked them. Shan followed Kew as they wove through the fighting, her gaze never still as she scanned for archers, or fighters getting too close to their party. She almost tripped over Kew when the dragon stopped, breathing fire towards a party running towards them. The group dived away and the guards hurried them forward. More buildings burned including the Office of Internal Scrutiny.

Kew led them to a circle of men protecting two people on the ground. They parted to let them through. Blood rushed from a gash in a soldier's chest and a woman had her hands on him, her eyes closed.

Kun laid Daiyu on the ground and a moment later the

woman sighed and took her hands off the soldier. The soldier sat, touching the place where his wound had been but it was gone. Shan gaped at her. What kind of sorcery was this?

Geriel has the gift of healing, like you have the gift of blending.

She hadn't known it was possible. "Can you heal Daiyu?"

Geriel turned to them, her thick rough cotton dress tunic identifying her as Rhoran. Shan's grip tightened around the sword and Kun's hand shot out and stopped her. "She's an ally."

Geriel nodded. "Kun it is good to see you again," she said, her accent a little strange. She rested her eyes on Shan. "Kew tells me Daiyu was poisoned?"

The concern on Geriel's face warmed Shan. "I think so," she said. "She fell ill from some soup, but was recovering until she drank tea given to her by her maid."

Geriel rested her hands on Daiyu and closed her eyes. She nodded. "It is a poison and it has spread fast. This might take a while."

The soldier Geriel had healed got to his feet and swayed. One of the guards in the circle steadied him. "Take my place and rest. I'll go out."

Shan's shoulders were tense as she waited. The fighting was far too close. How could they make it stop? "Where's Bao?"

Kun raised an eyebrow at her. "I don't know."

This was no time for games. "Can you end the fighting?" she demanded. "If the emperor has gone to his summer palace, surely you can take over, make an announcement, stop your people from killing each other."

"No one will pay any attention to me. They wouldn't hear me."

Geriel opened her eyes. "Kew, can you fly to Temur? Tell him to give you the horn and the voice amplifier."

Kew nodded and left the circle to take flight.

"Where is the khan?" Kun asked.

"They wait a league or so from the palace. They didn't want to frighten the people or make it seem like they were invading." Geriel closed her eyes again and after a few more minutes she sighed. "The poison is gone." She shifted away. "You can wake her now. It's probably best that mine isn't the first face she sees."

Kun gently squeezed Daiyu's arms, the look of concern on his face causing Shan's heart to squeeze. "Daiyu, you need to wake."

Her eyes fluttered and then widened. "Kun?" She flung her arms around his neck and he hugged her back.

Shan swallowed the lump in her throat.

"I must go," Geriel said. "There are others who need my help. When Kew returns with the horn, use it to get people's attention and then use the amplifier to speak. Lien and Bao are here somewhere, and they will come to you."

A few guards stayed behind with Daiyu, but most followed Geriel into the battlefield where she stopped to heal another fallen soldier. Such a contrast from what Shan had been taught. Geriel wasn't a barbarian, she was a healer, a peace-maker, healing both servant and soldier.

More was going on here than Shan was aware of. She stood and scanned the area as Kun helped Daiyu to her feet. "What now?"

"The steps of the Hall of Clarity are the best place to make a declaration," he said.

Shan handed him the sword and asked Daiyu, "Are you all right now, my lady?"

"A little weak still. What's going on? I don't remember much after you killed Zhi."

Shan swallowed. Too many deaths. Her hands were still stained red. "The palace erupted in violence."

"Wouldn't we be safer inside?" Daiyu asked.

"Some of the buildings are burning," Kun said, taking her

hand. "This way."

They went around to the front of the Hall of Clarity, their guards fighting off anyone who approached them. Bao's supporters might not listen to Kun so any speech Kun made wouldn't work without Bao by his side. They reached the top of the steps and Shan scanned the areas of fighting below. Every now and then groups fell to the ground as if pushed and when they leapt to their feet again, their weapons were gone. Her skin prickled. Even though she strained her eyes, it was too dark to make out the features of those who fought, but many of the groups were fighting hand to hand with no weapons.

A shadow in the sky caught her attention. "Kew is back." The dragon carried two items in her front paws. As she came in to land she said, *Catch.*

Shan reached out and caught the horn and a conical shaped object made from leather. Kew landed.

"Kew, can you find Bao?" Kun said. "Tell him to come here."

Kew was silent. *It is difficult with so many thoughts. Bao is not as familiar to me as Geriel.* Finally she said, *Blow the horn. He will come.*

Geriel ran up. "Let me." She took the horn from Shan and blew three long notes. Some of the fighters turned towards the hall.

Kun held the amplifier to his mouth. "Lay down your weapons." His voice boomed through the courtyard, but few paused.

Kew roared, the amplifier picking up the sound and it echoed through the air. Smoke snorted from her nose and the fighters swung towards the sound.

Kun smiled and tried again. "I am First Prince Kun. Prince Bao will join me shortly. We should not be fighting one another."

The men in the courtyard glanced at each other as if

uncertain what to do.

Suddenly a Bonamese woman appeared by Kun's side, a little out of breath. Shan's heart lurched and she reached for her hair pins, but Kew said, *This is Lien, former state princess of Bonam and current Tribal Mother of Rhora.*

Bao's sister. Shan lowered her weapon as Kun continued, "With the emperor away, it is up to me to end this violence. Put down your weapons and gather in front of me."

The nearby burning building bathed the area in flickering light. Bao ran around the corner of the hall, panting. Shan's heart raced. He was bleeding from a cut on his head and his clothes were covered in blood. His eyes met hers and they widened, but he didn't stop on his way to Kun's side. Kun handed him the amplifier and Geriel stood behind him and placed a hand on his neck.

He took a moment to get his breath back before speaking. "I am Prince Bao, son of Emperor Huang, thought dead these past eighteen years." He swallowed. "Please stop fighting each other. We can resolve this without more violence."

Geriel removed her hand from Bao and he stood straighter. She murmured, "I will search for more injured." A couple of Chungson men joined her as she went to examine the bodies lying in the courtyard.

As people lowered their weapons, Bao continued to speak. "Many people questioned why I would not reveal myself for so long and the truth is I didn't know who to trust. It was not Rhoran barbarians who attacked the carriage my parents and I were in, but General Ying who recently died." There were a few gasps from the men who had started to gather. Shan scanned the area. Guards stood between the crowd and the princes but a well-aimed arrow could hit either of them.

Shan moved along the front of the Hall of Clarity to check what was happening in the rest of the outer palace. Men continued to move towards Bao's voice, keeping distance between themselves and the men they'd been fighting.

"I was too young and too scared to return home and I found refuge with a friend. But now it is time for me to reclaim my birthright. My uncle, Emperor Xue did not believe the rumours, and I could not get access to see him. I had hoped he would be at the palace, but when I arrived I discovered servants about to be beheaded for spreading the truth."

A couple of people grumbled.

"What's the mood like, Kew?" Lien asked.

Uncertain. Some hope, some worry about where this change will leave them.

Kun took the amplifier. "Neither of us wants you to fight each other. Things will change but there is no need to fear. I have spoken with Prince Bao and he assures me he wants the best for Bonam."

Shan walked back to the princes and a soldier strode around the far corner of the hall holding a notched bow. "Get down!" She lunged for the group, but she was too far away. Lien spun and disappeared, but the arrow had already been released. Kun dived at Daiyu, taking her to the ground which left Bao standing alone. The arrow pierced his shoulder as he leapt away and landed heavily on the pavement. Shan fell to her knees beside him as Kun yelled into the amplifier, "Geriel!"

The crowd shouted and Lien called, "Calm them."

Shan didn't hear what Kun said, she only had eyes for Bao and the blood pouring out of the injury in his back. Her heart raced as she pressed her hands over the wound, her fingers splayed around the arrow, and he groaned. "Don't complain," she snapped. "I'm saving your life."

He grunted but she didn't think it was in laughter.

The arrow was buried deep. Could it have reached his heart?

"Don't die on me."

He turned his head to the side. "Would you…miss me?"

Relief filled her. He couldn't be too injured to ask such a foolish question. She didn't answer.

Geriel pounded up and dropped to her knees, pressing her hands to Bao's chest. Kun was still talking to the crowd, assuring them Bao would be all right. Shan glanced up and saw the archer lying dead.

"Lien, help me pull the arrow out," Geriel ordered.

Shan moved back and Bao gripped her hand. She squeezed his fist and murmured, "This is really going to hurt." Before he could respond, Lien and Geriel pulled the arrow from his back and blood poured from the wound. Geriel closed her eyes, pressing her hands over the injury. The flow of blood slowed and the torn skin knitted together, until fresh skin was left in its place.

Shan could barely believe it. "That is incredible." A sob nearby caught her attention and she found Daiyu with her back against the building, hugging her knees and sobbing. Guilt filled Shan. Her responsibility was to her lady, not to Bao. She let go of his hand and crawled to Daiyu. "My lady, what is wrong?"

Daiyu waved her hand at Bao. "Everything. People are shooting at us and killing each other… my brother's manservant is a prince…"

Shan wrapped an arm around her shoulder. "I don't understand it all, either. I'm sure they'll explain it to us in time."

The crowd cheered and she looked up to find Bao back on his feet. "We must extinguish the fires and collect our dead," he called through the amplifier. "Then please go back to your residences. Any ministers should come to the Hall to speak with us." He paused. "I know you are worried, but neither Prince Kun nor I want any harm to come to you."

After a little prodding from some of the Chungson guards, the crowd disbanded, some hurrying to help those putting out the fires and others arranging for the dead to be collected.

Bao let out a deep breath.

"Let's get inside," Kun said.

"What about the inner palace?" Shan asked. "Will they have heard you?"

The princes exchanged a glance.

"I'll go and disarm them, and then talk to the empress and the consorts," Lien said. "They know me. Others who were here will return and word will spread."

Bao nodded. "Be careful, Kixi."

Lien vanished and Daiyu gasped. "Does she have your gift, Shan?"

Kun stared at her. "You have the gift of speed?"

Shan shook her head. Is that what Lien had? She could move so fast she seemed to vanish. She must have been the one disarming the men in the courtyard.

"What is your gift?" Kun asked.

"She can vanish," Daiyu said. "That's how we escaped the palace. No one could see us."

"I would like to see it," Kun said as he helped Daiyu to her feet. "But first please get us some food."

Shock and disappointment swamped her as she stood. It had taken only seconds for things to revert to normal. No thanks for rescuing him or Daiyu, no concern about her welfare. She bowed. "Of course, Your Highness. Can my lady stay with you?"

"Yes." He wrapped his arm possessively around Daiyu and she leaned into him.

They entered the Hall of Clarity, and Kun directed her towards the servant hallways. Inside she found people huddled in fear. They watched her warily and she held up her hands to show she was unarmed. "It's all right. The fighting has stopped. Prince Kun and Prince Bao are meeting with the ministers to decide the future. They need food and drink so if someone could show me the way to the kitchen, I'd appreciate it."

"Shan!" A voice called from the back and people moved aside to let her through.

"Ting." Her heart swelled. "I thought you were dead."

She hugged Shan, her thin frame surprisingly strong. "No, the fighting started before the execution began and we ran."

"I'm glad you're safe." Hope leaked through her fatigue. She smiled. "Now if someone could lead me to the kitchen." She couldn't afford to keep the princes waiting. The innocent were safe for now, but her job could be in jeopardy if she was too slow.

Chapter 16

By the time Shan had returned with food and drink, the main hall was full. The Prime Minister sat next to the princes at the head of the table and around it sat officials. None of them acknowledged Shan or any of the people who served them food.

Where was Daiyu?

As she served Prince Kun, she murmured, "Your Highness, where is my lady?"

He glanced at her. "Sleeping in one of the guest rooms. Stay here in case we have need of you."

She wanted to check on Daiyu, make sure she was safe and not too anxious, but she couldn't. "Yes, Your Highness." She went to stand by the wall.

Geriel and Lien entered the room with Kew at their heels and the ministers muttered in outrage, one man saying, "What are they doing here? This is not women's business."

"Lien is the khan's representative." Bao gestured them to the front of the room. "Please give us your report."

"The fighting in the inner palace is over," Lien said. "The eunuchs are battling the fires and the empress and consorts have found places to stay."

Geriel stepped forward. "I have healed everyone I could, but there are a large number dead."

"Filthy Rhoran scum," one man muttered.

Bao glared at him. "Rhora is no longer our enemy."

Kun added, "Geriel healed many of our people today and several moons ago when there was fighting. We should be grateful to her."

More mutterings and the two women came to where Shan stood. Lien lowered her voice. "These men are all in positions of power because Xue gave it to them. We need to watch them carefully so they don't attack either Kun or Bao."

"Bao would be wise to get rid of them all and employ his own men," Shan said. "Especially with the emperor still out there."

Lien nodded. "This is not what we had planned, but Bao couldn't ignore the fact the emperor was going to behead people because of him."

"This wasn't planned?" Shan asked.

She shook her head. "We underestimated how unhappy people were under Xue's rule. The momentum around the rumours of Bao's survival took on a life of its own."

"Was Kun aware of what was going on?"

"Yes, but we didn't know if he could be trusted."

"Still don't," Geriel muttered.

I sense no subterfuge in him, Kew said. *He wants nothing more than for Bao to be emperor, and to marry Daiyu and live somewhere safe.*

"Will Anming still agree to the marriage?" Shan asked. Her stomach twisted as she continued, "Or will he want Daiyu to marry Bao?"

Lien glanced at her. "Bao will choose his own bride, but not until the emperor has stepped down. We need to find out where he is."

"I heard he was at the summer palace," Shan said.

"Kew, can you reach Anming and ask him to check it out?"

Kew nodded and a few minutes later she said, *He'll send one of his men.*

"Is Lord Anming in the city?" Shan asked.

"Yes. He didn't want to send too many of his men in case the emperor noticed and attacked Chungson."

Shan scowled. "Then why didn't he warn us?"

"Didn't Wei slip you a note?"

"No." At least not that Daiyu had told her.

"Perhaps he didn't have a chance. Anming was very worried."

He asked me about his sister as soon as I contacted him, Kew confirmed.

Shan closed her eyes as sadness flooded her. They cared about Daiyu but not her. It didn't matter how many times she put her own life in danger to save Daiyu that would never change. She should be used to it by now.

Bao waved his hand as he emphasised a point, and had the ministers' complete attention. He held a crowd, his leadership natural. She should have seen it before, should have realised he didn't come from a poor background. No wonder he had rejected her. She was nowhere near good enough for him.

Exhaustion stole the last of her energy and she slumped against the wall.

"You should go to bed," Geriel said.

Shan shook her head. "Prince Kun asked me to stay in case they need anything."

Geriel scowled. "Then he can get it himself."

"That's not how things work here," Lien said. She smiled at Shan. "We'll manage. Get some rest."

Shan hesitated. If she left she'd be defying a direct order. "I can't."

"She should be free to do what she wants," Geriel growled.

Lien sighed. "Come with me." She pulled Shan to the

table. "Cousin, I'm sending Shan to bed."

He frowned and then nodded. "Very well."

Shan bowed. "Thank you, Your Highness." She caught some concern in Bao's gaze as she turned to go, but she wouldn't be fooled by it. He hadn't cared about her well-being when he'd asked her to spy.

Geriel was right. She should be free to do what she wanted.

But freedom for the poor was the last thing on any of these men's minds.

~*~

"Shan, wake up." Someone shook Shan and she opened her eyes to find Daiyu staring down at her. Startled she sat and ran a hand through her hair.

"I am sorry, my lady. I must have overslept." Her heart raced as she noted the brightness of the day. "Can I get you some breakfast or water for a bath?" The room was strange. Larger than the servants' quarters with only two beds not four and the ceilings were high. In the corner stood the half-finished painting of Prince Kun. Memories flooded her. The riot, the struggle to save Daiyu, Bao being shot. Her muscles tightened. They were in the Hall of Clarity. "I'm sorry, my lady. I wasn't sure where to sleep last night. I hope you don't mind me taking one of the beds."

Daiyu placed a hand on her arm. "Not at all. Calm yourself. I do not blame you for oversleeping with everything that happened last night. Kun has said we may return to the Jasmine Palace."

Shan stood and brushed her clothes, her hands hesitating over the splotches of brown blood. Her body went cold and the hairs on her arms stuck up on end. She'd killed three people last night. Her vision blurred and she blinked rapidly.

"Are you all right?" Daiyu asked.

"Of course, my lady." She gritted her teeth and looked

around for the bag she'd brought with them. She'd been too tired to change the night before. "May I quickly change?"

Daiyu nodded.

Had anyone thought to check the state of the Jasmine Palace? As she tidied her hair and dabbed some jasmine oil on her wrists, she said, "Perhaps I should send someone ahead to clean."

"I'm sure it will be fine. Shall we go?"

Either Daiyu had forgotten about Zhi, or she assumed someone would have dealt with her, just as her room was magically cleaned whenever she left it. Shan followed her into the large hall where Kun and Bao spoke with Lien and Geriel.

Shan kowtowed. How could she suggest they clear the palace before taking Daiyu inside? Her mistress had already been through enough, she didn't need a reminder. But it wasn't her place to speak first and she had returned to her position of servitude.

"Rise, Shan." Kun barely glanced at her, but held his hand out to Daiyu, and Bao spoke with his sister.

She tensed at a movement in the corner, but it was Kew getting to her feet. Maybe the dragon could warn them.

Kew trotted to her. *I can hear your thoughts. What did you want to ask me?*

There may be a dead body in the Jasmine Palace. Could you ask Kun or Bao to send someone ahead to check?

Kew tilted her head. *Why don't you ask?*

It is not my place.

Kew snorted. *I'd forgotten about the protocol here. I will tell them.*

A moment later Kun glanced at her and then called a guard over and murmured something to him. The guard ran off.

Kun took Daiyu's arm and they walked outside, followed by Bao, Lien and Geriel. Shan made up the rear. Outside the Hall, the courtyard was mostly empty. No bodies lay on the pavement and though the stench of smoke lingered, the buildings were no longer alight. Some servants trotted around going about their daily tasks but there were few officials.

"Is it always this quiet?" Daiyu asked.

"We've asked people to stay indoors for the morning," Kun said. "This afternoon we'll start meeting with the various departments to explain the decisions made last night, but this morning we need to deal with the inner palace."

Shan mentally urged Daiyu to ask what decisions had been made, but Daiyu stayed silent.

A group of workers were pulling down the burnt structure of one of the pavilions and some servants carried boxes from a burnt building to a storeroom nearby, salvaging what they could.

At the Gates of Heavenly Virtue the guards stood aside to let them through, bowing deeply to both princes.

The inner palace buildings were closer together than in the outer palace and there was evidence of the fighting in the blood spatter on the walls and the blackened buildings. Servants scrubbed at the walls but were forced to stop and kowtow as the princes walked past. Neither man seemed to notice.

They stopped outside the Jasmine Palace and Kun spoke to the guard he'd sent ahead. He turned to Daiyu.

"My lady, I am told the palace is a mess. We will need to find you somewhere else to stay. Perhaps Shan can gather your things and bring them to my palace in the meantime?"

"Oh, of course." She turned to Shan. "Pack what you can and Hai can carry it."

Anger rose. "No, my lady."

Daiyu blinked and stepped back at her tone. "You won't pack my things?"

"I won't have Hai carry them. Your other servants tried to poison you at the empress's request. None of them should be anywhere near you."

Bao cleared his throat. "We have pardoned everyone for their actions of last night,"

Shan said nothing, didn't even glance at him. He might be naive enough to think his word was enough, but there would be those who were waiting for the emperor to return, some who might already have orders from the emperor.

"We'll help carry Daiyu's things," Geriel said. "It shouldn't take long. Send someone with a cart." She didn't wait for permission from either man, simply walked into the palace.

Envy filled Shan at Geriel's confidence and freedom. She bowed to Daiyu and followed her in.

Instruments had been smashed, clothes were flung all across the room and furniture was upturned.

"They made a mess." Lien's voice made her jump.

Shan bowed low. What was a state princess doing helping her?

"No need to bow," Lien said. "I am no longer Bonamese and the Rhoran culture is far more casual about protocol. We do not bow and we speak our minds."

Shan hesitated before asking, "Doesn't your husband mind?"

Geriel laughed. "Her husband encourages it," she said. "It took my husband a little time to get used to it, but he is Bonamese." She looked around the room. "Where do you want us to start?"

Unease filled Shan. The idea of ordering around two women who were clearly of a higher standing than she was so foreign. "Let me check the palace, find out who is inside first."

Lien smiled. "I'll do it."

"No, my lady. It may be too dangerous."

"Call me Lien. You don't need to worry, I'm a trained assassin and can protect myself." She disappeared.

An assassin? The surprises kept coming. Geriel placed a hand on Shan's arm and she jolted. "You are our equal, no matter what the others may think. You have my respect. I heard how you saved Daiyu from the highway attack. Bao was very complimentary."

Shan doubted it. "How well do you know him?"

"I spent some time with him in the mountains while I was searching for a cure for the Trader's Curse. I also saved his life after he'd been shot by Kun's men."

"Kun?" Then he wasn't to be trusted.

"It was a misunderstanding." She glanced over her shoulder. "Lien and Kew trust Kun, but I find it strange he would turn on his father."

It made perfect sense to Shan. "The emperor is brutal. He was going to kill all those servants based on the word of their peers, with no evidence. There is a culture of spying and fear here, and perhaps Kun recognises it." She paused. "Though I am not certain I can trust him, he does appear to genuinely care for my lady."

Lien returned. "The palace is empty."

Good. "There are some trunks in the utility room. I'll get them and we'll see how much we can salvage."

"I'll fetch them; you start," Lien said.

Shan's heart pounded as she walked into the bedchamber. Zhi's body was gone but Shan could still picture her there, lying still, eyes open, dead. She shivered.

Geriel asked, "Are you all right?"

She swallowed, still staring at the faint smear of blood on the ground

"Did you kill someone?"

"Yes. She was trying to poison Daiyu." Perhaps she could have done it differently. What if Zhi hadn't been the one to strike her, or Yun had been the one to poison the tea? Maybe she'd killed the wrong person.

"It is hard to take a life," Geriel said. "But sometimes it is necessary to save another."

Shan glanced at her. "You save lives."

The healer's smile was sad. "But I have taken them as well."

Lien walked in carrying one of the trunks. "We both have."

It was comforting to know she wasn't the only one —that these women understood and wouldn't judge her. She sighed. "Could you gather Daiyu's clothes?" she asked Lien. "Geriel, put anything broken on the table in the receiving room, I will go through my inventory and mark off what we need to replace."

Daiyu would be devastated that the precious guzheng was smashed. Shan fetched her list, and when she returned, she packed the unbroken items into trunks, marking them off her list.

"Bao tells me you're an artist," Lien said as she folded a tunic.

Shock speared through her. "Why would he mention me?"

"Anming was worried about Daiyu, and Bao assured him she would be fine as long as you were with her. He thinks highly of you."

Shan's heart hurt. "Not any longer." She bit her tongue. What was she saying? This was Bao's sister she was talking to.

"You must have worked together a lot," Geriel said. "He was Anming's manservant, wasn't he?"

She nodded. "We saw each other daily when Anming was in residence."

"How long have you worked with Daiyu?" Lien asked. "Were you there when Bao first arrived?"

"Bao was already at the manor house when I was sold to Daiyu about sixteen years ago." Her heart squeezed at the memory. The first time she'd seen him she'd been struck by how good looking he was. "He taught me the protocols of the house." She'd been thrilled to be placed in such an important position and for Bao to be so kind to her. She'd let her feelings get the better of her.

"But you two aren't friends?" Geriel asked. "I would have thought working together so closely would have bonded you."

Shan closed her eyes, glad her back was to them. "The servant's life does not encourage friendship. We have no autonomy and therefore a wrong word or action could have us cast out in the street with nowhere to go. We cannot trust anyone."

"Surely Bao wasn't like that," Lien said. "He knew Anming wouldn't cast him out."

Perhaps if she told them something, it would be enough to stop the questions. "He was very kind. Friendly and helpful, giving me tips about how the family liked things to be done." She turned and smiled at them.

"What happened?" Geriel asked. "You've barely spoken in the past twenty-four hours."

Curse her for being observant and nosy. Should she confess her mistake? These women might understand, and if nothing else, it would hopefully stop them from asking anything further. She sighed. "I fell in love with him," she said. "We used to spend our free time together in the garden and eventually I found the courage to suggest that we ask Anming and Daiyu for permission to marry." Her cheeks flamed and she focused on the flute in her hands. "He pretended to agree with me, but the next time we met in private I asked him about it, and he laughed as if it was a joke. Said we could never marry." Told her she'd imagined more to their relationship.

"Somehow Anming's father found out and was going to send me away, but Daiyu argued with him until he gave in." She owed her position to Daiyu. "After that I avoided Bao as much as I could, and he made no effort to see me." She blinked back the tears in her eyes. She'd been more alone than ever. She forced a smile. "I was very naive back then, thinking we could have some control over our lives."

Sympathy and speculation covered their faces. "Maybe it's a Bonamese thing," Geriel said. "Jie was cold and critical when he realised he cared for me."

Shan shook her head and laughed. "Bao does not care for me." If he did he wouldn't be so contradictory, hugging her after the highway attack and then asking her to risk her life further when they were at the Sun and Moon. Then she frowned. "There was a Jie at the manor house a couple of moons ago. He had been rescued from some Rhoran warriors."

Geriel smiled. "That is my husband. He's Bao's best friend and the Rhoran were taking him to Chungson to verify Bao's identity."

"How long have the Rhoran been involved?"

"Since the emperor betrothed me to Temur," Lien said. "A mistake he probably now regrets."

Geriel laughed. "Yes, he keeps making them. Infecting the Rhoran with a deadly disease just made us more determined to stop him. But we need to find him and make sure he can't gather an army to retaliate."

Shan nodded, glad they were aware the emperor wouldn't simply give in. "I worry the palace will not be safe for the princes," she said. "The empress and the concubines won't support Bao, unless he agrees to marry them all. They won't want to relinquish the power they have."

"Bao doesn't want concubines," Lien said. "It was never the way when my parents ruled. Father had Mother as empress and that was all. He didn't need multiple women."

Then there would be only one woman she would be jealous of.

Lien finished packing Daiyu's clothing and closed the trunk before helping Geriel collect other broken items in the receiving room.

Shan scanned the bedchamber. Everything had been packed, but there was a lot of missing jewellery. She went into the next room where the table was piled with broken instruments. A wooden box caught her eye and her heart sank. "Oh."

"What's wrong?" Geriel asked.

She picked up what was left of her drawing chest, careful not to catch her skin on the splinters. The beautiful case was beyond repair. Over on the floor, pieces of parchment were crumpled and dirty and a bottle of ink had smashed and stained the floor. Gone. It would take her years to save for a new one. She picked up one of the pieces of parchment and turned it over. The picture of her mother and sister had a black smear across it, obscuring part of their faces. She folded it carefully and tucked it into her top.

"Shan?" Lien asked, touching her arm.

She blinked and shook her head. "I am fine. There's nothing to be done about it." She returned to her list, puzzling together the pieces on the table to figure out what was broken. When they were finished only five trunks were needed for Daiyu's things. Had the seamstress had time to make any of Daiyu's outfits they'd ordered?

Outside, the cart was waiting. "We'll take these and then ask for the palace to be cleaned."

"What about your things?" Geriel asked.

Shan glanced at the broken drawing chest. "I didn't bring much with me. I'll check what is left." She went into the servants' quarters, fading before she entered in case someone had sneaked in while they were cleaning. The rooms were empty and she quickly retrieved her few remaining clothes, stuffing them in a bag.

When she returned to the main room, Geriel said, "How did you vanish like that?"

She froze. She hadn't thought to wait until she was in the

hallway to fade, hadn't considered these women might not be trusted. "It is my gift, like you can heal and Lien is fast."

"How does it work?" Lien asked.

Nerves prickled her skin. She'd never explained it to anyone before. "I imagine myself blending into the furniture or disappearing. My skin tingles when it works."

"Does it exhaust you?" Geriel asked.

"Not normally." She walked towards the entrance. "But last night I extended it over Daiyu and it took a lot of energy."

"We can help you with that," Geriel said. "The dragons taught me how to access a limitless supply of our gift."

"Dragons?" Sure, she'd seen Kew but she hadn't known there were more.

Lien smiled. "We have much to tell you. I think you're going to be a valuable part of this team."

Shan blinked at her, her heart full of hope.

Lien looped her arm through Shan's. "Let's rejoin the others."

Chapter 17

At Prince Kun's palace, Shan arranged one of the guards to take Daiyu's trunks through the servants' entrance.

"Come this way," Geriel called, waiting for her on the palace steps. Tension tightened Shan's muscles. Geriel might see her as an equal but neither prince did. They wouldn't like her entering through the front door.

"Come on." Geriel trotted down the steps and grabbed Shan's hand.

Shan pulled back. "I can't. It's not proper."

"That's stupid. If they don't like it, they can complain to Lien." She chuckled. "She'll set them straight."

Reluctantly Shan allowed herself to be pulled up the steps into the receiving room which was full of people. Kun and Bao sat at the head of the table together with Lien and Daiyu. But the other woman at the table made Shan gasp and fall to her knees in a kowtow. The empress.

Her ears strained for the order to have her removed from the room. Conversation continued. No one seemed to notice she was there.

"Shan, stand up," Geriel hissed.

She couldn't. While there was still a possibility the emperor would regain the throne, she had to behave appropriately around the empress. Even if the empress would later sentence her to death. Yun would have told her Shan had killed Zhi.

Geriel tugged on her arm, but Shan didn't move.

"Would someone please give Shan permission to stand?" Geriel called, her voice loud and piercing.

Mortification heated Shan's body. This wasn't the way a servant should behave. She was tempted to fade so no one would see her.

"Stand, Shan," Kun said.

Keeping her head lowered, she did as he asked, not daring to raise her gaze, not wanting to see their attention on her.

"Join us at the table," Lien said.

Shan glanced up and the empress hissed in outrage. "She is a servant. She has no place here. She killed one of Daiyu's maids."

"Shan protected her lady," Kun corrected.

Bao hesitated, looking between her and the empress. "The empress is right," Bao said. "Shan is a servant."

Hurt stabbed Shan, hardening her heart and she didn't look at him.

Daiyu gestured for Shan to stand by the wall with the empress's maids. Humiliation filled Shan and she fought not to let it show. Bao had once been her equal, her friend.

No, she corrected herself. He had always been heir to the throne, he'd once played at being a servant. Anming had probably never made him do any work.

As she took her place next to the empress's maids, their joy at her put down shone in their eyes. No matter. Their opinions didn't matter to her. Geriel's face had gone red and the look of outrage on it soothed Shan. Lien shook her head slightly at the Rhoran woman and gave Shan a sympathetic glance.

For all their talk about her being an equal, Lien wasn't willing to make a scene.

Perhaps it had simply been talk to get Shan to open up to

them. Just like Kun's seduction.

A servant brought a pot of tea to the table and she poured the empress's cup first.

"Oh, Imperial Princess Fen had a pot just like that," Lien said, reaching for it. "May I have a look?"

"Is that necessary?" the empress asked. "I'm sure my daughter had many teapots."

Lien smiled. "She served Temur and me tea when we returned to the palace to get my things."

"Must you bring up painful memories?" the empress asked. "They never found the highway robbers who killed her."

"Is that what the emperor told you happened?" Lien asked, gesturing for the maid to hand over the pot.

With a fearful glance at the empress, the maid handed it to Lien.

"That is what happened," the empress said.

"Now isn't the time to go into that," Bao said, his tone firm.

Perhaps the emperor had ordered Fen's death as he'd tried to kill Daiyu on their journey here.

Lien examined the teapot. "It's exquisite." Suddenly she fumbled and dropped it, smashing it on the floor. "Oh no, I'm terribly sorry."

A maid beside Shan ran to clean the mess.

"Shan, could you fetch us another pot of jasmine tea?" Lien asked.

Back to being a servant. Nothing had changed. "Of course." Shan bowed and exited through the servants' door. She met another maid in the hallway who directed her towards the prince's private kitchen. In a short time she returned to the main room where they were discussing the emperor's absence.

"He said nothing about where he was going?" Kun asked.

"He rarely confides in me," the empress said. "He was

unhappy after Fen's death and kept me at a distance until he wanted me to meet Lady Daiyu and teach her about the palace."

"Could he be hiding in the palace somewhere?" Geriel asked.

"I can't imagine it," Kun said. "It would be beneath him to hide."

"I'll get my men to check," Bao said.

Shan raised her eyebrows. So he respected Geriel's thoughts. Was it because she was married to his best friend? Shan stepped forward to pour the tea. Officially the empress was the highest ranking person in the room, but in reality Bao was. Whose cup should she fill first? Lien noted her hesitation and gestured with a slight tilt of her hand to Bao. Shan inclined her head and poured Bao's cup. When she was done, she returned to her place by the wall.

They talked for over an hour. Although the princes listened to the empress, they ignored her suggestions. Finally Bao stood, signalling the end of the meeting. "Aunt, I am relying on you to keep the concubines in order. Until we can find the emperor and settle this matter, no one may leave their palace except a servant to fetch food for every meal."

"This really is preposterous," the empress said.

"It is for their own safety," Kun said as he stood. "People are uncertain and that breeds fear. We would hate for any harm to come to them."

"Then you really shouldn't invite barbarians into the inner palace." She rose and swept out of the room, her maids scurrying after her.

"She's formidable," Geriel said. "Do you really think she doesn't know the truth about Fen's death?"

"I don't even know for certain," Kun said.

"I killed her," Lien said.

What? Only Shan's training kept her from showing her surprise.

Kun flinched and then sighed. "I suspected as much. I didn't know she was with the army until it was too late to turn back. Ying was sure she and the others could take care of themselves."

"They did some damage, but weren't well trained. Fen's temper got in the way. She shouldn't have been left in charge."

Shan had no idea what they were talking about.

A messenger came to the door and said, "Captain Ru and his men have arrived."

"Good," Bao said. "Jie will be with them. I must go. Kun will you come with me?"

"Yes."

"Wait a minute," Lien said as they were about to leave. "Don't you want to know why I dropped the teapot?"

"Do not be concerned, sister, I'm sure it's replaceable."

Lien growled and stalked to her brother. "Just because you're in the imperial palace does not give you the right to suddenly dismiss everyone who isn't male." She glared at him. "You forget that I represent the whole of Rhora, and without me, you would not have thousands of Rhoran warriors to protect the city." She took a breath. "I know more about this palace than you do. That teapot had a secret chamber in it which can be filled with poison. Didn't you notice how guilty the maid looked when I asked to see it?"

Bao shook his head.

"You think the empress wanted to poison us all?" Kun asked.

Lien turned to Kew who was resting in the corner. "Kew, did you sense it?"

The dragon yawned. *Yes. There was definitely poison in it.*

Kun went pale and Shan's heart went out to him. It couldn't be easy knowing your mother had tried to kill you.

Even Bao seemed a little shaken. "Should I have tasters?"

"Kew can sense most things and what she can't, Geriel

can cure," Lien said. "But you must be less trusting. That's why I sent Shan to get the tea. We can trust her, unlike the empress who must suspect where the emperor is even if she's not certain."

"If she won't talk, does it matter what she knows?" Bao asked.

"Perhaps Shan can help," Lien said.

They all turned to look at her and she had the urge to fade.

"She can sneak into the empress's palace and listen to what she says to others."

"She should stay with Daiyu and protect her," Bao said.

Kun interrupted. "If the empress wants us dead, it is not safe for Daiyu to stay here. Could she stay with one of your tribes until this is over?" he asked Lien.

Daiyu gasped, a look of horror on her face.

Lien smiled at her. "Forget everything you know about Rhora. They are lies spread by the emperor to make us the enemy. My people are welcoming and kind." She turned back to Kun. "Yes. I can spare some men to protect her on the journey. It will be a long ride though. Can you ride, Lady Daiyu?"

Daiyu nodded. "But wouldn't it be simpler if I returned to Chungson?"

Bao shook his head. "The emperor could easily waylay you as he did on our journey here. Far safer if you are beyond his reach."

"Then I will take Daiyu with me now," Lien said. "Geriel, can you stay here and teach Shan what you know about the gift?"

Geriel nodded.

"Wait! Won't Shan come with me?" Daiyu asked. "I will need a servant."

"Of course," Bao said.

"No," Lien replied. "Daiyu will need to learn to do things

for herself as I did. Shan's skills are needed here." She didn't wait for her brother's agreement. "Kew, go with Bao and Kun and tell them if anyone is lying," she continued. "When I return, I'll help you search the palace to ensure the emperor isn't here. I know of a number of secret rooms." She took Daiyu's hand, brushed past her brother and strode outside.

Shan appreciated Lien's faith in her, but no one had asked Shan what she wanted to do.

Or if she wanted to be involved.

Right now she wasn't sure whether anything would change under Bao's rule.

~*~

Geriel waited until Bao and Kun had left before she asked, "Do you mind staying here? I imagine no one has told you much about what is happening."

Shan shrugged. "I am used to doing what I'm told."

Geriel frowned. "That doesn't make it right," she said. "If you had a choice, would you have gone with Daiyu or stayed here?"

She hesitated. "I do not know. I would like to see Rhora, but I can see how I could be useful here." She paused. "And my best chance of having any freedom is if Bao becomes emperor." Though it wasn't guaranteed.

"Either he or Kun will be emperor one way or another. My people won't let Xue live after what he's done to us."

Shan wanted to know more, but she still wasn't used to asking out of turn. Before she could respond, Geriel asked, "Are there any gardens in the palace?" She hunched her shoulders. "Being inside these walls makes me uncomfortable."

Shan had heard rumours of how the Rhoran lived, but she wasn't certain how much to believe. "What are your towns like?"

"We have no stationary towns. We live in yurt villages

which we can pack up and move with the season. The steppes are our backyard and the sky is our ceiling."

"I would like to hear more about it one day." It was so foreign to what Shan was used to. "The emperor has a garden, but no one is allowed inside without his permission."

"I'm sure Bao will give it to us," Geriel said. "Show me the way." She picked up her bow and quiver and slung them onto her back and then checked her belted sabre was in place.

Having Geriel armed lessened the tension in Shan's shoulders. A couple of guards fell in behind them as they left the palace. Geriel paid them no attention, and it wasn't Shan's place to question them, to find out if they were palace guards or men who had come with Bao.

"Geriel!"

The call had them both spinning around. A Bonamese man jogged towards them and the guards stepped in front, blocking his way.

"Jie!" Geriel pushed through the guards and ran to him, flinging her arms around him. "What are you doing here?" They kissed and it was so shocking Shan couldn't look away. Such displays of affection should only be done in the home.

"I had to make sure you were all right. Letting you come here on your own was torture."

She raised her eyebrows. "Letting me? You had no choice in the matter. My skills were needed."

He winced. "You know what I mean. I wanted to come with you, but I had to lead my own men."

Geriel nodded and grabbed Jie's hand, pulling him towards Shan. "This is my husband, Jie. Shan is Daiyu's maid."

Jie smiled at her. "I've heard how you saved Daiyu on your journey. Bao praised you highly."

This man was Bao's best friend. She bowed, not sure what his correct title was. "Pleased to meet you, my lord."

Geriel laughed. "Just call him Jie." Then she turned to him. "Are you a lord?"

Jie grinned. "I am, which makes you a lady."

Geriel shuddered. "No thank you. Not if people are supposed to bow to me."

"Where are you off to? Wouldn't it be safer to stay in Kun's palace?"

His wife snorted. "We're going to the emperor's garden so I can teach Shan what the dragons taught me about the gift."

Jie frowned. "The emperor's garden is for imperial family only."

"Seriously, you people with your classes and segregation." Geriel tossed her braid over her shoulder. "I hope Bao puts a stop to all that nonsense."

Shan liked Geriel even more as she spent time with her.

Jie ran a hand through his hair. "All right, *tián xīn.* Lead the way. I hope you will let me guard you while you teach."

She beamed at him. "It would be my pleasure."

Shan led the way, a little uncomfortable with the level of affection they showed each other. They even walked hand in hand. If Jie was a lord, and Bao's best friend, he'd been brought up to know better. But perhaps this was the Rhoran influence. What would it be like to live in a place where everyone was your equal? Perhaps if she proved herself useful enough, Daiyu might permit her to leave and she could go and live in Rhora. Did they permit outsiders? They must because Lien and Jie had married into the tribe.

She walked over the bridge into the garden and towards the rock garden. It was the most defensible spot she'd seen.

"Can we stay by the stream?" Geriel asked. "Or is there a waterfall somewhere?"

"I don't know."

Jie grinned. "I do. Bao and I used to play in here when we were kids." His eyes were wide as he looked around. "It's barely changed. There's a small waterfall this way." He strode down one of the paths.

Geriel's smile took over her face. "I'm glad he's here."

Shan hesitated. "If I may ask, my lady, how did you meet?"

"Don't call me that. My name is Geriel and I won't be called by some Bonamese title which tells no one anything about me."

"Sorry, Geriel." She clasped her hands together. "This is all so strange. I don't know how I am supposed to behave."

"Behave as if we're friends, because I think we're going to be." She grinned. "I met Jie while searching for a cure to Trader's Curse. He was hiding from the emperor because he was supposed to be dead."

"Why?"

"He led an attack on Rhora and it was sheer luck that he wasn't killed. Kew recognised him and Lien begged for his life, so that's when we sent him to Chungson to verify Bao's identity. After that he hid in the Dragon Mountains and that's where I went to find a cure." She lowered her voice. "I thought he was very attractive but stuck up and cold when I first met him."

Jie had been in Chungson only a few moons ago. "You can't have been married very long."

"Less than a moon," Geriel said. "But we were betrothed for a moon before that. He travelled with me around Rhora, making sure all the tribes had been cured."

Jie left the main path and they walked into an area with a small pond. At the top of the pond were several rocks and water trickled over them into the water below.

"Perfect," Geriel said. She sat cross-legged on the grass bank and patted the spot next to her. "Sit with me."

Shan scanned the area. The bushes and shrubs surrounding them were high enough so she couldn't see past them and there was a wooden seat on the far side where someone could sit in contemplation. Jie sent the guards to opposite sides of the pond and took a post at the entrance. He would see that no harm came to them.

Shan knelt next to Geriel.

"First, show me what you do again," Geriel said.

Shan focused her energy and faded, holding the illusion in place.

"Wow." Geriel stretched her hand out and touched Shan's shoulder. "Oh, you're still there."

Shan released her gift and nodded. "It's only an illusion. If someone touches me they feel me."

"You need to be careful of stray arrows or swords."

"Yes."

"All right. Who taught you how to use it?" she asked. "I'm told the gift isn't common here."

"I taught myself. My master before Daiyu discovered I could do it and made me practise until I could fade easily."

"Do you visualise anything when you use it?"

"I just draw it from my energy."

Geriel nodded. "That's what I used to do. I'd been taught the gift is finite and if I used too much at once I could lose it, but now I know that's not true."

"You said the dragons taught you?"

"Yes. I was searching for the cure in the Dragon Mountains and one of their healers came to help. She had met Lien when Bonam invaded Rhora and disturbed their other home."

Bonam had invaded Rhora? No, she could ask questions about that later. She was here to learn. "What did they teach you?"

"The gift is endless, but you must pull it from the energy surrounding you. Dhalin taught me to visualise a never-ending waterfall and draw my gift from that."

Shan closed her eyes and the *shush* of the water soothed her.

"Focus on the sound of the water and visualise a

waterfall," Geriel said. "See your gift mixing with the water and becoming one."

Shan followed her instructions, slowing her breathing and bringing the image to clear focus in her mind, the golden light making the waterfall glow.

"Now reach out and make yourself disappear."

Shan smiled. "I think of it as fading," she said. "Fading into the background, unnoticed as a servant is meant to be."

Geriel snorted, but said, "Good, you've disappeared. Now see if you can push it out over me."

Shan opened her eyes, still connected with the waterfall and energy pulsed through her. She touched Geriel and the illusion slipped along her fingertips, over Geriel's hand and then her body. "Done."

"It feels tingly. Are you sure I'm fully covered?" Geriel said.

"Ask your husband." Jie was facing away from them, his attention on any potential threats.

"Jie, can you see me?" Geriel called.

Jie turned and frowned. "Where have you gone? Geriel it's not wise to go off on your own."

Shan dropped the illusion before he could get upset and he stepped back in shock. It took him a second to recover. "That's your gift?" he asked Shan.

She nodded.

"That could be useful. How far can you stretch it?"

"Slow down, Jie. She's only just getting started," Geriel said. "How do you feel?"

"Fine, but it doesn't normally tire me immediately." She wanted to test her limits. "Let me see what I can do." She'd never considered stretching it further than over a person. She reconnected with the waterfall and tried to push her illusion out towards Jie. It didn't budge, didn't want to extend from her fingertips. Perhaps she had to be touching him.

He stood on the grass, a gap of several yards between

them. Shan placed her hand on the ground and then she pushed the illusion over the blades of grass. Her hand shook at the effort. The blades didn't always touch each other, so she dug into the soil and connected with that.

Geriel gasped. "The soil has disappeared."

The grass looked as if it was floating on nothing, but it was difficult to spread the illusion across thousands of tiny grains. Her heart raced and she panted. Halfway across to Jie, Shan gave up. She let go of the illusion. "It's too difficult," she said. "I have to have direct contact with him."

"It might get easier the more you practise," Geriel said. "How do you feel?"

"Like I've been running for leagues."

"OK. Relax, keep drawing from the waterfall, let the flow become automatic, until you can do it without thinking."

She did as Geriel suggested, drawing more from the waterfall and the heaviness lessened.

"Someone's coming," Jie said.

She dropped the illusion and she and Geriel stood. "Should we hide?" They couldn't get through the bushes without making a sound.

Jie motioned them back, out of view of the path. "Can you hide all of us?"

The guards moved closer to them, alert but without drawing their weapons.

"I don't know. I've never tried to fade five people at once. I might not be able to hold the illusion in place if we have to move."

"Try it." Jie turned to the guards. "No matter what you see, don't move, don't make a sound unless I order it."

The men nodded and the three men encircled Geriel and Shan. "I need you all to touch my shoulder." She took a deep breath and drew from the waterfall. This time the illusion slipped over her like silk floating to the ground. She pushed it out, through the connection of hands and then glanced back to ensure everyone was covered. She'd done it!

Her gaze locked on the entrance to the pond. No one should be there. Kun and Bao had ordered everyone to stay in their palaces.

She waited, drawing constantly from the waterfall, trying to keep her breathing steady. If she started to pant, whoever it was might hear her.

Footsteps clomped on the path nearby. They weren't trying to hide their passage. Perhaps they didn't expect anyone to be in the garden.

"Let's stop here," a female said.

Yun. Shan stiffened. Her concentration wavered and Geriel hissed, "I can see the guards."

Shan recovered them. "That's Yun, the maid who tried to poison Daiyu," she murmured.

"Do nothing." Geriel took her hand.

Yun and Hai came into the garden, Hai carrying a box overflowing with Daiyu's jewellery.

"We can't hide here forever," Hai said. "Someone will find us."

"We just need to hide long enough for them to reopen the gates. Then we can escape."

"Shouldn't we have stayed with the empress?"

Yun turned on him. "Don't be stupid. We only got out of there alive because the prince called for her. She'll probably kill us so we can't tell anyone what she ordered us to do."

"But Prince Kun pardoned everyone who fought last night."

"The empress isn't the prince," Yun said. "It won't take them long to reopen the gates. They'll need to get food for everyone since the kitchens burnt last night."

Shan froze. That was bad. Without food, people would soon get upset, would demand action. Did Bao know about it? If the emperor was smart, he'd attack the palace now, before they had a chance to restock. How many men did the emperor have under his command, and how many served Bao?

"We've got nothing to eat," Hai pointed out. "We should have grabbed food as well as the jewellery."

"There must be food in the garden, fruit trees and such."

Hai glanced around. "I don't like being here. If someone finds us, we'll be in so much trouble."

"We're already in so much trouble," Yun said.

Shan had heard enough. She wasn't going to let them steal Daiyu's jewellery. Some of the pieces had been given to Daiyu by her mother and grandmother. Waiting until they faced the pond, she dropped the illusion and stepped forward. "I don't believe those things belong to you."

They gasped and spun around.

Yun darted towards the exit but Jie stepped onto the path blocking it.

Hai put the box on the ground and stepped back. "I didn't want to take it. It was all Yun's idea."

Yun glared at him and then narrowed her eyes at Shan. "Do you really think Daiyu would be this loyal to you? The minute you do something wrong, you'll be gone like the rest of us."

Shan said nothing. It was a possibility she had accepted long ago.

"You are both under arrest." Jie gestured for the guards to restrain the pair.

"The prince pardoned everyone!" Yun said.

"For things they did last night," Shan said. "You kept the things you stole from Daiyu, knowing you were supposed to return to your palace.

"We didn't know," Hai said.

"We heard you say you did," Shan replied.

"Take them to the prison," Jie ordered. The guards nodded and marched them away.

Shan went to the box of jewellery and dug through it. "It

looks like many of the missing pieces are here. Can we take them back to the prince's palace?"

"Of course," Geriel said. "It will be a good opportunity to use your gift while walking."

"That would make you useful," Jie said.

Geriel poked him. "Shan is already useful."

He grimaced. "You're right. I apologise."

Shan smiled, pleased someone recognised her worth. "It is of no matter." They walked back through the garden. "We should make sure Bao knows the kitchens have burned and the palace is short on food. He should bring some in as soon as possible."

Jie nodded. "You're right. As soon as I see you safely back to the palace, I'll find him."

Geriel raised her eyebrows. "We don't need your protection, Jie. We can take care of ourselves."

"I know." He squeezed her hand. "But I feel better being there for you."

It was so very sweet. Shan wanted to know more about how a Bonamese lord and a Rhoran healer came to fall in love. They came from such different worlds.

Geriel sighed and fell into step beside him.

Shan followed them. Could she use her gift on others while they walked? She checked no one was around and then faded.

"How well do you know your way around the inner palace?" Jie asked, turning to her. His eyes widened and he stopped walking, and she almost crashed into him. She touched his arm and he jumped.

She bit back a laugh. "Sorry. I'm practising as you suggested."

He blew out a breath. "OK, maybe some warning next time."

"Keep walking and I'll try to cover both of you. In answer to your question, not well. I've walked around it, but I don't know who lives in every palace, or even what all the buildings are."

"We should find a map," Jie said. "There must be one somewhere, maybe in the library."

Shan pictured the waterfall. It was harder to do without the sound of running water nearby, and she couldn't close her eyes while she walked. Perhaps she should simply try the way she always had, without the visualisation. It was the way she knew best.

Drawing her gift to her, she touched Geriel and Jie's shoulders.

"That takes some getting used to," Geriel said. "One minute Jie is there and the next he isn't."

"I'm still here."

Shan controlled her breathing, long, slow breaths as the effort to hold the illusion in place intensified. They were at the bridge leading back into the main inner palace now and a couple of servants hurried along paths. She wouldn't be able to hold it for much longer. "Stop," she whispered.

Geriel stopped immediately, but Jie didn't. Shan stretched her arm after him, squeezing his shoulder to make him stop, but her grip was loose. The illusion stretched, pulling her energy. If they suddenly appeared in front of the servants, they'd never be able to explain it and word would spread, letting people know what she was capable of. Her fingers brushed his back. "Jie, stop!" she said a little louder.

He stopped and a servant looked their way. Shan slid her hand firmly onto his shoulder.

Curse it. She pressed Geriel forward to Jie. Standing in a circle, all close together eased some of the effort, but sweat still beaded on her forehead. She wouldn't be able to hold it much longer.

"I need to drop the illusion, but I can't in front of people," she whispered. "We must find somewhere to hide while I do it."

"How about that building?" Jie asked.

"Which one?" If he was pointing, she couldn't see it.

"On the left with the blue door."

"OK. We need to walk slowly, keeping together." She could hear the strain in her voice. Her muscles shook and her head spun as she pushed them towards the wall. As soon as she was sure they were out of sight of everyone, she dropped the illusion.

And then collapsed to the ground.

Chapter 18

A cold cloth touched Shan's forehead and she flinched awake. She frowned, blinking as Geriel's face came into view.

"Good, you're awake. Can you sit?"

"What happened?" Her head spun as she sat and the room blurred before coming into focus. She was back in Prince Kun's bed chamber.

"You used too much of your energy holding the illusion. Were you using the waterfall?" Geriel handed her a dry biscuit.

Shan shook her head. "It was too hard to visualise while we were walking. I have to keep my eyes open."

"You should practise," Geriel said. "Your gift is invaluable."

She wanted to be useful, wanted to show she had more value than simply serving. "Where's Jie?" She nibbled on the biscuit.

"He went to tell Bao about the kitchens. He apologised for making it more difficult for you."

"It's all right. I'm learning my capabilities. The hardest thing is anticipating any sudden movements you might make. I have to stay connected to you."

"So Jie doesn't suddenly appear from nowhere?" Geriel asked with a laugh. "I told him he needs to listen to you."

Shan smiled. "Thank you." It was strange not having Daiyu here, not needing to wait on her. "Do you know if Daiyu made it to the Rhoran camp?"

"I'm sure she has. Lien was with her and she's the best fighter we have, so if they ran into trouble, Lien could deal with it." Geriel poured a cup of tea and gave it to Shan.

Shan sipped it. "How is a princess also an assassin?"

"The emperor discovered she had the gift of speed, so he taught her to fight. She can disable a whole battalion of soldiers in minutes."

Quite amazing the emperor would teach a woman to fight, but perhaps he recognised the ways he could use her. "Will she be returning to the palace?"

"Yes. She's determined to defeat the emperor and protect her brother. They've only just reconnected after eighteen years and they have a lot of catching up to do."

"She didn't know Bao was alive?"

"No. She thought he died with her parents. She mourned him for years."

As Bao had mourned for her. She remembered him talking about losing his parents and sister, but had never told her how. "It surprises me that Bao is using so many women in his strategy."

"He's using the best people he can and we are the best at what we do." Geriel grinned. "He's also using people he trusts." She handed Shan a cup of water. "You must know him better than us. Was he dismissive of women in the past?"

"Not until our misunderstanding, and then he was coldly polite, acting as if he was more important than me." She sighed. "I guess that's because he is."

"Nonsense. He may have been born to the right parents and in the right gender, but he is not more important than you." She sighed. "See, that's why we elect our leader in Rhora. None of this born to inherit rubbish which means you could get a terrible ruler."

Surprise spread through Shan. "You elect your leader?"

"Yes, Temur was elected a few years ago and he'll stay our leader for as long as he continues to do a good job. Lien is joint leader which is another reason why she'll return to the palace. She needs to ensure the Rhoran voice is heard and she can agree to tactics without having to go back to Temur."

The more Shan heard about the Rhoran culture, the more she admired and envied it.

"How are you feeling now?" Geriel asked.

"Better." The food and water had helped. She swung her legs off the bed. "Shall we practise?"

She would master her gift and help them defeat the emperor.

And if Bao admired her as much as Jie and Geriel said he did, then maybe he would listen to her and help the lower classes. Maybe she would finally be free.

~*~

It was late evening before the others returned to the palace. Shan had spent the day practising making Geriel invisible and could now hold the waterfall visualisation while they slowly walked. Any faster messed with her focus and meant she dragged the gift from her own energy which was far more difficult. A couple of times Geriel had had to revive her when she'd gone too far.

It was incredibly helpful having a healer close by.

As the princes walked in, Shan's body acted on instinct, kowtowing to the men. Bao had said she was a servant, therefore she would act like one, no matter if the others treated her like an equal.

It was Kun again who said, "You may stand, Shan."

She did so, keeping her eyes lowered, not wanting to see Bao's expression. He probably hadn't even noticed. She moved silently to her place by the wall.

"She shouldn't have to grovel like that in the first place," Geriel growled. "Bao, I hope you're planning to change such a humiliating act when you're emperor."

"It's meant to show respect," Bao said.

"So why don't you grovel to her?"

Shan lifted her gaze. Bao's mouth was open as if the words wouldn't come.

"You were a servant for years, weren't you?" Geriel continued. "Surely you understand how demeaning it is to be treated as lesser just because of the job you do or the family you were born into."

"Anming never made me kowtow."

"Why, because you were a prince, or because he made none of his servants do it?"

In Chungson a simple bow was sufficient.

Bao was silent a moment. "None of his servants kowtowed, but he wasn't emperor."

"Neither are you, yet, but he was the ruling lord of Chungson." Geriel turned to Lien. "Should we really be supporting a country whose rulers treat those less fortunate than them so badly? There is no community, no support, just the poor being treated poorly and the rich getting away with it."

Lien raised a hand to calm her. "It is difficult to change when they haven't been exposed to different cultures or a different way of living. Perhaps I should have brought Bao to live with us after the curse was cured."

"You're saying your way is better?" Kun asked.

"It's fairer," Lien said. "But it wouldn't be easy for Bonam and Chungson. Those who have power will cling to it and that will make it dangerous for anyone who wants to make changes."

Geriel frowned but nodded. "While it is just us in the room, there is no need to treat Shan like this. Shan, come and sit next to me."

"We need food," Kun said.

"Then get it yourself. You're not incapable," Geriel said. "We've been working hard this afternoon and are exhausted."

Shan moved to get the food but Geriel's glare halted her. Best not to upset a friend who was standing up for her. She sat while Kun gaped at Geriel.

Lien sighed. "Jie and I will get us something." She gestured for Jie to follow which he did without complaint.

Kew flopped by Shan's feet, breathing out a puff of smoke. *Can I have some too? I'm too tired to fly.*

"Of course," Lien replied.

Shan glanced at the dragon, but didn't dare speak aloud. *What did you do today?*

I listened to all the ministers and officials argue for their jobs and promise their fealty to Bao. Most of them will change their loyalty to whoever is in charge. Only a few were truly happy to see the emperor gone.

That would have been tedious.

It was. Kew glanced at her and winked.

That's right, Kew could hear her thoughts. She would have to be careful with them. Would Kew tell Bao how she felt about him?

Only if you plan to betray him. Your other thoughts are safe and private from him.

Relief filled her. There were some things she'd rather he didn't know.

Lien and Jie returned with food and water which Kew checked for poison before they ate.

"How much food is in the kitchen?" Bao asked.

"Not a lot," Lien said. "I stopped a few servants leaving with more than their rationed portions. The empress won't be having five courses tonight."

Kun winced.

"I've sent men to purchase more food for the palace," Bao said. "It will take a few days to arrive from the neighbouring provinces, but I don't want to starve the people in the city."

"And what of the people in the country?" Shan hadn't realised she'd spoken until everyone turned to look at her. She fought the urge to lower her gaze and instead looked Bao right in the eyes.

"They should have surplus. It's harvest time."

"Many harvests failed this year in Chungson," Shan said. "I hope it wasn't the same in Bonam."

Bao glanced at Kun.

"I believe we had a good season," he said.

Lien and Geriel were already eating so Shan picked up her chopsticks and ate a dumpling. It was delicious. She hadn't eaten anything fresh all day.

"We should all report," Lien said. "I took Daiyu to where our Rhoran troops are waiting. Sukh agreed to accompany her back to the main tribe."

Geriel smiled. "I hope Father won't be back in time for the fighting."

"Did Temur have anything to report?" Bao asked.

"No. The nearby villagers have been friendly and some of our people are trading with them." She smiled. "After Jie and Ru explained what was going on, they've been very welcoming."

It was comforting to know people supported Bao.

"What happened here?" Lien asked.

"I taught Shan how to focus her gift with a technique the dragons taught me," Geriel said. "She's getting stronger. She can now make us invisible while we walk slowly."

"Show me," Bao ordered.

"Manners, Bao," Geriel chided. "You could ask nicely."

Shan didn't want to push him too far. She stood. "Geriel, do you want to walk around the table with me?"

"Sure."

Shan held her hand and it was slow progress with Kew tracking them the whole way. "Can you see me, Kew?" Shan asked.

I can sense you and hear your thoughts, so I know where you are.

Interesting. "Does the emperor have any dragons?"

Not any more.

Bao walked towards her voice, reaching out his hand. Testing her. She touched him, pushing the illusion over his arm and the others gasped.

"I can still feel you." His tone was too intimate.

She dropped the illusion and stepped back. "Yes. I can't completely disappear. People can still bump into me."

He studied her a moment. "It's impressive."

High praise indeed. She hated the surge of pleasure the compliment gave her.

"I would appreciate it if you would continue to practise and strengthen your ability," he said.

"Yes, Your Highness."

He hesitated and then sighed. "Call me Bao when we're amongst friends."

She nodded, not trusting herself to speak.

"How did your day go?" Lien asked.

Bao and Kun exchanged a glance. "The ministers know I support Bao fully," Kun said. "I told them I expect their full cooperation."

"We've listened to hours of reports and complaints," Bao said. "I think many of them see this as an opportunity to get things Xue wouldn't give them."

Lien smiled at him. "This is just the start, brother. As emperor you will have a lot of meetings, reports and complaints."

He nodded, a wry expression on his face. "My biggest concern is where Xue is. My men have searched the palace and I have people going to the summer palace to see if he's there."

"I'll check the secret rooms after we've eaten," Lien said. "I don't imagine he's still here but there is a small chance."

"Didn't anyone see him leave?" Jie asked. "Surely the emperor would have had a full bodyguard and no one but the imperial family leaves the palace in a palanquin."

"I have people in the city asking questions," Kun said. "All the ministers agreed that Xue said he was going to the summer palace."

"How long until your people get back?" Lien asked.

"It's a day's ride there," Kun said, "but a palanquin can't travel that fast. Our rider should have caught up to him by now, if that's where he went."

Bao nodded. "We should have news by morning."

Someone knocked on the palace door and Shan went to answer it. Wei stood there, panting. "A message for Prince Bao."

Shan let him past and he bowed to the table. "I've just received word from Lord Anming. An army of soldiers are marching on Chungson and there are reports the emperor is with them."

Bao swore. "He knows Anming is supporting me. How many in the army?"

"Thousands."

Shan's heart froze. What would happen to her family? Was her sister at the manor house?

"Where are the Chungson troops?" Kun asked.

"Anming has already ordered his soldiers in Bonam to head home," Wei reported.

"What?" Bao stood. "Where is Anming?"

"He was stationed just outside the city."

Kew sat up and closed her eyes. *Where exactly?*

"Near the western gate."

I can't find him. What is your message and I will search for him?

"Could it be a trap?" Lien asked. "How trustworthy was

the person who brought the message?"

"As trustworthy as myself," Wei said. "I have fought with him many times."

"The only reason to attack Chungson is to draw troops away from the imperial palace," Bao said.

"Kun, you need to address the Bonamese soldiers in the city," Jie said. "Make sure they understand you support Bao and they are to follow your orders in the emperor's absence."

"After the failed invasion of Rhora, the emperor punished many of his generals and stopped including me in military matters," Kun said. "I'm not sure they'll listen."

Lien winced. "That was probably my fault. I told him Fen was Ying's daughter and suggested he ask the empress about your parentage."

Kun gaped at her. "My sister was Ying's daughter?"

"He said she'd inherited the gift from him, so he must have believed it. Only the empress would know for sure."

"That's why she was sent to the summer palace," Kun said. "He let her return when the betrothal was arranged."

"A chance to redeem herself," Bao said.

They were getting off the topic. "What are you going to do about the attack on Chungson?" Shan asked. "The emperor said he'd recalled troops from the border. Maybe that's where he sent them."

"How do you know that?" he asked.

She glanced at Kun. "I overheard it."

Bao rubbed his face. "Anming never should have ordered the withdrawal without discussing it with me. I don't know what he was thinking."

Anger stirred. "He was probably thinking about protecting his people." Did Bao care about Chungson or only Bonam?

Indecision crossed his face.

"I could send some of my people," Lien said. "They can ride fast and catch up with the army, stop them before they reach the border. Are there any open plains between here and Chungson which would work for a battleground?"

"Let me get a map." Kun went into another room.

It took an hour before they had agreed on a plan. Lien would send half of the Rhoran warriors to fight the army heading for Chungson. Kew would locate Anming and ask him to return his men to Bonam as soon as possible.

Shan didn't like it. Though she had heard of the Rhoran prowess on the battlefield, the commoners would be scared when they appeared, would be afraid they were invading no matter what Bao or Kun said. The poor didn't trust those in power.

"The peasants won't like it," she said. "They'll think they're being invaded and some may even try to stop the Rhoran from passing. You'll need to send word ahead."

Even that wouldn't necessarily work. Not everyone could read.

"We don't have much choice," Bao said. "The longer we leave it, the closer the army gets to Chungson and the longer the Rhoran will be away. We have to strike quickly." He gave Kew leave to go. "Lien, I want you to check every hidden room in the palace. If Xue is here, I want him found." He turned to Shan. "Shan, I need you to sneak into the empress's palace and listen to her conversation. If you don't hear anything about the emperor's plans, move to the next concubine palace and the next until you hear something."

She nodded, surprise filling her. He was actually using her.

"Jie, take Geriel into the outer palace. Introduce her to people, make sure they see the Rhoran aren't barbarians to be feared." He turned to Kun. "You and I need to take control of any soldiers still left in the city and ensure we have the support of those inside these walls."

He looked at each person in turn, finishing with her. "Be careful. Report back to me when you're done."

The intensity in his gaze warmed her, reminding her of the days they'd been close. Shan nodded.

She would see he claimed his throne.

Chapter 19

Dusk was falling as Shan walked out of the palace with Geriel. "Remember to draw from the waterfall," Geriel said. "I don't want you falling unconscious and revealing yourself."

Shan nodded. "I'll be careful."

She walked to the women's quarter, not bothering to hide her passage. Better she save her energy for when she really needed it. She smiled at the couple of servants she passed.

"How can you smile?" one girl demanded. "Yesterday was terrifying and today we're under the rule of a man who says he's the true heir. Where does that leave us? How many of us is he going to kill because we were servants of the emperor?" The girl brushed away a tear, her hands shaking.

"I smile because I know Prince Bao." She hesitated. Though she wasn't certain it was true, she would give this girl hope and maybe if she told others, it would lead to more servants supporting Bao. If the uprising yesterday had proven anything, it was the servants were stronger, more powerful than they thought. "Bao worked as a manservant while he was in hiding so he knows what life is like for us. When he becomes emperor, I am sure he will ensure our lives are better." Her heart wanted to believe it.

"Really? He was a servant?"

Shan nodded. "I must go, but don't worry. I am sure Bao will be a fair and just emperor." That at least she could say with certainty. Even if he didn't get rid of kowtowing, he wouldn't stand there making his servant's skin blister as Xue had done to Zhi.

The girl beamed at Shan, her posture straightening. "Thank you. That gives me hope. May I tell others?"

"Of course."

She continued through the maze of roads until she neared the empress's residence. Checking to make sure no one was around, she visualised the waterfall, drawing her energy from it and then faded.

Shan circled the residence. Two guards stood at the front door and two at the servants' entrance. There wasn't enough gap between the guards at the servants' entrance to allow her to squeeze through, but she wouldn't be able to open the front door without anyone noticing. Though she might still hear something.

Careful to place each foot quietly, she climbed the steps and walked past the guards. One man turned as she went past him and sniffed.

"What's wrong?" the other guard asked.

"Thought I could smell jasmine," he said.

"Probably from the garden."

Shan winced. She would have to make sure she didn't use any oils or lotions in future. She peeked through the front window. The empress sat at her table and three women sat with her—all concubines.

They weren't supposed to leave their palaces. Had their homes burnt, or were the concubines plotting with the empress? She leaned forward but their voices were murmurs.

She had to get closer.

She manoeuvred back past the guards and went around the side of the palace which had no doors or windows. The eaves met the gutters and she couldn't reach them without a chair and that would be far too noticeable.

Walking around the palace again she stopped across from the servants' entrance. The concubines would have to come out at some stage, but if she waited for them, she wouldn't hear what they were discussing. How could she draw one of the guards out in order to slip by them?

Would they investigate a noise? Probably not. They would be far too disciplined for that.

A distraction would be better.

Did you say distraction? Kew's voice sounded in her head.

Shan jumped. *Yes. Aren't you on the way to find Anming?*

Just coming back from telling Temur the orders, Kew said. *What can I do to help?*

Flying over the empress's palace might be enough. I need the guards to step away from the servants' entrance.

Be there soon.

Shan kept her gaze on the two soldiers until one of the guards gasped and pointed. "Dragon."

The other man stepped forward and scanned the sky. "That looks like Kew, but she never had wings that size."

Shan didn't wait to hear the response. She slipped between the guards and to the door. Checking they were still looking at the sky, she sneaked into the empress's palace. *Done. Thank you.*

You're welcome. Be safe.

Taking a moment to calm her heart rate, Shan stayed by the entrance, waiting to see if anyone had heard or bothered to investigate.

No one came.

She tiptoed along the corridor and paused outside the receiving room. Voices were raised but still not loud enough for her to make out individual words. The ceiling was her best chance. She slipped into the utility room, glad the palace layouts were all similar. With no one inside she dropped her illusion and climbed onto a barrel of water in the corner. She pressed the ceiling panel up as steps came down the corridor and stopped outside the door. Her pulse leapt. Not enough time to lift herself into the roof. She slid the panel back into place and faded as the door opened and a serving maid came in with a teapot.

The girl would have to lift the lid Shan stood on in order to get water for the pot. Curse it. She should have made the barrel disappear as well, but it was too late now. Shan braced her hands against the walls and moved her feet to the edges of the barrel. She could stay there and hope the maid simply thought it was stuck. No, there was a crowbar in the corner and the space wasn't large enough for Shan to get off the barrel without bumping into the maid.

The maid put the pot on the table nearby and approached her.

What other option did she have?

Shan glanced up. Perhaps if she lifted the panel a little, she could hang from the braces.

The girl reached for the lid.

No time to hesitate. Shan slid her hands along the panel, lifting it on either side. Her fingers gripped the roof as the maid lifted the lid and Shan brought her knees to her chest, swinging slightly. The maid stepped back, placed the lid on the ground and then picked up a ladle from the table and scooped the water. Shan's fingers burned but she didn't dare lower her feet back to the barrel in case she missed the edge and wet them. Arms straining, she watched the girl carefully put the pot back on the table and then dry the ladle.

She clenched her teeth. *Hurry up!*

As if she had all the time in the world, the girl picked up the lid, turned it around until she was satisfied it was the right way and then replaced it on the barrel. Before she'd turned away, Shan lowered onto the lid, holding her breath. She breathed out of her nose as the maid finally exited the room.

Shan sighed, rubbing her aching arms. Sliding the panel across, she lifted herself into the roof cavity, her arms straining at the effort. With the panel back in place she took a moment for her eyes to adjust.

Night had fallen and it was dark and dusty inside the ceiling, but heat still hung in the air from the warm day. She crawled towards the receiving room and stopped as soon as she heard the voices.

"These are dark times, but we can make it through," the empress said.

"Yes, Your Majesty," chimed the three concubines.

Shan faded and raised one of the panels a crack to see which women were with the empress. They weren't familiar to her, but she would remember the pinched lips of the youngest one, the tiny scar on the right cheek of the woman who sat next to the empress and the sallow skin of the other.

"Return to your palaces. The emperor will save us."

Shan held her breath but all that followed was the concubines rising and bidding the empress farewell.

Her spirits fell. She was too late.

How was the emperor going to save them? Did the empress know his plan? The only thing she had confirmed was the empress couldn't be trusted to obey Bao and she hadn't doubted that. She stayed where she was as the empress rang for her lady's maid.

"I want a bath."

"My apologies, Your Majesty." The maid's voice shook. "Prince Kun has rationed the water. We are not permitted extra water for bathing."

Shan held her breath, her muscles tight.

"I gave you an order," the empress said. "To disobey means death."

The maid gasped. "I am sorry, Your Majesty. Please forgive me," she begged. "I'm sure I can get you water for your bath."

"See to it."

Shan heard the maid exit the room and then her sigh. She wanted to whisper for the maid to get the water from the stream which ran through the emperor's garden, but she didn't dare. The empress would probably hate the idea of bathing in river water but it would stop the maid being punished.

Instead she stayed where she was, waiting to see if anyone else came to speak to the empress.

Time ticked slowly by, and her knees began to hurt from the wooden panels. It didn't appear as if the maid had found water for the bath.

Shan couldn't stay here forever. She crawled back to the utility room and made sure no one was inside before she climbed down. Brushing off some of the dust she'd collected, she faded and opened the door. The hallway was clear. At the exit she peered out the door. The guards weren't watching, but a maid paced outside the door, wringing her hands.

She must be the woman the empress had asked to get her a bath.

"Ancestors help me." The girl fell to her knees. "I need water for the empress."

Shan made sure she was completely covered by the illusion and then slipped out the door. She tiptoed to the maid and whispered, "Fetch water from the stream which flows through the emperor's garden."

The girl gasped and turned her head, looking for the voice. Shan stepped back to avoid the maid bumping into her.

"Thank you, ancestors," the girl said as she stood. She hurried to the guards. "Move aside."

The guards shifted and Shan stayed close behind the maid as she strode past them. Then she headed for the next palace.

~*~

It was late before Shan returned to Kun's home. Despite the concubines' house arrest, many of them had gathered together to talk. Most appeared to be more concerned about themselves rather than where the emperor was and a number were very cagey about whether they supported Bao's claim. They were smart. Until the whole business settled with one man left, it made sense to hold their tongues.

The only interesting piece of information she heard was reference to a surprise the emperor had planned. One of the concubines assured the others that he'd known Bao would come to the palace and he'd made plans to counteract that. Was she referring to the attack on Chungson?

Lien was the only one in the palace when Shan walked in. "Did you hear anything useful?"

"A little." She told Lien what she'd heard. "Did you find anything?"

"The emperor's not here, but it appears many of the rooms haven't been used since the secret bodyguard was killed. A lot of sandbags have been left behind."

"Secret bodyguard?"

Lien smiled. "Sorry, I forget you don't know. When I have more time, I'll tell you the whole story." She yawned. "We should get some sleep while we can. It's going to be a tiring time."

Shan hesitated. "Should I return to the Jasmine Palace?"

"No. We'll all sleep here. I asked a couple of eunuchs to bring in more bedding and to put it in Kun's bedchamber. We'll sleep in the same room."

Shan gaped at her. That wasn't proper in the least.

Lien laughed. "You and I will sleep on the opposite side of the room from Kun and Bao with Jie and Geriel separating us. Come on, we should check the bedding to make sure no one left any nasty surprises for us."

Shan's skin crawled as she entered Kun's bedchamber which had been rearranged so all the furniture was against the walls and several mattresses were on the floor. She checked those closest to her, flinging back the covers. The room was clear.

Lien stood at the door. "I'll stand guard until the others arrive."

Shan frowned. "But Bao's trusted guards are at the entrances."

The woman rolled her shoulders. "I remember the politics of the palace. People will change their allegiance the moment they think there's something in it for them."

She was right. "You should also watch the roof," Shan said. "The panels lift which is how I escaped and rescued Daiyu." She yawned, exhaustion filling her.

Lien's eyebrows rose. "I never thought of that. Thank you."

Shan was glad she could help. She chose the furthest mattress from Kun's bed and went to sleep.

~*~

The next morning Shan woke with the sun. Beside her Lien still slept and across the room Jie and Geriel curled into each other and Kun snored quietly. That meant Bao was on guard duty. She didn't want to see him, but her bladder needed emptying.

She couldn't see him from where she lay, so she faded and stood, creeping to the entrance. He stood just outside the doorway, staring out the window, his focus elsewhere and sadness on his face. She paused, taken back to the days when he used to confide in her and they'd talk for hours.

No more.

She headed for the servants' entrance.

"Aren't you going to say good morning?" Bao asked.

She whirled around with a gasp. He had turned towards her but wasn't looking directly at her.

"I can smell your jasmine oil."

She was tempted to keep walking, but he'd check her bed and see she wasn't there. She ran a hand through her hair and brushed her clothes before she dropped the illusion and he focused on her. "Good morning, Bao." She bowed.

"Why are you sneaking around?"

"I didn't feel like conversation today."

He studied her. "Where are you going?"

"To freshen up."

"Go on then."

She scowled. She didn't need his permission to wash. He was infuriating.

Taking her time, she cleaned herself and put on a new outfit. It would be nice to have pants and a tunic dress like Geriel and Lien. Then she wouldn't have to worry about exposing herself when she climbed into roofs. But perhaps today would be a day without spying.

When she returned to the receiving room, Bao was still the only person awake. She wasn't sure what time the rest of them had gone to sleep, but now she had him alone, she had a question for him. "Do you know what happened to Zan?"

He glanced at her. "I sent men to retrieve your sister from your farm. She should be at the manor house by now."

"Did you give my parents any money?"

"Yes." He approached her. "I won't let your family suffer, Shan." The intensity in his gaze made her nervous.

"Thank you." She cleared her throat. "Would you like me to keep watch?" she asked. "I was going to sketch the faces of the concubines who were plotting with the empress." She retrieved some paper from Kun's writing desk.

He hesitated.

"I am capable of defending myself and keeping watch," she said.

He sighed. "I know. You're capable at everything."

She blinked at the unexpected compliment. "Then get some rest while you can." She sat at the table, making sure she kept her back to the wall opposite the bed chamber. From here she could see all doorways.

He walked to her and she tilted her head to look up at him.

"I'm sorry," he said.

Her skin prickled at the serious expression on his face. She couldn't get drawn in by it. "For what? For reminding me of my place with the empress? Or for wanting to get rid of me and send me with Daiyu?" The words shot out of her like arrows and she bit her tongue to stop them.

He shook his head, and his brows drew together as they did when he was annoyed. "If the empress knows how important you are, you'll become a target," he said. "And I wanted you to go with Daiyu to keep *you* safe."

Her anger vanished.

"I won't apologise for that." He ran a hand through his hair. "But I do have to apologise for the way I treated you after you told me you wanted us to marry."

She pushed back her chair, ready to run. Her face flamed. Why bring it up now? "I misread the situation."

Bao shook his head. "You didn't misread it." He sighed. "But you did make me realise how serious we had become. When Anming's father found out, he told me to break up with you and wanted to send you away. I knew no distance would stop you from loving me, so I had to make you dislike me. I wanted you to stay at the manor house, where you were safe."

Why tell her this now? Why not continue as they had been? Her heart beat uncomfortably fast. She stood, stepped away from him. "That hardly matters now. You'll be emperor soon."

Concern filled his expression. "Do you think I'll be any good? Is it right I rule a people because I was born to it?"

She was tempted to be flippant, not liking that he seemed to care about her opinion. But her body warmed at those remembered days when they'd shared secrets and been as close as two people could be. "If you remember what it was like working for Anming, remember what people less fortunate than you are struggling with, and do your best to help them, then you might be a good ruler."

He smiled suddenly and it lit his whole face. "That's one thing I always liked about you, Shan. You never lied to me." He paused. "Will you continue to tell me the truth, continue to point out when I'm making a mistake?"

Her breath caught in her throat. She swallowed hard. "Are you giving me permission to tell you when you're being an idiot?"

He laughed. "Yes."

"Then I'd be pleased to."

They shared a smile and it was so like the early days that tears pricked her eyes. She blinked and sat again, picking up some charcoal. "Now go, rest while you can. You'll get little in the coming days."

"I will. Thank you, Shan."

He walked towards the bedchamber and at the door he turned back to her and his smile was so sweet her heart ached. All at once the intervening years fell away and it was just as it had been before they had broken up. Her heart filled with love for him and she ducked her head before he could see it in her eyes.

It was cruel to mention those days, unkind to remind her how much she'd loved him. In the end, all it brought was heartache for her.

No matter what happened, the emperor would never marry a lady's maid.

Chapter 20

Over the next two days Shan was busy spying on people for Bao. The waterfall visualisation came easily to her now and it wasn't hard to hold the illusion around herself. In the evenings she continued practising with Geriel or whoever was around to expand the number of people she could comfortably cover. So far she'd been able to cover the whole table of people as long as they were all touching its surface, but it became more difficult as they began to move. Still she pushed herself because they still had no idea what the emperor was planning. If he attacked, her gift might save them all.

Kew hadn't returned yet. Bao had asked her to act as communication between the Rhoran troops and Anming's men, and guide them to the army, so that meant the dragon wasn't here to monitor people's thoughts. It left Shan the job of following those who had had meetings with Bao and Kun and listening to the conversations they had with people afterwards. So far she hadn't learnt anything alarming. Just complaints about having to get used to a new ruler's quirks and rules.

The core group, as Shan had begun to think of them, now sat at the table, discussing their day. Geriel spoke. "I don't like the feeling in the city," she said. "There's tension there, but I'm not certain if it's people's reaction to me as a Rhoran, or if something more is going on."

"People are always uneasy with change," Bao said.

"Maybe."

"Should I go into the city tomorrow?" Shan asked. "I can listen to what people are saying."

"That's a good idea," Lien said.

Bao frowned. "I don't like the idea of you going alone."

"It will be easier for me if I don't have to hold the illusion over more than one person."

He appeared unhappy but nodded. "All right."

After they ate, it was Shan's turn to clean the dishes. Kun had ordered his servants to clean the palaces that had been damaged, which left them without servers, but Shan didn't mind. It gave her a few minutes to herself, time to contemplate all that had happened in the past few days. Since their talk, Bao had been kinder to her, making sure she had the support she needed and including her in their conversations. Thankfully, they hadn't been alone together since then because Shan wasn't sure how to behave around him. What had been the point in telling her he'd cared for her? It solved nothing.

She scrubbed at a stubborn spot on one of the bowls, taking out her frustration on it. She shouldn't still be pining after him. She was smarter than that.

The door opened and Bao walked in. "Need a hand?" His smile warmed her.

"No. I'm fine." She focused on the task as he stepped closer and picked up a towel to dry the items she had already washed.

"Then please indulge me," he said. "I find a mindless task like cleaning dishes quite soothing. It gives me time alone with my thoughts."

Was that a hint he didn't want her to speak? "Me too." She washed in silence, but her thoughts were no longer calm.

His presence next to her was too large, too noisy. He smelled like musk and the scent took her straight back to when they would chat about their day and discuss how best to serve Daiyu and Anming. She would always look forward to Daiyu spending time with her brother, because it meant she had time with Bao. She'd forget she was working, forget she had little freedom and simply enjoy being with him.

Bingwen had warned her not to get involved with anyone, had said relationships would do nothing but threaten her position, and he'd been right.

She placed another bowl on the bench and her fingers brushed Bao's. She jerked away.

"You haven't told me I'm being an idiot in the past few days," he said. "Does that mean you think I'm doing the right thing?"

"I don't spend all day with you," she said.

He laughed, a joyous sound. "You're right. Maybe I should have you with me when I speak with the scholar's guild tomorrow."

"I'm going into the city," she reminded him. "Have you spoken to any of the merchants or tradespeople?"

He frowned. "No. The officials speak for them."

She snorted. "Don't you remember Official Kim in Chungson? He never reported what his members wanted, only what he thought Anming wanted to hear. It wasn't until the weavers protested that the truth came out."

Bao swore. "I'd forgotten about that."

"Take your guards and talk to the people personally," she said. "They need to see you care."

"Will they tell me the truth though?"

Probably not. There was too much fear. "Did the man at the Sun and Moon know who you were?"

Bao shook his head.

"But you spent time with him, didn't you?"

"Yes."

"Then perhaps you can go to him and tell him who you are. He can help to spread the truth and gather information for you." What other options did they have? "I could hide you and we could walk through the dining hall in the outer palace. You would hear what your subjects are saying to each other." She placed the last plate on the bench and then rinsed her hands.

"Can you take me tonight?"

Many of the artisans and officials might still be eating, but it may also be too busy to move easily. "If you follow my instructions exactly," she said. "If I have issues with the illusion, you need to leave when I tell you to, no matter what we might be hearing."

He nodded. "I'll obey your every command."

She ignored the thrill that went through her. "Let's tell the others what we're doing." She gestured for him to leave the room first and then followed him back to the receiving room.

Kun and Jie insisted they take guards with them, so they arranged to walk to the Hall of Clarity as if he had another meeting. Once inside, Bao ordered the guards to leave them. Shan didn't appreciate the sly smile they gave each other. She waited until they were gone and then set out the rules. "I need to hold your hand," she said. "You keep pace with me, stay close by my side. Try not to make any sound. If you have to speak, murmur into my ear."

He nodded and held out his hand.

She hesitated before she took it and the warmth of his palm made it hard to focus on her waterfall. Annoyed at herself, she pretended he was Kun and the illusion slid over them. "This way." They left the room via the servants' entrance and went outside. The dining hall was on the opposite side of the grand courtyard and she walked at a steady pace, wanting to go faster to get this over with but aware her illusion might not hold if she did.

There had been other times when she'd walked hand-in-hand with Bao. The first time had been when they'd both had a rare afternoon off, and they'd gone to the river. She'd slipped on the mud on the banks and Bao had caught her before she'd fallen to the ground, steadying her and then keeping hold of her hand as they walked along the river's edge. The sun had been shining and birds flew between the bushes. She'd thought the day couldn't have been more perfect.

She sighed.

"What's wrong?" Bao's breath on her ear sent shivers over her.

"Nothing," she whispered back, mortified that he'd heard her. She was supposed to be setting an example.

They reached the dining hall and the murmur of voices floated out of the windows. It was late, but people were still eating. Everyone had a set dinner hour so their role was always covered. The door opened and a couple of men walked out, talking about going to bed. Shan pulled Bao inside and away from the door, scanning the room. The tables were only half full. Some people ate alone, and others gathered in groups. There wasn't a lot of space between the tables, so it would be difficult to get too close without risking someone bumping into them.

People nearby spoke about the pavilion they were rebuilding. No point going closer to any of the large groups. They wouldn't be foolish enough to announce their opinions about the change of rule to so many people. But there were three pairs speaking. Each couple sat close together and while from a distance it looked as if they were chatting, there was a stiffness in their posture or one or the other regularly checked to see who was around.

Shan tugged Bao's hand in the direction she wanted to go and skirted the tables until they were close to one of the pairs. Up close the two men looked similar, perhaps they were brothers.

"I tell you, no one will notice if we leave," the older of the two said.

"They've seen us since the riot," the younger said. "They know we didn't die."

"But this is our best chance to go home. Our family needs us."

"Our family will be punished if we're caught. We can't risk it."

Shan's heart went out to them. They had probably been ordered to work at the palace against their will. She squeezed Bao's hand and moved to the next pair.

The black ink covering their fingertips suggested they were scholars.

"There must be some way to authenticate Prince Bao's claim," the thin man said.

The rotund man chuckled. "Anyone who has been at the palace for more than twenty years can authenticate his claim. He looks like his parents and he knows things no one else would know. Yesterday he told me a story about the day his father told him to research Chungson in the library. He got into such mischief misfiling books and I told him off." The man sipped his drink. "I thought I'd lose my job, but the young prince never said a thing to his father about it."

"So what should we do?"

"Do? There is nothing for us to do. We obey the orders of Prince Bao."

"But the emperor will return. I overhead someone say the attack on Chungson was a ruse."

Bao's hand tightened on Shan's.

The rotund man straightened, knocking over his drink. He swore, trying to mop it up. "When? Who said it? Have you told the prince?"

"No. I have no proof. I don't know the men who said it."

"Still, we should tell him." The man stood and Shan

pulled Bao out of the way so they didn't touch him. "Come on. We'll send him word." He tugged the other man to his feet and dragged him away.

If the Chungson attack was a ruse, what could they do about it?

"I was terrified of Master Li as a child," Bao murmured to her.

She wanted to know more about the young Bao, but there was one more pair still talking. A soldier and a guard had carried their trays past the empty tables on the edges to one almost in the middle of the room. No one else sat around them, perfect for ensuring no one overheard their conversation.

"This way," she whispered, carefully weaving between the tables.

"When's it happening?" the guard asked as they approached.

"Tonight," the soldier replied. "They need darkness to sneak in. Be ready for the signal."

The guard hesitated. "How many are still the emperor's men?" he asked. "I've heard many people say they like the princes. Will we still have the same support inside the palace?"

"We don't need their support," the soldier said. "As long as we get the gates open, the emperor can bring his army in."

Bao stiffened beside her and Shan stifled a gasp. If the emperor had an army with him and the gates were open, Bao would be defeated for sure.

The guard nodded. "I have my men on the gates. They're ready."

"Good." The soldier hailed another soldier who was looking for a table. "Come join us."

He did and the conversation turned to the clean up of the palace.

"Let's go," Bao murmured.

They moved outside and Shan inhaled the cooler air.

"I can't believe—" Bao's voice was too loud.

"Shush," she whispered, dragging him back towards the Hall of Clarity.

"We need to go back to the palace," he said.

"First we need to get your guards otherwise they'll ask questions. If rumours spread that you disappear or sneak around, people will be even more nervous than they are."

"There's no time." He jerked his hand out of hers and stepped back, appearing in front of her in the darkness.

She lunged after him, grabbing his hand. "Don't be an idiot," she hissed, checking no one had seen him reappear. "It will only take a few more minutes."

He huffed and increased his pace, causing her to jog to keep up with him. Her visualisation faltered and she dug in her heels, yanking on his hand, desperately trying to keep the illusion in place.

"What?" He spun around.

"Stop. I need to focus." She squeezed her eyes closed, hearing the water trickling and seeing the rainbow glistening in the falling water.

"Sorry." He relaxed his hold on her hand which helped calm her fear.

When she was sure she had control, she moved forward, keeping her strides long and fast, and he kept pace with her. They arrived back in the room they had left and she dropped the illusion, her heart still racing.

"Are you all right?" he asked, reaching out to touch her arm.

She stepped back. "No thanks to you," she said. "You ignored my instructions and made it far more difficult."

"I really am sorry." His eyes shone with contrition.

"Then think in future." She walked towards the main door. "Come on, we need to hurry."

They strode back to the inner palace where they woke

Kun and the others. "We overheard men say the emperor is attacking tonight," Bao said. "The guards on the gates will open them for his army."

"Then we change the men on the gates," Kun said.

"How does he have an army?" Jie said. "They're supposed to be attacking Chungson."

"Maybe he didn't send all his men," Lien said. "We only had a messenger's word the army had been seen."

"We heard someone say it was a ruse," Shan said.

Kun swore. "Where are they hiding?"

"It doesn't matter. We need to replace the men on the gates with men we know are loyal," Bao said. "And tell them to be wary of attack from within and without."

Shan didn't like how many variables there were. There were three main gates into the imperial palace, with only the inner palace not having a gate to the outside. The moat around its walls would give them some protection, but not if the gates were opened and the bridges were lowered. Then they didn't know who on the inside to trust. Would the guards on top of the walls defend against the emperor's army, or let them pass?

Cries of alarm sounded outside and there was the scrape of swords being drawn. Shan whirled around.

Lien! Geriel! At Kew's cry, they all ran outside.

"Stand down," Bao ordered the guards, pushing past them to where Kew panted on the ground. "What happened?"

Lien knelt by the dragon. "Are you all right?"

Kew nodded. *Tired. I've been flying all day.*

"I didn't think you could," Geriel said.

Kew snorted. *Had to. Discovered there was no army headed to Chungson. Only a battalion of soldiers which Anming defeated easily. The real army is here. I saw groups of men entering the city as I flew over.*

The guards had been telling the truth.

"I'll get Tadashi and Ru to double the men at the gate

with men we can trust." Jie ran off.

Geriel brought a bowl of water to Kew and while Kew drank, Geriel placed her hands on the dragon.

A few moments later, Kew sighed. *Thank you.*

"Come inside," Bao said. "We need more information."

The Rhoran warriors are heading back to the city, but it will be at least a day before they arrive. Anming has sent some of his men home to protect the pass into Chungson and the rest are returning here.

"We could do with more eyes in the city," Bao said.

"Or over the city," Kun added. "Will any other dragons come? If they could fly above the city, reporting troop movements, it would be very valuable."

I do not know. I can't communicate with them from a great distance. I'd need to fly closer.

"I'll go into the city," Shan said. "Let me out now, before they attack. I can search and report back." She turned to Kew. "How close do you need to be to hear my thoughts?"

I can hear Lien and Geriel from leagues away, but others like you, from not too far. Also the city is full of thoughts and that makes it hard to distinguish one from another.

"Then we set up a system," Shan said. Her mind whirled. Fireworks would be too noisy, and she couldn't climb onto roofs and wave a torch, but maybe... "Sky lanterns. If I see the emperor's men, I'll release a sky lantern. You'll be able to see it rising in the sky and you'll know at least where they're coming from."

Bao shook his head. "They'll be coming from every direction if he's smart."

He was right. "Then I find the commanders, listen to their plans and return before they attack."

"You might not find them fast enough," Kun said. "The city is huge."

Kew suddenly leapt to her feet, her skin changing to black. *It's too late.*

Chapter 21

A roar went up and a bell clanged the alarm. Lien vanished and Geriel yelled, "Weapons!"

The others ran into the palace, returning a short time later armed with swords, bows and quivers of arrows. Shan only had her hair pin daggers.

Lien returned. "The gates are secure. The men trying to open them from the inside are dead, but there may be more who will try."

Bao nodded. "You stay on the top of the walls and monitor the gates. Kew, can you send word to the Rhoran about the attack? We need to get them into the city before the emperor closes the outer gates."

Kew took off, flying north.

"Kun and I will rally the soldiers and guards inside the palace. We'll close the gates to the inner palace. Geriel, you and Shan stay here and monitor what happens, keep people calm. I'll send a few men to help you. We know the empress is up to something, so watch her."

Shan nodded, her heart pounding.

"There are more weapons in my cupboards," Kun said. "Take what you need."

"Be careful," Bao said. As they ran towards the gates, Shan prayed for them all to be protected.

"Come on." Geriel grabbed her arm. "Let's see what weapons Kun has for you."

They ran inside and found a cupboard full of knives, daggers, swords and bows.

"Can you shoot?" Geriel asked.

"Yes, but I haven't practised in years." She slid a couple of knives into her belt. The sword would be too heavy and the bow too cumbersome. She prayed she wouldn't have to use them.

"You know the palace better than me. Should we split up?"

Shan shook her head. "You'll be attacked on sight because you're Rhoran. Better you stick with me and I can hide us if necessary." Her mind whirled. "Let's go to the empress."

Geriel followed her out of the palace. "Do we need to worry about anyone getting over the walls?"

Shan glanced at them. "Lien is up there."

"You're right. She'll deal with anyone."

They strode towards the empress's palace. As they passed other palaces they found the concubines and servants huddled at the doors.

"What's going on?" one woman asked.

"The palace is being attacked," Shan said. "Stay inside and lock the doors." She frowned. "Where are your guards?"

"They ran off when the bell tolled."

Hopefully that was customary for an attack on the palace. If not, then they were gathering somewhere. Shan drew one of her knives from her belt, the cold metal giving her comfort.

"It's not far." Shan took Geriel's hand to stop her and then faded, sending the illusion over them. "This way."

The empress's palace was quiet, though two guards still stood at the entrance. Shan peered through the window at the empress calmly drinking tea. She knew what was happening, but Shan doubted they would get any information out of her. Shan tugged on Geriel's hand and drew them away from the palace.

"Where now?" Geriel whispered.

"We'll do a full search of the inner palace," Shan said. "Make sure there are no surprises." She dropped the illusion and they strode through the streets, reassuring anyone they saw, and sending people back to their lodgings if they were out. No one walked with any purpose, all were frightened.

"Don't they have any plan for being attacked?" Geriel asked.

"They'd have no need to think they would be. The imperial palace is meant to be the safest place on earth. No one would dare attack the emperor."

Geriel laughed. "Except the emperor's been scared we'll attack for years. Maybe his plan was to escape and let the city burn."

She was probably right. They rounded a corner and Shan's heart lurched as she placed a hand out to stop Geriel and whipped the illusion around them. Luckily none of the two dozen guards in the small courtyard were facing them. What were they doing?

"You know your positions," the captain was saying. "Do nothing until you get the signal."

The men took the bags they were handed and dispersed, some heading straight for them. Shan and Geriel ducked down a corridor so no one bumped into them. When they were safe, they checked around the corner again. The captain spoke with the First Consort.

"This way," Shan said, moving after one of the guards.

The men in front of them split up, two heading towards the southern wall and two for the eastern wall. She paused. The emperor's garden was along the eastern wall. Why would they be going there? She followed that group and Geriel kept close by her side, her bow in one hand and an arrow in the other, ready to attack. Shan had no doubt Geriel would hit whomever she fired at.

The guards crossed the bridge and then went separate ways. Her instincts told her one of the guards was probably going to the room where she had found Kun, but where was the other going? She followed him, being careful in the dark not to tread on any leaves across the path. He eventually stopped by one of the pavilions and sat on the seat inside, placing the bag he had by his feet.

"What's he doing?" Geriel whispered.

Shan shrugged. The guard scanned the area, his hand on his sword, but didn't look overly concerned. What was in the bag? Food, or something else?

Perhaps she could get close enough to look inside. No, he'd have to move for that to happen. "What now?"

"We should go," Geriel said. "The injured will need my help."

In the distance men shouted and women screamed. Shan's muscles tightened. The others would be fighting, maybe dying. Geriel should definitely be out there healing as many people as she could. They moved away from the guard and when they were far enough away, Shan dropped the illusion. "We should tell Bao."

Geriel nodded. "He might be able to spare some men to investigate." Suddenly Geriel froze, a look of horror on her face.

"What is it?"

"Kew," she said. "Bao's been injured, but Kew's too far away to help." Geriel started running and Shan followed, pulling up her dress to increase her stride so that she could keep up with the healer. Her heart pounded with exertion and fear. How badly was Bao hurt?

"Where is he?" Shan yelled.

"He's on the wall," Geriel said. "Lien says there are stairs up in the servants' entrance."

They ran over the bridge. "This way." Shan pointed to the

door in the wall. How many guards were inside, and whose side would they be on?

Geriel stopped outside and Shan held her hand, composing herself to bring the illusion over them. It was dark and people were too focused on what was going on outside the walls to notice them.

"Stairs are on the left," Geriel said.

Shan opened the door and six guards whirled towards them, drawing their swords. The access to the top of the wall was directly to her left but a guard stood in the way. They wouldn't be able to make it past.

"No one's there," the guard blocking their way said.

"Check it," another ordered.

Shan and Geriel stepped away from the door as the man moved slowly out and looked in both directions. His bulk still blocked the entrance. Damn it. They didn't have time to wait. As he stepped forward, she pushed him hard and he cried out, stumbling forward. Shan and Geriel ran for the stairs as the other men laughed.

"Tripped over your own feet?" one called.

"Someone pushed me."

"No one was near you."

Their voices faded as Shan pounded up the staircase and finally burst out onto the walkway on top of the wall. Geriel took the lead and Shan was forced to drop the illusion. Her breath came in gasps as they reached Bao. Jie had a cloth pressed against the wound in Bao's stomach, his hands covered in blood, and guards surrounded them.

"What happened?" Geriel asked Jie.

"One of the guards stabbed him." He gestured to a dead man behind him.

Good.

"This is going to hurt," Geriel told Bao and closed her eyes.

Shan grabbed his hand. This was too familiar. How many

times would he be shot or stabbed before people finally accepted his rule?

"You're supposed to be in the inner palace." Bao gritted his teeth.

"I would be if you hadn't been stabbed." His hand shook in hers and she stroked his brow. "Geriel will heal you and you'll get the reputation of being unkillable."

"That would be useful," he said.

She smiled into his eyes, glad he was focusing on her and not the pain. Finally Geriel lifted her hands from him and sighed. "Done."

Jie helped Bao to his feet and Shan stood. From here she could see over the wall into the city below. Soldiers grouped below with battering rams, and makeshift bridges trying to breach the moat. Lien appeared, slightly breathless. "Sorry, I had to defend the northern gate again."

Bao nodded. "Kew, what's the status with the Rhoran?"

The city gates are closed so they can't enter.

Bao swore. "Wei's men were supposed to still be in the city to keep them open, but he pulled them all inside when the servants revolted."

"Do you have any loyal men in the city?" Shan asked.

"Maybe but we have no way of getting a message to them."

"What about Kew?"

Lien shook her head. "Kew can't land in the city without risking being shot and anyone who hears her voice in their head will think they're going crazy." She turned to her brother. "I'll go. I can kill whoever is on the gates and open them."

"How will you get outside without being shot?" Jie asked. "You're fast, but you can't descend walls that quickly."

"Maybe this is a mistake," Bao said, running a hand through his hair. "If we let the Rhoran in, they'll kill the soldiers. I don't want to kill my people." Real pain tinged his voice.

"This was always the plan," Lien said.

"I'd hoped Xue would see reason, or the people would. Using the Rhoran was always the last resort."

He cared. Bao was an emperor worth fighting for. Shan stood taller and studied the city, careful to stay close to one of the merlons to avoid being shot. She wouldn't be able to avoid getting wet, but if she could carry dry clothes, and descend where there were fewer troops, she'd have a chance. "There's another option."

Everyone turned to her.

"Send me into the city. No one will see me, and I can open the gates."

"Lien could go with you," Jie said.

She would love to have company, but Lien was needed here. "No. She needs to find those guards we spotted, figure out what they're doing." Quickly Shan told them what she and Geriel had seen. "They might be in some of those secret areas Lien knows about." And if the gates were breached, Lien would be needed to fight.

"You can't go alone," Bao growled.

His concern helped to calm her racing heart. She would do this for him. "It will be easier and faster on my own. Kew can monitor the city and I can tell her anything I hear from the soldiers. I might even discover where the emperor is. How do you open the city gates?"

Bao described the gate mechanism to her. "It's heavy. I hope you can do it on your own."

So did she. She examined the moat again. "I just need to get across the water. How deep is it?"

"About ten feet," Jie answered.

Too deep for her to wade and she couldn't swim.

Lien gasped. "When I searched the palace, I came across a storeroom full of old things. I saw that boat we used to play in. Do you remember Bao, we'd row it on the stream bordering the emperor's garden?"

He nodded. "It was just big enough for the two of us as children, so it should be big enough for Shan."

If they could find a place along the wall where there weren't many troops, she should be able to get across without too much trouble. It was still dark, and if they tied the boat to a rope, the others could lift it back to the walls when she was over.

"I'll need a hand lifting it," Lien said.

"And we'll need rope long enough to lower it," Shan said.

"I'll help Lien." Geriel and Lien jogged away.

"I'll find the rope," Jie said.

Suddenly Shan was alone with Bao.

"Do you really think you can shield the boat and yourself?" he asked. "If the illusion drops, you'll be an easy target."

Her skin prickled. There wasn't a lot of choice. "I can do it."

"You open the northern gates and then you return." He gripped her hands. "I want you safe behind these walls. The men who enter can open the rest of the gates."

His concern touched her. "I will."

"Your Highness!" a guard yelled, running towards him. "They've got fire arrows. They're trying to ignite the buildings."

Bao hesitated, looking at her.

"Go," she said. "I'll be back soon."

"Take care." He pulled her close, kissed her hard and then ran after the guard.

Shan touched her lips and prayed to her ancestors to keep him safe.

~*~

Shan found a spot on the south side of the palace with few soldiers outside. There was no gate to breach, and the moat was wider, close to a hundred and fifty feet, so only a few men would be required to monitor the walls. Lien and Geriel arrived with the small wooden boat. She would just fit in it. There was a metal ring on the bow for them to tie the rope through, but not one at the stern.

"We'll have to lower you and the boat separately," Jie said. "Can you hold the illusion over both?"

"I need to be touching it."

"We'll keep it next to you." Jie tied ropes to two of the merlons and then tied one rope to the boat.

"We'll lower you," Lien said, handing her the end of the other rope with a loop in it. "Put your foot in there."

They moved to the edge of the wall and when they each took hold of the rope, Shan covered them in the illusion. She peered over the edge and her head spun. It was a long way down, a long way to fall. She gritted her teeth. "When I get off the boat it will reappear. You'll need to pull it back up quickly."

"We will," Jie said.

"Be careful," Lien said. "If you need any help, call Kew to you."

I'm on my way back.

"I'll be fine." Shan climbed on top of the wall and placed her foot in the loop. Jie and Geriel held the end of her rope and Lien held the boat. She gripped the rope with one hand and the boat with the other. "Ready." Slowly they lowered her down the wall. Her heart pounded as she focused on the illusion covering herself and the boat, trying not to think about the drop below. As they reached the water, the boat wobbled with her weight and a little water seeped in through the joints on the bottom. She knelt and retrieved the paddle they'd tied on, then she tugged the rope she'd been lowered on so they could retract it.

It was dark, but there could easily be soldiers nearby watching. In the distance people shouted commands, but around her was relatively silent. The dip of the paddle into the water made a soft sound. It couldn't be helped. She paddled as quickly as she dared across the wide moat.

Something cold touched her knees and she glanced down. Water still seeped through the joints of the boat, not quickly, but enough to wet her knees and her feet. She was only a quarter of the way across. If it kept leaking at this rate, she might not make it across, and if she did, she would have to discard her shoes, else she would leave a trail of wet footprints behind her.

She increased her pace.

Movement on the banks in front of her caused her to pause. As she strained to make out who was there, the water reached her calves. She kept paddling, risking a glance behind herself to make sure the illusion was still in place. It was, but the moat rippled showing the boat's path.

She froze. There was no way she could cover it. Hopefully no one noticed. Only fifty feet to go.

The figures took shape. Two soldiers, one tall and broad, the other small and lean, staring at the moat. The broad man said something, but his words didn't carry to her. The other pointed to the left of Shan and then to the right.

They'd seen the ripples. And if they were smart they could work out where she was, even if they couldn't see her.

Ancestors, please don't let them be smart.

She willed her strokes to be silent as she came closer and closer to them. They moved along the bank, back and forth between the ripples, not allowing her any place she could quietly disembark. They would hear something, the boat tapping the edge of the bank, the water sloshing as she stepped out.

She couldn't risk changing direction. The water was seeping in faster now and her lower legs were wet. Her options were speed or killing them, but dead bodies would lead to an increased guard presence and she might never get back into the palace.

Almost there. The guards had separated, each at the furthest end of the ripples. She slowed the boat and the bow bumped against the brick edge of the moat, the sound as loud as a shout. The guards turned towards it.

Quickly she disembarked, tugging on the rope so Jie and Geriel could pull it back. She crouched, paddle in her hand, one hand still on the boat covering it in her illusion as the men converged on her, the broad soldier with an arrow notched to his bow.

"You see anything?"

"No, but you heard that sound."

"Yes."

Shan couldn't move without them hearing her. Instead she stayed crouched on the edge of the moat, breathing softly. The second she let go of the boat, they would come closer and she'd be trapped. The boat jolted as it began to move away from her. It was being pulled back. She eyed her path around the men and then stood, water trickling down her legs, and let go of the boat. It reappeared and the broad guard swore and released an arrow towards it. "Where did that come from?"

She ran as the lean guard pulled his sword and swung it around, the blade sweeping so close she felt its wind.

"Get it!" the man yelled, lunging at the boat. Shan dodged him and headed for the nearest building, her footsteps loud in the night.

Both men yelled and she glanced back. They were staring at her wet footprints.

"How'd he sneak past us?" one called.

"I don't know, but he won't get far." The guard with the bow pointed it in her direction and shot. The arrow whizzed towards her and she ducked, prying off her shoes.

Then she ran.

Chapter 22

Shan weaved through the empty streets, her heart pounding as she tried to lose the guards. An arrow brushed her arm, ripping her dress and making her stumble. She looked back. They were about twenty yards behind her but her footsteps weren't as obvious now. Staying on her toes, she ran quietly down the paved road, but her clothes still dripped, leaving a faint trail. Where could she get dry clothes?

The buildings were all dark, people long since gone to bed or in hiding.

At the next intersection she stopped and squeezed out the excess water from her dress and slippers. The men ran past as she struggled to quieten her breathing. Then one stopped. "Wait. The trail's gone."

They backtracked to the intersection and Shan slipped past them holding the illusion tight, the waterfall feeding her strength to keep it in place. Her lungs burned wanting to draw huge mouthfuls of air, but any sound would alert them to where she was. She held her breath, keeping close to the building wall, hoping its shadow would help to hide any trail she left.

"Which way?" the lean guard asked.

The broad man studied the puddle of water and then stood. "You go that way and I'll go this way. Yell if you pick up the trail."

She kept still as they walked only yards away, her chest hurting as she slowly breathed out through her mouth. One soldier looked in her direction.

She waited until they were almost out of sight before she moved, heading back the way she came, sticking to the trail she'd already left, her heart thumping. Her body shook. That had been too close.

She turned towards the outer gates. She was supposed to go north but the western gates were closer after her mad dash, and Anming would be coming from that direction. The Rhoran could easily ride to the other gate. She continued her journey, scanning the shops she passed, hoping for a clothing store. She spotted one and tried to open the door, but it didn't budge.

She slipped her damp shoes back on. It was only a few hours until sunrise and it would be far more difficult avoiding people in the streets during the day. Though maybe she wouldn't have to hide herself, maybe she could blend into the crowd.

Shan, I can sense you. I'm above the city.

She'd forgotten about Kew. *Can you hear me?*

Yes. What do you need?

Good question. *Are the streets clear to the western gates?*

I'll have a look.

Shan kept moving. She glanced at the sky but she couldn't spot Kew anywhere. That was good. If she couldn't spot Kew, then archers wouldn't either.

She kept to the wide streets, not willing to duck down the dark alleys even though she was cloaked.

The roads are clear ahead of you. Kew's voice made her jump. *But there are many guards in a couple of streets to your left. Some of them surround the emperor's palanquin.*

Her mouth dropped open. *Where?*

Not far from where you are.

Her skin prickled. What was more important—getting the gates open or learning the emperor's plan? Bao didn't want his people killed, so perhaps they could avoid further fighting if they knew what the emperor was going to do. It would only take a few minutes to investigate. *Can you direct me?*

Yes. Go left at the next intersection.

Shan followed Kew's instructions and winced as she stepped on a rock which stabbed through her soft slippers. She wished she had boots like Geriel.

Around the next corner.

Shan took a moment to calm her rapid heart rate and draw more energy from her waterfall. If her illusion failed, she'd be dead. As she stepped around the bend, she gasped. The whole street was full of the emperor's personal guard, blocking the street in both directions. The palanquin sat between them in front of a large house about halfway along, and lanterns illuminated the whole street. No one would be able to sneak up.

Taking note of which side the house was on, she moved back along the street, hoping to find the rear entrance. An alley ran behind it, but it too was well-lit and full of guards.

What other options did she have?

The neighbouring houses were close to each other, near enough for her to hop from one roof to another, but they had high walls. Climbing wasn't her strong suit.

Why had she thought she could do this? Lien or Geriel would probably be able to scale the wall with ease.

Shan retreated to a few streets away where she'd noticed a tavern. Ducking around the back she found a couple of small barrels. She lifted an empty one. It might be tall enough to help her over the wall.

She carried it back to the illuminated street and placed it at the base of the wall she wanted to climb. It creaked as she stepped onto it and one of the guards looked her way. She stayed still, watching him until he turned.

She lifted herself onto the top of the wall and the barrel appeared below her. The fabric of her dress rasped against the brick and she paused, lying along the wall. The guard who had heard her wandered over, frowning at the barrel in the shadows, and then checking in both directions and on the roof before returning to his post.

She sighed and moved onto the roof of the building, shielding her eyes from the light of the lanterns so she could see better.

As she reached the apex of the roof, she froze. A dozen guards were strategically placed around the courtyard and the one closest to her was staring straight at her, his sword out. She swallowed, waiting for him to attack, but after a minute, he lowered his sword and stepped back. He kept his gaze in her direction.

Were all the courtyards between here and the emperor's building full of guards? The clay tiles creaked under her feet and they'd be able to follow her progress. It would only take one diligent guard like the one by the moat to fire an arrow. Then she'd be in real trouble.

Temur's calling me, Kew said. *They're under attack.*

Fear hit her. The emperor must have more troops outside the city. *Go.* She should have gone straight to the gates and opened them. Then they would have had somewhere to run.

It was too late now.

A lantern was lit in the room across the courtyard. She crouched and could see into the room where a man was dressing with the help of a manservant. It was early for anyone to be rising. The rich yellow of the man's silk outfit made her pause. Only the emperor wore yellow. She squinted, hoping to get a better look. He moved out of the room and along the corridor, the lantern his manservant carried bobbing in front of him. Lights were lit in the central building and a soldier came outside. "Guard the building."

The soldiers below her left their posts and walked to the

central building, taking positions outside on the verandah. The bobbing light entered the lit room. From this angle, she couldn't see much.

Getting off the roof would be tricky. The tiles on the edge looked brittle and overhung so she couldn't shimmy down one of the posts that held the roof in place. She would have to lower herself and hope the tiles didn't break. After she'd confirmed the man was the emperor and listened to his plans, she could sneak out again by the front door.

She crawled to the edge. At each creak of the tiles she paused, waiting for the guard below to lose interest before moving again. After the third creak one of the guards said, "I'll check that out."

He moved towards her, sword out.

She was right at the edge of the roof and some clay crumbled under her hands, showering the ground. She held her breath, heart thumping.

The guard examined the clay, then looked around and disappeared under the roof line. A moment later he was back, carrying a table with him. He placed it directly below her and she crawled back, the tiles protesting as she did. A moment later the guard appeared before her and hefted himself onto the roof, his sword out.

He was less than two yards away and she was in his direct path, yet she didn't dare move.

The guard crouched and moved slowly closer, his gaze scanning the roof. Shan pressed back onto her heels, leaning as far back as she could without overbalancing and he stopped only inches away.

The blood pounded in her ears as his breath blew towards her face. He stared straight through her, frowning. Could he sense her presence?

"Anything?" someone called quietly.

He shifted back. "Nothing. Probably just a cat."

Shan didn't move until he climbed down and returned to

his place on the verandah. Her clothes were drenched in sweat and her skin was tight. How could she lower herself if they investigated each noise?

She couldn't stay here all night. Instead of crawling this time, she stayed on her feet and took long steps to minimise the number of creaks. At the edge of the roof, she lay down and lowered her head and chest to peer underneath the eaves. A beam ran along the edge. If she could reach it, she could swing down.

After checking the guards hadn't moved, she reached for the wood, wrapping her fingers around the rough edges. It didn't offer much to grip. She curled her fingers more and then somersaulted off the roof. Her core strained to control the movement but the momentum was too much. Splinters tore into her fingers as her legs swung off the roof and towards the wall. Her grip loosened and she hit the wall with a thud, the air knocked out of her, and her illusion wavered.

As one, the guards drew their swords.

Shan staggered to her feet, gasping for air as the guards stalked towards her. She pulled the illusion to her and forced herself to move along the verandah, her footsteps heavy. Curse it. She clenched her teeth and straightened her spine, limping towards the building the emperor was in. One guard stepped onto the verandah in front of her, his steps slow, gaze running back and forth. He swung his sword in front of him, the arc covering the whole width of the walkway.

Behind her, another guard walked towards her doing the same thing.

She'd be trapped between them if she stayed here.

She took a moment to steady her breathing and then crouched and moved towards the man in front of her. She kept her illusion tight against her and watched the motion of the sword. Timing was everything.

The sword swept towards the courtyard and she rushed past the guard, her footsteps soft. He gasped and whirled, reaching for her, his fingers just brushing her collar. She didn't stop although the man yelled, "I felt something."

The door next to her opened and a man stepped out. "What's going on?"

Shan slipped past him into the building. The room was an office with a desk and chair in it, but otherwise empty. She went through the interconnecting door into a room without lights. Good. She gave herself a moment to breathe and calm her pulse. That had been too close.

Outside guards murmured.

"We should tell the emperor."

"Tell him what? That we heard something but no one was there? He'll think us incompetent. Get back to your post."

Shan smiled as she moved through the darkened room. The emperor was definitely here. She pried open the door to the next room which looked to be a bedchamber, but if someone was inside, they still slept. She crept in, closing the door behind her. This was a corner room which meant the emperor was in one of the rooms to her right. If this house was set out like most Chungson houses, the door should lead to a corridor. She opened it and light spilled into the room. Behind her the person in the bed stirred. Quickly she went into the corridor, and closed the door behind her. She crouched. The light was coming from the lanterns outside on the verandah. Large windows at waist height showed the guards were back at their positions. She crawled along the wall below the window until she reached the room she'd seen the emperor enter.

"It's taking more time than we anticipated to build the bridges across the moat," a man said.

"I don't want excuses, I want action."

Shan froze. She recognised the emperor's refined tone.

"I want the usurper dead. I want those gates destroyed by morning, or I'll take matters into my own hands."

She frowned and was pleased when whoever was with the

emperor asked, "Heavenly Majesty, what do you mean?"

The emperor chuckled. "I knew the usurper would eventually come here and I took precautions."

Her skin prickled.

"What kind of precautions?"

"I received a report recently that explained a province was unable to show honour to the ancestors on Ancestor Day because someone had accidentally lit the bag of powder on fire before they could make the fireworks. It exploded and destroyed the whole building it was in."

Nausea stirred in Shan's stomach.

"I ordered bags of this powder to be placed in rooms along the walls of the palace. I have people inside, waiting for my signal to light them." The satisfaction in his voice made her sick.

"But won't that kill everyone inside?"

"They're all traitors," the emperor yelled. "They deserve to die."

"What about the empress?"

"She betrayed me as well."

The guards in the inner palace! Her mouth dropped open. Lien had mentioned seeing a lot of sandbags in the secret rooms she'd searched. She had to get word to Bao.

Kew!

No answer. Maybe she was too far away to hear.

Kew!

Nothing. She had to get back to the palace, had to warn the others. She crept along the wall, heading for the main entrance.

Thud.

Pain ricocheted through her head as the outside door swung open, hitting her hard.

Someone gasped and she glanced up, her head spinning, vision blurry. The guard stared straight at her.

She struggled to move, to check her illusion was in place,

but couldn't focus. The dizziness wouldn't settle.

Then his fist powered towards her and brought with it more pain and then darkness.

Chapter 23

The cold sting of water on Shan's face woke her. She gasped, her eyes shooting open and then she closed them again as her head pounded like a dinner gong. She groaned, blinking to clear her vision. She lay on a polished wooden floor, an unfamiliar wall in front of her. She tried to move her hands to wipe the water from her face and found she couldn't. They were tied behind her back.

Fear pierced the remaining blurriness and she rolled over. In front of her stood an imperial guard holding an empty bucket of water. "She's awake."

Dim sunlight streamed through the large windows overlooking the courtyard. She'd been in the house, listening to the emperor's plan… her gut clenched. He was going to blow up the palace, killing everyone inside. Panic filled her and she struggled to sit only to discover her feet were bound together as well.

"Leave us." The emperor.

Shan twisted to face him. He sat behind her on a plush recliner, his expression cold. She froze, fear making her immobile. She would die.

The guard bowed and left the room. Shan wanted to call him back, beg him not to leave her alone with this man. Not that it would do any good. She swallowed hard and watched the emperor, waiting for him to speak.

"Imagine my surprise to see my son's whore outside my room," the emperor said. "I never thought someone as beautiful as you would be so devious. Did my son put you up to this, or were you working for Anming the whole time?"

She didn't speak. The rope around her wrists was tight, its rough cord biting into her skin, but she moved her hands trying to loosen it.

"I order you to answer me."

He might not know she could turn invisible, but she couldn't do it while she was tied up. It would take him only seconds to find her. She scanned the room for something sharp as she answered, "Heavenly Majesty." She bowed as well as she could in her position. The room was virtually empty. Aside from the chair the emperor sat upon, there was a desk in the corner and nothing else. She would have to use her wits.

"Answer me," the emperor hissed.

She managed to kneel and bowed lower. "Please forgive me, Heavenly Majesty. I never should have sneaked into your home. I was looking for you, but I did not know if you would see me."

"Were you going to kill me?"

She gasped. "No, Heavenly Majesty. I wanted to tell you what I overheard Prince Kun say." She glanced at him, keeping her expression sincere and innocent. The knives at her belt were gone.

"You would betray your master?"

Inwardly she winced. Technically when Daiyu married Kun he would be her master. "I am loyal to my emperor first."

"What did you hear?"

She frantically scrambled for something she could tell him. "I heard him mention the usurper, Bao," she said. "He said the Rhoran barbarians supported him."

"I know this. The barbarians are outside the city."

"Oh."

"When did you leave the palace?"

"Days ago after my lady, Daiyu told me to find you," she said. "I told her what I'd heard, and she said you must be told immediately. But you had left the palace and I came looking for you." She bowed again. "I'm sorry, Heavenly Majesty. I know I am not meant to leave the inner palace, but I didn't know who to trust. If the prince had said such things…" She imagined Zan dying to bring tears to her eyes. "I tried to catch you, but I didn't know where you'd gone and then the gates closed, and I was trapped in the city." The shake in her hands was real. This was her only chance to live.

"Lady Daiyu told you to find me?"

"Yes, Heavenly Majesty. She was horrified and confused. She loves Prince Kun, but her loyalty is to you."

The emperor was silent, studying her.

"What else did my son say about the usurper?"

She really didn't want to get Kun into trouble. "He suspected the usurper had men inside the palace and they would try to kill you."

"And was my son happy about that?"

"No, Heavenly Majesty."

"Then why would you think the prince wouldn't tell me his fears?"

"He said no one could know." She slumped as if she suddenly realised the truth. "Oh, but he must have told you which is why you left the palace." She sniffed as tears rolled down her cheeks. "Please forgive me, Heavenly Majesty. I am a foolish servant. I only wanted to help."

"How did you find me?"

She swallowed. "I've been wandering the city for days and then I saw your palanquin."

"How did you get past the guards?"

Too late she realised what a mess she'd made of her

excuse.

"They didn't stop me when I walked past."

The emperor picked up something from his lap. One of the knives she'd taken from Kun's cupboard.

Fear gripped her. She had to get word to the palace somehow. Had to warn them about the explosion. *Kew!* She sent out the thought as loudly and widely as possible. *Kew, the palace is in danger. The emperor has explosives inside.*

He twirled the dagger in his hand. "You walked past and they saw you and did nothing?"

She nodded. They both knew she was lying anyway. *Kew!*

Who are you? The voice in her head was deep, male, unfamiliar.

Shan hesitated. *My name is Shan.*

He must be a dragon, but whose side was he on?

Bao is a friend, the voice said. *I am Riltien. The dragons are closely watching what is happening. Kew is helping the Rhoran, but I can take a message to Bao.*

Relief filled her, then the emperor stood and her attention flicked to him and the dagger.

"You're lying," the emperor said. "I don't know how you got in here, but it wasn't through the front door." He stopped in front of her and she tilted her head to see the restrained fury on his face. "You are going to tell me exactly what my son and nephew are up to."

Shan, are you in danger?

It was difficult to concentrate on both voices at once. *Tell Bao—*

The punch knocked the breath out of her and she sprawled onto the ground. Pain made her stomach convulse and she groaned as she picked herself up.

The emperor smiled. "Now I have your complete attention, tell me, have you seen my nephew?" The next punch made her dry-retch.

She nodded, closing her eyes. *Tell Bao the emperor has placed firework powder in the walls.*

"Where?" He held the dagger to her throat, pricking it.

He has people willing to light the bags. The palace walls will explode, killing people inside.

You are in pain. Do you need help?

No one could help her here. *Just tell Bao. Hurry. The emperor will give the signal when he is tired of waiting for the soldiers to breach the walls.*

I will be back.

The emperor slapped her. "Is Bao really in the imperial palace?"

If the emperor had people inside he knew it was true. "Yes." She breathed past the pain. The dagger was her way out of her bonds. But how could she get it from the emperor?

"How many people support him?"

"I don't know."

He punched her again and she bent over gasping for breath. "Tell me." He played with the dagger.

She swallowed past the pain. "I was in the inner palace," she said. "The empress spoke of supporting you, she told some of your consorts you would help them." Shan forced herself to sit upright. "I saw guards gathering and then taking their position. One of them said to wait for your sign."

The satisfaction in his smile made her feel ill.

"And in the outer palace?"

"After the riot, people stopped fighting. I don't know whose side they're on. The officials and ministers are all very wary."

"But they do not fight?"

She shook her head.

Anger filled his face and he hit her again. "Why not?"

Pain blossomed making her head spin. "I do not know."

He breathed deeply. "What did my son say to you?"

She shook her head, trying to shake off the pain.

"Nothing, Heavenly Majesty."

"You must have heard something in those nights you spent with him. You were not there for very long."

More of his spies. She lowered her eyes, hoping a blush would come to her cheeks. "We did not really speak, Heavenly Majesty."

"You expect me to believe that my son, a man who has never approved of my consorts and concubines, takes his betrothed's bridal companion to his bed within days of meeting her?"

Her body trembled. "It's the truth, Heavenly Majesty." She was ready for the next punch and she tensed.

"My men heard no sounds from the bed."

Kun had been right to worry about being overheard. "Was I supposed to make sounds? I didn't know. It was my first time."

He narrowed his eyes. "A beautiful thing like yourself was still pure? Does Anming not have eyes in his head?"

"It's true, Heavenly Majesty." Her body throbbed with pain.

"And what of Bao?" the emperor asked. "What time did you spend with him?"

"None, Heavenly Majesty. I saw him from afar as I sneaked out of the palace and that is all."

"What does he look like?"

Hope sprang. "I could draw him for you," she said. "I have been told my drawings are quite realistic." She would need her hands free to draw.

He studied her. "How accurate would a drawing be if you only saw him from afar?"

"I could try."

He walked to the desk, playing with the dagger again. She shifted her hands, trying to loosen the knots, keeping an eye on the emperor as he shuffled papers on his desk. When he turned back to her, she stilled.

"Guards!" he called.

Two men rushed in and bowed.

"Tie her to the chair, leave her hands free."

Shan winced as they jerked her to her feet. Nausea swelled in her stomach and she swallowed hard to keep it down. They dragged her to the chair and tied a rope around her waist, the thick cord pressing on the bruises. She jiggled her feet to stop the tingling in them, closing her eyes as more pain washed over her.

"Leave us." The emperor placed a piece of parchment and some charcoal in front of her. "Draw."

He still held the dagger and stayed out of her reach. There wasn't anything else on the desk that was any use. She picked up the charcoal and her sleeve fell to her elbow, exposing the ribbon garrotte on her wrist. It wouldn't cut through her ropes, but maybe her hair pins would if they were still in her hair. She didn't dare draw the emperor's attention to them by trying to fix her hair. She started the long strokes which would be Bao's face. She could draw him in her sleep, his face was so familiar.

The rope holding her to the chair cut into her and she sat as still as possible, but perhaps there was something sharp under the desk she could use to cut the ties on her feet. Subtly she shifted, probing for anything within reach.

The chair legs were smooth.

"You draw well," the emperor said.

She blinked, bringing her attention back to the parchment in front of her. Already Bao's face had begun to take shape. "Thank you, Heavenly Majesty."

I have spoken to Bao. He is searching for the powder now.

She flinched at Riltien's voice, her hand drawing a line across the parchment. She coughed, wincing at the pain but kept coughing until the emperor handed her a glass of water. "Thank you," she rasped and took a tiny sip. Then she brushed the hair on her face back and encountered her hair pins. She could use them against the emperor if she was fast. Though one yell from him would have the guards in the room. She continued drawing.

He wants to know where you are.

In the western quarter. If she didn't get away, they needed to know where the emperor was. *I am with the emperor. Kew saw his palanquin outside a house, but he's not in that one, he's in a residence three or four houses north.*

Are you hurt?

I am alive.

That's not what I asked.

The emperor has tied me to a chair and beaten me.

I can not help. The streets are too tight and if I use my fire, I may cause the whole city to burn.

I will escape. Somehow.

Suddenly the emperor ripped the parchment from her. Shocked, she looked up at the satisfaction in his face.

"He has his mother's eyes and his father's dimple." He glared at her, throwing the picture onto the table. "You've been closer to him than you said."

Dread filled her. The portrait of Bao was rough, but captured every part of his essence, including the dimple which showed when he smiled. She was a fool. She should have concentrated on the drawing, on ensuring it had little detail but it was too late now.

The emperor shoved the chair around so she faced him. "How long have you known Bao?"

"I do not know him, Heavenly—" His backhand snapped her head back, cutting off her words.

"You could not have drawn this detail from seeing him from afar. Was he living in Anming's residence?"

She turned back to him, keeping her gaze lowered. "I do not understand."

He gripped her chin, squeezing it as he raised it so she was forced to look at him. "Was Bao at Anming's residence?"

"Not that I saw, Heavenly Majesty." She held his gaze.

He plunged the dagger into her shoulder and hot, flashing pain made her scream.

"You're lying." He twisted the blade and she gritted her teeth as warm blood slid down her chest. "Let's try again. Do you have any knowledge of Bao being with Anming?"

What was the point in lying? He must have his suspicions. She opened her mouth to tell him and her gaze caught on the picture of Bao. No, she couldn't do anything that might hurt him, even if he had hurt her in the past.

The emperor ripped the knife out and her head spun as he wiped it on her dress. Shan wanted to vomit. Her heart thudded, pumping more blood down her back.

"Do you support him?"

She glanced at him. "It doesn't matter who is emperor," she said. "My life won't change."

Speculation crossed the emperor's face and unease filled her. "It could."

"My duty is to serve my master." Bingwen had drilled that into her.

"And if I tell you I'm your new master?"

Her skin crawled, but she let her training take over, and bowed low. "Then I shall serve you however you wish."

The emperor stepped back and called out. Two guards entered and bowed. "Yes, Heavenly Majesty?"

"Clean her and get her out of those clothes then take her into my bed chambers. Tie her to my bed." He smiled. "Make sure her legs are spread."

~*~

Shan gritted her teeth to stop herself from begging the guards to let her go as they cut the ropes tying her to the chair and dragged her out of the room. Panic threatened to take over and blood continued to pour from her shoulder wound. Her vision blurred. She fought to stay conscious as they entered a large room with a bed in it. They dumped her on the ground and one guard stood above her while the other went to the side table and poured water into a bowl.

"You're a pretty one." The guard watching her was attractive, his uniform pressed to perfection and his posture erect.

She said nothing. These guards wouldn't dare disobey the emperor, so there was no point wasting her breath. Her hands were free, but her legs were still tied and her energy was waning. If she pulled the illusion to her, was she strong enough to hold it in place while she undid the ropes?

No, the guards were too close anyway.

Two large windows were open, looking out on the courtyard and letting a gentle morning breeze waft into the room. Getting stuck in the courtyard wasn't her first preference. With her injured shoulder, she might not be able to climb onto the roof.

The other guard approached with a cloth and the bowl. He was younger than she expected for someone guarding the emperor. He must be incredibly skilled. Placing the bowl on the ground he drew a knife from his belt. She flinched. "Hold still. I need to expose your injury." He sliced the dress from her neck, along her arm, his movements precise and clinical. The top fell away and the warm air touched her skin. Only the silk wrap around her breasts protected her modesty. He tucked the blade back in his belt and wet the cloth, washing the blood away from her skin and then pressing hard against the wound.

She hissed at the pain, but her attention was on the dagger only a hand-span away. If she grabbed it, she would have to kill him. The older guard stood by the bed watching, a smile on his face. She needed him to turn away even just for a moment. "May I have some water?"

The guard frowned and walked to the side table. As the younger guard rinsed the cloth in the bowl she gathered her energy in the waterfall. Then she grabbed her hair pin. He glanced at her, eyes wide, mouth open to yell, but it was cut off as she slit his throat. He slumped against her and she grabbed his dagger, then pushed him away and faded. She rolled away from his body as the other guard turned and gasped. She sawed frantically at the ropes while the guard scanned the room for her, fear on his face. The emperor would kill him for letting her escape.

One more strand to go.

It snapped as the guard drew his sword and swept the room with it. She gritted her teeth, using the wall to help her stand. Speed was better than stealth. She dashed across the room and leapt out the window, pain spearing through her as the wound reopened. The verandah was still full of guards and the sun bathed the courtyard with dawn light.

The table the guard had used to get onto the roof earlier was across the other side of the courtyard. Behind her, her guard finally shouted the alarm. "She's escaped!"

Shan dodged several men and stumbled around the perimeter of the courtyard, keeping to the shadows, praying the table wasn't too heavy.

When she reached it, the other guards along this section were watching what was happening around the emperor's bed chambers. She lifted the table and gritted her teeth at the pain. Three steps. That's all. Drawing more energy from her waterfall, she shuffled across, placing the table in the corner of the courtyard. She checked the guards' positions. One man was looking her way, a frown on his face.

No time to lose.

She climbed onto the table and stretched her hands up to the tiles. She hissed at the pain, but pushed through. There was no way to stop the noise she would make. Speed was essential. On the count of three, she hefted herself up, her chest hitting the roof and her legs kicking behind her. Guards shouted and an arrow hit the roof right next to her palm. She shifted her hands, pulling herself onto the roof, and scrambled across to the peak, her heart racing. As she ducked down the far side, something pierced her leg and pain exploded through her.

Chapter 24

Agony ricocheted through Shan's leg and she gasped for breath. She retched, crawling further away from the courtyard. Reaching back, her fingers connected with the wooden arrow shaft sticking from her thigh and the warm blood welling from the wound. Behind her voices yelled. They would be on the roof in a matter of seconds. She gritted her teeth as her body throbbed. The waterfall. Her gift. The pulsing pain made it difficult to focus. She forced the image to her mind and dragged her gift over her just as a guard climbed onto the roof. He stood, drawing his sword.

Curses. Several yards of tiled roof lay between her and the alley which ran along the back of the houses. It was her best chance, but moving fast would be noisy.

She kept her eyes on the guard as she pressed back to her heels, careful of the arrow shaft, and another man climbed onto the roof. "Where is she?"

"She's got to be here somewhere. Get some more men up and send some around the rear."

If they looked closely they'd see the drops of blood. She stood, her head spinning. It was about three yards to the back alley. Neither guard on the roof had a bow and arrow. She could make it if she didn't stop, didn't hesitate at the edge. She would have to jump and hope she didn't injure herself when she landed.

Taking a long breath, she ran, ignoring the torture of the arrow jerking with each step. The guards spun at the sound and yelled, swiping wildly towards her. One blade swept by, chilling her.

The edge of the roof was only steps away. She glanced down, noted the guards pouring into the road from both sides. She'd be trapped. At the last minute she lengthened her stride and jumped, leaping for the house on the opposite side of the street. Her illusion wavered and behind her men yelled.

She wasn't going to make it.

She stretched out, reaching for the roof.

Let me see you and hold still.

Shan dropped the illusion and sharp claws wrapped around her biceps and lifted her, carrying her the extra distance to the roof.

"Dragon!" one of the guards yelled.

Her feet touched the tiles and Riltien let go. *Run,* he ordered.

He flew away, ducking and weaving through the arrows. Shan pulled her illusion tighter and ran across the next roof, looking back only when she was halfway across. The two guards who were on the roof of the emperor's residence were looking towards her, but were unable to breach the gap.

Drop your illusion, Riltien said. *Let me help you across the next few streets and then I'll find you somewhere safe to come down.*

She did as he asked, dropping the illusion as she leapt across three roads.

Follow me.

She pulled the illusion to her again and followed his diagonal path across the roofs, focusing only on the next step and then the next until she reached a road with a junction.

I'll help you down.

Again she dropped the illusion and held out her arms so Riltien could lower her. A woman nearby screamed in fright. Shan winced. There would be guards here in a matter of seconds. Not caring who saw, she pulled her illusion to her again and vanished.

I can't help you with the arrow, Riltien said as he let her go and rose into the sky again. *Kew can't come so I've called for another dragon to heal you, but she will be a while.*

Shan blinked. It was harder and harder to comprehend what he was saying. She touched the arrow and her hand came away bloodied. Drops of blood dripped to the ground below. She would leave a trail.

"Need to find a bandage." She stumbled along the road. The streets were relatively empty, people not willing to venture out until they knew what was going on. All she needed was to find a blade and she could chop what remained of her dress into strips.

She stopped. Her hair pins. She reached up, hissing at the pain in her shoulder and withdrew her remaining blade. Then she pulled her skirt towards her and leaned her shoulder against a wall to help her stay upright as she sliced the fabric.

Breathing was difficult. *Riltien, find me somewhere to hide.*

Getting back to the palace would be impossible and she still needed to open the western city gate. Her body ached and each movement was harder than the last. She folded one length of fabric into a soft pad and prayed she had the strength to pull the arrow out and not faint while she did it.

The tavern on your left has a path to its back courtyard.

She stumbled forward, found the path and entered the brick courtyard. The shutters on the windows were closed and the doors were shut. She was alone.

Sighing, she perched on the edge of a barrel and grabbed the base of the arrow. She clenched her teeth and yanked back. "Argh!" The scream ripped from her and she pressed her lips together, dropping the arrow and fighting the waves of nausea. She slapped the pad against the wound, and then wrapped her makeshift bandage around her thigh. She tied it as tightly as she could and then wiped her bloody hands on the barrel.

Shan closed her eyes, wishing she could sink to the ground and rest, but she was still too close to the emperor's residence. She gave herself a moment as she examined the other barrels in the courtyard. One was marked as water and had a ladle resting on its lid. When the pulsing pain in her thigh lessened, she pushed herself off the barrel and limped over.

The container was half full.

She dipped the ladle in and cautiously sipped the contents. Water. She drank deeply, two full ladles before her stomach cramped. When the pain subsided, she washed her shoulder wound and her face and arms. There was little she could do about her clothes, her modesty protected only by the silk binding around her breasts and the one sleeve still in place.

Next to the door into the tavern sat a crate full of peaches, perhaps an early morning delivery. She took one and bit into its soft flesh, closing her eyes as the juice ran down her throat. The sugar gave her a little more energy and she ate quickly.

A high-pitched whistle pierced her ears and a loud bang echoed in the sky. She stumbled away from the building and lifted her gaze to the smoke trail in the sky above her. Sparks of light floated towards the ground. Fireworks.

Her stomach clenched. Was that the emperor's signal? Had Bao found the powder in time?

She hurried back to the street, no longer leaving a trail of blood behind her, but every step was painful. She had no more time to rest, no time to wait to be healed. Opening the gates was vital. The allies could enter and help protect Bao. She had no idea which way she was heading.

Riltien, can you direct me to the nearest gate? He circled high above her, out of range of any arrow.

Turn left at the next intersection.

The intersection was twenty yards away. As she shuffled towards it, soldiers came out of houses and fell into lines. She held her breath and pressed herself against a wall. The street was no longer empty. Soldiers filled it, six abreast. Someone up ahead called out an order and the men marched forward, turning right at the intersection… heading for the palace.

Riltien, can you tell Bao? Soldiers are moving on the palace.

Yes. I'm watching them. They're coming from all sides.

There were even more men inside the city than they had realised. Shan could do nothing but stand there, watching in horror as the line of men continued past her.

Suddenly a loud boom echoed through the air and the ground shook. She lay her palms against the wall as she fought for balance. The soldiers around her exchanged startled looks and a few drew their swords.

Shan wanted to be ill. The emperor had attacked.

Riltien!

The wall without a gate has been destroyed and so have many of the palaces inside. The emperor's men are crossing the moat now.

The southern side of the palace was where the emperor's concubines lived. They would have all been in their palaces, as Bao had ordered. How many were dead? She itched to move forward but the soldiers kept coming.

For how long had the emperor been syphoning troops into the city?

Go in the opposite direction of the troops, Riltien said. *I must see if Bao needs my help.*

The line of troops still spread out as far as she could see. Exhaustion tempted her to close her eyes and rest, but the moment she lost her focus, the soldiers would see her, and they wouldn't ignore a half-naked woman in the street who suddenly appeared from nowhere. Especially one who must look like she'd been in a fight.

She focused on her breathing, on counting the number of soldiers marching past.

Bao didn't have enough men inside the palace to fight them.

She needed to let the Rhoran in. But were they still fighting whoever had attacked them?

Riltien, are the Rhoran still fighting?

Yes, they have almost defeated the men from Laksung.

The vassal state from the east. *What about Anming's men?*

They will arrive at the western gate by midday.

Then she had only a short time to get across the city and make sure the gates were opened. Could she risk walking alongside the soldiers for the short distance to the intersection?

She had to.

Her thigh throbbed and she checked the wound, saw the blood colouring the bandage.

She kept her hands on the brick building, the rough surface keeping her grounded. Then she slid along it, gauging the small gap between her and the marching men. Each step was as quiet as she could make it, but her mad dash across the roof tops had ripped her slippers into useless strands and the ground was already warming from the sun.

Fifteen yards to go.

The soldiers moved faster than she did, stepping in time, the rhythm hypnotic. Her head grew heavy and nodded of its own accord. Jerking up she dug her fingers into the wall and strengthened her illusion.

She shuffled faster, reaching the ten-yard mark. Checking the road behind her, she gasped. At the end of the lines of soldiers was a wide wagon and on top of it was a rectangular device which had multiple arrows pointing out of it. She had no idea what it was, but nothing with that many arrows could be good. Increasing her pace, she slid along the wall.

Sharp pain at her arrow wound made her gasp and flinch, colliding with one of the soldiers.

Fear wrenched through the pain and she leapt back as the man reached for her. "Something just hit me."

Her hand swiped a metal ring in the wall that must have been what she'd run into. She ran as the soldiers ahead glanced back. Five yards to go.

"There was someone there, I swear."

Behind her a man yelled, "Blood on the wall."

Shan winced. The intersection was just up ahead. She raced around the corner and hit something solid.

Correction, *someone* solid.

She stumbled back, tripping on her feet and sprawled on the ground. Her illusion shimmered and she strengthened it, rolling away from the general she'd hit. He yelled, drawing his sword.

Scrambling to her feet, she drew on her last ounce of strength and ran.

Shan's lungs strained and her muscles burned as she sprinted down the street in the direction of the gates. It wasn't until she reached the next intersection that she risked a glance behind her. The general still swung his sword, but no one followed her. She slowed, but kept moving. The sun was rising high above the horizon bringing illumination to the horror around her.

Riltien, how is the palace?

The emperor's soldiers have breached the walls, but only one wall was destroyed.

Relief filled her. *Where is Bao?*

Leading his troops to fight. The men on both sides are horrified by the emperor's actions. He killed many of his concubines.

She prayed to her ancestors to protect Bao, Geriel, and whoever else was still in the palace. She leaned against the wall to get her breath back and her head spun. Her thigh still throbbed and she placed a hand against her wound. It was warm with blood. How much blood could a person lose before it was too much?

She shuddered and prayed the gates were close.

Forcing herself forward, she continued down the street. People stood outside, staring at the smoke coming from the direction of the palace, but no one made a move to help.

The fear on their faces was clear.

She stopped when the scent of straw and horse dung reached her. A stables. If she could ride to the wall, it would be much faster. The next gate opened into an empty stable yard. She moved into the stables itself to find three horses inside and a servant calming one who was obviously still skittish over the explosion. Her steps were heavy and the boy spun around as she crunched through the straw on the ground, fear in his eyes.

Exhaustion whispered to her, enticing her to let go, to give in.

Her toes hit something metal under the straw and pain shot through her. She fell to the ground, dropping her illusion.

The boy jerked back in shock and so did the horse, whinnying in fright. “Shhhh, it’s all right,” the boy murmured, turning side on to soothe the horse but also to keep an eye on her. “Where did you come from?”

Shan pushed past the pain. “Please. I need to borrow a horse.”

“You’re injured.”

She nodded.

“Whose side are you on?”

Her answer could get her killed. “What do you mean?”

“That explosion came from the palace,” the boy said. “The man they’re calling the usurper was inside, so I guess the emperor is attacking it. Do you support the emperor or the usurper?”

She climbed to her feet. None of the horses wore bridles

or saddles. If the servant raised the alarm, she would have to run without a horse. Right now the truth was her best option. "I have met Prince Bao, the man they are calling the usurper. He is the son of Emperor Huang."

The boy gasped.

"All he wants is to reclaim his birthright. He could do it easily by bringing in his Rhoran allies, but he doesn't want to kill his people. He wanted to end this peacefully, but Emperor Xue will not give in."

"What do I care which emperor is on the throne?" the boy asked. "If I let you take a horse, my master will beat me."

"I understand." Her head still spun. "I promise to return your horse."

"I don't know you. Your promise means nothing."

What else could she say to him? She was in no state to fight. "Prince Bao will give Chungson their freedom and I hope he will also ban indentured servitude and give us the freedom to choose who we work for."

The boy glanced towards the house. "What makes you think that?"

"Prince Bao is a good man. While he was hiding from the emperor, he worked as a servant. He understands our life."

He hesitated and then said, "When will you return the horse?"

Hope filled her. "As soon as I can."

He left the horse he was soothing and crossed the room to fetch the tack. Quickly he saddled one of the other horses. "She doesn't spook easily," he said. "If there are any more explosions you should be fine."

"Thank you." She took the reins.

"Wait a second." He ducked into a small room off the side and came back with a pair of pants and a tunic. "I don't have shoes that will fit you, but these should."

Tears blurred her vision. "Thank you." She changed her clothing. "I will make sure the prince knows how you helped me."

The boy frowned. "Just get the horse back to me by nightfall." He gave her a leg up and she adjusted her seat.

Relief made her dizzy. "Thank you." She rode out of the stable yard, not bothering to draw her illusion towards her. She needed all her strength to cling to the horse. There were fewer people in the streets now, everyone knew there was nowhere to run, not with the gates shut, so they hid inside, probably praying the violence wouldn't find them.

Soldiers still marched on the main street to the palace, so she kept to a smaller side street, keeping at a walking pace, not wanting to attract any attention.

Dhalin should be here soon, Riltien said. *She will be able to heal you.*

As the walls grew higher before her, she dismounted and tied the horse to one of the metal rings outside a shop. No one was likely to take it. From here she would go on foot.

Shan took a moment to breathe. Her body ached, but she couldn't wait until the dragon arrived. She reached the outer wall and turned to look along it. She gasped. The gatehouse was immense with a four-storey archery tower looming over the wall. A dozen guards stood outside and Shan pulled her illusion to her. In her fuzzy-headed state, she hadn't considered how many people might be guarding the gate.

A guard came out of a doorway to the left of the gate.

"What's happening out there?" a soldier asked him.

"Smoke's coming from the palace," the guard said. "The emperor must be attacking it."

"What was that explosion?"

"One of the palace walls coming down."

The soldier shuffled his feet. "Should we go and help? The emperor might need us."

"If we leave the gate unguarded, the emperor will kill us," the guard said.

"The people in the city need us to keep them safe from

the barbarians outside," another soldier added.

Shan stepped away, out of sight of the men. Maybe that was her way inside. She released her illusion. She was injured enough for the story to make sense. She stumbled out from the building, and headed towards the gate. "Help. Please, can someone help me?"

A couple of the soldiers drew their swords, but the one who'd spoken of helping the people stepped forward. "Stop there. Who are you?"

It wasn't difficult to bring tears to her eyes. "I'm a maid from the imperial palace." She staggered forward. "The fighting is horrible. The usurper…" She sobbed.

"Did you walk all this way?"

She nodded. "No one would help. Everyone is hiding inside." She gripped the soldier's arms. "They attacked me." She showed him the wound on her shoulder.

"Come with me." The soldier placed a hand on her lower back and led her to the door next to the gate. "We've got supplies inside. We'll patch you up."

Shan didn't have to fake her relief. "Thank you."

The door opened onto a common room with a long table and chairs in it. To one side a fire was lit and someone was cooking meat in a pot. "Can you manage some stairs?" the soldier asked.

Shan nodded.

A flight of stairs brought her into an infirmary with two single cots in it and a window which looked back at the city. "Sit," the soldier said. "What's your name?"

"Ting," she lied.

"I'm Wang." He poured water into a bowl. "Tell me what happened at the palace." He wet a cloth and began to clean her scratched and bloody hands.

"After the usurper took control, he confined us to the inner palace. I am the First Consort's maid and she did not like being told she wasn't allowed to go anywhere."

The soldier nodded. "Taking orders can be difficult sometimes."

"We managed until this morning when the south wall of the palace exploded. My mistress had ordered me to get her some soup, so I was by the kitchen when it happened. The whole ground shook."

"It must have been scary."

"It was." She hissed as he wiped a sharp-smelling oil over her palms.

"Sorry. It will cleanse them. What did you do then?"

"I ran back to my mistress but there was nothing but rubble where the palace once stood."

Wang's eyes widened. "Did anyone survive?"

"I don't know. The emperor's men were crossing the moat. They shot at me so I ran."

"The emperor's men shot at you?" He seemed incredulous.

"Yes. I was terrified and I hid until they had all entered the palace and then I sneaked out the hole in the wall hoping to find someone who could help me."

He rinsed the cloth and cleaned her feet. "These aren't a maid's clothes."

She shook her head. "I had to rip mine to make bandages." She glanced at him. "I stole these, but I promise I'll replace them." Across the room was a dagger, but she didn't want to kill this kind man. She would wait until he left and then continue up the stairs to the winch room.

"I need to loosen your tunic to examine that wound on your shoulder," he said.

She hesitated. "I also have a wound on my thigh."

He glanced down. "Then you should remove your pants so I can look at it."

"Thank you." She stood and pulled down her pants, blushing when Wang stepped back. She unwound the bandages over her injury and Wang took the pad away and she flinched at the pain.

"It's started bleeding again. Let me clean it."

The cool water soothed and stung at the same time.

"I'm amazed you got this far. How did you get the arrow out?"

"I pulled it out."

"That takes strength."

Shan, where are you?

Riltien's voice made her start.

"Sorry. I'm almost done."

She blocked the pain and answered, *I'm inside the western gate complex.*

Dhalin has arrived. Can you get out in the open?

How many guards are on top of the wall?

Too many. She won't be able to land without being shot.

Then hopefully Wang's bandaging would hold. *I'll contact you when I'm out.*

"This needs stitches," Wang said. "Let me find my comrade. Stay here."

As soon as he left, Shan pulled up her pants and limped to the bench. She tucked the dagger into her pants pocket.

A bell clanged loudly somewhere outside, making Shan jump. Voices shouted and people ran up the stairs outside the room. *Riltien, what's going on?*

The Chungson have arrived.

This could be her chance. She stepped forward and the arrow wound pulled. She touched it and her fingers came away bloody. Wang wasn't likely to be back with his comrade. She grabbed some silk bandages from the bench, wadding one up and placing it over the wound and then wrapped another around her thigh to keep it in place.

People still shouted but no one ran up the stairs. Shan peered out of the room and then started up the stairs. She didn't bother to shield herself as she climbed. The stairs were narrow and anyone coming down them would hit her.

At the next level she peered into the room. It was empty of people but full of swords, shields and barrels of arrows. She continued ascending. The next room contained projectiles designed to be dropped on anyone who dared try to breach the walls.

As she climbed the staircase, the voices grew louder. Her wound pulled and ached as she climbed but the top must be close. She rounded the turn and entered a long room which stretched the width of the gate. Inside was a large spindle with a chain around it.

"Who are you?"

She gasped as a guard strode to her from the corner of the room. Curse it. "I am Ting. Wang was kind enough to see to my injuries, but then the bell clanged and he left and I wanted to see what was happening."

"You shouldn't be here. Leave."

She bowed. "Of course. I am sorry."

She went back down the stairs, past the bend and then drew her illusion to her and returned to the room. There were two guards inside, the one who had spoken to her and another across the room who didn't look like he was old enough to be a guard. There were metal grids over holes in the floor and buckets full of steaming liquid next to them. Her heart jumped. If Anming breached the gate, they would pour whatever was in the buckets down on the men riding through.

The winch was right in front of her, but even if she managed to raise the portcullis, someone would come in and lower it again as soon as she left to open the gate.

Anming says he has men inside the city. If I can get word to them, they might be able to storm the gate.

Which left her to lift the portcullis and defend the room from the soldiers. Luckily there was only one entrance. She went back to the door she had entered and examined it. It was thick and heavy with a brace that allowed it to be locked from the inside. A last line of defence.

She glanced over her shoulder. Both guards paced along the top of the gate. Perhaps she could close the door without them noticing.

"I wish this place had a window facing the outside," the younger guard complained.

The one who'd told her to leave scoffed. "Why, so it's easier for invaders to get inside?"

"That's not what I meant. It's difficult not knowing what's going on."

Shan wrapped her fingers around the edge of the door and pulled. A sharp squeak made her wince.

"What was that?" the guard who had stopped her earlier asked.

"I don't know."

"Then check."

The younger guard strode over and Shan slipped back, away from the door. He yanked it forward, checking to make sure no one hid behind it and it let out an awful squeal.

"Ugh, would you oil that thing?" the guard in charge complained.

"Han took the oil earlier." The younger man moved the door back and forth a couple of times and the other guard swore.

"Stop that, or go find the cursed oil."

The man glared at him and then muttered, "I'll be right back."

Shan waited until he left the room and the other guard had turned away. Then she slammed the door shut, wincing at the noise it made, and slid the bar into place.

"What?" The other guard strode towards her, his sword drawn. She ducked out of the way and grabbed the dagger from her pocket, wishing there was something heavy she could use to hit him over the head. As he scanned the area she held her breath. Then he muttered and sheathed his sword. Before he could lift the bar, she slipped behind him and ran the dagger across his throat. The man's scream cut off midway and his arms flopped back as he fell against her.

She stepped back, letting him fall to the ground, blood rushing out of the wound and over her hands. She vomited, her whole body clenching at the horror, and she squeezed her eyes closed.

How many more would she have to kill?

Forcing her eyes open again, she checked he was dead.

Wiping the dagger on her pants, she breathed through her mouth to avoid smelling the blood. *Riltien, I'm winching up the gate.*

She returned to the spindle and pushed the handle. It rattled but barely budged, its massive weight burdensome. Her stomach sank. There was no one else who could help her. She pushed her whole weight against the handle and it shifted a little. Relief filled her as she shoved again, and this time it slid a little easier. She kept rotating the handle and slowly the gate raised.

Someone pounded on the door. "Why have you shut the door?"

The younger guard. It wouldn't be long before he raised the alarm, or someone realised she was opening the gate.

She pushed again, ignoring her pain, focusing only on the cold hard metal her fingers wrapped around and the slow progress of the gate.

The guard pounded on the door again. "What's going on?"

She didn't look at the man lying dead on the ground. It had been necessary. The emperor had attacked the palace; Bao and Geriel might be fighting for their lives.

Shan increased her pace and finally the chain filled the spindle and she couldn't wind any further. The gate was up. She set the lock into position so it didn't fall. *Riltien, the portcullis is open.*

Anming's men in the city are still on their way.

She pulled her illusion to her and peered out of the window. Soldiers were lined outside the gate, more alert now for anyone approaching. The thick wooden gates were braced shut with a heavy beam of wood.

More banging on the door and shouts. The door was sturdy, designed to keep people out as a last defence against someone raising the gates, but she had no idea what weapons the Bonamese had at their disposal. Could they make the door explode like the wall at the palace, or would that be too dangerous?

Thump.

Something hit the gates and she felt the vibrations. *What's happening?*

Anming is trying to open the gates with a battering ram.

She heard the *swoosh* of arrows being released. Did they have the manpower to take on the men at the gate? Did they have the time to waste while the emperor could be defeating Bao?

Her body tingled with nerves and fear.

Shan looked out the window again. She was four levels above the ground, but the window was just wide enough for her to squeeze through. If she could find a rope or a chain, she might be able to climb down, lift the brace while the soldiers faced the city, waiting for an attack.

She searched the room and eventually found a length of rope in a chest. She tied it to the chest and tugged on the knot to make sure it held. Then she covered the rope in her illusion and lowered it out the window.

It dangled about one level above the ground. She would have to jump the remaining distance, but at least it meant it would be difficult for any soldiers to reach it to climb back up.

Tell Anming I'm going to try and open the wooden gate.

How?

I'll climb down. There's rope.

She felt Riltien's surprise. *Be careful. You have no wings.*

She smiled. Testing the knot again, she climbed onto the window ledge. It was a squeeze, but she managed to loop her feet around the rope to hopefully slow her descent. It was a long way.

Ignoring her rapidly beating heart and sending a prayer to her ancestors, she lowered herself from the window.

She hung there, yards from the ground, her muscles burning. Letting go of the rope, even for a second, to lower herself further, seemed like a foolish thing to do. Below her, the soldiers shouted and she twisted to see men charging towards the gate.

Were they Anming's men?

Shan uncurled her top hand and moved quickly, grabbing a section of rope a little further down. She used the section wrapped around her legs to slow her as she slid down the rope, every muscle in her body straining with the effort. The clang of metal on metal and shouts told her the fight below had begun but she didn't look, couldn't lose focus.

Then the rope ran out.

She was far higher off the ground than she thought she'd be, maybe three yards, but without the rope around her feet she held on by her upper body only, and her grip was failing. She couldn't climb back up.

Checking the ground below her was clear, she let go.

Chapter 25

Shan fell, hitting the ground with a thump, pain shooting through her limbs at the jolt. Her hand appeared before her and she struggled to fix her illusion as the piercing pain made it hard to concentrate. Luckily, she'd landed behind the soldiers fighting to protect the gate. She stepped towards the cross bar but pain ricocheted through her ankle and she stumbled forward, just managing to balance before she put weight on it again.

She glanced down, withdrew the illusion from around her foot and saw a blue tinge around the puffy skin. Curse it. There was nothing nearby she could use as a crutch. Gritting her teeth, she hopped, taking her time to regain her balance, and then hopped again until she reached the gate.

Shan panted, the pain in her foot radiating through the rest of her. Her illusion flickered again, harder to hold with the layers upon layers of pain inside her. Not much further now. All she had to do was lift the thick, heavy chunk of wood bracing the gate.

She hopped into place and lifted, her arms straining at the weight.

It didn't budge.

Sobbing in frustration, she crouched, placing her shoulder under the beam and lifted again. The full weight of it pressed into the dagger wound on her shoulder and she closed her eyes at the pain. Balancing on her good foot, she pushed up, the beam raising above the notches.

Shan pulled it towards her but it didn't budge. She followed the beam along the gate to where the other side still rested snuggly in place. Someone else needed to lift it at the same time as she did.

Shan dropped the beam back into place and turned, examining the fighting behind her. Anming's men were outnumbered and she couldn't spread her illusion over them without touching them.

Riltien, I need help.

One of Anming's men glanced towards the gate.

He is going to try and get around the soldier. Can you hide him?

When he touches the gate I can.

She pushed the illusion across the beam as the man ducked under the swing of the soldier and ran towards her. He touched the beam and the illusion covered him. The soldier he was fighting gaped in shock.

Shan lifted the beam again, her body straining, and the man lifted the other side. The weight of the beam made her stumble back, her ankle screaming in agony and she dumped the beam on the ground.

It's clear, Shan told Riltien.

Stand back.

She didn't have the energy to move. Anming's man was already pulling his door open, but Shan's head swum with the pain, making it impossible to tell her body what she needed it to do.

Shan, stand back. Anming's men are coming through.

And she'd be in the way.

She hopped and lost her balance, falling to the ground, then crawled away, dragging her useless ankle behind her.

With a crash, the gates burst open and men charged through. The Bonamese soldiers had no chance, only time for the look of horror to cross their faces before they were cut down.

The riders were a mixture of Chungson and Rhoran men. Some galloped along the main street, heading for the palace and others broke off to the right and left, probably heading for the other gates.

Shan crawled so her back was against the wall as a few warriors dismounted and headed for the gatehouse.

Drop your illusion, Riltien said. *Chinua is looking for you.*

Shan didn't know who Chinua was, but she released the illusion and used the wall to help herself stand. A young Rhoran man strode to her. "Shan?"

She nodded.

"You're hurt."

"I twisted my ankle when I jumped." She motioned to the rope dangling above them. "And I was shot and stabbed."

He shook his head. "Come with me. I'll take you to Dhalin to be healed." Without waiting for her response, he swept her into his arms and carried her to his nearby horse. As she mounted, she remembered the horse that had carried her here.

"Go that way," she pointed. "I need to get my horse."

"What you need is to be healed. You're as pale as smoke." He kicked the horse into motion and thundered through the streets of the city. It was all Shan could do to hold onto him as her head spun. Chinua stopped outside a city park, helped her to the ground and carried her over the grass to some trees.

A large shadow passed overhead and she glanced up as a green dragon came into land.

"Dhalin." Chinua nodded a greeting.

Shan couldn't speak. This dragon the size of a tiger had a regal presence.

Place Shan on the ground. She has almost as many injuries as Lien did fighting Ying.

Shan winced as Chinua placed her on the ground. The dragon approached her and placed a paw on her arm. *Stay still. This might hurt.*

A gentle probing and then a sharp pain in her thigh. She gasped and clenched her teeth.

The arrow wound is healed. Now your ankle.

Chinua stood guard, bow and arrow at the ready as he scanned their surroundings. They weren't near the palace or any of the gates so it was unlikely there would be soldiers here.

The bone is cracked, but Geriel taught me how to fix them recently, Dhalin said.

More pain and then Dhalin stepped back. *How do you feel?*

Shan rotated her ankle and felt her thigh. "Better." Exhaustion still clouded her, but most of the pain was gone.

Dhalin frowned. *You are still hurt.* She touched Shan and the throbbing shoulder wound and the scratches on her arms from Riltien's claws disappeared.

Thank you.

You are welcome. I am needed elsewhere. The dragon stepped away and the wind from her wings brushed Shan's cheek as she flew away.

"Wow," Shan breathed.

"They're incredible, aren't they?" Chinua held out a hand to help her to her feet.

She nodded, her mind racing. "We need to get to the palace."

He grinned. "I'd love to fight the emperor but I'm under strict instructions to keep you safe."

She frowned. "Who asked you to do that?" She headed towards his horse.

"Lien gave me my orders, via Riltien, but they came from Bao. He wants you kept out of the fighting."

She raised her eyebrows. "Without me, you'd still be on the other side of the wall."

"I know. I'm impressed. I thought most Bonamese women were fragile and weak." He mounted and then pulled her up behind him. "Don't tell Lien I said that."

"I did what I had to." She wasn't going to stay here when she could help Bao, but first she needed her own horse. "Can you take me back to the gate? I left a horse there and I have to return it before nightfall."

"Sure." He nudged his horse in the right direction.

The sun now shone directly overhead, scorching her with its rays. The horse's hooves echoed loudly in the stillness. Shan's skin crawled. Being alone out here didn't fill her with comfort, even with a Rhoran warrior for company. "Do you want to go a little faster?"

Chinua increased the pace and she directed him to where the horse was still tied up, waiting. She slid off Chinua's horse. "Thank you."

"Where are you taking it?"

"The stables are closer to the city." It took her two attempts to mount.

"We should go back to the gates. They should be secured by now."

Shan looked at him, hoping she was reading him right. "Neither of us wants to be at the gates. You can either come with me and protect me or explain to Lien how you lost me." She gathered her energy and faded.

He chuckled. "I like you. Let's go."

Shan dropped the illusion and they headed towards the palace, the smoke from the fires their guide.

~*~

Shan returned the horse to the stable, and at her suggestion, Chinua left his horse there too, though he swung his bow and arrows onto his back. It would be easier to sneak into the palace under her illusion without horses.

The sounds of battle grew louder as they drew closer and

the stench of smoke was thick. They walked around a corner and the street ahead was full of men fighting. Chinua placed his arm out, stopping Shan. "We won't get past without being attacked. Can you make us invisible?"

"I could, but it won't help. There's not enough room to squeeze by. We're likely to get hit by a stray arrow or swinging sword."

He glanced up. "What about if we go over the rooftops? Will they hold our weight?"

"Yes, but the gaps between the roads are too wide to jump."

"I hate cities," Chinua grumbled.

"Maybe not all the streets are full." She led him through the streets, heading to the south, trying to find a path through, but it was pointless. There was fighting everywhere, Rhoran on their horses and Bonamese soldiers on foot. Frustration filled Shan. She had to get to Bao. Directly in front of her was the wagon she'd seen with the arrow device now shattered and leaning on only one wheel. At least that couldn't hurt anyone.

Suddenly a loud horn wrenched the air. Chinua froze. "That's the call for retreat."

Riltien, what's happening? She pressed herself against a building as the Rhoran galloped past, heading for the gates.

Bao has called for a cease of fighting. He has asked the emperor to meet with him. He doesn't want his people dying. The emperor has agreed to accept Bao's surrender.

"The emperor will use Bao's empathy against him," Chinua growled.

Shan agreed. "We must get to him."

The Bonamese soldiers were seeing to their fallen comrades.

Will the Bonamese guarantee our safety if we bring in our healers? Riltien's voice boomed in her head and around her the soldiers stopped what they were doing and glanced around, hands going to their weapons.

Shan saw Dhalin circling above. She stepped forward. "The dragons can heal people," she called out and the soldiers whirled to face her. "They want to help those who are injured." She pointed out Dhalin. "Will you guarantee their safety?"

A captain stepped forward. "Whose side are they on?" He eyed Chinua with animosity.

Annoyance filled her. "Does it matter? People are dying and they want to help."

Prince Bao has asked us to help. He does not want his people to die, which is why he ordered the Rhoran to retreat. He wishes to speak to the emperor face to face so they can settle this without more bloodshed.

"Why should we believe you?"

Dragons do not lie.

"How convenient." Someone nearby moaned in pain and the captain sighed. "Send them in."

Dhalin landed behind Shan and Chinua and folded her wings. *This way.*

She went to the first man, who clutched his stomach, blood covering his hands. The man trembled.

Calm yourself. I will not hurt you. Dhalin placed a paw on his leg and a few minutes later the man pulled his hands away from his stomach.

"She really healed me." He stood and lifted his armour for the others to see. "Thank you."

Dhalin inclined her head and moved to the next person.

Riltien landed next to her and the Bonamese backed up, giving him space. *I shall guard Dhalin. You are needed at the palace. They have arrested Bao and speak of beheading him.*

Fear pierced Shan. "Come on." She hurried forward, only to be stopped by the captain, his sword drawn.

"Where do you think you're going with that Rhoran scum?"

"The palace."

"Didn't you see? They retreated like the cowards they are."

"They retreated to spare your lives." Behind her, she heard the rasp of a sword being drawn. She glanced at Chinua. "Put it away."

He glared at the captain but did as she asked.

"We can help end the hostilities," she said to the captain.

He laughed. "A servant and a barbarian? All I see are people attacking my emperor."

She didn't have time for this. She reached out for Chinua, placed her hand in his. "I'm sorry, but we need to go." She vanished them and tugged Chinua past the captain who had stepped back in shock then hurried down the road that led to the southern wall. People milled in the distance and as they got closer Shan discovered more dragons had arrived and were helping the injured. She hadn't known there were so many.

Chinua waved to one. "Nice to see you again, Falin."

"Shush," Shan said. "He can't see you."

But I can sense him. Let us hope the next time we will all be at peace, Chinua.

Beyond Falin was the remains of the southern wall. A huge hole had been blasted into the side and rubble filled the moat, making a jagged bridge for people to cross. Inside the wall, palaces still burned but those closest to it had been demolished.

How many had the emperor killed?

How many had died in a battle between two people, arguing over something that should have been settled at a meeting? Power was addictive, it corrupted.

Several Bonamese soldiers guarded the bridge into the palace.

They are not letting anyone through, Falin said.

They would have to sneak in. Shan tugged Chinua to follow her and then ducked behind a building, releasing the illusion. She kept her voice low. "We need to sneak past and the rubble may be loose. Be ready to avoid any attack."

His expression was a little wary, but he nodded.

"This way." She held his hand and spread the illusion over them.

They weaved around the makeshift medical bay and it wasn't until they were almost at the bridge that Shan paid any attention to the guards. She smothered a gasp. They were the guards who'd seen her cross the moat. They knew what she could do.

She tugged on Chinua's hand and stretched to whisper in his ear. "These men almost caught me when I left the palace. If they hear us, they will shoot." She examined the rubble bridge, mapping out a path. Sticking to the larger boulders would be safer and make less noise. She gave the nearest soldier a wide berth and then stepped onto the rubble. Staying slow and steady so Chinua could keep up with her, she crossed from one boulder to another, wincing occasionally when a sharp stone stabbed her feet. When she got inside she would find some better shoes.

About three-quarters of the way along, Chinua slipped and rubble clattered into the water. They ducked as arrows sped their way.

"It has to be that person again," one of the soldiers said, scanning the bridge, an arrow notched.

"It might be the stones settling," another said.

Shan measured the distance. "Fast?" she whispered.

"Yes," Chinua replied. "Keep low."

She ran as fast as she could, keeping her steps light and then ducked behind one of the boulders in the palace grounds. Chinua was right behind her. She let out a breath.

"Which way?" Chinua asked.

"I'm not sure where everyone is. We'll check Kun's palace first." And she could get some shoes and clothes that fit her properly.

She kept the illusion around them as they weaved through rubble and past buildings, avoiding soldiers and guards alike. Several female bodies were lying on the ground nearby, and as they walked past, another limp, dusty body was pulled from the wreckage. She clenched her teeth.

A mound of bricks had replaced the empress's palace and people were frantically searching for her.

Shan wanted to be sick. The emperor only cared for his throne.

She swallowed hard and increased her pace, hurrying along the roads. No guards stood outside Kun's palace. She stopped Chinua. "I need to get some shoes."

He nodded and she opened the front door. A quick search revealed no one was in the main rooms. She dropped the illusion. "Stay here."

She ducked into Kun's bed chambers where she'd left her bag, but her gaze caught on Geriel's bag. The Rhoran clothing would be far more suitable. She changed and returned to Chinua.

"Kew says they're in the main courtyard," he said.

"All right. It's not too far."

Chinua smiled. "I'm familiar with the outer palace. I was here each time the emperor tried to kill Lien."

A story for another time. She pulled the illusion around them as they exited the palace.

They continued along the road and the shoes felt like cushions on Shan's feet after so long barefoot. Near the Gates of Heavenly Virtue a group of soldiers were being guarded by the emperor's men. It appeared everyone inside the imperial palace walls had surrendered.

Kew, is Lien all right? Surely she would have defeated the emperor's soldiers.

She is fine. Bao decided to surrender because too many outside the walls were being killed. There was a pause. *Bao is not happy with either of you.* Kew sounded slightly amused. *He wants you to both leave immediately.*

Chinua chuckled softly. "He's not usually so tense."

As they walked, Shan asked, "How do you know him?"

"I met him a couple of moons ago when I was helping Geriel find a cure to the Trader's Curse," he said. "Then we travelled together when he went to meet with my khan."

The whole palace was in shambles with bodies lying on the ground and buildings burning worse than after the riot. Shan's heart ached. This wasn't what Bao wanted.

They walked past the large hall and the courtyard came into view. All of the people fighting for Bao had been gathered together and were sitting in a large group being guarded by the emperor's soldiers. "Can you see Bao?" Shan asked, scanning the men.

"On that platform to the right," Chinua answered.

Sure enough Bao stood defiantly on the platform they had set up when he and Kun had spoken to the palace only a few days earlier. He wore leather armour and dirt or blood covered his clothing and face. With him were a distinctly unimpressed-looking Lien, Geriel, Jie, Kun and Wei. Geriel was arguing with the soldiers surrounding them.

She wants to help heal the injured, Kew said.

Where are you?

Flying above, out of arrow range, keeping an eye on everything. Manalin is offering to negotiate the peace between the emperor and Bao.

"Manalin?" Shan asked.

"Another dragon," Chinua said. "He knows Xue and spent some time at the imperial palace when Bao's father was emperor."

Right. "Will the emperor listen to him?"

"I don't know. The dragons received their land and stolen babies back when we signed a peace treaty with Xue. He might still be mad about that."

Shan had so many questions.

"How do we get past?" Chinua asked.

A good question. The soldiers encircled the prisoners and there wasn't a lot of space to squeeze past. "Let's get closer." Shan continued to visualise the waterfall, able to keep the illusion over her and Chinua easily. It helped that he moved in time with her, stopping any time she stopped.

They halted only a yard away from the group. Jie argued with one of the men guarding them. "We fought side by side," he said. "You know who I am and what I'm like. All my wife wants to do is help heal these people."

"I'm under orders, Jie," the man said.

Shan examined the circle. Maybe she could swap Chinua for Geriel. They both wore brown clothing. *Kew, can you share my plan with the others?* She didn't dare speak it aloud as they were too close.

Bao orders you to leave, Kew said. *But Geriel and Chinua are ready when you are.*

Geriel and Jie returned to sit with the others, Geriel with her head lowered as if in defeat and Jie's arm around her.

Shan squeezed Chinua's hand and they crept between the guards. Chinua sat in the space next to Jie. The guards' attention was on what was going on around the courtyard rather than on their prisoners. Shan placed her other hand on Geriel and quickly spread the illusion onto her while dropping it from Chinua. He sat with his head bowed and Geriel stood.

"Be careful," Jie murmured.

Shan glanced at Bao, still standing proudly, but his hand trembled and deep fatigue darkened his face. "Have faith," she whispered before retracing her steps, pulling Geriel with her. After they cleared the guards Shan relaxed.

Geriel hugged her fiercely. "I was terrified when Riltien said the emperor had captured you," she whispered.

"I'm fine now. Dhalin healed me."

"Good. Now let's go to Bao's men. Some of them look badly injured, and Xue's general insisted the dragons heal his men first."

They walked across the courtyard. The sun was viciously hot and the ground must be scorching. "Does Bao have a plan?"

Geriel scoffed. "Kind of. He hopes by surrendering, he can finally force the emperor to face him and see the truth."

"Only if the emperor doesn't kill him first."

"Lien should be able to prevent that."

They fell silent as they reached the men. How were they going to do this without freaking the men out? Geriel couldn't just put her hands on them and hope they stayed calm.

"There's Tadashi," Geriel murmured. "This way."

Shan let herself be pulled to a man who was busy wrapping a bandage around an injured soldier.

"Tadashi let me," Geriel said and crouched.

"Geriel, thank the ancestors." Tadashi looked over his shoulder and frowned.

"I'm here. You just can't see me. The guards wouldn't let me go, so Shan sneaked me out. See if you can identify all the injured and I'll heal them."

Tadashi shook his head. "I should be used to these kinds of things by now." He turned to the injured man whose eyes were wide with incredulity. "Don't worry. You'll feel Geriel's hands on you and it might hurt a bit, but she'll heal you." He stood. "Anyone else injured?"

"Hey, sit down," one of the Bonamese soldiers called.

"I'm seeing to my injured comrades. Unless you'll allow the dragons to help us."

The man scowled. "Fine."

Men raised their hands and slowly the three of them made their way through the group, Tadashi explaining what was going to happen and then Geriel healing major and minor injuries. Word spread through the assembled men and those who could walk came to them. It was impossible avoiding people bumping into them, and a couple of times Shan lost touch of Geriel and she suddenly appeared for everyone to see, but the emperor's soldiers didn't notice.

Around mid-afternoon, Geriel was done and they made their way back to the others. Chinua still sat with his head bowed as if he was upset. The guards hadn't noticed he wasn't Geriel.

Kew, can you tell Chinua we're ready to swap?

He's sleeping. I'll get Jie to wake him.

"Figures," Geriel murmured. "He gets to rest while we do all of the work."

The emperor is leaving the house, Kew said suddenly. *He's agreed to let Manalin negotiate the surrender, but I still don't trust him.*

Neither did Shan. "Let's get you back," she whispered to Geriel and increased her pace. As before, Jie and Chinua made space and Shan swapped the illusion.

Though Geriel had given her a boost of energy, it was getting difficult to hold her gift. She pulled Chinua in the direction of the dining hall.

"I need to eat."

The dining hall was empty, but the kitchens were busy with scents floating out and people calling to each other. As far as they were concerned, it was business as usual. Shan stepped to the side, out of the doorway as she entered the kitchen, keeping Chinua's hand firmly in hers. The cooks were plating hundreds of steamed buns and she quickly transferred four to one plate and picked it up, covering it with her illusion. "Grab a jug," she whispered to Chinua and after he did, they went back outside. She scanned for a place to hide so she could drop the illusion for a short while.

"It looks like they're moving Bao and the others," Chinua said.

Shan spun to look. Sure enough, they were moving to the edge of the platform. Other soldiers carried large wooden blocks onto the platform—chopping blocks. Her blood ran cold. "They can't mean to behead them!"

"I'm sure that's exactly the emperor's plan," Chinua said.

Her head spun and Chinua swore, pulling her around the side of the building. "You've dropped the illusion."

Her mind whirled. How could they save the others? "We should kill the emperor." She stuffed one of the buns in her mouth, needing the energy.

Chinua's smile was devil-like. "I like your thinking."

No, Kew said. *Bao will not approve.*

"I don't answer to Bao," Chinua said.

"Neither do I." Anming was her master. Shan swallowed the bun with a gulp of water as Chinua ate as well.

"The emperor must be coming through one of the gates," Chinua said. "He'll want to be here to witness Bao's death."

Lien tells you not to do anything too foolish.

An interesting choice of words. She obviously didn't trust Xue either.

"He'll need to make an example of Bao," Shan said as she ate the second bun. "Show people what happens when they defy him."

The emperor is marching his soldiers into the palace.

Her muscles tensed. All those soldiers she'd seen outside could easily massacre those inside. She grabbed Chinua's hand, sending the illusion over them, and then moved back around the building to scan the courtyard. A general approached one of his commanders.

"This way." She jogged towards them as the commander saluted and then said something to the general.

The general looked around and Shan slowed, stepping quietly as his words reached her. "He wants us to behead the usurper after the surrender has been signed." His voice was low.

Shan held her breath.

"Won't that defy any agreement they reach?" the commander asked.

"It is not up to us to question the emperor," the general said, but the frown on his face showed his concern. "I need your men to be ready for the response from the rebels. The emperor said to use all force to stop any further rebellion."

"He wants us to kill them?"

The general was silent. "Be ready," he repeated and then moved away.

Shan tugged Chinua away, her energy spiking at the emperor's orders. She would not let the emperor win, would not let Bao be killed.

"We need a plan."

Chapter 26

Shan and Chinua moved back towards the Hall of Clarity. *Which gate is the emperor coming through?* Shan asked Kew.

The northern one. He's in his palanquin.

They wouldn't be able to get a clear shot from a distance. "We'll need to get closer," she said to Chinua.

There was a clear path all the way to the northern gate, but before they had a chance to move towards it, soldiers started marching through, ten abreast, taking up positions in the courtyard.

Chinua swore. "We should grab Bao and the others and run."

Shan agreed, but, "Bao won't leave those who fought for him behind."

A loud gong reverberated through the courtyard as the emperor's palanquin carried by four sturdy servants moved through the gate, soldiers surrounding it on all sides.

The emperor is inside.

The palanquin reached the main bridge which spanned the river winding its way through the courtyard and the emperor disembarked, his golden robe a spotlight amongst the black-clad guards. Sixteen men surrounded the emperor as he walked to the platform.

Shan scanned the crowd as they moved closer, searching

for anyone else who might seek to harm Bao, looking for signs of a bow or a quiver of arrows. The soldiers stood erect, in parade position, waiting for orders. She checked the rooftops and scanned the outer walls where guards watched the proceedings, but no one had their weapons ready to fire.

Chinua prodded her and she realised she'd been gripping his hand too tightly. The emperor didn't glance at the crowd or any of his guards, but walked slowly over the central bridge and onto the platform, his guards falling into line behind him.

He is satisfied about something.

Shan's muscles tightened, her shoulder blades itching as she waited for something, anything, to happen. The emperor held no weapons, had none on his body that she could see. His guards were another matter, all carrying swords at their waists.

Two dragons swooped to the ground, Kew and a sandy-brown one which was bigger than Dhalin.

"Manalin," Chinua murmured.

Bao bowed a greeting at the emperor from where he was, still surrounded by guards, but the emperor did not respond. Instead he stepped away from Bao, and Manalin stood between the two parties. *I am Manalin, friend to Emperor Huang and negotiator for today.* His voice sounded in Shan's mind and all the soldiers flinched as one. Other dragons flew in and landed on rooftops. It was a sight to see with them all as big as tigers and in various colours. She recognised Dhalin, Riltien and Falin from earlier, but there were another five dragons watching proceedings carefully.

Intimidating, but their presence comforted her.

"What is the meaning of this?" the emperor demanded.

My kin are here to ensure justice is done.

Shan stood next to the platform and kept her gaze moving through the crowd and along the wall. A whistling sound chilled her and Chinua yelled, "Arrow!"

Before she could find it, the arrow pierced Manalin's chest and he bellowed in rage. Geriel ran forward, only to be stopped by the guards and the dragons roared, fire coming out of their mouths. Lien disarmed their guards so Geriel could get to Manalin as the emperor called, "Find the archer." His guard surrounded him, but Shan didn't miss his smug smile.

"We need to get onto the platform," Chinua said. "The emperor has more up his sleeve."

The soldiers still stood in rows in front of them, not daring to move out of formation, but a couple shuffled their feet and many were alert, eyes darting back and forth waiting for the next attack.

Lien guarded Geriel as she worked on Manalin.

The emperor is certain Manalin will die, Kew growled, smoke puffing from her nose, facing the guards who surrounded the man.

Forever silenced from telling the truth about Bao's parentage.

He underestimates Geriel's skills, Dhalin said. *Manalin will recover. Watch the emperor. He has more planned.*

"We must continue despite this horrible turn of events," the emperor announced. His voice wasn't loud enough to carry further than to the first couple of rows of soldiers.

Kew, where did that amplifier end up? Shan asked.

I returned it to Temur. Her gaze flicked to the dragons on the roof. *Falin will fetch it.*

"We must wait until Manalin is healed," Bao said.

"You are in no position to dictate this meeting, Imposter," the emperor responded. "I hereby charge you with pretending to be a member of the imperial family, and charge your men with treason. The punishment is death."

No. Manalin climbed to his feet, his cold gaze on the emperor. *It is you who should be charged with treason.*

The emperor took a half step back before recovering and

standing tall. "How are you healed?"

Geriel is a powerful healer.

"Sorcery!" The emperor pointed at Geriel. "Arrest this barbarian for sorcery."

Lien disappeared and seconds later reappeared with over a dozen swords which she dumped at her feet. The guards surrounding Bao and the emperor were now weaponless. She smiled sweetly at her uncle. "I think this is fair, don't you?"

The emperor glared at her. "More sorcery."

"No, Uncle. You know exactly what I can do. You had me trained."

A movement in the sky caught Shan's attention and Falin flew in with the amplifier in his claws. He dropped it above Lien and she caught it and spoke into it. "I am Lien, Tribal Mother of Rhora and previously State Princess of Bonam. I vouch that this man," she pointed to Bao, "is my brother, Prince Bao of Bonam, son of Emperor Huang and true heir to the throne."

Gasps went through the assembled crowd.

Jie took the amplifier from her. "I am Lord Jie, childhood friend to Prince Bao, and I vouch that he is who he says he is."

Xue's face was red. "Arrest them! They are imposters as well."

One of the emperor's guards stepped away from him. "I recognise Lord Jie and the princess. They are telling the truth."

The emperor seethed, but before he could say anything, Jie pulled the guard out of reach of the other soldiers.

Step forward, Prince Bao, Manalin said.

None of the soldiers tried to stop him as Bao moved next to Manalin. Lien and Jie flanked him, and Shan pulled Chinua with her to stand behind Bao, wanting to be near in case he was attacked. She could at least help by making him vanish.

Manalin continued. *Eighteen years ago, I travelled with Emperor Huang, his wife, the empress, and Prince Bao to Chungson. It was the final stage in our cultural exchange, and I was to meet the king before returning to my kin. The emperor was worried about Xue's ambition and asked me to take Bao to Chungson should anything happen to him.*

The crowd murmured and Shan checked the rooftops again and then scanned the crowd.

We were attacked by a group of men dressed like Rhoran soldiers, but the man leading them was the one who became General Ying.

Behind her Shan heard gasps.

I was able to rescue Bao and I took him to Chungson to the king until we could ensure Bao's safety.

Bao took the amplifier from Jie. "Before we could discover who we could trust, Xue invaded Chungson and I had to hide. He made Ying a general and it was clear that he had been behind the order to kill my parents."

Xue watched him as if he was bored. This was not a man concerned about his life or position. What else did he have planned?

"It was only when Lien married the Rhoran Khan Temur and defeated the general I felt confident that I could claim my throne."

The emperor's eyes shifted behind Bao, and Shan whirled around. Before she could focus, something hit her and pain exploded in her chest. She clutched her breast, felt the hilt of a dagger embedded in her skin. Gasping for breath, the illusion dropped away and she fell to the ground.

Chinua yelled but his words made no sense and Shan's vision blurred. Blood pumped over her hands and her head spun. Geriel's hands covered hers.

"Don't you die, Shan," Bao said.

Her head tilted back and she saw him, crouching next to her, fear in his eyes. Behind him the emperor smiled and drew a knife from his sleeve.

Shan opened her mouth to warn Bao, but the red hot pain

of Geriel's healing robbed her of speech. She struggled to stay conscious, to get her thoughts out. *Kew, emperor—knife.*

The emperor raised the blade and stepped forward. The knife plunged towards Bao's exposed neck.

Flames exploded between Bao and Xue and fear gripped Shan. She reached up and screamed in pain.

"Stay still." Geriel grabbed her arm and lowered it.

"Bao," she gasped.

Geriel glanced over and her jaw dropped. "He's fine, but the emperor has a blade sticking out of his throat."

Good. Shan closed her eyes and embraced the darkness.

~*~

When Shan woke, Geriel was by her side. She lay on a bed with walls surrounding her and she frowned, trying to get her thoughts in order. The last thing she remembered was Bao talking to the crowd. "What happened?"

"You were stabbed, but you saved Bao's life." Geriel smiled.

Memories of the searing pain and the emperor reaching for his knife flashed through her.

Shan sat, pushing Geriel out of the way. "He's all right?"

"He's fine," Geriel soothed. "Not a scratch on him."

Then where was he? She exhaled. "Who threw the knife?"

Geriel scowled. "It was Wei. Turns out he's been working with the emperor since we met him in the Dragon Mountains. He didn't want peace with Rhora."

She'd assumed he'd been in the palace working for Anming. But that explained why the messages hadn't got through. "What about the emperor?"

"Dead. I was too busy healing you to see to him." There was satisfaction in her gaze.

"Who killed him?"

"Lien. Kew warned her and she grabbed the dagger from your belt and struck before he could kill Bao."

Shan sighed. "Does this mean it's over?"

"There's a lot more to be done. The soldiers in the courtyard almost rioted when they realised the emperor tried to kill Bao and was now dead. Luckily Bao was able to calm them and asked them to stand down. He told them changes would be made in Bonam and he would review his father's policies and go from there. Most of them were happy, but I think we'll find that a bunch of Xue's supporters will have left the city by the evening." Geriel smiled. "Since then, Bao's been in the hall with the ministers arguing that Lien should not be punished for killing the emperor."

Shan shook her head. "What are the Rhoran going to do now?"

"We'll stay for another quarter moon to make sure none of the emperor's supporters try to do anything, and to witness the coronation. I don't think there will be trouble since Kun supports Bao and he's the only other person in line for the throne, but a whole horde of Rhoran outside the city is a good deterrent."

"Wasn't there another prince?"

Geriel shook her head. "The explosion crushed the children's palace. They're still looking for survivors, but it doesn't look good."

Her heart clenched. How horrific. How could Xue have done that to his children? "What happened with the Laksung men the Rhoran fought?"

"We defeated them," Geriel said. "Their lord has asked for independence as well. It turns out that Xue told them the Rhoran would be weak because we'd been infected by the curse. He neglected to mention we'd been cured."

Perhaps this was the end of the fighting. Life could go back to normal, whatever that would be. "Will you send word for Daiyu to return?"

"I imagine so. Kun and Anming will decide. Do you want to get up? We can find something to eat?"

"Yes." They walked out of the room. Shan clenched her hands together, her shoulders stiff. What would life be like for her now? She'd helped Bao, hoping for the best, but the unknown made her belly swirl. It might be a half moon before Daiyu returned and she would answer to Anming until then. Would the marriage between Kun and Daiyu go ahead?

So many questions.

They walked past the entrance of the grand hall. Inside, Bao sat at the head of the table and his ministers sat around him along with Kun and Anming. "Manalin confirmed Xue was behind the murder of my parents," Bao was saying. "Lien merely carried out Xue's sentence while also saving my life. There will be no more discussion on the matter." He drew himself up and glared at them as if daring them to disagree. The look was one of an emperor, a leader. He'd been training all his life for this and it suited him. Her heart ached, pleased he had got what he wanted, but she would probably never see him again after she left the palace.

She continued past and they went outside. The courtyard was now empty with only a few people going about their business, moving between the nearby buildings. "How long do you think it will take them to rebuild?"

Geriel shrugged. "Bricks and mortar are foreign to me. When the Bonamese attacked our camp, it only took us a few days to rebuild, but I guess this will take a lot longer."

And that was just the surface damage. How long would it take to fix the emotional damage Xue had inflicted on his people?

Geriel led Shan to Lien, Chinua and two Rhoran men she didn't know. Lien smiled at them. "I'm thrilled to see you, Shan. How do you feel?"

"I am fine. Geriel is a gifted healer."

"She's our best," one man said.

Geriel blushed. It was odd to see the confident young

woman embarrassed by the compliment. Shan hadn't thought anything would bother her.

"This is my husband, Temur," Lien said, indicating the man who spoke. "And his friend, Amslan who is also a gifted healer."

"We are heading to the camp outside the city for dinner," Temur said. "You're welcome to join us."

Shan hesitated. She was curious about the Rhoran people, but she didn't have permission to leave. She probably shouldn't have left the hall without checking with Anming, but the Rhoran way of living was growing on her.

"That sounds great," Geriel said. "The walls always feel like they're closing in on me. Do you know where Jie is?"

"He's helping Bao," Lien said. "They'll be a while. Are you coming, Shan?"

She stepped back. "I would like to, but I need to ask Lord Anming's permission."

"I'm sure he won't have a problem. You did save Bao's life after all." She paused. "Unless you'd feel more comfortable staying here."

Shan didn't know her place here anymore. "I'll come."

"You can ride with me," Chinua offered.

Warmth spread through her at their easy acceptance of her. "Thank you."

They walked to the stables and with a little bit of help, she mounted behind Chinua. She rested her hands lightly on his waist and they rode out of the palace with the others. The mood in the city was cautious. A few people glared at the Rhoran, but others waved and called out greetings, thanking them for bringing Bao back. Word had obviously spread quickly. It wasn't long before they exited the gates and crossed the meadow to where the Rhoran had set up camp. A few cooking fires burned and people sat around chatting. As they neared, a sentry called out, "Welcome back! Does this mean there'll be no more fighting?"

"None today, Ganbold," Temur replied. "And hopefully none for a long time."

How strange. "Shouldn't they bow or at least call Temur by his title?" Shan murmured to Chinua.

He laughed. "That's not our way. We're all equals, all have our value to the tribe." He halted his horse near where the others were tethered.

She dismounted. "What's your value?" She winced at the way it sounded. "What I meant—"

Chinua chuckled. "Don't worry. I know what you mean. I'm a warrior and a fast rider. I often take messages between the tribes."

Tents were set in neat rows offset from each other and men and women wandered through, calling out greetings. Some gathered together chatting and working—fletching arrows, sharpening sabres or making new bows.

One of the fletchers looked up at them and raised a hand. "Greetings! How did it go?"

"The emperor is dead, Cheren," Lien called. "My brother is in charge."

The man cheered.

At the cooking fire, Chinua handed her a plate. "Help yourself."

Geriel explained what the dishes were and Shan tried a little of everything.

What a strange culture where men and women were treated equally. Would Chungson or Bonam ever be like that? Could she ever hope for a better life?

A small part of her hoped Daiyu had fallen in love with someone while she'd been with the Rhoran, so that Shan could stay here too, but it wasn't likely. Most of their men were here and Daiyu had been besotted by Kun.

Geriel introduced her to people who came to the fire to talk to them. None of them greeted her with disdain or suspicion. They all seemed pleased to meet her.

Shan's heart ached. For over two decades she'd been taught the Rhoran were savages and yet they were far kinder than some of her own people had been. The thought of going back to her old life where she had to be subservient and quiet, serve without being noticed, made her want to run away. But then what would become of her sister and family?

She would have to send a message to them.

"Would you like to stay here tonight?" Geriel asked. "I'm sure we can find you a bed."

She was already going above her station by coming here for dinner without telling anyone. "I should go back."

"I'll take you," Chinua offered.

They rode through the darkness and into the city. At the palace, Chinua rode her all the way to the bridge across to the Hall. She slid off. "Thank you."

"You're welcome. I'll see you tomorrow." He turned his horse and rode away.

Shan crossed the bridge and went inside, nerves filling her again. Without the Rhoran to support her, she was back to being a servant. Perhaps she should return to the room she'd woken in. She passed the main hall. The ministers had left and only Bao, Kun, Anming and Jie were still seated at the table. Bao looked up and stood. "Where have you been?" His demand echoed through the hall and Shan flinched. So this was how it was going to be.

She bowed low before entering the room. "Geriel invited me to have dinner with the Rhoran."

"Who gave you permission?" Anming asked.

Her blood went cold. She bowed to him. "No one, my Lord. I did not want to disturb your meeting, and Lien didn't think you would mind."

"Lien is not in charge," Bao said.

No, of course she wasn't. Anming was Shan's master. She never should have forgotten it.

Jie spoke. "The Rhoran have a different culture which

does not include asking permission to go for dinner." He smiled at Shan. "We were all worried something might have happened to you."

She inclined her head. "I am very sorry for concerning you. It will not happen again." She turned to Anming. "My lord, do you have any duties for me to carry out?"

"See there is fresh water in my room," he said.

Bao frowned at him.

She had no idea where he was sleeping, but she didn't dare ask. "Of course, my lord. Anything else?"

"No. Then you can go to bed."

"Thank you, my lord."

She walked out of the room, head held high, but her heart shattered.

Nothing had changed.

Chapter 27

The next morning Shan woke early and hurried to organise breakfast. She had no idea who had stayed in the hall overnight or what the plans were for the day, but that was beside the point. She had a job to do. She couldn't afford to make a mistake and be fired. Her pulse raced, but her steps were slow. After everything she had been through, life had not changed, had perhaps even become worse without Daiyu to care for.

She found the servants' quarters and thankfully Ting was inside and knew what to do. Together they prepared food and then she carried it into the main hall. When breakfast was ready, she hesitated. Normally this was when she would wake Daiyu, but she didn't know where everyone was sleeping, or if they wanted to be woken.

The door across from her opened and Bao walked in, dressed in rich silks. Her heart skipped a beat and she frowned as she bowed low. "Good morning, Your Highness."

"I told you, you don't have to do that when no one is around," he said, walking to her.

She pulled out his chair. "Anming made it clear last night that I was his servant," she said. "I daren't do anything I might be punished for. I can't afford to lose my job."

"Anming won't dismiss you."

Anger rose. "You don't know that." He was clueless about the fear she lived with. His life had just got infinitely better and hers was balanced on a knife's edge. She stalked over to get the soup tureen for him.

"Shan, don't be like that."

She dumped the bowl in front of him. "Like what?"

"Don't be upset." He placed his hand over hers.

She snatched her hand back. He could pretend nothing had changed, but everything had. "Of course I'm upset," she snarled. "You want a different relationship with me in private than you want in public. How is that not supposed to upset me?" She swallowed hard and willed the tears away. "I'm not your equal, Bao, I never will be, so you need to stop pretending I am."

"What do you want from me?" Bao demanded, meeting her anger with his own. "I'm going to be emperor. There are expectations on me too."

His ignorance took her breath away. "But the difference between us is that you have the power to change things." She couldn't stay here, not when the others might walk in at any moment, not when she wanted to cry and yell and behave in a manner that would get her fired. She headed for the door.

"Don't walk away from me."

She ignored him.

"That's an order, Shan."

She tensed. It was simple for him to exert his power when he didn't get his own way. She kept walking. "Then it's lucky no one is around to see me disobey it."

~*~

Shan made sure there were several people in the main hall any time she went in there during the day. She and Ting served meals, kept the drink jugs full and snacks on the table while Bao and Kun arranged Bao's coronation and spoke to the various people in the palace who ran things. Lien and Anming were part of much of the discussions as representatives of Rhora and Chungson, and Bao had ordered papers to be drawn up to give Chungson and the other vassal states their independence. It would be his first act as emperor to sign it.

She sighed. At least that would be good for her family. Without the emperor's control, maybe life could go back to how it had been. If Anming thought to change it.

"We need to talk about marriage," Anming said.

Shan flinched and glanced at the table.

"Daiyu was engaged to Kun when he was the heir. We need to decide if the engagement stands."

"I won't marry Daiyu," Bao stated. "She's too much like a sister."

Anming nodded. "I thought as much. Kun, what are your thoughts?"

Shan hated they were discussing Daiyu like she was a commodity, as if she had no choice in the matter, even if she didn't.

"I can't marry anyone when I don't know what my standing will be." He glanced at Bao. "We haven't discussed that."

Bao smiled. "I've been thinking about it. There's a dukedom which was given to Ying's family after he killed my parents. I thought you might like it. You can keep the title of prince if you wish, but your heirs will be dukes."

Kun smiled. "I know the area. It's lovely. Thank you."

And just like that, Bao had tossed a family out of a house they may have lived in for two decades, without thought of where they would go or what they would do. It wasn't their fault Ying had murdered the emperor.

Kun turned to Anming. "Then if you are happy for your sister to marry a duke, I would be pleased to continue with the engagement."

"I am pleased."

Shan gritted her teeth. Why had she fought so hard to put Bao on the throne when this was what he did? She'd thought he would be more aware of people's feelings.

"Should you not perhaps ask Daiyu whether she wants to marry Kun?" Lien asked.

The men stared at her in surprise and Shan smothered a smile.

"It is her life you're deciding," Lien reminded them.

"You had no choice in your marriage," Bao said.

"That doesn't make it right," she said.

Daiyu would want to marry Kun, but Lien had a point.

"We can't change everything overnight," Bao said.

"But you can make steps towards change."

Anming sighed. "I'll ask her when she returns. Has she been sent for?"

Lien nodded. "One of my riders left this morning. He might catch up to them in a few days, depending on how fast Daiyu was able to ride."

"Then we need to talk about Bao's marriage," Kun said. "The sooner you produce heirs, the better. Xue's supporters will forget about trying to put me on the throne if you have heirs of your own."

Bao's gaze darted to Shan and her heart ached. "I'll be too busy unravelling the mess Xue made to marry."

"It won't take long," Kun argued. "Decide on a wife and others will prepare the ceremony. They were already preparing my wedding. We just need to work out who the best strategic match is."

Strategy not love.

"I won't marry any of Xue's supporters just to get them on side," Bao said.

"Is Laksung likely to be a problem?" Anming asked. "They attacked on Xue's orders but have been too scared to accept your invitation to these meetings."

"That will be seen as rewarding Xue's supporters too," Lien said. "Perhaps you should set an example, brother. Marry who you want to marry, show people it is all right to marry for love rather than position."

Jie looked at Shan and she lowered her gaze to the ground. What had Bao told him about her?

"The same rules don't apply to emperors," Bao said. "Father always said that. We must be beyond reproach."

"Marrying for love won't cause reproach," Lien said.

Before Bao could comment, Jie said, "You have lived with the Rhoran for too long, Kixi. You've forgotten the strict social structure we abide by. Even when your father was alive, people married their own class. Bao must marry a duke's or minister's daughter if he wants the support of the highborn."

Though she'd known it was coming, it didn't make it any easier. Shan wanted to block her ears, or leave the room, but she had no choice.

"Shan," Lien called. "Could you send for Tadashi? Oh, and check whether Jie's parents have arrived yet. If they have, send them here."

Shan bowed low, full of gratitude. "Of course." She hurried out of the room. Once outside she breathed deeply to calm the storm in her stomach. Listening to them discuss who Bao was to marry was more painful than all of the injuries she'd sustained while fighting for him. She blinked rapidly and swallowed to control the emotion. She had a job to do.

Tadashi wasn't guarding the hall so she scanned the courtyard and then headed for the barracks. She knocked and said to the soldier who opened it, "Tadashi is needed in the main hall. Is he here?"

"Wait a minute." The soldier left and returned a minute later with the man.

"How can I help?"

"Lien asked for you in the main hall."

He gestured for her to lead the way.

"Do you know if Jie's parents have arrived?" She didn't know who they were or why they'd been sent for.

"They'll be in the guest quarters if they have." Tadashi pointed to a building not far from the hall.

"Thank you." She left him at the entrance and continued to the guest quarters. Once inside, the servants directed her to one of the rooms. She knocked and bowed when an older man with greying hair answered the door. "Forgive my intrusion, sir. You are Jie's father?"

The man nodded.

"Lien has requested you and your wife go to the main hall."

"Princess Lien?"

Shan shook her head. "Lien, Tribal Mother of the Rhoran."

He smiled and he looked like his son. "Lovely." He called to his wife and Shan accompanied them back to the main hall. She wished she could have stayed away longer.

When they walked in, Jie stood and greeted his parents before introducing them to the others in the room. Jie's mother's eyes were damp as she held back tears greeting Bao. "We thought you were dead."

"Shan," Jie called. "Could you go to the Rhoran camp and get Geriel? She hasn't met my parents yet."

Shan nodded and hurried away. Thank the ancestors Jie and Lien were kind.

Shan borrowed a horse from the stable and found Geriel shooting arrows at targets on the outskirts of the camp. Geriel waved at her. "What are you doing here?"

"Jie sent me. His parents have arrived, and he wants you to come to the palace."

Geriel bit her lip. "Oh. I've been dreading this day."

"Why?"

"What if they don't like that Jie married a Rhoran? What if they're really stuffy and proper and look down at me when I hug him?"

Shan understood her concerns. "His mother had tears in her eyes when she met Bao," she said. "That shows she has some emotion."

Geriel nodded. "Good. Let me fetch my horse." She whistled loudly and one of the horses nearby trotted over.

Shan stared at her. "Wow."

Geriel laughed. "My father communicates with horses. He told Khulan to come any time I whistle like that and she does it most of the time."

Everything Shan learnt about the Rhoran made her want to learn more.

Geriel mounted and they turned back to the city. "What have they been talking about this morning?"

Shan's mood plummeted. "Marriage. Whether Daiyu should still marry Kun and who Bao should marry."

"I thought you would marry him," she said.

Shan's mouth dropped open then she laughed. "What made you think that?"

"When you were stabbed, he wouldn't leave your side until I convinced him you were fine and resting." They rode through the city gates. "And while you were away in the city spying on the emperor he was distracted and short-tempered. When Riltien said you'd been shot he was going to order the gates to be opened and his soldiers to search for you."

Shan couldn't speak. That couldn't be right.

"Plus, he's always looking at you when you walk away."

Keeping his feelings secret. "It doesn't matter. He is the emperor and I am a servant. He must marry a duke or minister's daughter."

"Pfft. With all their rules, it's a wonder anything gets done," Geriel said.

The guards at the palace waved them through and they left the horses in the stable. Geriel clutched Shan's hand. "I'm so nervous I want to be sick."

Shan smiled. "No matter what happens, Jie loves you."

She relaxed. "You're right. Bao has already given Jie the title of ambassador to Rhora and Temur granted me the title of ambassador to Bonam so we'll be able to spend time in both countries."

Shan prayed to the ancestors that Jie's parents would like Geriel.

Geriel stopped outside the hall and patted her hair. "Damn, I didn't think of what I'm wearing. Do I look all right? Do I smell like horses?"

Shan gave into her urge and hugged her. "You look lovely." Although she didn't want to go inside, she opened the door and smiled at her friend. "You'll be great." She let Geriel go in before her and paused by the door. She wanted to turn invisible, but Bao had spotted her the moment she walked in. She headed for the wall where she could stand until she was needed again.

Jie was already on his feet, hugging Geriel and introducing her to his parents. His father nodded a greeting, but his mother studied Geriel for a moment and then hugged her. "I'm delighted my son found himself a wife."

Tears glistened in Geriel's eyes as she hugged her mother-in-law back and Shan sighed. Everything would be fine for her friend.

Lien smiled and then said, "I think we should take a break and have dinner."

Shan moved from the wall as Bao agreed. She went into the servants' area and arranged for dinner to be brought to the main hall as soon as possible. On her way back she almost ran into Bao. He steadied her as she stumbled, and her heart jumped. She stepped back, pressing her lips together and bowed.

"Can I speak to you privately?" Bao gestured to a nearby room.

She couldn't refuse, but maybe she could use the opportunity to have her say. The room had been set up as a makeshift bedroom much like her own room. She stayed close to the door, wrapping her arms around her waist. Before he could say anything, she said, "You're being an idiot."

He frowned. "What?"

Her muscles tight she continued, "You kicked Ying's family out of a home they have lived in for two decades without thought of what is going to happen to them."

"Ying killed my family," Bao growled.

"Yes, but his family didn't. Where are they going to go? How are they going to live?"

"I don't care."

She put her hands on her hips. "You should. They're exactly the type of people who could rise up against you if you don't treat them with any respect."

He paced the room, silent and then faced her and sighed. "You're right. I'll ask Kun to see they have somewhere to go."

Good. She turned to go.

"Wait!" He grabbed her arm. "I'm sorry, Shan."

Surprise made her look at him.

"I've acted badly towards you since we arrived in Bonam."

"It's been longer than that." She winced and pressed her lips together. He was no longer the man she'd loved, he was the emperor. She shouldn't speak to him so familiarly.

He flashed a smile and her heart squeezed. "I love that you're honest with me."

Love? She ignored the skip of her heart. "I shouldn't speak to you so. You're an emperor."

He nodded and studied her silently. "I wanted to tell you who I was, so many times."

"But you never trusted me enough."

"I couldn't afford to."

And yet she had shown him her gift which was equally dangerous. "But you could afford to play with my heart even though you knew nothing would come of it." Those days they'd spent together had given her hope and happiness. They'd dreamed of changing the world, making things fair for all people.

"I was foolish. I never wanted to hurt you." He took hold of her hand and she wanted to yank it back but a part of her liked the warmth of his touch. "I thought we could never be together, but after you left today I spoke to Tadashi and Jie's parents and they said there have been emperors who have had commoner wives."

She smothered her hope. "What about servant wives?"

"That too. What I'm saying is, they convinced me that we could have a life together, if you will forgive me."

Shan's legs went weak and she braced herself against the wall behind her. "What?"

"I have loved you for years, Shan. You brought light into my life, which had been desolate after my parents died. You gave me joy and hope and made me smile again." He pulled her closer. "I want to spend my life with you."

She couldn't be hearing this right. There had to be a condition. "As your consort?"

"No. I want you to be my wife, my empress."

Her head spun and she placed a hand on her heart.

"You can rule by my side the way my mother ruled with my father."

This was happening much too fast. She couldn't keep up. "You want to marry me, make me an empress, allow me to rule with you?"

"Yes. Will you do it?"

Did he realise he was offering her everything her heart had ever desired? She was almost too scared to take it. What if this was all some kind of dream? She pinched herself and winced. Not a dream then. Her heart expanded until it felt as if her chest would explode. She flung her arms around his neck and kissed him. "Yes. Yes, I will marry you."

His arms wrapped around her and he kissed her back. His taste and touch were achingly familiar, flooding her with memories of the times she'd been happiest.

When they broke apart her head was spinning. "I love you so much, Bao." She kissed him again, not quite believing this was true.

He laughed, the sound wrapping her in its warmth.

"Think of all the good we can do together," she said. "Servants will finally have the freedom to live their own lives, families won't have to sell their children anymore, the world can be a much better place."

Bao stepped back and frowned. "Slow down. I need to nurture relationships with people before we can make too many changes."

And by people he meant those who were wealthy. "For how long?"

"A year, maybe longer."

Nausea burned in her stomach. Could she become empress knowing people like her were still being treated badly, still having no say in their lives? She'd wanted to marry Bao for years, but everything was different now. She swallowed. "I understand." He smiled in relief but before he spoke she said, "But I can't marry you until those changes are made."

His mouth dropped open and hurt flashed in his eyes.

She squeezed his hand, needing him to understand. "I can't be empress, having clothes and money and servants waiting on me when I know some of those servants have no choice in being there, and that others are being badly mistreated. I can't enjoy that life knowing farmers are still having to sell their children to support the rest of their family. I'm sorry, Bao. I just can't."

"I can't make those changes immediately."

She closed her eyes, breathed deeply, her heart breaking.

"Then I can't marry you." She walked out of the room.

Tears blurred her vision and Shan blinked rapidly. She needed air, needed space to cry. This was all she'd ever wanted.

"Shan, wait."

She pulled her illusion around her and increased her pace.

"That's not fair, Shan."

She didn't care. She rushed out of the closest exit and inhaled the cool evening air. The pavilion across the way was still standing and the garden surrounding it would help her find peace.

She trotted up the steps and went to the seat. No, she was too upset to sit still. She turned and found Bao right behind her.

Shocked, she stepped back, out of his reach.

"I know you're here somewhere, Shan. Please show yourself." He scanned the pavilion. "I'm going to feel like a real fool if you're not here," he mumbled.

He shouldn't be outside without his guards. She dropped her illusion. "How did you know?"

"You always run to the garden when you're upset. There's not a lot of choice here." He stepped closer. "Please don't run from me."

The tears spilled down her cheeks and Bao pulled her into his arms. "I didn't mean to make you cry."

"It was always my dream," she sobbed. "But I can't take it."

"I know." He rubbed her back. "I didn't realise how strongly you felt about it." He sighed. "I don't want to marry anyone else, but I can't make too many changes at once. Not until I get to grips with how the country is run."

She sniffed. "I understand, really I do."

He swore. "Forget about producing heirs," he muttered. "We can have a long engagement," Bao said. "We'll get married a year from now and we can spend the time learning how to rule Bonam. You can focus on the poorer classes and I can appease the rich. I don't know what the finances are like, but perhaps we can offer temporary assistance to anyone who is in urgent need and then work towards a sustainable solution. Then before we marry, I'll sign a law which will free indentured servants."

She pulled back to look at him. "Will that work? Won't people try and talk you out of it, won't they hate me?" Would Bao hate her for insisting on change?

"Let them talk. I won't marry anyone else and what you want is the right thing to do. We just need to prepare everyone else for the change."

It wouldn't be easy, but she desperately wanted to agree. "Do you really mean it?"

"Yes. I'll swear it in front of everyone in the hall, in front of the whole palace if I need to. Please, I can't imagine ruling without you by my side. You're my love, my compass, my conscience."

Shan's heart swelled and she cupped his face. "I have always loved you, Bao." Her next breath shuddered from her. "Yes, I will marry you."

And together they would heal Bonam.

Epilogue

A baby's cry drew Shan's attention and she crossed the room to the crib where her beautiful three-month-old son lay. She picked him up, crooning to him. Zan looked up from where she'd been embroidering. "He is the most cherished child I know," she said. "He barely gets a chance to cry."

Shan smiled at her. She couldn't believe two years had passed since Bao had become emperor and a year since she had married him. Two years full of hard work, difficult decisions but most importantly, love. One of the first thing she'd done after peace had been restored was invite her sister to Bonam. She'd come gladly and become Shan's assistant and close friend.

Anming had made certain Bingwen could no longer prey on the poor, arresting him for spying on the royal family, and Zan and Shan had celebrated the day they'd received the news. Shan was pleased Anming's title of king had been restored and Chungson was now its own country again. Anming was busy changing laws and had made certain his farmers had been supported throughout the seasons.

Bao walked in looking far too serious in his golden ceremonial robes. She'd asked whether he could change the imperial colour, because it reminded her of Xue, but Bao had insisted. This was the colour his father had worn. She wouldn't argue with that.

"Is our boy awake in time to meet everyone?" Bao asked, coming over and kissing her and then kissing Huang's forehead.

"He's awake. Have they all arrived?"

"They're waiting at the hall."

Shan gestured for her sister to follow and together they left the emperor's palace and walked towards the Hall of Clarity. Guards fell in beside them, but kept a respectful distance and Shan smiled and acknowledged the workers they passed.

"You've made such a difference here," Bao said. "There's been such a shift in the atmosphere since we wrote the new law and gave servants more rights."

"Workers," Shan corrected. "They're workers now."

He smiled. "They are."

All of the buildings had been repaired and more small gardens dotted the outer palace. They crossed to the Hall of Clarity where inside, the main hall was full of people.

"Let me see my nephew," Lien said and hurried over.

Behind her Temur smiled. "He'll have another cousin to play with next year."

Shan handed Huang to Lien. "Congratulations."

"It's been too long," Geriel complained. "You were still pregnant the last time I saw you." She engulfed Shan in a hug.

"You're the one doing all the travelling," Shan said.

"And she loves it," Jie said. Behind him stood Anming, Daiyu and Kun. Shan hesitated. Even after two years she was never certain how to address them. She used to be their servant and now she was empress.

They're as unsure as you. Kew bumped her leg in greeting and Shan stepped back.

"Your wings are even bigger now."

I flew all the way here with the others.

Manalin, Riltien and Dhalin were all waiting to the side for the others to welcome them.

Shan held her hand out to Daiyu. "How are you?"

"Well, thank you." Daiyu bowed.

No, that would never do. "Don't bow, it makes me uncomfortable. You're my cousin and friend." Shan hugged her and then welcomed Kun and King Anming.

You look well, Dhalin said. *May I greet your baby?*

"Of course." She took Huang back from Lien and knelt so the dragons could reach him.

He is strong, Manalin said.

Riltien lifted a lip. *Not yet, but he will be.*

Shan smiled.

He has the gift like his mother, Dhalin said.

Everyone turned to her. "You can tell already?" Geriel asked.

Dhalin nodded. *Look.*

Geriel touched Huang's cheek and closed her eyes. "You're right." She grinned at Shan. "You two will have your hands full with him."

Shan didn't mind. As long as he was healthy and happy.

"Dragon!" a young voice cried.

Shan looked across to where one of the servers was shushing her little girl, fear on her face. They had set up creches for the children so parents could continue to work if they wanted to, but this little one had obviously gone exploring. Shan stood and held out a hand. "It's all right. Would your daughter like to meet them?"

"No, it's fine," the server said, trying to shepherd her daughter back through a door.

They'd come a long way in the past two years, but it would be some time before the poor truly trusted the changes.

The little girl slipped past her mother and ran over. "I'm Fen." She bowed.

Shan's heart warmed and she inclined her head. "I'm Shan. This is Dhalin, Manalin, Riltien and Kew." She indicated each dragon in turn.

This little one is strong-willed, Riltien said, approval in his tone. *She will go far.*

Dhalin nodded. *This new generation will grow up with less fear. They will take Bonam to new heights.*

Shan exchanged a glance with Bao. It was just as they hoped, a stronger, happier country.

"Of course," Ting said as she handed around drinks. "Bonam hasn't had a decent leader in twenty years and now it has two."

Shan smiled at her friend. Ting had travelled back to Laksung to visit her family after Xue had died, but had decided to return and work for Shan. Her family was allowed to visit her whenever they wanted, and she could return home twice a year.

"Thank you," Bao said and raised his cup. "To friends and family."

Temur raised his. "To peace and understanding."

Geriel clinked hers against Jie's. "To health and happiness."

"To equality," Shan said and glanced at Bao. "And love."

Thank you for reading!

I hope you enjoyed the book. It would love it if you could leave a review wherever you bought it from, if you have time. Reviews let me know what you thought of the story and help other readers decide if they want to read the book.

Acknowledgements

I started plotting The Servant's Grace on a road trip across Australia, from Perth to Melbourne, with fellow author Michelle Diener. We were heading to the Romance Writers of Australia conference and had plenty of spare time driving the almost 3500 km. I had originally planned for the heroine of this book to be Daiyu, but as I brainstormed with Michelle I realised it had to be Shan. After I worked that out, the story came to me quickly. I want to thank Michelle for being such a fantastic travel companion and helping me with my plotting.

I also want to thank my team; Lana Pecherczyk for the beautiful cover, Ann Harth for her wonderful editing suggestions, Shona Husk for drawing the map of the world, and Teena Raffa Mulligan for her copyediting.

Stay tuned…

A new fantasy series will be coming late 2021.

Sign up to my reader group to be kept up to date with the latest release dates. You'll also get a copy of The Prince's Wish, a short story which tells the tale of Bao escaping the emperor's plot to kill him.

https://www.claireleggett.com/readergroup

CPSIA information can be obtained
at www.ICGtesting.com
Printed in the USA
LVHW092100250121
677440LV00016B/549/J

9 781925 696721